Jenny Dawson was a radiographer in the NHS for most of her working life. She lives in Lincolnshire.

Jenny Dawson

THE BED THAT I LIE ON

AUSTIN MACAULEY
PUBLISHERS LTD.

A CIP catalogue record for this title is available from the British Library.

ISBN 9781786296184 (Paperback)
ISBN 9781786296191 (Hardback)
ISBN 9781786296207 (eBook)

www.austinmacauley.com

First Published (2017)
Austin Macauley Publishers Ltd.
25 Canada Square
Canary Wharf
London
E14 5LQ

Acknowledgments

An especially big thank you to the wonderful people at the Durham Mining Museum for accepting my ignorance and introducing me so generously and kindly to an industry of infinite worth which has all but disappeared. As always, I would like to thank my writer friends for their grace and patience as listeners and readers, and my sister for her unfailing support. Thank you again to the amazing staff in Gainsborough Library for putting up with my frequent hauntings. Last but not least, I would like to thank my publishers for their forbearance and helpfulness.

Contents

Beginning on the Fourth
Day of January

'We will go on foot, my dear,' he said. 'You need not distress yourself thinking you will be driven through the streets of Durham in a carriage so that all and sundry may stop and look at you.'

'Will I be coming back here, sir?' I said.

'That is for you to decide, my dear. The door will always be open.'

'I will pack then, sir. It will not take long.'

'We are a household of drab dissenters,' he said. 'We would each of us make it our wish if we could to travel lightly through this life.'

Then I came back into this room for the last time and packed all of my world, being one other gown, a change of undergarments, two pairs of woollen stockings and two books, one having the title *Evelina* and the other a journal, empty of words. And the thought came to me that I might as well be as the Republicans were in France who made their own almanac, where every season was known by its complexion. So I begin on this, the fourth day of January in the year 1812 when I will, as the winter twilight settles over Durham, leave myself behind in the house of Sainte Agathe, and walk out of the door as a different woman, who is to be wed to a man called

11

Nathaniel Chark, a coal master, whom she hardly knows, but whom she has consented to marry; and that when the next day lightens over the city she will awake in another house, and in another life.

The Whole Kingdom of
This World

On the second day, being the Sabbath and the fifth in January, Mr Chark brought into the chamber early a poor young woman, whose name he said was Willow, but if that was the name by which her kindred knew her or her name by Holy Baptism he did not know. Not that the matter need perplex me, he said, for she was an unfortunate soul without speech or hearing brought up from the dwellings of the miners, to whom he had promised to give employment, as he had in the time of his late wife.

Then he walked around the room scarcely stopping to take breath as he spoke of the accommodation there, asking eventually if all were to my comfort. To which question I had no time to give an answer before I was caught up in the same perambulation and taken to the high window, where we stood side by side, Mr Chark and I, like any man and wife, though we are not, until the poor creature Willow, who could be asked nothing on account of her infirmities, drew back the heavy brown curtains.

And it came to me that I was being shown the whole kingdom of this world, for there below us lay glittering in the morning's frost the fair city of Durham and the country beyond; and rising up out of the mist like three great incubi the mines, of which I had heard much but seen nothing, for all was in darkness when I was brought to Mr Chark's dwelling the night before.

'Clara, my dear,' he said, calling me for the first time by my baptismal name, 'you have brought with you, as it were, the first morning in the creation of the world. See how the sun shines on us. We will be happy, will we not?'

To which I would with all my heart have answered in the affirmative, yet glancing up at his face I saw in the instant that this "we" of whom he spoke did not include himself, so darkly were the sorrows of the world written there. And I asked instead to be reminded of the names of the mines, which I knew well enough but feigned not to. That being the first deception I visited upon my betrothed, and I pray the only one. Then he told me again, with infinite patience as if he were speaking to a little bairn, their names, of Thayne, Blennowe and Shackleton.

'But they are asleep this morning,' he said, 'for all the men must be given the opportunity to attend holy service, whether they wish to or not. And as for myself, I may close the pits on the Sabbath day yet I cannot make those that work there go to service. We will be happy, will we not, my dear?' he added. Saying which he bestowed a chaste kiss on my forehead and the same on the quiet brow of the poor creature Willow, then left the chamber.

And I resolved in the instant that regardless of the lackings of Willow, whom I take to be my maid, I will address her nevertheless in words, as if she can both hear them and give answer to them, which she cannot. For on

14

this second day of my beginning I have no other in the city of Durham, unless it is the present volume, which is like Willow my maid in that it receives my words without question and gives back none in return.

Yet, for all his words on the subject of closing the mines on the Sabbath to enable the men to attend holy service, Mr Chark had made no mention of himself attending, nor either of me attending, wishing not, as I supposed, that he should be seen at the dissenting chapel in the company of a woman to whom he is not yet wed. So I resorted to continuing the perambulation around the room, which I understood to be my chamber, for I had been left here with my worldly possessions, such as they were. And there also was the little soul Willow following me with her eyes as I walked, being now my maid, though I had nothing for her to do. And thus we were, I walking and Willow following me with her eyes, bright and black as gems of coal, until she took herself to stand beneath a portrait hanging on the west wall and catching the low gold slants of the morning sun.

'Who is that, Willow?' I said, and I saw that the bright black eyes brimmed with tears. 'Who is that, Willow?' I said again, though I knew well enough that the portrait was of the late Mrs Chark, as I knew also that she had passed out of this world in childbirth, and her bairn also. And I thought there was no end to my knowing, almost as if I had come this way before, though I have not.

Then my maid Willow put into my hand a looking glass, turning it towards my face. For she had seen what I had not, that the portrait on the wall and the face I now looked at in the glass, being my own, were the same but for the arrangement of the hair and the dress; and were I to do my hair as hers was done and to wear her gown, we would be as one.

'Does the master see this likeness?' I said to my maid. 'Would you be so kind as to put this back where you found it, Willow? I cannot remember where it was.'

She took the looking glass from me and softly pulled at my sleeve so that I would follow her to the dresser, where she painstakingly laid down the glass as if there was no other place for it. And I saw on the dresser, for the first time, a brush and a white tray of hair pins, both the brush and the pins still carrying small wisps of hair, which were little dulled by the passing of time, although I knew that it was a matter of nearly two years and a half since the first Mrs Chark had lived.

'Does Mr Chark not see this likeness?' I said again, forgetting now that Willow was without hearing, yet not wishing for an answer and fearing not only that he could see the likeness but had been seeking it out until he found it. For I could conceive of no other reason for my presence in this house, waiting for the next day, to be wed to a man I do not know.

Nor does he know me, in spite of his protestations that we will be happy. And the last question hung on the air between me and my maid Willow, whom I now noticed as if for the first time as a woman similar to myself in years, but whose hair as it springs from under her cap is already whitened like that of a woman carrying a score more of years, and who would have been as myself in height but that her poor back is twisted, with one shoulder higher than the other by the measure of a six inch rule, and one leg the same. Yet she is a sweet creature with a winsome face and black sparkling eyes, who, even as these observations came to me, dropped a curtsey and hurried from the room.

So I took again to walking around the chamber, not least to keep warm, for the fire had sunk in the grate, and the sun, which a short time before streamed across the floor, had now gone and a dark mist had settled over Durham, turning the shining day into near night although it was little past noon. And in the course of my perambulations, for I will always think of these walks around the chamber as perambulations, though it is an odd word in these times, I came to the tall press in the corner, which on opening I found to be already occupied. I closed the door quickly, for although there was no one there to see I found myself suddenly a thief and an incomer, as indeed I am.

Presently Willow returned with coals to mend the fire. Following after her was another young woman, similar to her in body, who asked what I would take for luncheon, to which I answered that I would be happy to have the same as she herself was having, not knowing what to say for I had never as far as I could remember been asked to make such a choice.

So the fifth day of the year of our Lord 1812, and the second of my beginning, wore on, cast as it was into an early gloom; it being the Sabbath day with no merriment abroad in the city, nor anything but silence within the house, from which I understood that Mr Chark is a severe observer of the Lord's day, imposing the same on his household. And I saw before me a procession of Lord's days walking away to my life's end, with nothing but silence in my head and nothing but religious texts before my eyes. Yet it did not matter, for my first life had been no better.

Thus we were, Mr Chark (for I cannot think of him by any more familiar name) reading what serious works he would in his study, and Willow and the housemaid the same in their room, for there would be no converse anywhere, with Willow bound to silence by her own infirmity and the housemaid bound to silence by Willow's infirmity, until the clock in the hallway chimed three hours after the noonday, and I was brought back to myself, not by the voice of the clock but by a strange and dense oppression – I have no other word for it – in the chamber in which I sat.

And going to the window, for the curtains were as yet not drawn against the evening, I saw the same oppression covering the city of Durham; in form like a mist, yet it was not, being thick and terrible with great soots gathered up in it, and reaching as it seemed from the door of our dwelling on the Rose Pavement as far as the mine of Blennowe, being the most distant, like a strange dense night having fallen before its time. Yet in the house I heard nothing, as if everyone within its walls was unaware of the fearsome pall of the mist lying over Durham; only, and far away, I heard the quiet closing of an inner door and then what I thought to be the opening and closing of the side door which gives onto a garden with outhouses and a coal shed.

After some brief time, for I did not hear the clock strike again, there was a deafening crack as if the whole world was being torn apart, and before my eyes I saw the nearest mine – called Shackleton – wrapped in flame, and great fiery rocks hurled high into the sky.

Then even as I watched the whole of the city of Durham woke, and all in it as far as I could see left their dwellings, not one going empty handed but carrying gifts as if they were bound for the stable at Bethlehem. For some bore gifts of ropes and some of bed or table cloths and some pails, and everyone was on foot running, as I thought, towards the stricken mine of Shackleton, though it lay nearly a league distant. And all the time flames poured out of the pit and fires rained down, and soots fell on those who had left their dwellings and gone to help.

And I had no other thought than to put on again the cloak and hood, which was not mine, but in which I had arrived at Mr Chark's house short hours before, and follow after the good people of Durham, though I did so with empty hands. So I left the house to its silence, joining the thoroughfares of St Giles Gate and Framwell Gate, which though crowded with citizens were quiet but for the sound of their clogs ringing on the stones, and the clang of pails and the drag of the ropes, and the hooves of whatever horses had been brought.

Thus we made our way, and even though I was not known to any in the place, there were some who stopped to look at me, as I thought, but whether it was for the fact that I went empty-handed or because I was not wearing clogs but the leather boots of a lady I could not tell. Yet this I knew from the few words being spoken, that the north pit of Shackleton had gone up; and it was not known if those who worked there were down already, it being the end of the Sabbath observance and the mine about to set to for the week.

And I heard also that the master had made the journey down to Shackleton in the hour before noon. For certain people who had been returning from morning worship at that time spoke of the sun turned red and a menace in the air, and of seeing the master running hatless out of the city.

All of which talk, though it was little enough, I caught along the way, until we were met with a blockade. And those that manned it, being as I understood certain people of standing in the city, said we could go no further, the way ahead being perilous with the heat and the poisoned gas from the mine, but that any offerings for the rescue effort would be most humbly and gratefully received and taken down to the north pit and put to use. And there was nearby already an array of such utensils, being received by colliers, who said to each one of those who gave, 'Thank you, mun; thank you, mun; thanking you most kindly, mun.'

Then the citizens of Durham turned round and went back home, knowing nothing more, neither if there were men down the pit, or if indeed the master was still at the scene. For of Mr Chark I heard no more but that he had gone running hatless down to Shackleton in the hour before noon. And I was perplexed in my mind, not having any name to call him by but "Mr Chark", who is my betrothed, whose name is Nathaniel, yet in my mind I call him neither my betrothed nor Nathaniel, but only Mr Chark, the sombre master of Blennowe and Thayne and Shackleton, on account of whom I feel the dismay and shame of a kept woman, being not yet wed to him.

With these thoughts and thoughts like them running in my mind I was scarcely conscious of a drag on my sleeve, which indeed I had been trying, unawares, to shake off for no little time before that which was impeding me spoke, and in a voice like no other I have heard in my life, so hoarse and broken was it.

'Please, mun, if you please, mun,' the voice was saying. Yet when I looked I saw only my maid Willow, who had tight hold on my sleeve and was guiding me up the steep cobbled thoroughfares, though I had not known it; and was even then, though I was hardly listening, letting her difficult words fall, as water splashed from a pail falls onto the ground and runs away.

'They say the master is after the affairs at the north pit, mun, and will be home presently. Though I do not know what presently is, whether it be presently before the Lord's day is through, or whether presently on the morrow, or the morrow after, for such is oft the case when the mine blows.'

'Thank you, Willow,' I said, not finding the heart to make reference to the fact that she who had been brought to me without speech or hearing had now found what she could of her voice somewhere in the throng on the Lord's day.

'Miss Wellow, mun,' she said. 'Marion Wellow.' After which her words left her.

The Mine Under the Earth

The housemaid is known by the name of Cecilia and is cousin to my maid Willow, both having a deformity of the back, but Cecilia less so. There is in addition in Mr Chark's household one other: a gentleman of uncertain years who names himself as Bertie-mun, though I am hard pressed to make out any other word that comes from him, so pitifully scarred is his face. These three souls make up the entirety of Mr Chark's household, and poor maimed creatures they are, in body if not in mind, for all are of a sweet and peaceful nature.

As to Mr Chark himself, I knew nothing more until today, for my maid Willow, once back in the confines of the house, returned to her silence. But this I did know, that for the whole of yesterday, the feast of the Epiphany, which is a short enough day being little after St Lucy's, the city of Durham lay under a shroud of smoke, through which sudden spurts of flame from the north pit of Shackleton mine continued until after dark to leap into the sky, it being clear and starlit above the smoke.

And it was a disquieting sight to look down from the high window of the house on the Rose Pavement and see the city laid out at our feet. For I had a notion, which has come back to me many times since, of the heaven above set with silver stars, and the earth beneath it under a pall of dust, and the mine under the earth like the worst imagined pit of hell, in which black pit there might still be men fearfully trapped. And as this thought comes to me, so also, from some distant and forgotten place, does the childhood prayer:

"Matthew, Mark, Luke and John
Bless the bed that I lie on
Four corners to my bed
Four angels round my head
One to watch and one to pray
And two to bear my soul away."

For no one had yet said anything to persuade me that none were trapped, even though I wandered around asking for news, if not from Mr Chark's household, who were much occupied with Monday wash day, then from the walls and the closed doors and the high ceilings of the silent house.

And hearing nothing I was left with the conclusion that there were colliers who lay smothering and voiceless in the thick darkness, with the pit roof bearing down on their heads and the pit floor hard under their backs, waiting for their release into the next world even while harnessed to this one. For all in the county of Durham know the workings of the mines, and trust that those who labour there are "born to it", wishing for no other station in life than that which the Lord God who dwells high above the stars, and the master of the mine who dwells high above the city of Durham, has ordained for them.

So passed the day of the Epiphany in the year of 1812. And for all that I have words and more to spare for this volume, my speech nearly fails me in the presence of Mr Chark, to the extent that I hardly know how I gave my consent when he asked for my hand in marriage, though I suppose I did. And I don't know if he does this deed for my benefit only, to make of me a virtuous woman. For I am to believe that he is a kindly and good man, with, and I have to say this, a pleasing face, which I can scarcely bring myself to look at.

In such a way the newborn year woke to the next day, being this, the seventh in the month of January, and when Willow came into my chamber I asked how Mr Chark was, though she could not hear; whereupon she straight away dismissed herself with a curtsey and must have summoned him, for in a little time he was in the room.

'What is that, my dear?' he said, meaning this volume, which lay open on the desk. I handed it to him, but seeing that it was a journal, he closed it and gave it back to me saying, 'Please forgive me, Clara, my dear. I have no wish to intrude on your private thoughts.'

Then he told me about Shackleton as if I knew nothing of the events of the day before, saying that the north pit had blown, and although it was thought that none had gone down, it being the end of the Sabbath observance, one was unaccounted for by the name of T Spence. And, as certain of the pulleys were kept swung out of the way yet nearby in the case of such a contingency, the horse-whim was to be put to work so that men might go down to see if any soul was still there. For although he knew well enough every man by name he could not bring to mind a T Spence, nor could his overman, the one collier called Spence having the Christian name of Charles.

'Which is where I am expected within the hour, my dear,' he said, 'for the business is best got over with.'

Then I gathered up what courage I have, which is little enough, and addressing Mr Chark for the first time by his name, Nathaniel, asked if I might go also. To which he answered that with all his heart he would discourage me, but it had always been the custom in Durham that the womenfolk of the mines were present when a rescue party went down and he could not but give his consent; and, indeed, the presence of a woman who was of the master's household might help, he said.

'And had it not been for this wretched affair, we would have been wed, and I would not have been searching as in darkness for a way to describe your station, my dear,' he continued, 'and I would not have had recourse to a clumsy way of words. For I don't know why God has seen fit to visit a further calamity on this household. Your maid will guide you down to Shackleton,' he added, 'for the thoroughfares are steep and ill-paved. Forgive me, my dear, for I never could use one word where ten would do.'

As Mr Chark was delivering this speech, and making his customary perambulation around the room, the doorbell rang at the front of the house, and Willow, for all that she is lost in her hearing, ushered in a visitor, Mr Chark appearing to see no incongruity between my maid's impairment and her readiness to answer the bell.

The visitor took me by the hand and looked at me with a fleeting recognition before introducing himself as Mr Tregowan, who, by his dress, I took to be a dissenting minister. And a spasm of fear passed through me that he might be in Mr Chark's house on account of our marriage, which had been delayed after the accident at Shackleton; and which, had it been my choice, would have been well to be delayed longer, if not forever, for the nearer the day approaches the more frightened I become. And the thought came to me, suddenly and unasked for, that I had unwillingly and unwittingly brought the disaster with me by wishing for a delay in my marriage, just as surely as I had brought dishonour into the household with me.

Yet in the event the minister was present to accompany Mr Chark to Shackleton, since there were those in the streets of Durham and among the colliers who had scant liking for the master, though all knew that it was not he who caused the north pit to blow. And it was hoped, also, the minister said, it being the Sabbath day observance, that the man who was missing by the name of T Spence might be discovered elsewhere and not down the mine; even should he have gone to a den of strong liquor it would be well, if his life had been spared.

'Though we have to search,' he said, letting go of my hand, 'for did not the shepherd go out and leave the ninety-and-nine until that which was lost was found?'

And I did not know how to answer, if indeed the question needed an answer, or who Mr Tregowan meant by "the shepherd", unless it was that man who would be lowered down to search, nor did I like to ask, nor even think of anyone who drew breath under heaven to be sent down into the poisoned damp of the mine.

'We had best go, Patrick,' Mr Chark said, 'for likely they will have brought the Spedding up from Thayne by now.'

Then Mr Chark and Mr Tregowan set off, it being one hour and a half before noon, with a veiled sun glancing through the pall of smoke that still hung over Durham, though less so than yesterday. And there remained with me in the house my maid Willow, the housemaid Cecilia, and the gentleman who was known as Bertie-mun, being the total of Mr Chark's household.

Presently we also set off, arriving near to Shackleton at I do not know what hour, except that the sun still peered fleetingly through the cloud, as if in doubt of our endeavour and ready to close its one eye completely should some fearful sight be uncovered.

There we stood on a shallow hill, yet sufficiently raised to enable us to see below the whole number of the colliers of Shackleton and their womenfolk, and to the west side of us their dwellings. And many of the citizens of Durham were there, some of whom had gathered on the same low hill as ourselves, where already, while the weak sun still swam in the sky, the first of the frost struck up through our boots.

Farther away, and nearer into Shackleton, the horse-whim had been brought and men assembled round it to work the pulleys. And I found myself searching with my eyes for the man whose task it was to go down, thinking to see the overseer. But I couldn't see, and I heard nothing from those who stood nearby, only that from lower down and closer in to the mine there arose on the quiet air, which was not air for we could scarcely breathe, a gasp of horror, by which I understood that the descent had begun.

Then after no time, word passed that the men who had been down were back again, but whether it was that the missing collier, T Spence, had been found, or whether the overman and the others who went with him could proceed no farther on account of the poisonous gases in the pit, no one knew. Having heard the tidings, which were no tidings, some of those watching from a distance prepared to return home to their dwellings. But as soon as they made to leave they were brought back by further word that the rescuers were to go down again to retrieve the man whom they sought, who, it was said, was not far in.

And even as we stood waiting, the sun, such as it was, dipped below Blennowe, fell over the edge of the world, and was gone; there being only the lanterns of the rescuers on the surface to light the proceedings, and few enough of those on account of the afterdamp which hung on the air, which we could taste, far away as we were. For this reason also, there was little talk, as everyone wished to keep the poison out of their mouths. Nor was there anything to talk of, either good or bad.

So we waited, with the cold from the frozen earth striking into our bones, for few had come there clothed for a long watch at nightfall in the dead of winter, until word came up that the horse-whim had stopped and the rescuers were back up. And there was no more, only that the crowd was asked in the name of God and the King to go quietly and peaceably to their own dwellings. Which we for the most part did, stumbling in the dark and ice, and with the cold in our limbs, until we were well up into Durham city.

But some did not go quietly and certain murmurings ran along the lanes that there was mischief afoot, and a certain matter that was being kept secret from the people.

And for the first time I heard the name of Chark vilified.

The Lees of the Tap Room

It being a Wednesday, and the north pit is still sending up smoke and sporadic spurts of flame, as if it were some malevolent dragon crouching next to the city of Durham. And for all that it was a new day it was like an extension of the day before, as no one slept well, for the reason that certain of the city's people had gathered on the Rose Pavement below the house during the night, and had made themselves known not by knocking on the door but by their perpetual shufflings and coughings. For I have to say that coughing and wheezing is pitifully common among all who live in the shadow of the mines and take in their rancid breath.

This went on until the break of day when, no doubt because lights were seen in the house, there was a ringing on the front bell and a battering on the door. Then, after some time had passed, Cecilia the housemaid knocked and entered my room, begging me to go down, for the master had brought in those who were outside to get warm and give them gruel and toast, to which Willow and she by themselves were unequal, Bertie-mun being occupied building up the fires.

'Seeing as how you are dressed, mun,' she said. 'And some would say that the master is a wily gentleman, for they outside are angered on account of what is afoot at Shackleton, but they cannot properly vent their rage, being now guests under his roof. But I do not say myself that he is wily, mun. I only repeat what others say of him, in order to warn you what you will like as not hear of him. If you will please to follow me, mun, for I doubt you have seen the scullery. Nor indeed have I in its present state, full of folks starved with cold and the steam rising from their toggery, with a will in them to fire off like the north pit given half the chance.'

And it occurred to me then, that Cecilia could well have the same tendency as Mr Chark, that she could not use one word where ten would do, and that between them, the master and the housemaid, they made up for the speechlessness of Willow and Bertie-mun.

There were seated round the table nine guests, for guests they had now become, muffled against the cold to such an extent that I didn't know if they were men or women. And whatever might have been their grievances outside, they had been struck down with silence, being under the master's roof and being helped to a hot gruel.

And the scullery was thick with the cloying steam from damp clothes, for though many may bathe themselves before the Sunday observance, the same is not so with outer coats, which go on without sight of the wash tub until the seams fall away. Nor, I thought, was I in any way otherwise, for I had arrived under this roof with little more than the garments I stood up in. Nor, I believe, is Mr Chark any different, despite the fact that he is the master, for being a dissenter he goes clothed in the same black from day to day, changing to another black only on the Sabbath.

'Iyeseetoast thanye,' said Bertie-mun, and placed in my had a wedge of bread, while heaping coals into the grate, from which I understood that the feeding of the citizens had been done before. 'Juswonside, mun,

30

thasnuf,' he continued, then to those seated at the table announced, 'Maspresly,' which did not perplex them at all, for to a person they hastened to finish their eating and drinking and straighten their coats, while Cecilia continued to fill bowls with gruel and Willow stirred the pot, neither appearing to notice as the door opened and Mr Chark came in.

And I would gladly have been as unconcerned as they were, for I did not wish to appear discomposed; though I was, and I did my utmost to carry on toasting bread, making a poor enough pretence at it. For, to tell the truth, yet I have no one to tell it to, I am lamentably discomposed in the presence of Mr Chark.

'Why, Clara, my dear,' he said, 'thank you.' For without knowing what I was doing I had placed the toasting fork in his own hand. 'Gentlemen,' he continued, 'this young lady and I would have been wed had not recent tragic events overtaken us and made any manner of celebration unseemly. I would ask you to explain your presences, for we must attend to the matter in hand.'

'Roger Priest, sir,' one of the men said presently. 'Priest,' he said again as if he had not been heard the first time, and rose to his feet awkwardly, sending a plate clattering to the floor as he did so. 'Roger Priest, sir, and I beg you and your good lady to excuse our presences. Not to beat about the bush, sir, we, the folks of Durham, suspect tomfoolery down at yon Shackleton. Being firstly, sir, why them fires are not yet quenched, and secondly, sir, that collier you went on search for, was any soul brought up or not, sir? For we believe we are being maintained in ignorance. For if a soul were brought up, sir, them fires must needs be damped and yon pit sealed, and if a soul were not brought up, sir, for what reason?'

Roger Priest finished his speech but remained standing, his hat in his hand, until the others did likewise, and were all on their feet with their hats in their hands, as if they were still outside Shackleton mine awaiting the return of the rescuers. Then Mr Chark, drawing me to his side, addressed them in return.

'Gentlemen of Durham,' he said. 'The fires have not been quenched because the missing collier has not been brought out. The missing collier has not been brought out because a stenting had to be strengthened to preserve the lives of the rescuers, and that is nearing completion. When the sorry task of recovering the lost collier is done, north and south pits will be closed over and the fires will starve for want of air. Any questions, gentlemen?'

'We would know the age of the collier, sir,' said Roger Priest.

'That I do not know, Mr Priest. I know only the name of one soul reported missing, that being T Spence, who may or may not be the collier still down.'

'If that's a wee bairn, thou wilt pay, Mr Chark,' said another man. 'Brim Salter at your service, sir.' Having said which, he spat into the fire.

A murmur arose amongst the others. Mr Chark said nothing, nor did the men, for all their shame. Neither did they make to leave, but seated themselves again in silence, while I continued to toast wedges of bread, on which matter I had no option for Bertie-mun continued to slice the loaves and pass to me the rudimentary fruits of his labours.

All of which might well have gone on for some time, for my maid Willow passed around the toast regardless of the words that had been said, and Mr Chark dealt out gruel to those who had drunk up, beginning with the man called Brim Salter, about whose person I detected the lees of the tap-room, which cannot have been welcome in a dissenting household though no one appeared to notice. And the words of Cecilia came back to me, that some think Nathaniel Chark to be a "wily gentleman", about which I can think nothing; for I do not know him; whether he is a "wily gentleman", or whether he is a Christian gentleman, following in the footsteps of the Saviour and returning unkindness with kindness.

'About the age of the soul to be recovered from North pit I know nothing, Mr Salter,' he said. 'Nor do I know rightly if it is T Spence, who is unaccounted for, who is still down. But I may say this, that all those who work the mines will feel gratitude if the citizens of Durham see fit to attend the recovery at midday, as a gesture of fellow feeling, and place themselves at a discreet distance in decency and quietness as a token of respect. Thank you, gentlemen.'

At the high noon of day, though there was little of either, for the sun swung low in the sky and what there was of the day was lighting some other region above the pall of smoke that still hung over Durham, all came out of their dwellings and stood as they had before, which indeed was only short hours before. Then, as the cathedral church chimed the hour the rescuers began their descent. And I was standing again with my maid Willow on the ridge, looking out on nothing but the black clad crowd beneath, for all had gone in their Sunday best. And it seemed no time, though the sun had long gone, before word went through the crowd, as quiet as the breeze before daybreak, that they were back with a covered pallet on which lay the missing collier, brought up into the fair world again where the whole city stood watch. And further word passed that the lanterns of those waiting on the surface at the mouth of the north pit were promptly and utterly extinguished so that no onlooker might bear witness. And yet further word passed that he who was brought up out of the north pit of Shackleton was a woman.

The Floor of the Pit Both her Couch and her Pillow

It is now seven days since that last entry, and in the intervening time the citizens of Durham have been, as I am told by Cecilia, dismayed to the last degree. For although the community of colliers has long been accustomed to the presence of women in the pit, the city's people, even if they knew of the practice, had buried the knowledge, as being beyond bearing. And so it is, for what woman can easily contemplate the humiliation of one of her own, to be dressed as a man and harnessed to a cart, so that the very straps assault her body. And I will confide this to my journal, for I could not say things of such intimacy to anyone, how does such a woman manage at the time of her monthly courses? Or is the toil so extreme that she has forgotten that she is a woman? Or could it be that her body also no longer obeys the laws of nature?

Often in the night as well as the day my mind has returned to the collier Tessa Spence, for that was her name, and I have always seen her trapped on a narrow shelf with the roof of the pit closing down on her, and no light to guide her to her rest.

One day Mr Chark, seeing these matters writ large on our faces, for I understand from Cecilia, who talks for the rest, that all in the household are preoccupied in the same way, gathered us together, being Willow who cannot hear, Cecilia and Bertie-mun, and myself, and said to us that Tessa knew nothing of the catastrophe at the pit, as sleep would quickly have overtaken her in the presence of the firedamp. Yet he said nothing of why she was there during the Sabbath observance when every other collier was on the surface, having not yet gone down. Nor did any one of us ask why, Cecilia no doubt because she and Willow and Bertie-mun are of mining families where the question would not be asked, and I because I stand on the threshold of the coal master's house, neither belonging nor not belonging.

And the face of Tessa Spence has appeared to me many times, how to my mind she was; hardly less pale in her difficult life than in the time after her life when she lay under the low roof of the pit with her pale hair curled about her face, and the floor of the pit both her couch and her pillow. And always the same words come back to me,

"Matthew, Mark, Luke and John,

Bless the bed that she lies on…"

It has come to me also, and so powerfully that I know it to be true, though doubtless it will remain a secret Tessa carried to her grave, that she was with child. Why I am convinced of this I cannot say, except that I have seen in the face of Tessa Spence as she comes to me in my imaginings the same inwardness that I have perceived in the face of the portrait that hangs in my room; regarding which I asked Willow, my maid, who can neither hear nor answer in return, if the first Mrs Chark was with child when the portrait was done. To which Willow shook her head, although she cannot have heard the question.

And, as I have described in these pages the mortal appearance of poor Tessa Spence, I will today make portraits, as well as I might, of the rest of Mr Chark's household, if only to rid myself of the gloom that has enveloped me. For I feel myself to be as Tessa was, trapped in the darkness, no one having wondered why I am absent, or even noticed.

First, Willow, my maid, who is otherwise called Marion Wellow, who in the house has no speech or hearing, yet whose voice I have heard as a silver bell turned hoarse, and whose black coal eyes shine with kindness and merriment. For the rest, she is pitifully made, with her poor feet out of line with her head on account of a bend in her back, both sideways and forwards, so that I cannot imagine how she walks in a straight line, yet she does.

The housemaid Cecilia has the name Hacker and I don't know how this is, as I am given to believe that she is kindred to Willow, and neither is wed. She is in all respects as my maid Willow, but to a lesser degree, less contorted and less pitifully put together. And whereas my maid Willow would be silver in speech (though she does not speak) Cecilia is of a more humble metal. And as I know little about the names of metals, there I rest my analogy.

Bertie-mun is above middle height and slender, yet strongly built. He has hair the colour of straw, as much as he has remaining, part having been lost in the pit fire which also took from him his expression. For, and it pains me to say this, poor Bertie-mun has no expression at all on his face, so thickened and misshapen are the contours of it, and so unmoving are his eyes and mouth, where facial expression would otherwise reside. And Cecilia has told me that Bertie-mun does not take refreshment with her and Willow for fear of offending their presences with his dribblings and splutterings. 'Though we wouldna mind, mun,' she added.

Now there is Mr Chark, whose name by baptism is Nathaniel and to whom I am betrothed, and whom I know to no greater extent than I know Bertie-mun, or Mr Priest, or any of the other citizens of Durham who have been given hospitality in my presence; and indeed, were I betrothed to anyone else I believe I could feel no more anxious than I feel being betrothed to Mr Chark.

Nathaniel Turner Chark is forty-one years old. He is master of three mines: Shackleton, Blennowe and Thayne. He was wed at the age of thirty-five, his wife being by baptism Arabella. Yet he called her at her own insistence Enid, that being a family name, for she thought Arabella too precious a name for herself, Enid being a brown, unremarkable name, she said. Arabella Chark died in childbed and her little infant soon after her, as if on finding the world a desolate and unforgiving place without his mother he would make haste to follow her, but not before he had been baptised Herbert by Mr Tregowan. And Bertie-mun, whose name is Herbert Tull, stood godfather to the little bairn.

Thereafter, Nathaniel Chark sank into melancholy, which manifested itself not in any outward show of mourning for he took himself to his duties at the mines within seven days, but in the mask of grief which settled on his face as if carved there, which face would otherwise have the quiet grace of an angel from heaven, for all that his station in life is an abomination to many.

This I know of Mr Chark because Cecilia has told me. Yet she has not expressed any opinion as to his nature, and it has crossed my mind that maybe she holds no opinion, one way or the other, for she is not called upon to marry him.

'Do you find Mr Chark fair of face, mun?' she said today after another such instalment.

'Yes, Cecilia,' I said. 'I do.'

'Then, miss,' she said, 'Mr Chark is also fair by nature, and if you hear otherwise 'tis only because he believes in his heart that a coal master does no ill.' Saying which, she took her leave.

So it is left to me to describe myself, of whom I know nothing. Only that I was born, for I am here in this world. Only that my name is Clara Thomas, for they tell me so. And only that I am betrothed to be married to Nathaniel Chark, to which union I must have given my consent, though I do not remember. For the rest, I find nothing that I recognise. And if I were not Clara and thought of my name as a colour, as Arabella considered that the name Enid would be brown and unremarkable, my colour would be white. It is as if I am a blank, as the unwritten pages of this journal are. And I say this in honest truth, not in any sense of humility for we are given to believe that God made all whatever their station in life to be something, but because so little of my former life belongs to me.

I am as I arrived here, in possession of little. Indeed, when I look in the glass I see a stranger, to whom, if I passed by her in the thoroughfares of Durham I would not so much as say good morning, so utterly is she unknown to me. For it was not until my maid Willow took me to the glass and showed me my likeness to the portrait of Arabella Chark that I saw the woman who is myself. And although I would ask Willow anything (though she has no hearing) and although I would listen to anything said by the housemaid Cecilia (for she needs not to be asked her opinions, which she gives freely and unsolicited) this I cannot ask. Why? Though why I do not know.

'Some would think the master asked you to be wed to him on account of your likeness to Mistress Enid, mun,' said Cecilia, 'but 'tis not true. They think after that manner because 'tis the only sense they can find.'

All this I write in fear, as Mr Tregowan came today, and, taking me by the hand with great kindness, asked if tomorrow would be a suitable day for me to be wed, saying I need have no anxiety for the ceremony would be done in the drawing room, with only Willow and Cecilia and Bertie-mun as witnesses, the clerk of records, and Barbara, who is Mrs Tregowan. And I said yes, for I could do no other.

If Such a Fleeting Thing
Could Be Called a Marriage
Ceremony

This being a Friday, the seventeenth of January, and all
night long again they were covering the north pit of
Shackleton, the work having lasted five days and nights
for the men were driven back by the heat and the
presence of choakdamp. I know this from Cecilia, who
told me also that certain men of ill intent had been out in
the thoroughfares of Durham, for the city people do not
rest easily in the knowledge that women are sent down
to work in Shackleton mine, and most likely also in
Thayne and Blennowe. And indeed I knew as much,
having been awake through every watch of the night,
and hearing close enough to the house the clack of boots
and clogs and the hardly muffled voices of those who
were abroad in the streets and the lanes.

'I came not to tell you that particular, mun,' she said,
'but to let you know that Mr Tregowan is arrived and
Mrs Tregowan would speak with you. She means well,
mun,' Cecilia added as she went out of the door.

And it came to me that the housemaid Cecilia, for all
her plain speech, sees some good in everyone and is at
pains to persuade all to do the same, as if she is afraid

that they might otherwise miss whatever kindness there may be in others.

Presently Mrs Tregowan came in, preceded by a small tap on the door, and advanced towards me with both arms outstretched.

'My dear Arabella,' she said, and promptly blushed furiously. 'I'd best start again, my dear,' she said, and disappeared hastily out of the door.

She returned some seconds later, with much the same confusion, and indeed more, for further wisps of red hair had sprung out from under her bonnet.

'How can you forgive me, dear?' she said. 'They told me you are named Clara, and I immediately make a silly mistake. I'm Barbara, but you have my permission to call me anything that comes into your mind after what I've done, my dear. I'm here to acquaint you with the practicalities of married life, but after the error I've just now perpetrated I may say whatever I have to say and you won't believe a word of it.'

Then, taking my hand and gazing at a point somewhere above my eyes, she said, 'Is there anything you need to know, my dear? No, I thought not; you are too gentle and ladylike a spirit to ask. But I have to tell you, my dear, that it isn't too bad. No, not too bad at all once you are accustomed. Nathaniel is a good man and a gentle man, though he is a coal master. The only fault I find in him, and it is but a slight one, is that perhaps he talks a little too much, by which I mean that he has the habit of using ten words where one would suffice, not that he is unguarded in his speech, for he is not. If you need anything else, my dear Claribell, all you have to do is let me know.'

And seeing that Mrs Tregowan was about to dart out of the room, and wishing to detain her in the hope that she would tell me I know not what, for one is in ignorance of what one does not know, I asked her if I should wear the gown I had on, which was dark blue, to which she answered, 'Yes, Claribell, my dear darling, you need only bring yourself. Are you acquainted with the works of Mr Handel, dear? I thought you would be.'

Having said which, she went, leaving me with the conviction that if I wished to know anything I could not ask Mrs Tregowan. For whatever she knew she was too reticent to tell, for all her cascade of words. And I resolved in the future to rely on the housemaid Cecilia, whose homely words fall like the rain from heaven, unasked for, and always in season.

After Mrs Tregowan's departure, for all that she arrived in great haste and urgency as if the ceremony was about to take place immediately, a silence fell on the household, during which time I watched the sun reach the summit of his climb and begin his descent; for the smoke is disappearing from above the city of Durham and the light of the mid-winter days, although dilute, might be seen again. And I do not know how I can write so carelessly of the journey of the sun when my own matters weigh so heavily on my mind, unless it is that God set the golden sun in heaven as a thing of permanence to remind those on earth that the events of our lives, for all their great importance, pass by in the twinkling of an eye. Which thought also brings me no manner of comfort.

So passed today, and somewhere in it, when the sun had dipped behind the church of St Saviour, I was wed, if such a fleeting thing could be called a marriage ceremony. We were gathered in the drawing room, though I fail to remember how I came to be there, where Mr Tregowan read the service and Mrs Tregowan sang an air by Mr Handel; during which time Willow my maid and Cecilia the housemaid, and Bertie-mun, all being witnesses, studied between them the whole geography of the walls, ceiling and floor rather than look at Mrs Tregowan as she sang, or indeed at each other's merriment, until Willow my maid, who is quite without hearing, disappeared totally with shaking shoulders into her handkerchief, and took herself away from the proceedings.

I am to suppose that I am wed, yet what I most dread, though I do not know with certainty what it is, has not happened. For I found myself after the wedding breakfast, which took place when the candles were already lit for the night, back in this room, nothing having been asked of me but to wear the same blue gown in which I had arrived under this roof. Yet I had seen a flicker of merriment light Nathaniel Chark's eyes. And whether it was caught from Willow, or caught from the words of the service, I do not know. Only that he kissed me, and left.

In this way I have remained, seated alone by the window and watching the city of Durham sink into its rest, until the night-watchman passed by calling the hours and beseeching the citizens, some of whom he had surely awoken from their slumbers, to look up and rejoice in the stars, for the pit was sealed and the smoke had cleared from over the city.

And I was in this way occupied, craning my neck to look up at the stars, when I heard below the front door opening and steps on the Rose Pavement, which I supposed to be those of Bertie-mun returning from an errand. But presently Cecilia knocked, dressed already in her nightgown and cap, and said that the master had been detained long in overseeing the measures in place for the quenching of the fire at Shackleton, having just then gone back there. For which reason, instead of his presence in person, he had written a letter.

'And if I were in your shoes, mun, I would find a letter more to my liking than its writer, bringing in the cold and the smoke of the mine at this time of night,' she said, 'even though I were wed this very day. Good night, mun.'

Seeing Myself by the Window Looking Up at the Starry Heaven

"My beloved Clara," the letter began. "If I did not bear in mind your dread of our wedding night I would be hard pressed to find in my heart words sufficiently contrite to account for my absence at this time. As it is, I have entrusted Cecilia with this letter, who will no doubt remark to you in her blunt way that if she were you she would rather see the letter than the fellow who writ it, bringing in the cold air and the smoke of the mine at this time of night.

"Suffice to say that I have been detained at Shackleton ensuring that the last of the fire is quenched, so that the north and south pits may be afforded the free flow of air again and men may be set to work. I append hereto a sketch of the pit so that you might better understand the workings of a mine and the perils of an explosion in such a place, which is at the best of times sour with firedamp." (There followed here a neat drawing of the north and south pits, ruled out and labelled.) "The absurdity of including a representation of a colliery in what I hope you will receive as a letter of my most ardent love, my darling, is not lost upon me, and I hope and pray that some sense of the ridiculous rests with you also. May God bless you, my dear Clara. Your most loving husband, Nathaniel."

I took the letter to the window, reading it over and over again, as the rare and precious document it is, for surely I am the only woman in the whole history of the world who has received a love letter on her wedding night with a sketch of a mine "appended hereto". Yet by no means a "sketch" for it had been done painstakingly and minutely, with the headings and stentings and stoppings labelled in a fine, neat hand.

Then for the first time it came to me that, just as I am fearful of Nathaniel Chark, so also is he fearful of my fear. And indeed, it may not be that I am fearful of my husband, Nathaniel Chark, who would rather be down a coal mine on the night of his marriage than at home, but of any husband. Yet I was in the end diverted and touched by the sketch appended hereto, and went to my bed with the letter under the pillow, with the notion that were our marriage to proceed in the form of letters all might yet be well.

It was as I thought towards the dawn, though still dark, when I awoke, imagining myself to be standing at the window looking up at the stars as the night-watchman had bid us do. Yet as I came into the conscious world I discovered myself still to be lying in my bed and some other standing by the window, looking not at the stars but into the room where I lay. And I did not know whether this was man or woman, angel or adversary, only that their person as it advanced towards me obliterated all the stars in heaven and I saw nothing else, not in the room I was in or of he or she who came upon me, who appeared only as a black shape expanding until it filled the whole of my vision. Which was the last

I knew, until I awoke and the pallid dawn crept over the sill and across the counterpane, and my maid Willow blew out the candle standing on the dresser; who seeing me awake went out of the chamber and returned with Cecilia.

'Happen you heard a commotion, mun,' she said, 'or happen you did not, but there was one. It was they in Durham asking an inquest on Tessa Spence, for it is not practice to hold one when the cause is known. The master requests your company in the drawing room after you have broken your fast, mun,' she added as she was going out of the room.

And if I write down every word of this audience (for I have no other word for it) with my husband, Nathaniel Chark, it is because I remember every word of it as it was spoken by him, as if at some time in an unknown future I might wish to remember all his words, as I might wish to remember also the room in which those words were said, and the listening garden bound in winter outside the window.

And thus I will remember, in the drawing room: a table, a writing desk, four high-backed chairs, a sofa, a fireplace with a tiled surround depicting exotic plant species, two walls given over to bookshelves, one to an oak door opening into the hallway, a tall window looking onto the garden, where the cold gripped the blackened leaves in the rose bed and touched the lawn with frost.

Thus Nathaniel Chark, who also happens to be my husband, though I am at a loss to understand how or for what reason it happened: standing behind one of the four tall chairs with his left hand resting on the back of it, graceful of person and dark haired, the stars in whose eyes registered my entry, so that I was hard pressed not to look round to see who might have entered the room behind me.

'My darling Clara,' he said, 'pray be seated. There are matters for discussion which would be much easier accomplished if I could look into your sweet eyes,' he added, taking a seat at the desk opposite to mine, and gently lifting my chin. 'That's better. I can see your lovely face now.' He placed a number of papers on the table between us.

'I'm afraid it is my habit to study the pattern in the carpet and the grains of wood in the desk most of the time. I know them well,' I said.

'Look at me, Clara,' he said, 'even though I come a poor third in fascination when compared with the grains of wood and the pattern in the carpet.'

'Indeed you don't, sir,' I said.

'And what was that last word, Clara?'

'It was Nathaniel,' I said.

'That's better. And what am I to call you, my dear?'

'You may call me anything you please, Nathaniel. Mrs Tregowan called me first Arabella and then Claribell.'

'For which I am deeply sorry, my darling,' he said. 'Truly and deeply sorry. What must you have thought of us?'

'Cecilia said Mrs Tregowan means well. Cecilia sees good in everyone, and I'm trying to emulate her.'

'Then I will continue to call you Clara, my dear. And I fervently pray that your intent to emulate Cecilia and see good in everyone may extend eventually to me also, unworthy fellow though I am.'

'It does already, sir,' I said. 'If you sit here much longer you will be as I am, thinking little of yourself and studying the grains of wood in the desk.'

'Then we must give ourselves, frail creatures that we are, something else to study, must we not?' he said, sliding towards me a paper on which I recognised the drawing of the north pit of Shackleton mine, like in all respects to the sketch appended to his letter of the previous night, but indicating a fire at the foot, and with certain arrows directed downwards and upwards.

'This is the mine again,' I said, 'and a fire, and some arrows.'

'Odd though it may seem, darling, we keep a fire burning at the base of the pit so that the heated air may draw in the cool air and so ventilate the mine, which is what the arrows mean. That is how a mine works.'

He passed another paper across the desk, which was like the other but that a large area of the mine was scored through, and a cross was marked at one of the intersections. 'Something went terribly wrong, darling,' he said. 'There was, as we suppose, an accumulation of firedamp which led to an explosion. It was the Sabbath day, yet Tessa Spence was there. We have only to be thankful that there were no more, yet one is one too many. There have been murmurings among the citizens demanding an inquest.'

'Cecilia told me.'

'My darling Clara, I wish not to place my troubles on your shoulders. It is sufficient that you are intelligent of what has passed. Your own opinions on the matter I respect, whatever they are, and I do not ask you to tell me. All I ask of you, and forgive me for this will come as a surprise to you, is your presence at the Sabbath day school.'

To which I said, 'Yes, Nathaniel,' not knowing what I had consented to, yet it could be no greater or worse thing than consenting to wedlock, even with this man who seemed to me at that moment, though I did not know him, to have the face of an angel and a temperament to match. While these matters were going through my mind, he was still speaking, and it came to me that Mrs Tregowan could be right, that for a man of such quietness of spirit, Nathaniel Chark does talk a lot.

'Nathaniel, I will be present at the Sabbath day school,' I said, 'if someone would instruct me as to what to do there.'

'That is well, Clara,' he said. 'Thank you.' Then taking my hand he continued. 'My dear, do you have any recollections of the night just gone?'

'Why, Cecilia came in with your letter …'

'…saying that you would be better with an epistle than the presence of the writer, bringing in on his person the smoke of the pit and the cold night air.'

'Yes, she did, Nathaniel,' I said. 'Those were her words. Then I read the letter and saw the sketch of Shackleton mine, and I reflected on the neatness of the drawing as well as on the tragedy of the poor young woman. Then, and I do not know if I had yet retired to bed, but the night-watchman was round exhorting the citizens of Durham to look up and see the stars again, for the smoke from the fire at the colliery had cleared. And it was no time later that I was in a dream seeing myself by the window looking up at the starry heaven; yet it was not me, for the figure detached itself from the window seat and came towards my bed; and the nearer it approached the more it occupied my sight, so that soon all was filled with its black shadow. After which I knew nothing until I awoke and Willow was there, and the dawn light was creeping in at the window. It was nothing but a dream, Nathaniel. I believe I have had it before, though I don't remember when.'

He rose from his chair and walked over to the window, standing some minutes there looking out into the garden, until I wondered if I had been dismissed, or if he had forgotten that I was there.

'Nathaniel, I will leave you to your thoughts,' I said, though not to my husband.

He turned in the instant. 'How long have I been standing at the window in a brown study while you have been there waiting, Clara?'

'An hour at least, Nathaniel,' I said, whereupon he scrutinised his pocket watch for some time and sat down opposite me again, taking my hand.

'Six and a half minutes,' he said. 'We left your story as you were describing a dream you had last night, which you say you have had before. You did not tell me if this dream frightened you or not. Clara, my darling, you are talking to me and not to the grains of wood in the desk, as we have already decided. Look at me. Were you frightened in the night?'

'I don't remember.'

'Forgive me. I ask too many questions.'

'You do not ask too many questions, Nathaniel. I think I am frightened all the time. I am frightened but I don't know what I am frightened of. I am not frightened of the Sabbath day school,' I added, for the spirit of darkness had suddenly been lifted from me. 'I don't know what the Sabbath school is, but I am not frightened of it.'

'Neither more do I know what the Sabbath day school is, for I have never been there,' he said, and the stars danced in his eyes, 'but I'm sure it's very frightening. Clara, my darling, I am reluctant to ask you this, that you move out of your room into the one adjoining mine, by which you may well draw the

52

conclusion that there is to be an intimacy you do not wish for. That will not be so. These matters come to pass only in the Lord's good time. I ask you for the reason that Bertie-mun heard you cry out in your dream, which is why you found Willow watching over you when you awoke.'

'Bertie-mun?'

'His room is beneath the one you have been occupying,' Nathaniel said, going over to the window again. 'It is snowing, my dear, and all in Durham are baying at my heels demanding an inquest on poor Tessa Spence. They are making their demands in vain.'

'How so, Nathaniel?'

'It is not custom and practice, darling.'

'Never?'

'Never, darling. I beg you not to vex yourself with questions like these. God knows, I am perplexed enough myself.'

'She is not yet laid to rest?'

'No, she is not. her remains are in the keeping of certain of the mining people until the matter is resolved.'

'And if it is not resolved, what then, Nathaniel?'

'When Tessa is laid to rest and the mine is made safe, then it will be opened again and the men will be set to work. Not until. I have told you more than I intended, Clara. Forgive me, darling. I am much in need of forgiveness. That is Cecilia. Come in, my dear. We are done with what we were talking about.'

'Begging your pardon, sir,' said Cecilia, standing by the door as if she was ready to leave if she found herself a trouble, 'there are ruffians at your gate, sir, who care nothing for the poor young woman who were brought up from pit if you'll pardon my saying so, for all know it was a young woman. You would be best to take Bertie-mun with you, but I cannot find him. If it pleases you, sir, Willow and I will settle Mistress Clara in the other room. Were you to take my advice, sir, you would not answer the door, but you will do exactly as you please, sir, with respect, for you always do.'

'Yes, that would be for the best, Cecilia, my dear, if you and Willow would kindly see to it that Clara is settled in the other room. If Bertie-mun is not here, so be it. How many are outside?'

'Happen twenty or twenty-five or more, with strong liquor on them, sir,' said Cecilia. 'Only so long as you do not read to them the riot act again, sir, though I know you will do exactly as you please, with respect. 'Tis anachronistic, sir, that's what they say.'

'And what do you understand by the word anachronistic, Cecilia, my dear?' said Nathaniel.

'I will let you know rightly when I have studied it up in Mr Johnson, sir,' said Cecilia, selecting a volume from the shelf of books. 'But in practical terms I understand the former King George to be passed away, and the present King George ails in his intellect, for Bertie-mun told me. They will but laugh at the riot act, sir. And before you say to invite folks in again, sir, there are many in their cups, as you will find for yourself when you see the spewings and shittings at your gate, begging your pardon for my plain words, sir, and you also, mun, but it is so. If you leave them be they will disperse in time for they are low folk brought in to foment a quarrel with you, being the master, sir, and when the liquor runs out they will go, for none in Durham will sell to them.'

And I was waiting for my husband to enquire of Cecilia what she understood by the word foment, but he did not, for before he could say anything there came from the parlour, which is at the front of the house, the sudden crash of breaking glass.

Whereupon my husband said, as if it were but a small matter, 'I must see what they are about.'

And as the drawing room door was opened I had a strange sense that he who had been in my room during the night was at that moment in the hallway, although it was only a dream I had in the night and there was no one there. Only my maid Willow stood at the foot of the staircase with an empty pail in her hand, who on seeing Nathaniel made in dumb show the act of throwing water from the pail, though there was no knowing if she had done as she wished him to suppose, for there was no one left outside to bear witness. And all was quiet as if nothing had happened, except a pane gone in the parlour window and a clod of frozen earth on the carpet wrapped in paper, which my husband glanced at and put in his pocket.

'You will find no glass to sweep up, Cecilia, my dear, for it is outside and I will ask Bertie-mun to do it,' he said.

Every Voice but My Own

Being the Lord's day again, my husband and I went to the dissenting chapel, taking with us Willow, Cecilia and Bertie-mun, all muffled against a biting wind from the east which had blown the snow off the by-ways in some places and made great drifts in others, and had set the trees creaking and rattling above our heads.

But in spite of the bitter cold the chapel was full to overflowing, there being some fifty-five there besides ourselves; whether for the praise of the Lord or because Mr Tregowan kept a stove burning I do not know, but Cecilia said it was for the latter reason. And I suppose I will learn one day why, in spite of us all being ready a full hour before the time we had to set off, my husband, who in all other respects is deliberate and prompt in his habits, would dither and delay until we were all but late, leading us in and stationing us at the back with a sea of worshippers in damp garments before us.

After a while a steam made up of many homely fragrances filled the chapel, which is a plain white room furnished with forms and a table at one end, and a wooden box by the side of it so that Mr Tregowan might be seen by each one as he offered up the psalm: "I was glad when they said unto me, we will go into the house of the Lord". Behind me the voices of Cecilia, Bertie-mun and Willow, though she is without speech, and

56

beside me the fine tenor voice of my husband Nathaniel were raised to the Lord. Every voice but my own.

And on this the nineteenth day of the first month of the year 1812 and the sixteenth day of my own beginning, in the plain white room of a dissenting chapel with the hiss of the stove and the windows running with steam, I asked the question of myself: was I glad to be in the house of the Lord? And the answer came back to me emphatically that I was not.

Then I took to studying not the grains in the wood or the patterns in the carpet as was my habit, but the weave in the cloak of the good woman standing in front of me, following its intricate journey across her back until the criss-crossing stopped at a seam, and the voices in the chapel fell silent, and I needed no longer make a pretence at being glad. For if the truth be told I felt a desolation I had not in my entire vocabulary a word for.

Presently the service came to an end, as all things in this transient world must, and Nathaniel took off his own cloak and wrapped it round my shoulders, saying that I would feel the cold badly after the heat of the chapel, which I was not used to in the same way that everyone else was; and if I could tolerate such an encumbrance I might be introduced to members of the meeting as his dearly beloved wife. Yet seeing that I was suffering under the necessity to the study grains of wood in the bench and the warp and weft of a weave, though I did not say a word about such things to him, he said that introductions were no matter of urgency and might be accomplished at any time. And as if to make up for the deficit in my social intercourse that morning he filled our walk home with talk of each one there without malice and with so much good humour that I was in the end laughing in spite of my sadness.

'For we are all of us quaint creatures,' he said, 'and I sometimes wonder about that, my dear Clara, for by this time in history the Lord has had plenty of practice that he might have set the pattern to rights. Which is not to make light of the Lord's handiwork,' he added, and a sudden melancholy fell on him, by which I understood that his thoughts had returned to Tessa Spence, as well as to the missile thrown into the parlour, which had with it, so Cecilia said, a letter of ill-intent.

'It is the Sabbath day school, Nathaniel,' I said in an attempt to lift his spirits, for I had come early to the conclusion that he is much like me, and ready to sink into the doldrums at any time of the day. And I don't know whether it is better that he and I are not sailing in the doldrums at the same time as each other, or whether it would be companionable to find another soul swimming in that dreary place.

'Willow and Cecilia will assist you with the Sabbath day school, as they assisted Enid,' he said presently. 'And, my darling, I have just committed the final and terrible injustice of naming her, when I had promised to myself not to injure your feelings by talking of her in your presence. I will not do so again, as the Lord is my witness.'

Then I said to Nathaniel that he had my leave, though I could not speak for the Lord, to talk of Enid as often as he wished, and I told him also that when I first arrived in his household Willow had drawn my attention to her portrait and pointed out my likeness to her. To which he said nothing, and I feared I had delivered a mortal hurt in wishing to do the opposite.

'I don't know why we must go to chapel,' said Cecilia later, 'for it casts a gloom over all of us and the master most of all, and I'll be bound every one of them other folks there, with all of us reminded once a week of our sinfulness and whatnot. The slates in the schoolroom is out ready, miss, and Bertie-mun has set the chairs. 'Tis like chapel, for they will trudge miles through the snow to sit by a stove.'

'What do I teach them, Cecilia?' I said.

'Just their letters, mun,' she said. 'Those will do as well as anything. 'Tis what miss Enid did.'

'And do they not know their letters by now, Cecilia?'

'Some does and some doesn't,' she said, 'but Miss Enid disliked that some should run away with their learning and others was left behind. Therefore, until all have their letters that is what they study. They are waiting, mun.'

And indeed, I looked out and saw a huddle gathered at the gate and Bertie-mun grappling with the lock, which had frozen fast since the time we returned from chapel. Then I saw that Bertie-mun had left the scholars shivering and stamping their feet, and had come back inside, making such a long time of it that I was afraid the Sabbath day school was abandoned for the afternoon. Yet at length he returned with a pan of hot coals, which he gave to one of the scholars to hold while he worked on the lock.

Then suddenly they were all of them in the school room, and the huddle separated itself into seven distinct persons, whom I could not recognise to be either men or women, or indeed bairns, so wrapped against the cold were they, and so grimed in their faces; and all of them with the same aroma, compounded of the pit and the odours of the body and of Sunday soapings. And neither do I know how I must have appeared to them, for had not Willow pointed out my likeness to Enid's portrait, I would not know how my face looks, nor my person; but that looking down at myself, which is neither tall nor otherwise, nor sturdy nor yet angular, I know only that I am dressed today in a louring grey, the colour of the smoke that has only recently cleared from over the city of Durham, and the colour of the doldrums in which my husband and I are sunk. But, for all that, I was not afraid of the Sabbath day school.

'Good day,' I said.

'Good day, mun.'

Seven voices replied, yet still I could not have said if they were those of men or women, for all the voices were equally low and gritty as if the dust from the pit had entered the wind pipes of their owners.

'We will do our letters today,' I said, 'but first I must learn your names. You see, I have a hard task, for I have seven names to learn and you have only one. I am called Clara. One by one, if you would be so kind.'

'William Darbyshire, mun.'

'Frederick Pennell, mun.'

'James Sowerby, if you please, mun.'

'Alfred Baines, mun.'

'Amos Frost, mun.'

'Bartholomew, mun, for I have no other.'

'Gregory Parrish, mun.'

To each of which I said thank you, while wondering how it was that at least three of the gentlemen scholars had the form of women and appeared to be wearing bosoms under their coats, about which I made up my mind to enquire of Cecilia afterwards.

I asked the scholars to write each one his name on the board, which they did, all of them, and then identify the letters of the alphabet, which they did, all of them;

then the common words, cat, dog, mat, tin, man, hat, cap, which they did, all except two of the scholars who foundered at first, righting themselves immediately.

And thus we proceeded swiftly through the lesson, which was not a lesson, for there was nothing to teach; and we might at the end have had all of Mr Johnson's dictionary up on the board, but that Cecilia came in with heels of bread to give the scholars. With which distribution the Sabbath day school may well have drawn to a close, but that while Cecilia was occupied with the heels of bread I wrote on the board the words Shackleton, Blennowe, Thayne, colliery, Spedding, Durham, firedamp. And all the scholars foundered, knowing the words well but not the sight of them. And each one looked in wonderment at the strange patterns, which surely meant nothing but toil and dark and hardship, and the fearful prospect of rampant fire under the earth.

'You mean you noted some of the gentlemen scholars have bosoms, mun,' Cecilia said when they had gone, which was all she had to offer on the matter. And I did not then like to suggest to her that the scholars without exception would be equal to the entire works of Mr Richardson in the near future, only so long as those works did not contain the words which concerned them the most, as belonging to the colliery.

'You have taught class before, mun,' Cecilia continued, which remark threw me suddenly into the greatest bewilderment, for though I might have taught class before and have a passing acquaintance with the works of Mr Richardson, those things seem to me to belong to some other life and not to my own.

Then the thought came to me that, whether or not I am in the doldrums, I am all the time like a ship drifting on the sea without any anchor, not knowing where it has come from and not knowing where it is going. And in the instant it came to me that my husband Nathaniel is the same, his first wife having gone from this world, and not knowing if his life might be regained. For we are both of us in ships drifting on the open sea, but whether we are in the same ship or not, I do not know.

'You have taught class before, miss,' said Cecilia again. 'The master told me you had. Happen you are too humble to say so of yourself, mun.'

I don't know if Cecilia expected some kind of response, but I gave none, for I wondered, if I held my peace, she might tell me other things about my life I had lost hold of. But there was nothing more on the matter, and Cecilia continued to collect up the slates, dusting each one clean if she saw any remains of the afternoon's class.

'You might have supposed you were going to occupy the chamber adjoining the master's,' she said as she was going out the door. 'But it is not so, as you will have found out, mun. You are in the room opposite on account that the master does not wish you to feel apprehensive of his presence. Begging you pardon for my blunt speech, mun. You need not be feared of him.'

Then, since Cecilia stood at the door as if she had something further to say, and although to speak the words filled me with a cold dread, I asked her why the master should think I would be fearful of his presence in the adjoining room.

'That I do not know, mun,' she said, 'lest it be that the rooms have a door between, and on account of the accident you suffered, mun, which I do not know what it was and by the look of you happen you don't either. You are as white as yonder snow, mun, and 'tis on account of my big mouth, for which I humbly beg your pardon.'

So saying, Cecilia left the schoolroom, asking me as she did so to go to the parlour where a fire had been made, as the stove in the schoolroom was left to burn out after the Sabbath day school. Yet I stood by the window looking out at the flakes of snow drifting down, for the easterly wind of the morning had dropped, and the day was closing into stillness.

There I turned over in my mind Cecilia's words, which led nowhere but back to my fear, until I had visited all of my life I could lay hold on, which was meagre, being like the portmanteau in which my possessions had been brought to the house of Mr Chark and containing little. And I could find no fear in it, unless it was in the dream on the night the watchman had exhorted the citizens of Durham to look up and see the stars and in the figure that cancelled out the stars.

So caught up was I in these wonderings that I had not heard the door of the schoolroom open, nor heard the steps across the floor; nothing, indeed, until a shadow glided over my shoulder and I could see in the window glass that I was in the presence of someone who had all the appearance of the intruder in my dream, who was even then wrapping a shawl round my shoulders.

'Clara, you are shivering, my darling. The stove has burnt down,' he said.

'Nathaniel, I'm sorry, I'm not cold in the least. I saw your reflection in the glass and you appeared somewhat like the intruder in my dream the other night,' I said.

'Am I like that intruder?'

'No, no, you are not, not at all. I meant no detriment to you in what I said. Nothing could be farther from my mind. Forgive me, Nathaniel, I am babbling like a brook and making less sense. How did you know I was here?'

'That wasn't difficult. We missed you at the table and I asked Cecilia.'

'Cecilia knows everything.'

'They are still waiting for you or me to say the grace.'

'Then we had best be present, Nathaniel, or we must all starve, and Willow and Cecilia and Bertie-mun do not deserve that. I am recovered.'

Yet I was not, and the figure in the glass stays printed on my imaginings, so that I have come to believe that it was not the reflection of my husband I had seen but the embodiment of someone other outside the window.

Nathaniel took my arm and led me to the parlour as if we were any married couple, which I am to suppose that we are, for Mr Tregowan read the words of the service, and Mrs Tregowan sang an air by Mr Handel in our honour, and the clerk recorded our union in the annals of this world.

In the parlour Willow, Cecilia and Bertie-mun were already seated at the table, and rose to their feet as we entered, for all of the household is present for the Sunday high tea. Though I have to say that the arrangement is not to their unmitigated delight, as the presence of Nathaniel, which is pleasant to his household in the homely light of day when they are his servants, is fearful to them when he makes himself their equal. And none had any conversation to offer, except for stray words which fell as the flakes of snow fell outside, drifting past one by one and going nowhere. Indeed, poor Bertie-mun had no talk to offer at all, as he is used to eating alone, and was all the time occupied with trying not to dribble, so out of the ordinary is his face. Then Cecilia, when the last attempt at talk had foundered and there was nothing to be heard but the sound of the coals settling in the grate, spoke.

''Twas but two or three days ago but it is as if it were a lifetime' she said.

'To what are you referring, my dear?' said Nathaniel.

'Why sir, to the broken pane,' she said, 'for Bertie-mun and me, we came expecting for there to be splinters of glass yet there was none, as you said, sir. 'Twas after them folks came demanding an inquest, sir.'

'Yes, Cecilia, I remember,' said Nathaniel.

'Then, sir, it was not broken from the outside,' said Cecilia.

'No, Cecilia, I have thought that also,' said Nathaniel.

'And happen there was a stone put inside to make pretence the pane was broken from the outside, sir.'

'Then whoever put the stone inside did not think as intelligently as you think, Cecilia, my dear.'

'And happen the stone had a letter wrapped to it, sir.'

'You are right, Cecilia, as you are right in all else, but the contents of the letter are not fit hearing for ladies. Is that all?'

'Yes, sir,' said Cecilia. 'Only begging your pardon, sir, and that of Mistress Clara, for Mistress Willow and Mr Bertie-mun are acquainted with the message of the letter, it said ...'

At which Nathaniel rose from the table, pushing back his chair and taking no pains to conceal the mask of darkness that passed across his face.

'That will do, Cecilia,' he said. 'Thank you, my dear. We will now say the departing grace.' Which indeed he shouted, as if the Lord were deficient in hearing, as well as in heaven. 'I will see you in the drawing room presently, Clara, my dear,' he added.

Then Cecilia, Willow and Bertie-mun began the clearing of the table, and for all that a gloom had descended on the evening with the allusion to the letter, my maid Willow was in fits of stifled laughter, which I supposed to be on account of the grace, sent loudly skywards as if the Lord is as she is, and unable to hear.

'I am afraid Cecilia spoke out of turn,' Nathaniel said on my arrival in the drawing room. 'Although it pleases me that the good souls in our household converse, and dear Cecilia means well, it vexes me when the affairs of the mine are discussed. I feel that I showed ill humour towards poor Cecilia, did I not?' he added, leading me to the fireside and taking the chair opposite. The warmth of the fire and the pleasant aspect of my husband's face settled in thought and illuminated by the glow from the hearth quickly took away every word I had, and I found myself hard pressed to keep awake.

'Your silence informs me that you think I did wrong, my dear.'

'I know nothing of the matter Cecilia spoke of,' I said, 'and as to your showing ill humour, I did not notice that either. Forgive me, Nathaniel, the warmth has made me drowsy, which is why I am silent.'

'Cecilia was referring to a morsel of paper wrapped round a clod of frozen earth which was found in the parlour after the pane of glass had been broken. The paper had certain writings on it which Cecilia seems to be privy to, though I do not know how.'

'Where is the letter?'

'I could not say, darling. I put it in my pocket, no doubt along with parts of the earth and stones, and it has gone.'

'Yet the earth and stones are still in your pocket?'

'No, my dear.'

'Then surely Cecilia, seeing that your coat was dirtied with earth from the garden, and intending to brush it down, found the letter.'

Nathaniel went over to the door and rang the bell. Presently Willow appeared.

'If you please, Willow, would you ask Cecilia to come to the drawing room, dear,' he said, forgetting her infirmity.

'Willow cannot hear, Nathaniel,' I said when she had gone.

'Yet she knows words,' he said. 'I have pondered on that often, that she cannot hear and yet she knows what is said. Cecilia, come in.'

Cecilia said nothing, but took a dirtied paper from her pocket, gave it to Nathaniel, and left the room. Without looking at it he threw it into the fire, where, caught in a down draught from the chimney, it fluttered half burnt onto the hearth, opening as it did so to reveal a rough script: "2 murdures Charke thow will pay wyth thy life"

'You have read what is written,' said my husband. 'Tessa Spence was with child. May the Lord forgive me, for I did not know.'

Long Destitute by Now

The windows have been sheeted in ice, and drawn out in ferns and feathers which have not melted all day; and it being Monday wash day, Cecilia was at the copper, and Bertie-mun at the wringer. And Willow was all day setting steaming linen on horses in the scullery, as, being my maid, she has little enough to occupy her. And I likewise, for I have been living in Mr Chark's house for more than two weeks and I do not know my duties, unless they are to take the Sabbath day class, which is only one day in the week. For Nathaniel orders the mine, Cecilia the household, Bertie-mun the heavy work, Willow the mistress (being myself), and the mistress (being also myself) is like a lost soul without a purpose; this especially on Monday wash day when everyone else is occupied and Nathaniel takes himself down to Shackleton to be out of their way and to avoid falling over horses of steaming linen.

And all were on foot as no carriages were out today on account of the ice, for which reason the viewer, whose name I cannot recall if indeed I ever knew it, went down to Shackleton walking to see when men may be put to work again.

'Once the matter of Tessa Spence is settled,' Nathaniel said, as if he had quite forgotten the letter of ill intent and its fearful contents.

Then it came to me that all those who work Shackleton mine, having been idle these fifteen days, will have been long destitute by now, and I decided to make this observation to Cecilia, who was still in the scullery, for all that she had remained silent since my husband's sayings of the night before.

'It will be some while before the matter of Tessa Spence is done, miss,' she said. 'And it could be that they who came setting up a mayhem at our gate were not from the mine but candymen an' ne'er do wells, but there are certain folks at the colliery also who will make use of any pretext to oppose the master. An I dislike to say this to you, miss, being his wedded wife, but it is so. As to them from Shackleton being in penury and hardship, happen they are, if being on half wages when full wages is scarce enough places a body in hardship. Pardon my blunt speech, miss, you being the master's wedded wife an' all. An' since you ask, for that you are bound to do, when the pit is opened up an' the men set to work again, happen they will be required to continue to work to half pay until the quota is made up. So I hear, mun, from them as work other pits.' Which speech, delivered as she stood in the door ready to make her departure, set me wondering how Cecilia, who is tied to the household and scarce goes out even on her half day's liberty, knows of these matters.

'Where do you hear such things, Cecilia?' I said.

'Why, at holy scripture, miss. Not that 'tis set down in holy writ what passes in the pits, for I doubt the Lord God knows, but from they that stay behind for instruction after service, for Mrs Tregowan does always leave us to our own devices while she visits the privy between the service an' holy scripture. Pardoning my plain speech, mun.'

'And what's to do for the colliers in hardship?'

Cecilia's face set in a dark fury. 'Begging your pardon, mun, what's to do is for the master of Shackleton an Belnnowe an' Thayne, who is your recently wedded husband, to give them miners a raise. And I know 'tis not Mr Chark only, for 'tis the going rate for pit work an' in yonder parts also. Besides which, they must needs have less of hours. An' less of bairns down pit.'

'It has struck me that certain of the gentlemen scholars are women, Cecilia, though they each of them give a gentleman's name.'

'I know nothing of such things,' said Cecilia, 'and whether the gentlemen have bosoms some of them, which you have remarked on before, miss, asking your pardon. But happen one wage don't suffice. An' happen your recently wedded husband is witless of the matter, miss. I like you not to be in the steam for it is like to clap to your lungs, mun, an' there is plenty around here with the consumption.'

'I am at a loss as to how to occupy myself, Cecilia,' I said. 'You and Willow and Bertie-mun all have the Monday wash to occupy your hands and I pass my days in idleness.'

'They also serve who only stand and wait, miss,' she said.

'What is that, Cecilia?'

'I do not know, mun,' she said. 'Happen 'tis from holy scripture. I've heard it of the master, for he is full of words, though not all is to my liking. If you please, miss.'

I followed Cecilia out of the scullery to the cupboard under the main stairway where, reaching inside, she took down the household keys from a nail; then up the staircase to the drawing room and my former chamber, and again up to the landing which is where my present chamber is, and opposite to it my husband's. Then, before I could find the words to restrain her, Cecilia unlocked the door of Nathaniel's room, leaving it standing wide. And although I did not look in, I caught from the edge of my eye all of my husband's widowed life: the cheerless couch, the cold hearth, the small table on which lay the Holy Bible and the writings of Mr Milton and Mr Bunyan; a desk scattered with papers, sooted as if from the mines; and two upright chairs.

'It is cold, Cecilia,' I said. 'It is colder in the master's room than in the pantry.'

''Tis so, miss,' she said. 'Bertie-mun would build up a good fire but the master wills it not.'

Then I thought of how Nathaniel had taken off his cloak and wrapped it round my shoulders after the Sunday service.

'Perhaps the master does not feel the cold,' I said.

'The master feels the cold as any other body feels the cold,' said Cecilia. 'He will never be done with chastising himself. If you please, miss.'

Cecilia removed a small key from the mantle shelf and started for the end of the landing, and for the narrow staircase leading to the upper corridor. And for all that Nathaniel would not have a fire in his own room, I noticed, as I followed her, that Cecilia's boots were newly mended, and her gown of a heavy woollen fabric, as is the gown of Willow my maid.

'That is not to say the master deprives us, mun,' Cecilia said. 'On the contrary. An' though I had rancour in my heart towards him yesterday eve that is but a passing thing which will blow away. Happen you thought this was a common closet, miss, an' I know not if I do right in showing you. But 'tis not to do harm to you, mun, for nothing would fret me more.' Saying which, Cecilia unlocked the door and went in, looking behind to see if I was following. 'Be not dismayed, miss,' she said. 'Bertie-mun would clear this room but that the master wishes it to be left. Though I know for a certainty that he has not visited it since you were in the house, mun,' she added, 'for I have looked to make sure the key on the mantle has not been disturbed, and it has not.'

'And if he had been here?'

'But he has not, mun. For the key is as it has been these weeks past. 'Tis Miss Enid's sewing press here, may the Lord bless her sweet soul. She was like to your good self and begged occupation, and Mrs Tregowan, for she means well, miss, set her to work with her needle for the bairns in Shackleton an' all. They's left as she left them. See the needle with the twine in, mun. With your leave, miss, I'll ask of Mrs Tregowan after next Sunday scripture if she might find occupation for you, for she means well, as I says.'

To which suggestion from Cecilia I gave my consent, or I believe I did, for she said no more and returned the key to the mantle shelf in Nathaniel's chamber. But in truth I felt a cold dread grip me, for Arabella Chark's room was as if she had stepped out of it for but a short time, leaving, besides an unfinished hem, a cradle ready for her bairn, with an embroidered counterpane, and the fortepiano uncovered as if for playing, with a book of the airs of Mr Handel open and annotated.

And it came to me that I was not in the house of the living but of those who have passed on from this world and left it behind. A feeling of terrible oppression descended on me, knowing also that my husband had been in the habit of going to his late wife's work room where there was a cradle made ready for their lost bairn. And knowing moreover that we were all of us in this desolate place together, Nathaniel and I, and Willow, Cecilia and Bertie-mun.

'Happen you are under the impression that we all of us live in a house of the dead, mun,' said Cecilia, 'but if you were to say such a thing to Mrs Tregowan, not that you will, if you take my meaning, she would say to you in return that Miss Enid is the more living of all, having gone to dwell with the Heavenly Father. Though I know not if that is the case,' she added, 'but if Miss Enid is anywhere, 'tis in heaven. That's the master come in, mun. We'd best be down the stairs.'

And I knew in my heart that Nathaniel would sense that the door to Arabella's work room had been open, and that he would, like Cecilia and I, breathe in the sleeping air from the closed chamber which now pervaded all the landings. Yet he said nothing.

A Dark Flame

The thaw is now four days in, and the first of St Joseph's thorn is in flower in the garden. I write "the" garden because I do not know how I will ever be able to think of the garden on the Rose Pavement as "our" garden, as if I were part of this household which I am led to believe that I am by all but myself. And all around a great weeping has set in, with every twig and every blade of grass bright with tears, and all the crevices and gulleys running with plaited streams of melt; which general lamentation I can only suppose to have been sent from heaven, for today Tessa Spence was laid to rest.

Mr Tregowan came early and was shown by Cecilia into the drawing room, where Nathaniel was seated at the desk occupying himself with correspondence and I by the fireside reading Mr Richardson; both of us, no doubt, having the appearance of contentment as if we were any wedded couple, which Mr Tregowan believes that we are.

'Mrs Chark, my dear.' Mr Tregowan stepped forwards, and it was again all I could do not to look behind me to see who else he might be addressing. 'Ah, Mr Richardson, I see.'

'Nathaniel kindly brought me the volume, which is less to his taste than mine,' I said. 'I fear I am a frivolous woman, Mr Tregowan.'

Whereupon my husband took my idle hand in his and said, 'My wife is so frivolous that she has asked to be present at Tessa's farewell, Patrick. The people of Shackleton will value that as a graceful and compassionate gesture, will they not? You may say what we were going to discuss between ourselves in Clara's presence.'

Then the talk between my husband and Mr Tregowan turned to the form of service, and I learned that Mr Tregowan knows about the letter of ill intent, and knows also that there are some who say, whether it is the truth or not, that Tessa was with child.

'Had there been an inquest the matter may well have been established,' said Mr Tregowan, 'but it is not the custom to cause additional distress when the manner of demise is known, as it sadly is with poor Tessa. So I propose to say words to the effect that she for whom we are gathered together is thought to have been with child, and commend both souls to the tender mercy of the Lord Jesus. "Thought" or "believed", do you suppose, Nathaniel?'

'I do not know, Patrick,' said my husband. 'You are the man of letters and must do as you think best. I know not the difference, except if it is that thought is from the head and belief is from the heart, but neither one is of use to Tessa Spence. I have much to answer for.'

'Come, come, my good man,' said Mr Tregowan. 'We don't want you in that dark place again, sir,' saying which, he cast a questioning glance in my direction.

'We are both of us in the doldrums from time to time, Mr Tregowan,' I said, 'though not in the same doldrums at the same time, is that not so, Nathaniel?'

'Ah, the doldrums. You are a student of Mr Coleridge also, my dear Mrs Chark,' said Mr Tregowan.

'Clara says rightly,' my husband said, ignoring entirely Mr Coleridge, 'and as we are not in the same doldrums at the same time, then we may help each other. As for the words thought or believed, you will say what is appropriate, Patrick, for the Lord will give you utterance. If we are to go on foot we should look to beginning our walk now.'

'Barbara would value your good company in the carriage, Mrs Chark,' said Mr Tregowan.

I said nothing, for the arrangement was very much to my disliking, not because I have any aversion towards Mrs Tregowan, which I do not, for she is a sweet soul who means well, as Cecilia has often pointed out, but because I did not wish to go in a carriage like a privileged woman. Yet that is not to say Mrs Tregowan behaves as a woman of privilege, for she does not, but that she is obliged to travel by the quickest means because the weakness of her bladder dictates that she cannot be long without the comfort of knowing there to be a privy nearby. So Cecilia has said, which leads me to believe that Mrs Tregowan's most intimate secrets are discussed freely among the scholars before holy scripture, as are the secrets of the mines.

And without intending it I tightened my grip on Nathaniel's hand, for I could say nothing of my reluctance to travel by carriage for fear of offending Mrs Tregowan, which was far from my wishes. Then as I was at a loss for words of my own, my husband asked for a moment's private conversation with Mr Tregowan outside the door, and when they returned the matter was resolved, that I was to walk to Shackleton hamlet with my husband, and Cecilia, Willow and Bertie-mun.

The morning continued to weep desolate tears from every high and low place, and from the sky also for a drenching grey rain had begun to fall, as if the whole of creation mourned the passing of poor Tessa Spence. And everyone in the city of Durham came out hatless from their front doors and followed us, being for the most part the very same who had offered assistance in kind after the explosion, until we were a great crowd who came down into Shackleton. For those who lived there were already out, men and women and bairns, the women wrapped in shawls and all soaked through and already dark clad on account of the soots that sank daily into their garments; and before whom stood a cart bearing Tessa's casket.

Then we came, all of us, to join the people of Shackleton. And certain among them raised voices in discontent on seeing the master there, which would likely have risen into a howl, but that seeing Mrs Tregowan being helped down flustered and red of face from the carriage they fell silent, and some reached out to touch her as she made her way towards her husband; who, seeing she had arrived, began to speak.

'Good people of Shackleton,' he said, 'we are gathered here today to bid farewell to our dear sister Tessa. Would Tessa's kindred kindly take up their places behind the carriage, and afterwards her good neighbours and friends. Be not dismayed, for the hearts of all the people of Durham go out to you, my dear brothers and sisters.'

But there were no kindred. Mr Tregowan asked again. Still none came forward. He asked a third time, his voice echoing the more loudly around the lanes and dwellings of Shackleton, as if any who were still in their beds might be woken up and summoned. Yet none came, and all was in silence but for the occasional stamping of the horse with Tessa's cart, and the sound of the falling of the rain. By which I suddenly understood that those who were her kindred might feel dismay that she had been found to be with child out of wedlock.

And it came to me also, though I do not know why, that although no one else was willing to go forward to follow behind her casket, yet I should do so myself, being a sister in her adversities. So I let go of my husband's hand as if I were casting myself adrift, and as if we were indeed in different ships on our sea of troubles; and I took up my place behind the cart on which poor Tessa Spence lay. Yet I was not alone, for no sooner had I done so than Barbara Tregowan stood by my side, who is surely a woman blameless before heaven and earth, which I cannot say for myself, for all that I have little recall.

So we set off for the waste tract of land that does as the burial ground for Shackleton, which was now seething and boiling under the torrential rain. And as we walked the conviction came to me that I could have been like Tessa Spence had not the master of Shackleton, who is despised for his station in life, taken me in. Which thoughts occupied my mind so utterly that I did not come to myself until we were at the side of the grave and Mr Tregowan was concluding the service.

'We commend them into thy safe and merciful keeping, Lord Jesus Christ. May they rest in peace. Amen,' not knowing if he had used the word "thought" or the word "believed" or neither, or, indeed, if it mattered.

And Tessa Spence might have gone forth in peace, but that the gathering was broken by someone crashing through it, forging a straight pathway, for none cared to stop him. And I recognised the man called Brim Salter, yet hardly Brim Salter, for he now had the look of a habitual drinker of strong liquor on him, being unwashed and unkempt, and his face unshaven and his eyes shot with blood. Then approaching Tessa's grave he stood tottering on the brink and would likely have thrown himself in, had not two of the colliers standing nearby restrained him.

Brim Salter stood there between them casting about, first up to heaven, and then sweeping the crowd with his eyes as if looking for someone to blame; until suddenly he broke free, staggering towards my husband with a great hand raised in fury. And before anyone could stop him, for the whole thing happened as in a flash of lightning, he had felled Nathaniel.

So Cecilia told me afterwards, for I remember nothing between seeing Brim Salter standing at the graveside drunken and reeling between the two good men from the colliery, and crossing the bridge of the Wear with my arm in Nathaniel's and Bertie-mun on the other side offering what consolations he could in his dribbling way. And I believe at that moment a dark flame arriving from I know not where sprang up in my heart.

"What Have I Done to You?"

I do not know if I was dreaming last night or not, for I have never known a dream in which the actors cough so piteously. It was a hollow, pained cough that I heard towards the midnight hour, and I thought also I heard footsteps on the staircase, then travelling along the higher landing, and returning. The dream, if it was a dream, continued for upwards of half an hour, the footsteps going three times up the staircase and along the upper corridor, and always the same hollow cough, which became worse as the journeys continued. Nor did I know how many there were on such a painful journey, whether only one or if there was a fellow traveller. After which I must have fallen asleep, as the next thing I knew was the sound of Willow drawing back the curtains, letting another day into the room.

And far from the weeping of yesterday the morning was golden and sunlit, as if heaven was giving welcome to Tessa Spence after her hardships in this world, which, having had such a thought, I spoke it aloud to Willow my maid although she has no hearing.

Yet before long the glittering day turned to darkness and misgiving in my soul, if not in the world outside the window, where all was carrying on as merrily as any fine day before the Sabbath. For as soon as my thoughts turned to Tessa Spence, then so also came back the aspect of Brim Salter, pale under the influence of strong liquor and his eyes shot with blood, who would have leapt into the grave had not two good men from the colliery prevented him, and who then turned his fury on my husband, though I have no recollection of it. Nor did Nathaniel refer to the incident for the rest day, which carried on as if nothing untoward had happened.

'I fear the master will now be feeling the soreness from yesterday's calamity,' I said to Willow.

'You might well say calamity, mun,' said Cecilia, who was now also in the room. 'I did knock, miss, but you did not hear. The master is in the scullery. He is asking for you.'

'Scullery?' I said. 'Why the scullery?'

''Tis where the apothecary cupboard is, mun. Happen you did not know of it for it is not our habit to ail.'

'You had a raw time of it on my account yesterday, darling,' said Nathaniel as I entered the scullery. 'Forgive me if I don't turn round to look at you, Clara. I wished that you should never encounter adversity as my wife, and this has happened when we are but short weeks into our wedded life. What have I done to you? Pray be so good as to sit by me, darling. The apothecary will be in attendance presently and will no doubt need your assistance.'

'Kindly cease your chatter, sir,' said Cecilia. ''Twill bring on the cough, which you well know. The master has a cough, mun, which is from being out in the rain without his hat.'

'Then half of all those who live in Durham and Shackleton besides have a cough this morning, Cecilia, if that is your reasoning,' said Nathaniel. 'The apothecary will be well occupied.'

'The apothecary is now here, sir,' said Cecilia.

Yet I saw only my maid Willow, who had lately come in at the door and was busying herself laying out on the table tinctures from the cupboard, and applying salves to the edges of my husband's wound. Meanwhile I sat by him watching for the hurt to show itself on his face, but it did not.

'Mistress Willow would ask for you please to remove the master's top shirt, mun,' said Cecilia, 'for you may do so being his wedded wife, but we may not with decency, being servants in his household. Pray leave off your chatter, sir. You'll bring on the cough.' For Nathaniel had made to protest and say that he would take off his own shirt, at which point a terrible and painful cough interrupted the words he would have spoken, and a line of bright blood started from the corner of his mouth.

'There, I told you, sir,' said Cecilia. 'Kindly let the mistress do it. If you please, mun,' she added.

So I did as I was bidden, loosening the laces of the shirt and opening the neck. And I had no doubt that the quaintness of the situation was not lost upon my husband either, that the first time I should undress him was to be in the scullery with the servants of his household looking on. For while this operation was taking place Bertie-mun had come in also, holding in his hand a glass phial and muttering a word which sounded to me for all the world like ooomimun.

'Place it on the table, if you please, Bertie-mun,' said Cecilia, for there was still no apothecary present, in spite

82

of Cecilia having announced him in the last quarter of an hour. And no one either remarked on what could only have been obvious to us all, namely that, extending from my husband's jaw to a twelve inch length below the bone they call the collar bone on the left side, there was a broken and bloodied bruise, the lower part of which appeared to be breathing of itself, for small bubbles arose and broke on the surface even as I watched, which I did until the whole scene swam before me and I could see nothing clearly.

'Had the master worn his thick coat it would have muffled the blow,' said Cecilia, 'but he would not. See, your good lady wife is like to weep, sir,' she added.

Then Nathaniel, with his right hand, brushed away the tears which I did not know were there, and asked again the question, to which I had no answer.

'What have I done to you, Clara, my darling?'

'We must seek the advice of the apothecary,' I said, for my tongue was suddenly loosened, yet I did not wish to alarm my husband by drawing the attention of Cecilia to the breathing wound. Then the apothecary, who had been present all the time, being Willow my maid, laid a salve and a poultice over the wound and bid Nathaniel take a potion, showing me the preparations and their labels: ULMI FOR THE WOUND and PULMONARIA FOR THE LUNG.

'For 'tis one or the other at them mines,' Cecilia said, 'the wound or the lung, lest it be the burn; and the master has both the wound and the lung, though not the burn, thanks be to God, and to do him justice he does not complain.'

I saw then that all the household realised the severity of the master's wound and had observed that it breathed by itself, though none would remark on this phenomenon in his presence; for he could not himself see it, and continued to submit to Willow's careful ministrations without a murmur, having been ordered by Cecilia to hold his tongue.

'We have to call the surgeon,' I said presently. Yet no one agreed, and it seemed to me that Cecilia and Bertie-mun exchanged glances, though I have not known them to do so before. 'Must we not send for a surgeon?' I said again. 'It is not that I would undermine the skill of the apothecary,' I added. Cecilia spoke by way of an answer, not to me but to Nathaniel.

'Happen the mistress does not know, sir,' she said. 'You may speak, so long as it is only a few words, for 'tis not in my place to tell her.'

'It is not fitting that we should send for the surgeon, my dear,' Nathaniel said, 'for the surgeon is himself most in need of healing. I am much recovered now. Thank you, my dear Willow. We must needs see to the opening of the pit, in which case we will have to ask you for the use of your hand, Clara, darling.' Which I assumed to mean assistance in walking and started from my chair, but Nathaniel was already striding for the door.

'The master talks in riddles, mun,' said Cecilia. 'Had he asked you in plain English to pen his letters for him you would have known his meaning, for he pens his letters with the left hand. As for the surgeon standing in need of healing, how is you to know the meaning of that, mun? But it is not in my place to explicate, though I could and more.'

'Then will not the justice be called at least?' I said.

'No, mun,' Cecilia said. 'The justice will not.'

'Then I must go and write letters, Cecilia,' I said.

84

'If you please, mun,' said Cecilia. 'And if 'tis not to your best liking, for it would not be to mine, what you have to put, 'tis as it is, for we can do no other.'

Then it occurred to me that Nathaniel is not the only one in this household who speaks in riddles, for Cecilia does also. And my maid Willow and Bertie-mun do not speak at all, which leaves us at the least in great confusion, if one or other of us is not in the doldrums, which Nathaniel and I habitually are. So I went to the drawing room, finding my husband seated at his desk, and with his sound hand blotting up an extensive spill of ink.

'I do not well at this, my dear,' he said without looking round, for, as I thought, the pain from the wound had become such that he could not turn his neck. And I touched his hair, which (I don't know if I have set down in these pages before, though I have thought so often) is dark and beautiful; as indeed his whole person is beautiful in my eyes, and not like my imaginings of a coal master.

'Come round and let me look at you, Clara, my dear,' he said. 'You are lovely this morning.'

'And you also, sir,' I said. 'Bertie-mun will help you with the ink. I will call him,' I added, for I felt suddenly frightened.

''Tis only a desk,' he said. 'It does not matter about the ink. When it is dried we will continue these letters. See, I am not neat with the right hand.'

'What will you have me do, Nathaniel?' I said.

'I would have you sit here a little longer so that I may see your loveliness, my darling,' he said. 'But I see also that those few ill-considered words have caused you to study the grain in the wood and the pattern on the carpet again, for which I am deeply sorry. Pray forgive me, Clara.'

'Are you much hurt?' I said.

'I am as you would see, if you were to cease studying the desk top, darling. No, I am not much hurt. I fear you are the more hurt for you were close by.'

'I do not remember anything until we were crossing over the Wear Bridge and Bertie-mun was assisting you. Cecilia told me what took place.'

'What did she tell you?'

'That Brim Salter cast up to heaven for someone to chastise and finding no one there turned his wrath upon earth, you being the nearest he found there. She said the justice would not be called in.'

'No man is responsible for his actions when strong liquor is on him,' Nathaniel said. 'Doubtless Brim Salter will today have but a poor recollection of what passed by yesterday.'

'And if it were not you, for you care little about yourself, but another who was hurt at the hands of Brim Salter would you not then call in the justice, Nathaniel?'

Then I watched in dismay and horror as the colour drained from my husband's face and the light in his eyes turned dark. And I would have gone to him, but that I sensed a great divide come between us, as real as if a door had been closed.

'We must to the work in hand,' he said. 'Forgive me, darling, I entered the doldrums for a moment but I have returned and I am recovered now.'

Yet my husband was not recovered; and the expression of melancholy I have often seen, and some other thing I had not seen and could not read, stayed with him.

'You have a fair and gracious hand, my dear,' he continued. 'I would ask that you write to Mr Higgs and Mr Thorley regarding my intention as to the opening up of as much of Shackleton as is viable. Pray tell me what grief it is you have, darling. The mine will wait for us.'

For we are like open books to each other, reading the writing there, although we do not always understand the language it is written in. So I asked my husband about the soundness or otherwise of Shackleton mine, which, situated as it is outside the boundary of the city of Durham, seemed far away from the drawing room in the house on the Rose Pavement in which we were both seated, together, yet separated as it were by a door closed between us. And to do him justice, which saying I have caught from Cecilia, Nathaniel gave an answer to the question I had asked and did not enquire further into my grief, grief being the word he used, though if it was or not I do not know.

'It is for the most part sound, my dear,' he said, 'apart from that area of the north pit affected by the explosion. And even that now is of little danger, but I propose to let it lie for a while.'

Then the image of Tessa Spence, which indeed is never far away, came into my mind, and the childhood prayer I find myself whispering nightly into the darkness: "Matthew, Mark, Luke and John, bless the bed that I lie on", until I do not know rightly who the prayer is for.

'We believe that poor Tessa did not suffer at her end,' my husband went on, 'though what she might have suffered before her end only God in heaven knows. We believe that she fell victim to the stythe, in which case she would have fallen into a deep slumber, may the Lord Jesus give her rest.'

87

And it was in my mind to ask why Tessa Spence had been there on a Sabbath day when the pit was resting and none were at work, but I did not ask, remembering Nathaniel's asperity when Cecilia, as he said, interfered in the affairs of the mine. Yet he nevertheless answered, as if I had spoken out loud what was in my mind, though I had not said a thing.

'Tessa's pilgrimage in this world is over now,' he went on, 'and it is not for us to speculate on why she was in the pit on the Sabbath day, for it will not help her. The matter is closed and we must get the men back to work.'

Which "we", as I understood, included me, for I was to write to Mr Higgs and Mr Thorley to the same effect, namely that of setting the men to work in the pit again.

'We will not endear ourselves to anyone, Clara, my dear,' Nathaniel said presently, 'for in order that all the men are set to work each must work half his time.'

'Then, Nathaniel, each will receive only half his remuneration,' I said, the words escaping me before I could rein them in.

'No, Clara, each will receive his full remuneration but will, until all of Shackleton is open, work half his time.'

'It is the same thing, Nathaniel.'

'It is different in principle, Clara.'

'But the outcome is the same. They will be working for half the remuneration.'

'Then am I to keep all those who work the afflicted part of the north pit idle at home while they who work elsewhere in the mine go back down?'

'No, Nathaniel,' I said, seeing that he had driven me into a corner with his argument. And for those five minutes I had quite forgotten the wound that breathed by itself. And, indeed, the colour had gone from my husband's face, whether for the reason of his injury, or because his wife was seated by his side opposing his wishes concerning the mine, I did not know.

'You are exhausted, Nathaniel,' I said. 'I have become your worst enemy. I am deeply sorry for taxing your strength further. Forgive me.'

'You did not, my dear,' he said. 'Do not be sorry for what you haven't done, or we shall both of us be in the doldrums. You will find your task arduous enough as it is, for the pen is used to writing with the left hand. I am recovered now, darling.'

Yet he was not, and before the ink was dry on the page he asked if Bertie-mun might take him to his room. 'I am too much for you to manage by yourself, darling,' he said, 'for I have the sensation of being on the deck of a rolling ship. Not that I was ever on board ship in the whole of my life, but it is as I imagine it, for I cannot even travel in a carriage without the pitch and roll of it reminding me of a ship.'

And so we came to my husband's room. And I saw it for the second time, the difference being that now a fire was lit in the grate and the window was closed against the morning's frost.

'I am suddenly all chatter,' Nathaniel said, 'and I have only to be thankful that Cecilia is not here to chastise me.'

'She is here, sir.' Cecilia's voice was on the landing. Kindly say what you have to say and cease your chatter, for you will make yourself badly.'

'Then if Bertie-mun would deliver the letters to Mr Higgs and Mr Thorley and afterwards ask Patrick Tregowan to call in his own time, I should be more than grateful.'

'You have had your say. Now hold your peace, sir,' said Cecilia. 'I will bid Willow apply a poultice on top of the other for it bleeds through.'

'Yes, Cecilia,' Nathaniel said. 'I believe it does.'

'Silence, sir,' said Cecilia. 'I have told you it does. I may seem harsh with the master, mun, but 'tis for his own good. He is a most obdurate gentleman. You'd best bide here while Mr Tregowan comes, if you would. Pardon my high manner, mun, for it is not you who is obdurate, only your lately wedded husband.'

Willow did not bring another poultice, and I was left with Nathaniel, Bertie-mun having gone out to deliver the letters, and Cecilia occupied with the household. So I remained there, watching my husband for spasms of pain, but there were none.

'What are you looking at, my dear?' he said presently. 'I am suddenly become as fascinating as the grains of wood in the desk and the pattern in the carpet. If you watch for pain, I haven't any. Do not be dismayed for me, darling.'

'You must not speak, Nathaniel.'

'No, I must not. Yet as long as you are beside me looking into my eyes, I might also look into yours. You look at me expecting to see pain, and I look at you and see only loveliness. I have to speak if only to tell you that.'

'But you must not speak, Nathaniel.'

'No, my dear, I will try not to,' he said. 'Yet there is a matter you should know if you do not know already. Bertie-mun and I have attended to the locked chamber at the end of the upper landing, for it was high time. And it is that which has opened the wound more than any affront offered by Brim Salter. Bertie-mun would not have me haul and heave, but I could not see the good fellow doing all the heavy work by himself. Begging your forgiveness, my darling Clara, for I never could make do with one word where a whole lexicon would suffice.'

After which he fell silent and I found myself wondering why he was at such pains to mitigate the insult done by Brim Salter, yet I said nothing. And we remained so, without speaking, until a commotion in the hallway announced the arrival not only of Bertie-mun with Mr Tregowan, but also of Mrs Tregowan and, as I understood from the diverse sound of their footsteps, one other, though I could not be certain. Then Cecilia came in, saying that Mrs Tregowan begged the pleasure of my company in the drawing room.

'For she means well, mun,' Cecilia added, 'whatever words she may say.'

And it came to me that the whole of God's world means well in the eyes of my husband and his household, to the inclusion of Brim Salter, who had lately inflicted a wound on Nathaniel that was becoming the more grievous with every minute that passed.

'Ah, my dear Claribell,' said Mrs Tregowan, 'how you must be suffering seeing your dear husband mortally wounded, for so they are saying he is. Patrick and I, Patrick being my husband, you know, never could have bairns,' she went on, 'and that is our own cross the dear Lord has given us to bear in this life. For we all have our crosses to bear, do we not, darling Claribell, and we must bear our crosses patiently. You look stricken, my dear, and it is no wonder after what you have borne.'

For my eyes had drifted, though Mrs Tregowan did not know it, to Nathaniel's attempts to write his letters using the wrong hand, which were still strewn about his desk; and the letter of ill intent, although he had immediately returned it to the fire, flashed before my sight.

'Be seated, my dear, for we must give our minds and hands some occupation in these troubled times. You must call me Barbara,' she continued, 'for all that it is a dreadful name and puts me in mind of Barabbas who was released in the stead of our Saviour.'

Then Mrs Tregowan talked of her proposed occupation for my hands and mind, which is, as Cecilia has intimated, needlework for the miners and their kindred. And I do not know how I will do it, for though I recall little of what my life has been, I remember well that I could never thread a needle or sew a straight hem. Yet Mrs Tregowan means to do generously by all of creation, even to the extent of imposing on the good women of Shackleton a needle worker whose efforts are far inferior to their own.

"Yes, We May Study This"

It is the Lord's day again, and it is five short weeks since I came into this household, and the thirty-seventh day; which are rather thirty-seven long days and five long weeks, for they are all of the life I can easily bring to mind; all of it except the distance of time between the injury done to Nathaniel at the graveside of Tessa Spence and the crossing of the Wear bridge on the way home. Which absent time I had only to ask Cecilia for, and she gave it back to me. And it crosses my mind that I could ask her for the rest of my life and she would give it back to me, with as little consequence as if she were giving me clean linen scented with lavender from the closet. And I suppose Willow and Bertie-mun would also have given back to me the absent mile of time between Tessa's graveside and the Wear Bridge, but that they do not speak, which is doubtless why Cecilia and my husband fill the house with words.

And I don't know if I speak or not, but I suspect I am somewhere in the middle, neither using a lexicon where one word would do, nor holding my peace entirely. For with Willow I am full of words as she has none, and with Cecilia I have few words as she has many, and Nathaniel fills with his words the silences that fall upon me. All this I write inconsequentially, trusting that what I most wish to put down will not flee from me for ever.

For I have been seated here at the window until the evening turns to night, and the night ushers out the ninth day of February in the year of our Lord 1812 for ever, and still I have no words. And I might as well, as I have said, be as the republicans were in France and devise my own calendar, beginning on the fourth day of January in the year 1812, that being the first day I woke up in this house and looked out of the window onto to a scene which bore no resemblance to any scene I had looked out on before; there being the three mines of Shackleton, Blennowe and Thayne lying dark in the mist under a glittering sky.

And while I am in my mind still standing at the window of my first room in the house on the Rose Pavement, which is high above the city of Durham, it seems to me that it would be but a small thing to step away from the window, and leave the room to which I had been taken, and to return to the place I had come from, which I will name here, as if for the first time, as being the house called Sainte Agathe. Where I can think myself to be, standing outside in the gathering frost, the door of the house having lately closed behind me for ever. And at my side is the gentleman I do not know, yet know as Nathaniel Chark, whose face I can hardly bring myself to look at, who has in one hand my portmanteau, if such it is being so small, and in the other my own hand; as if I might on a whim turn round and stand crying at the door for them to let me back in, knowing that is where I belong.

Suffice to say that I have become tonight the most abject of women, suspecting what I was before Nathaniel took me in, which did not haunt me before, but now it does. And, to compound my bewilderment, there has come into this house a "presence", for I can describe it in no other way, having not seen or heard or felt anything except the creak of the boards in the hall and the exchange of air as doors are opened and closed. Yet I know in the soul of me, when this presence is in the house, I become a most dismayed creature, with a revulsion against something in myself I have not a word for unless it is depravity. Which consciousness makes me also dismayed in the presence of my husband, for he surely knows what I am, having taken me in.

Yet Nathaniel, who knows my spirits to be low, as if I am living perpetually in the month the republicans called Pluviôse, believes that I am still feeling remorse for having questioned his intention to put the men back to work on half time, and so adding to his adversities; which he is at pains to assure me every day that I did not.

On the contrary, for this evening when the household was gathered at the table for high tea, with diminishing enthusiasm I have to say, he announced into the silence that a new poultice had been applied to the wound and that he is much recovered; which has become a refrain with him: 'I am much recovered.' After which he asked me to sit with him in his room and read from Mr Milton if I would, for he could not look down to see the print, and after which cursory reading, for it did not last for long, he took the volume from my hand and closed it.

'I fear you are in the doldrums, Clara, my darling,' he said.

'It is you who should be rightly in the doldrums, Nathaniel,' I said.

'Not so,' he said. 'I am much recovered. Tell me what it is that makes you sorrowful, darling.'

'I have become your adversity, Nathaniel,' I said. A look of puzzlement passed across his face and he took my hand.

'Clara,' he said. 'It is I who is more like to misplace words. You are tired, my darling. Surely you meant adversary, in which case we must let Mr Milton alone for a while. He is gloomy reading for a winter's night.'

'No, Nathaniel,' I said. 'I did indeed mean adversity. I was thinking of Mr Tregowan saying so often that adversity fortifies the soul, which took my mind back, for a reason I can't fathom, to the matter of remuneration for the colliers. I was not only your adversary but also your adversity in that I added to the troubles you have. Forgive me, Nathaniel.' And I would if I could have kissed the hand that held mine, but that the dismay still wrapped me round like a dark cloak, and the occasion passed.

'But Clara, my darling,' Nathaniel said, 'I gave you my leave and my blessing to differ from me, as I trust you give me your leave and your blessing to differ from you. It is the way we will survive. If we do not give each other this blessing, then we do not survive. There is something else, is there not?'

'I don't know.'

'But there is, my darling.'

'It is of no matter,' I said.

'It is of matter, Clara,' he said. 'It is of great matter.'

'I am ashamed, Nathaniel,' I said. 'I don't know why.'

'You don't know why,' he said. 'Or you cannot say why?'

'No,' I said.

'Which I must take to mean that you do not know and you cannot say.'

'Yes.'

'Then in the solitude of your room, could you at some time in the future write down in a letter to me what is troubling you, Clara? Since I now have to ask you to write my correspondence, a personal letter would pass unnoticed even by Cecilia.'

Which absurdity made me laugh in spite of myself and Nathaniel then wished me goodnight, now that I was recovered, he said, borrowing his own phrase, and calling me his "darling adversity". And it occurs to me that, that having found me in the house of Sainte Agathe, he surely knows the dismay that hovers over me, which I will not and cannot say, and which is like an incubus, even as the mines of Shackleton Thayne and Blennowe are incubi sitting darkly in the valleys outside the city of Durham.

And that takes me back to the Sabbath day school, which did little to settle my habitual confusion, for I was at a loss to decide whether the scholars were the same as those who have attended before, or indeed whether they were all men or all women or that both men and women were present. Nor do I like to ask them their names again and again, as if I doubt their truthfulness. And moreover, they answer to any name given to them, always reciting the same quota of names when they arrive.

The lesson proceeded as before until it was nearly done and all were about to receive a heel of bread on their departure, when the collier who had answered humbly and pleasantly to the name of Frederick Pennell throughout the class, though he wore bosoms under his coat, produced from his pocket a rough tract, dirtied with the soots of the mine, which I gathered to be from the many hands it had passed through before it reached his own.

'Begging your pardon, mun,' he said, 'for you was on the point of bidding us farewell, but we would study this.' And he placed in my hand the paper he had drawn from his pocket, which I unfolded and looked at, knowing that all eyes were upon me.

And I read, silently to myself: "... by which I mean that men are all of one degree, and consequently that all men are born equal, and with equal natural rights."

'What is this?' I said.

''Tis as you see, mun.'

'What would you have me to do?'

'We would learn of it, mun, saving your honour.'

Then I looked at the colliers seated in front of me. And my mind turned to my husband, born with a natural grace of person and spirit, the kindest of men, who wore his privilege lightly, then back to the colliers who had a tact and kindness of their own, and though they were rough-hewn and from the back lanes of Shackleton, the same in the eyes of whoever it was who had written what I saw before me.

And I said, 'Yes, we may study this.'

Full of Unknowing Tonight

As it has been Monday it has also been wash day, and all of this day, the seventeenth in February, I have been occupied with needlework, for no better reason than to keep myself out of the way. And although it is to a good end, being for the bairns of the colliers, my heart is not in it, for I can't thread a needle or sew a straight hem. Nevertheless, Mrs Tregowan encourages me in these deficiencies, saying I do well and use will come in time, for all that I say to her that I believe I am now twenty-eight years old and it has not come yet. And to tell the truth, though I would not say it to Mrs Tregowan, such dealings with white linen lower my spirits to the depths, as if I have already had my life's fill of white linen. And the damp fragrance of Monday wash day, which though to others is newness and cleanliness, creeps into every corner of the house, and also lowers my spirits.

So, engaged as I am in good works, my mind turns disconsolately back to the Sabbath school, for I don't know how to study the lesson asked of me by the scholars, which though it is short enough is undoubtedly from some inflammatory text, but I do not know what. And whoever I may enquire of among the scholars, though I do not, the answer would be the same: 'I dunnow, mun. It come to us.'

Yet I find, unaccountably, Cecilia and Bertie-mun now present at the Sabbath day school to learn and not merely to help set it up, and my maid Willow also, although she has no hearing. And I find that each one of the scholars from the colliery has the text by heart yet cannot read it. So I present the words one by one, using them in simple ways, so that anything written on the blackboard or on a slate will be out of place should my husband walk in during a lesson, which he has not done yet. For I have no doubt that he would construe the whole as an insurrection under his roof, at the same time as giving hospitality to the insurrectionists and sending them blameless on their way with a heel of bread.

Yet I write this without knowing, for although the *Times* lies on his desk, Nathaniel says nothing of the common affairs of men, as if to him the great world begins and ends in the city of Durham and its mines; which indeed it might as well for all that I am concerned.

And I am full of unknowing tonight. I don't know if I do rightly in permitting the scholars to study an inflammatory text. I don't know who it was who entered the house during the Sabbath day school, who opened the door of the schoolroom and seeing me, though not I him, closed it. Nor do I know how to answer the letter.

Written in a Laboured and Painful Script

I have lain awake the whole of the night hearing the coals fall in the grate and watching the candle gutter into darkness, listening every hour for the watch to be called out, and composing in the empty chambers of my mind a reply to Nathaniel's letter. For I thought he spoke lightly when he said I might write a letter if I could not tell him my troubles in words. Yet he did not speak lightly. And I don't know how I will write in a letter what I have not the words for in my voice nor in my much thinking.

Nathaniel's letter is on the table in the envelope in which he gave it to me, saying loudly at the same time, 'Clara, my darling, would you kindly reply to Mr Walsh and say that I will attend to the matter of the indemnities as soon as I am able. You may sign it with your own name, my dear,' as if the walls and indeed the whole of Durham had hearing and he wished all to know. For Nathaniel's natural voice is not loud, except on occasions when he says the grace on Sunday.

Enclosed in the envelope was indeed a letter from Mr Walsh asking about the indemnities, to which I had replied from my husband's dictation, each of us making pretence that I know the meaning of the word "indemnities". And Bertie-mun has taken the letter, so that Mr Walsh, to whom I cannot put a face although he is every week at the chapel, might even now be sitting in front of his fire reading it. All this being of small consequence and serving only to divert me from Nathaniel's letter, which lies folded inside that from Mr Walsh.

"Clara, my darling," it says, "Although you thought I spoke in jest I did not. If you would but write of the troubles of your heart I would answer as best as I may. For on the Sabbath just gone you had something on your mind you could not speak of, only that you said you were ashamed, and for a reason you either would not say or did not know. Pray tell me in a letter, my darling, what it is that afflicts you so. For I was always given to fear, and now that fear seems to me to be justified, that some event apparently over and buried may nevertheless surface again. And now I speak in riddles, and I have one riddle more, dearest Clara, which is this: if at any time you care to read to me from Mr Richardson I should count myself the most honoured of men. Your loving husband, Nathaniel."

All of which is written in a laboured and painful script, and now lies unfolded on the desk with each word illuminated by the morning sun. And I must attend to it. Yet misgivings overwhelm me at every turn as to what to write, and not least how to conclude; whether as "your loving wife" which the dismay I have for myself forbids, as surely as if a fiery angel were to fly down and seize the pen from my hand in the writing of it.

Then my mind returned to Mr Milton, who was ever a man to fill a fragile soul with gloom, and so to the eternal adversary. And so to "adversity", which word is my own, for myself. Yet whether to write "loving", I do not know, for that is to enfold my husband in angels' wings, which is a thought I cannot give room to on account of my dismay. And presently Cecilia will come in and tell me that Mrs Tregowan awaits the pleasure of my company in the drawing room, so there will be more threading of needles and more hems. And I kiss my husband's letter, for that at least I may do, and put it back in the table drawer.

'The master is asking if you care to read to him from Mr Richardson, mun,' Cecilia said, 'at your liking. And I told him happen you has enough to tax your poor eyes with all them sewings, and 'twill be a good thing when he gets back to the mine, for he is under our feet. Though to do him justice, he does not complain of his hurt. And Mrs Tregowan says she awaits the pleasure of your company in the drawing room, miss. Bertie-mun has built up a good fire, and I know you care not for yourself, mun, but Mrs Tregowan is badly with her troubles for she was three times at the privy in Sunday service, asking your pardon for my plain speech, mun. She awaits the pleasure of your company, miss.'

So I went to the drawing room, and meeting Willow on the landing asked if she had any remedy for troubles with the water that she could give to Mrs Tregowan. And I found Mrs Tregowan doubled over in a chair and red in the face, not having heard me enter the drawing room.

'My dear Claribell,' she said, 'I beg your forbearance if there is any odour about me. I have to wear rags when I am taken like this for I often do not reach the privy in time. And I might as well tell you, my dear Claribell, since all in Durham know of my malady, that I fear there is ribaldry when my back is turned. But it is the cross the Lord has given me to bear, which I bear gladly, though I could wish it were a different one.'

Then I asked Mrs Tregowan if she had seen a physician, to which she answered emphatically no, as if a physician were the last person in the world to make her well. 'For the Lord gives and the Lord takes away, my dear Claribell, and it is so also with the afflictions of the body. I am much recovered now, dear.'

And it came to me that not only my husband and his household, but his friends also, set great store by saying they are "recovered", as if the saying of it accomplishes the fact in the absence of a physician. So I suggested to Mrs Tregowan that, in the case of future attacks of the same, Mistress Willow might find some remedy laid by in the apothecary cupboard.

'That would be nice, Claribell,' she said. 'Now, tell me, my dear, do I carry an odour with me today?'

And I said that she did not, which was true, and on the contrary there was always the fresh air of the fields about her, at odds with the soots and the smoke pervading Durham.

'Thank you, Claribell,' she said. 'I may call you Claribell, may I not? That name puts me in mind of Mr Richardson's heroine.'

And I believe Mrs Tregowan would then have recounted at length the latest trials of Clarissa Harlowe, but that my maid Willow was at the door with remedies for troubles with the water.

'That is the case as I understand with certain poor souls on whom the Lord has placed such infirmities,' said Mrs Tregowan in Willow's hearing, though she cannot hear. 'They may not know the use of their ears or their tongues, yet they have other gifts. For though you have not left the room to make the request for remedies of Mistress Willow, she could discern what was in your mind even as she was about her duties elsewhere in the house. There, my dear Claribell, we have brought a smile to your pretty face, for which I am pleased, for I sometimes fear that you are not happy, dear.'

Then Willow showed Mrs Tregowan some remedies, and, as Mrs Tregowan was perplexed as to which one to take, gave her a bottle labelled *"Urtica"*, for which Mrs Tregowan thanked her most gratefully, forgetting as I thought that Willow has no hearing, until she added, 'for if it does no good it cannot do harm either.'

Whereupon Willow gave her a second remedy, of *Leguminosus*, or some such word, which was much crossed through and altered, being awkward for the pen and odd looking. And all of this brought us no nearer to sewing hems, but rather threatened to send Mrs Tregowan hurrying back home to try the remedies and leave me alone with the prospect of replying to my husband's letter. Which I have done, and I have written this:

"My dear Nathaniel, I have sensed in the house lately the presence of someone, which causes me great disquiet. I do not know if it is the presence of a living, breathing being, who otherwise is seen by all and walks abroad in the busy world, or if it is a presence known only to me in my mind; only that it brings on a feeling which I must describe as the deepest dismay; and worse than that, for it is of the soul as well as of the body. Forgive me if I also write in riddles.

Your loving adversity,

Clara."

Yet before the ink was dried on the page I was stricken by what I had written, and the face that looked back at me from the glass as I crossed the chamber was of a woman I did not know, whether harlot or penitent I couldn't tell. And it came to me again that my husband

and I are no more than souls to each other, although we are led to believe that our souls are given refuge in the earthly temple of the body. And I feel remorse, as if I have undressed my soul before an angel in comparison with myself, for all that my husband is a coal master, and would willingly send his men back to the pit on half pay. Yet the letter is written, and lies folded between pages 232 and 233 of *Clarissa*.

"Thow Willt Pay Ful Paie"

It being the Lord's day, my husband insisted that he was
so far recovered as to attend holy service. Yet I don't
know how much that decision had to do with the Lord,
or with a malevolent crowd gathered at our gate. For
whereas another man would look to his wellbeing and
not venture out, my husband is of the opposite turn of
mind and, seeing peril, will rush headlong into it. I say
this because all night from the first watch onwards there
was a growing assembly at our gate, at first numbering
fewer than the fingers on one hand, and then increasing
steadily, until by morning, which dawned heavy and
grey with a thick sea fret, there numbered some fifty
men or more hunched over small fires of coals and
stamping their feet in the cold.

And in the morning before dawn Bertie-mun, who
was abroad fetching coals from the out-house, was
summoned to the gate and a rough letter was thrust at
him through the slats; after which he returned to the
house, Cecilia said, much put about, being otherwise the
most peaceable of souls, on account of having heard
some lewd talk relating to the disfigurement of his face,
though what it was he could not or would not say. For
that phrase has joined the lexicon of Nathaniel's
household, along with "means well" and "much

recovered", and it occurs to me that we might as well all of us contribute to the lexicon as occasions arise.

And my mind has travelled many times every day to the letter I have written to my husband, which still marks the place between pages 232 and 233 in *Clarissa*. For although in the interval I have been summoned to write several letters on Nathaniel's behalf I have not yet read to him from Mr Richardson, and as he has not asked again I'm afraid he draws the conclusion that I wish not to, which I do not know if I wish or not. And as for that shame and dismay I feel, I have become almost accustomed to it, only so long as I don't have to be in the presence of the person, who is surely a "he", who causes it. For he, if indeed he resides in the temple of an earthly body, has been in the house each day until yesterday, and then not.

Before the dawn also, which was late in arriving on account of the sea fret, Cecilia knocked at my door and asked me to rise and dress, bringing with her a jug of warm water which enveloped her in smoke in the chill of the room.

'If you would please to make do with this, mun,' she said, 'and finish off later. For happen you don't know but there is a horde at the gate, and 'tis better to be clothed than not to be clothed, pardon my plain speech. Bertie-mun has built up a fire in the scullery. An' there is another note of ill intent, mun, not wishing to alarm you, but just so as you be prepared.'

The note was lying on the scullery table when I entered, and I had seen it before Willow could place over it the pile of clean linen she had in her arms.

'Willow, my dear,' said Nathaniel, although Willow has no hearing, 'Clara saw the last letter and she might as well see this,' at which Willow lifted up the pile of linen, and no one showed any surprise that she heard when she cannot hear. 'It is in the same hand as the other letter, is it not, darling? Take a look and see if it is not.'

"Charke, thow willt pay ful paie," the note said.

'What do you think, darling?' my husband said. 'Is it like to the other? We may take it that this is an unlettered scribe, may we not? Though I would condemn no man for being unlettered. I do not well in that respect myself.'

'Doesn't it look somewhat like your attempts to write your correspondence with your sound hand, which is not the hand you are accustomed to writing with, Nathaniel?' I said. He took the letter from me and held it to the firelight.

'Then you suppose the writer has a lame arm?' he said. 'Or does he conceal his natural script by writing with the other hand?'

'Yes,' I said.

'You do not know and you cannot say,' Nathaniel said, and although he continued to study the script I saw the stars twinkle in his eyes, by which I understood, inconsequentially and somewhere at the farthest edge of my reasoning, that the invitation to read from Mr Richardson remained. 'But as to Bertie-mun,' my husband continued, 'he suffered ribaldry of some kind on account of his disfigurement, which he will not mind my saying in his presence, and that leads me to the conclusion that those at our gate are not from among the colliers, or indeed from the city of Durham, for it is unlikely they would abuse their own on account of a calamity at the pit that might well have been theirs. The reason for these things are known only to the Lord.'

'If indeed the Lord knows them reasons either,' said Cecilia. 'An' if I was the Lord I'd have words in plenty of my own.'

'Cecilia heard what was said to Bertie-mun,' said Nathaniel, 'but she will not repeat the words for two reasons, firstly because in doing so she would inflict upon Bertie-mun the abuse a second time, and secondly,' here he glanced sharply at Cecilia, 'because she is a lady.'

'But I will say nevertheless that a piss-pot were launched, sir, which, may the Lord be praised, who happened to be awake at that there moment in time, fell short of its intended recipient.'

Then seeing the colour rise in my husband's face, I said that we had best begin to prepare ourselves for Sunday service if we were going, although it was still early, and the day was yet a wan face peering in at the window. And all the while my maid Willow had unaccountably been caught up in a fit of merriment, which she was at great pains to conceal behind her handkerchief, yet I was certain I saw her sweet speechless mouth form the shape, "piss-pot".

'It were best to ignore them at our gate, mun,' said Cecilia, 'and then they will go away. But the master would ever place himself in the way of peril, an I can do more than speak my mind.'

'It is always Cecilia's habit to speak her mind,' said Nathaniel, 'and I can do no more than let her have her say and then she will hold her peace.'

Yet neither my husband nor Cecilia spoke of the obvious alternative, which would have been to let ourselves out by the back way and not by the front gate which gives onto the Rose Pavement. For although Cecilia counts Nathaniel an obdurate gentleman, she herself is obdurate in persisting in doing that which she least wishes to do. Suffice to say that Willow, having much recovered from her fit of merriment, brought in my cloak and put it on a chair near the fire to warm. And in this way I was caught up in the general intention to attend holy service, and to attend it in the least commodious way possible.

And I persist in attending holy service although it sends me into the doldrums with its gloom and talk of sinfulness, if only for Nathaniel's sake. And so was added another custom of Nathaniel's household, for besides believing all others to mean well whether or not they do, and saying we are much recovered whether we are or not, and having in us that which we do not know and cannot say, there is also a penitential tendency to do what we do not wish only so long as doing so discommodes us as much as possible.

'I would not wish for myself to leave the house by the front door,' my husband continued, 'and certainly I would not wish all of you, whom I hold dear, to be importuned, yet we do best to show that we are not intimidated.'

In truth there was but a handful of men left at the gate, albeit that they had strong liquor on them. And a sudden sense came upon me that I was no more than an arm's length from that presence I had feared in the house, and knowing it Nathaniel drew me to his side, even though he had placed himself nearest to those at the gate.

Then a rough chant rose up, 'Chark, thou shalt pay,' which followed us down the Rose Pavement and until we were round the corner and onto the Wear hill, and my husband said, 'I knew but one of them and he is not of the colliers. They will have gone on their way by the time we return.' Which indeed they had for the reason, Cecilia said, that the hostelries had opened up their doors, which opinion she expressed in no small voice as we passed by the sign of the Fox, being the only hostelry on our way.

And I was suddenly in my mind inside the open door of the Fox, looking out, watching the household of the master of Shackleton going to and returning home from the Sabbath day service at the dissenting chapel. And a droll, forbidding sight we must be, dressed in black, with my husband and I leading, and Willow, Cecilia and Bertie-mun at the back of us, scurrying like some ten-legged organism through the streets of Durham.

But before our hurried walk home Mrs Tregowan took me aside, since, as she said, she was so far recovered in her affliction after Willow's remedies that she did not need the privy, and might well use her time in pleasantries as befitted the wife of the minister.

'My dear Claribell,' she said, 'you must never think ill of your husband, for he means well and he is a good man for all that he is the coal master, and also some are saying that they who have gone back to work do not receive their due remuneration. Yet we are but women, my dear, and coal belongs to the interests of men, and how the colliers are paid, that also belongs to the interests of men, which we women do not understand. And it is not a life I should like, burrowing in the earth, for I feel starved of air even in a carriage. But, Claribell, to the interests of women belongs the welfare of the colliers' kindred, and if it pleases you, my dear, you will accompany Miss Walsh and me on a mission of mercy.'

Which mission of mercy I am afraid will fall on me as a necessity, just as much as the sewing of straight hems and the threading of needles has fallen on me, and I have only to wait.

Yet the scholars who attended the Sabbath day school, for all that they were to be put on half remuneration by the master and the news of it was abroad in all of Durham, were as they had been, asking nothing but to study the text that had come to them, as they said.

And the text is so committed to my memory by now that I may say it word perfect as the scholars do: "... by which I mean that men are all of one degree, and consequently that all men are born equal, and with equal natural rights ..." Until I can believe that when I am taking my last breaths in this world I will be reciting this text, and when they ask me what it is, I will say, as my scholars do, 'I don't know. It came to me.'

As to the scholars who attend, they give the same names to me every week, which I don't question, those names being: William Darbyshire, Frederick Pennell, James Sowerby, Alfred Baines, Amos Frost, Bartholomew, and Gregory Parrish. Yet I doubt if they are the same scholars, for, as I have noted, Frederick Pennell sometimes wears bosoms beneath his coat, and sometimes not, and Amos Frost, though he presented himself at first as a grey-haired man, is sometimes brown haired and sometimes tawny. Which leads me to suppose that in the space of twelve months we may well have entertained in the schoolroom the entire tally of the colliers of Shackleton, all of whom will carry in their souls the text: "... by which I mean that men are all of one degree, and consequently that all men are equal, and with equal natural rights ..." And all will be able to read it, if they read no other thing. And if, in my last day on the earth, anyone were to ask of me, did you do well in teaching them this? I will say I did this even if I did no other thing good in my life. Yet I did not know if it was good or bad.

In the evening at a time when all in the household were, as I supposed, much recovered from the compulsory attendance at the table for high tea, I went to the drawing room, taking with me Mr Richardson's novel, and finding my husband seated there at his desk with the *Times* propped up in front of him, though I had not seen him read it before.

'I will read that to you, Nathaniel, if I may. And I have also Mr Richardson's work,' I said.

'Then we will hear from Mr Richardson, my dear,' said Nathaniel, 'for doubtless this fellow Napoleon will be marauding in the low countries for some years to come. It is the calamity of our times that men suppose they will be the more heard for the more noise they make.'

'So you did not know who they were at the gate this morning?' I said.

'They might have been the army of Napoleon Bonaparte for all that I knew of them,' said my husband, 'but that they had English ribaldry on their tongues. I knew only one, though it does not matter who he was for the liquor was on him and at this moment he will be in his chamber drowned in slumbers.'

'I am not sure that Mr Richardson makes fit study for the evening of the Lord's day,' I said.

'I know nothing of it, but it is a work Barbara Tregowan speaks highly of,' said Nathaniel. 'You do not like it, darling?'

'Yes, I do, Nathaniel,' I said. 'I like it very much, and the more so because you gave it to me. I merely said I don't know if Clarissa Harlowe's tribulations are fit study for a Sunday evening. I have answered your letter, sir.' And I gave my letter to Nathaniel before I could alter my mind, and with haste, as if it burned my fingers.

'Thank you, my darling,' he said. 'I will read it later, unless you wish me to read it in your presence.' I said to my husband that I would rather he read it later. 'And will you leave Mr Richardson with me as well?' he said.

'I will not, Nathaniel,' I said. 'It will corrupt your mind.'

'Then I must certainly read it when the Sabbath day is over,' he said.

As the River Wear Meanders out of Durham

Wednesday is Cecilia's day of liberty, and I have only once before known her to take it, and even then she returned after a short time away. Yet today she was absent for all of the daylight hours, returning as my husband did. And he had gone to Shackleton, being much recovered, which he has said so often that I do not know how much more recovered anyone can be. Willow was beating carpets in the back area, and Bertie-mun setting to rights the garden after the winter.

And all was in silence, until a loud knocking came on the front door, which was repeated and again repeated. Then, as no one, so I thought, was in the house but myself I went down, finding Bertie-mun there and the door open, yet on the chain, and someone on the steps, whom I could not make out, engaged in an unequal dialogue with Bertie-mun. Which I would have taken up, for Bertie-mun becomes the more flustered the more he is spoken at, except that on approaching the door I was, as it seemed, beaten back by the same shaming presence of which I have been aware often in the house of late. And I do not remember how the encounter came to an end, for when I came to myself I was back in the drawing room threading a needle and sewing a straight hem, which was not straight at all but meandered over the linen in much the same way as the River Wear meanders out of Durham.

Then Mrs Tregowan came in, saying, 'You look a little peaky, my dear Claribell, and no wonder for we live in troubled times.'

So I asked her if she had seen anyone about, to which she answered that she had seen folks in plenty.

'For they are not back on full time down at Shackleton as you know, my dear, and they wander about the thoroughfares of Durham like so many lost and weary souls, and most looking ill fed also. Though it is not the fault of your dear husband that there was a disaster at the pit and the men are still on half time, Claribell, my dear. You must not think that, darling.'

And Mrs Tregowan, seeing me propelled further into the doldrums by her speech, continued in her well-meaning.

'Yet all is not lost, my dear. When times are hard we open up the kitchen, for the Lord does not wish any of his children to go without.' And here Mrs Tregowan glanced towards the door, lowering her voice. 'The kitchen comes out of the profits of the mines, even if the profits be never so meagre, Claribell, as Patrick tells me. Yet this is not widely known for if the colliers knew they would not attend the kitchen. Men have ever borne a grudge against their masters, even in the time of our Lord. Now, dear, I have said more than I should, yet I could do no other, seeing you so troubled. What is the matter, Clara, my dearest?'

And hearing Mrs Tregowan lapsing into my proper name, which I was unaware she knew, it was in my mind to tell her of the caller at the front door. Yet I did not, for in her well-meaning she would have passed our talk on to her husband, and he back to Nathaniel. So I made some small talk about the manner of women, and to my dismay watched her poor face crease and crumple in anguish, so that I wished I had said nothing. For Mrs Tregowan, who is sympathetic in all things, is even more so when the trouble is below the waist.

'Oh, my poor dear,' she said, 'we must delay talking about our mission to the families of the miners until you are more able. Unless you wish to assist at the kitchen, my dear. But I will leave that with you.'

Having said which, she was gone, because she feared her presence to be a burden to me, suffering, as I wasn't unduly, from a malady below the waist, which nevertheless to Mrs Tregowan is the worst of misfortunes. Then I applied myself to the task of needlework, which was simple indeed, being the hem of a smock for a little bairn.

And I don't know what it was, whether that unmentionable malady which never does trouble me excessively, or the shaming presence at the front door, or that I had lately been into my old room for a pen and had seen again the portrait of Arabella Chark, but when I held up the tiny garment to inspect the hem I had made a fit of weeping came over me. And I was in such a state of misery that poor Bertie-mun, finding me in the drawing room when he came in to mend the fire, brought Willow in from her carpet beating, who promptly went out again and arrived back in the drawing room presently with a draught from the apothecary cupboard.

All this taking place in silence, as indeed the whole day passed in silence, the only sounds being the voice of the clock in the hall, and the voices of various doors and floor boards in the house as Willow and Bertie-mun passed to and fro.

Then as the dusk began to gather Nathaniel returned home, bringing Cecilia with him, for, as he said, she was at Shackleton to call on her kindred and he did not wish her to walk back to the Rose Pavement on her own when the day's light had gone and the lamplighter was not yet out.

'You look peaky, mun,' said Cecilia. And at that my husband took me to the lamp and studied my face, passing his hand over my hair.

'It is nothing,' I said.

'Then if you are sure it is nothing, you may read to me from Mr Richardson this evening, darling,' he said.

'Happen the mistress would do better to take herself to her chamber and lie down, for I know them signs when I see them,' said Cecilia. 'You are but a man, sir, with respect, and you know not, though I have to say you mean well.'

Then all of a sudden the daytime silence of the house was deafened with the noise of voices, augmented by other sounds of Willow making the table ready in the parlour and Bertie-mun bringing in the coals. And seeing a further contention arising between my husband and Cecilia, and on my account, I said I would do both of those things, namely lie down until called to the table, and read from Mr Richardson afterwards.

It was when the hall clock was striking nine that I went up to the room of my husband, who drew me over to the lamp again and, taking my face between his hands, kissed my forehead. For it is always so, that we are more like brother and sister than husband and wife, for a reason I can hardly fathom, except that I fear to be otherwise, and I believe Nathaniel fears the same. And if we could but remain as we are, all might yet be well.

Then he talked about the mine, saying that it would be three weeks at the least before the whole of Shackleton is opened.

'For when they brought in the Spedding mill the red sparks flew, which indicated the presence of foul gases,' he concluded, asking me then about my day.

So I began my account far off, saying that Mrs Tregowan had called about the needlework, and had spoken of the kitchen, where I might help if I would like to. Then by slow degrees I came back to the early part of the day, when the house was silent and a loud knock had come at the front door; and not knowing that Bertie-mun was there already I had gone down, finding there Bertie-mun communicating as best he may with the visitor, yet the chain was still on; and I told Nathaniel how, though I did not see who was the other side of the door, I felt the same troubling presence of which I had written in my letter, telling him also of my fear that he would conclude that my mind is unhinged. After which narrative my husband said he would discuss the matter with Bertie-mun as well as he was able the following morning, not giving me back Mr Richardson's novel, but instead a letter addressed to himself in a hand familiar to me.

'I would be grateful if you could write back to Mr Walsh, my dear,' he said loudly, 'and tell him that I am happy to go over the ledger with him at the time he suggests. Don't go yet, darling.' He lowered his voice. 'Far be it from me to tell you what to read and what not to read, yet I do wonder if Mr Richardson might not be deadening to the spirit. The work appears to contain subject matter inimical to your happiness, although Mr Richardson's moral aims I'm sure are laudable. Do by all means continue with it if you wish, for I cannot forbid you, and indeed I am much to blame for having brought the work into the house in the first place, may the Lord forgive me. And if I continue in this vein much longer you will begin to think I have read it. As to the other matter, darling, you need not ask my permission to go to the kitchen so long as you are recovered, or indeed to go anywhere.'

Then as I made to leave, thinking our interview was over, my husband gave me another book, as if it were a penance and not a blessing. Neither would he hear any words of gratitude. Yet he did not give back Mr Richardson's novel, and I am left to conclude that not only has he read it, but found in its later pages, which I have not yet read, something "inimical" to my happiness.

"Knowing Who My Master Is"

Heavy snow had fallen in the night, casting a white glow into the room, and the sun rose pale and late like any lie-abed. It being Tuesday all the house was filled with the sound, as I supposed, of the flat iron, and the thudding of it went on for much of the day, until Cecilia told me that it was the parlour casement banging, for it had broken loose of its moorings in a high wind that came with the light.

Yet I find myself recovered, which I said to my husband early, for he was intent on going down to Shackleton in spite of the snow.

'I tell the master he's not in his right mind,' said Cecilia, 'for he only has his one arm to walk with, and it being bad under foot and all. But he'll do as he wishes.'

On which my husband, hearing Cecilia's admonitions, remarked that he had two legs and one arm to walk with and would go to Shackleton nevertheless; and moreover he hadn't yet seen anyone in Durham walking on their arm, whether they had two or one.

'Happen that pit's worse than they gave the folks to believe,' said Cecilia when he had gone. 'Leastways, that's what they're saying down in Shackleton. An' turnips won't pay the rent,' she added inconsequentially.

'Before they know it they'll have the candymen at their doors carting off their goods. Not that they have much goods, if you'll pardon my plain speech, mun. An' I take down to them of my wages what I can, if you follow my meaning, but 'tis not all who have their kin in work. An also they be reluctant to receive aught from me, knowing who my master is. Pardon my plain speech, mun, he being your lately wedded husband. For that reason I go not often to see my kin for they think me to have gone over to Beelzebub, though 'tis he who gives them their pay. And 'tis nowhere else I could work, nor Bertie-mun nor Willow neither, for there is none that would have us.'

All this while Nathaniel's letter has lain in my desk drawer, which I have no need to read again for I have it by heart, as I have in my sight also the laboured script and the lines that either climb hills or descend into valleys, and the blots of ink like great boulders on the way.

"My darling, If I could say something to you I would, for I wish not to do you harm, my only desire being to protect you and keep you from hurt. Yet if I did not give you an answer to that concern which you addressed in your letter, even though I might tell myself that I did that which was for the best, the Lord in heaven would know of my dishonesty. Therefore (if you have followed the foregoing which I do not myself) I must tell you the truth as I perceive it, for who in this world knows what truth is? You will understand well whom I have to thank for that borrowing, darling. Suffice to say that what you describe as a shaming presence in the house coincides with the presence of a visitor in the house, if indeed the presence of which you speak and the presence of this some time visitor are one and the same. And in explanation of this presence, my darling Clara, I must say yet further, that the visitor of whom I speak was formerly a surgeon by profession, and now he is not. And although all in the house knew the degree of hurt I had, yet it was on my darling wife's suggestion that Bertie-mun brought him hither, though you did not know it. And now I do indeed ramble, as if I have got myself into a labyrinth and would wander around without direction seeking to find the way out of it. Yet there is one more thing before I close this epistle. I propose to tell you the whole sorry tale, yet as a tale, so that you may know, as it were at one remove what happened, and which closely involved yourself. But before doing so I must beg your permission. Is it your wish, my darling, that I tell you this tale in a letter? Or is it your wish to wait for the natural healing of the mind to restore to you full remembrance of these events? Or do I tell you in the presence of a trusted friend?

Your loving husband,

Nathaniel."

And in the end I wrote down, for I was late in the day seated at the desk in the drawing room writing an envelope, and my husband was seated opposite me reading the remaining correspondence, "Yes," sliding the page across to him.

Which he glanced at and said, 'Is that yes, I shall tell you, or yes, I shall refrain from telling you, or yes, I shall tell you, but only in the presence of a trusted friend? Or may it mean that you do not know, or you cannot say?'

'It means yes, I shall carry on reading the tale, Nathaniel, for I have started reading it already.' I said, as loudly as I might, for I was aware on the landing the unequal steps of my maid Willow, knowing at the same time that she could not have heard our speech.

To which Nathaniel replied, 'It is entitled *Sense and Sensibility*, by an anonymous author, and it is highly spoken of.'

Then I said to him that I did indeed like the book by the anonymous author who calls herself only "A lady", though we were talking nonsense, and that my spirits were much recovered on account of having abandoned Clarissa Harlowe to her trials and tribulations; all the while looking into my husband's dark and glowing eyes, so that if it were not as I have said with us I could believe that we were married.

Along the Cinder Path
Carrying With Me His
Blessing

The frost continues so hard by day that the winches at Shackleton, being fast with ice, look likely to fail, and all the men are laid off work again as a consequence. And some say they would go down if only for half a day's wage which is better than no pay, and others say that the winches are sound and working and talk of them being frozen solid is a ploy of Thorley and Chark to thwart the colliers. So Cecilia tells me, yet I do not know how she has come by this knowledge as she has not been abroad in Durham, nor indeed has Willow, the way down from the Rose Pavement being steep and icy in the extreme, like a mountainside. So my husband said, though he had never been on a mountainside in his life, he added.

'An' it's them laws, mun,' said Cecilia, 'and if it were not for them laws the men would be at the master's door making them demands.'

Then I asked her which laws she meant, and she said it was them combination laws which precluded the use of, and of the rest she was uncertain, for she had followed the first part of the talk, as it went on after holy service before Mrs Tregowan's return from the privy, yet not the second part of the talk when the laws were spoken of, how they were construed. But, Cecilia said, she would discover the rest at chapel on the morrow and inform me.

'That's if you would like to know, mun,' she added. To which I answered that I would, for I could do no other.

Then as she was leaving, Cecilia said, 'The master informs me that he has some letters for you to write, miss, an' it strikes me that if he has some letters for you to write he could well inform you of the fact himself, for he is much recovered if it were not for his arm, but his voice does not ail him, nor has it ever. If I didn't know the master to be a well-meaning gentleman I could think him to be a wily fellow, for them letters and all. He is in the drawing room at this minute, but he can wait.'

I didn't know whether that latter remark came from Cecilia or my husband, yet I went to the drawing room, finding him looking not "wily", though I don't know how a wily fellow would look, but pale and drawn.

'There are letters for Mr Higgs and Mr Thorley confirming the closure now of the sound area of Shackleton on account of the winch,' he said, and then, quietly, 'Pray sit down, darling. Naturally Mr Higgs and Mr Thorley know of the closure for they were at Shackleton yesterday when we discussed the matter. The men are in high dudgeon, but that can't be helped.'

'No,' I said.

'Meaning, of course, that it is impossible for you to comment,' he said. 'Yet I needed only to tell you of my troubles and I now feel much recovered.' And indeed, the colour had returned to his face, which, as I have said before, and would gladly write on every page of my life like a foolish young girl, I find lovely to look at. 'You are beautiful this morning, darling,' he said.

'And you, sir,' I said.

'But you have something to say, my dear,' he said. 'I see it written in your face.'

'You cannot read what is written there, sir,' I said.

'No, but you are about to tell me, darling.'

'I wished to ask you, Nathaniel, if I might attend the kitchen, for the colliers are off work and the weather is bitterly cold.'

'I have said before, Clara, you need not ask my permission in anything. I have surely mentioned the kitchen?'

'Then I may go today, Nathaniel?'

'Only so long as you take Bertie-mun with you in case you slip on the ice,' he said. 'And let me see you before you go to make sure you are warmly wrapped up, my dear. I would accompany you myself, but that the men have no wish to set eyes on the master at the best of times, and now times are at their worst. Even the coal master sees that, but it is beyond my capacity to rectify matters.'

So presently we arrived at an outhouse at the rear of the wool hall, which did as a kitchen, with its great hearth and brick ovens; having reached our destination without mishap as Bertie-mun took me along the cinder path behind St Giles where the snow was yet soft. And I had on not only my own cloak but also my husband's, which he had placed around me, as if I might be the entire way along the cinder path carrying with me his blessing, for all that he is the coal master and despised by the men. For no doubt the colliers and their kin see not a kind man but a dark browed tyrant when they look at him, an encounter with whom most would strenuously avoid.

Arriving at the entrance to the outhouse behind the wool hall Bertie-mun left me, and left me to the most desolating of scenes. For there inside, stretching as far as the eye could see, and indeed farther, for those at the back were lost in the fog of the room, was a queue of men, though some were women, filing alongside a vast cauldron and receiving each one a measure of stew and a ration of bread. And the fog in the room nearly stifled my breath, compounded as it was of the customary soots of Durham, and the smoke of the stew, and the aroma of those whose dwelling houses are too cold and whose spirits burn too low to permit of bathing.

'Ah, Claribell, there you are, my dear. You will see what has befallen us.' Yet what it was that had befallen I did not discover, for Mrs Tregowan's voice was smothered in the din of the place. Only that, taking my hand, she placed a ladle in it, seeing me no doubt at a loss and speechless. 'One spoon to each bowl, my dear,' she said. 'I will take your cloak or you will be overheated. Try to be accurate rather than precipitate, darling, for the good souls do not mind waiting. And when you are wearied we will put you on to the bread. I will ask dear Bertie to carry the coals for us if I can find him, for we are all ladies as yet.'

And in such a manner Mrs Tregowan continued her talk by my side, while in front of me was the queue of colliers, saying, each one, 'Thank you, mun. Thanking you kindly, mun.' Until the voices faded into a counterpoint like the ground bass in a work by Mr Handel, and I became conscious of, as it were, a descant sounding apart from the general noise.

For at my back, slicing turnips, were two other women, whose conversation, because of its difference, reached my hearing. And their talk was of a young woman who had perished in the north pit of Shackleton, who on account of her shameful condition had been cast out by her kindred, and it was likely had not come up after her shift for many a day, but instead had found her dwelling in the mine, for they discovered with her morsels of bread and a candle end.

Then all of a sudden I could no longer see the ladle I was holding, and the great queue of men drifted into a mist before my eyes. And I looked for Mrs Tregowan, but she had gone. For there remained nothing in my mind but the face of Tessa Spence, whom I had never seen in my life, lit by a guttering candle and making her bed for the night in the north pit of Shackleton; who remained there watching over me until I remembered late in the day the correspondence for Mr Higgs and Mr Thorley.

Yet there were no letters, merely envelopes in those gentlemen's handwriting, addressed to my husband. And between them a folded paper, on which was written in Nathaniel's difficult hand:

"Our narrative begins in the year of our Lord 1800, forgive me, darling, for I am no story teller, when they required a surgeon in Durham, the previous incumbent of that post having passed away of the phthisis. And none came forward but one, for work among the colliers is arduous for a man of physic – and he that at length came forward was a man with no testimonials but a torn script of some years' age from an asylum in the county of Lincoln. Yet the matter was pressing on account of an outbreak of fever in the hamlet of Blennowe and he was appointed, by a committee of three, myself being one; yet not Mr Tregowan, who is debarred from such an office as a dissenting minister. My dear Clara, do you wish me to continue?"

And here the story drifts away into silence, for there is no more, my husband having done that to me which all of my sisterhood well know to be the most tantalising thing, namely that he had begun a tale and not ended it.

The Night Music of the Melting Garden

It may well be Wednesday morning but all the days are the same. The white glare of the snow continues into the second week in March, as does the kitchen in the outbuilding at the back of the wool hall. For the men are still laid off. The winch cannot be released from the frost, and, indeed, the cold hardens as the days increase. And I am still going to the kitchen, wrapped in Nathaniel's cloak, which he insists would only serve to impede his progress in the snow.

'Having only one arm to walk with,' he says, though not in front of Cecilia. 'For she means well,' he adds.

As do we all, which words I have to repeat to myself daily, for I don't know if I mean well or not, or how great the divide is between meaning well and not meaning well. And I no longer know what either is, except that in the world of Nathaniel and Cecilia, being the only ones in the household with voices (which are used to such effect that they make up for Willow and Bertie-mun, who do not speak) to mean well is better than to do well. And although I attend the kitchen, I do not know if I mean well, or if I do well. Yet Mrs Tregowan, although she is troubled over many things, undoubtedly does well without stopping to speculate on the matter.

'I know you are wondering about the bairns, my dear Claribell,' she said today, which I do not know if I was or not, for I had not seen any, hidden as they surely were in the fog of the place. 'Do not you fret, darling, for they are born to it. Though there is one person,' she lay emphasis on "person" as if it were not the benign word it is, 'who from time to time inflames the matter of bairns working in the pit, as a sling and arrow with which to wound your husband's reputation. Which I fear he has succeeded in doing. Yet this person should not count himself as any great moral authority for he has been unwise in his time, though it is not befitting in a lady to repeat such gossip,' having said which Mrs Tregowan blushed furiously, for she is fair of complexion with hair the colour of autumn leaves. 'You did not hear that latter, did you, my dear Claribell?'

So I said to Mrs Tregowan, for I could do no other, that I had not, yet it came to me that I might ask her if the talk I had overheard about Tessa Spence making her dwelling down the mine when she found herself in a humiliating condition is the truth. But I did not ask.

And it is the eleventh day of March and my sixty-eighth under Nathaniel's roof; and the frost does not loosen, even under the pale sun, which glides daily towards the equinox, and fresh flurries of snow blow in from the sea, driven into peaks by the keen wind.

Yet the Rose Pavement is sheltered, so that any stranger coming here might suppose it to be a haven of tranquillity rather than the thoroughfare in which the coal master has his dwelling, were it not for a perpetual seething of men at the gate, to whom Willow carries out each day warm heels of bread. For if anyone were to offer ribaldry she would not hear, which they well know, and for that reason hold their peace.

All of this passes as a dream before me. Yet, and although I might travel as if I were a disengaged passenger, I am not, for lying in the drawer of my desk is a sheet of paper on which I wrote after my husband's last letter, "Yes, I wish you to continue your story," the key being locked on it so that I may not change it.

And I wait only for the occasion to say to my husband, 'If you wish, I may read to you from *Sense and Sensibility*. It will divert you from the matters of the colliery.' Yet I am not good at this subterfuge, for neither my husband nor I are any other than indifferent actors, and I have no doubt that this charade is fully known to Cecilia, though not the purpose of it.

'Nathaniel, if you wish I will read to you this evening,' I said as we sat at the table. 'You may find a passage to your liking,' giving to him the book, in which, between pages 96 and 97, was my letter.

'Then we shall read at nine o'clock, my dear,' he said. 'It will, as you say, divert our attention from the frozen winch.'

Which, even in the saying of it, provoked a huff from Cecilia, agitating as she was to clear the plates. And I felt like a frivolous girl, if indeed I ever was one, for I have no clear memory of being either a girl or frivolous. It is as if I were born into the world a woman of twenty-eight years, having consented, as I suppose, to a marriage with a man I did not know, and fearful to the last degree of the exigencies of the wedded state. Yet before I could begin any kind of apology for tarrying so late at the table, Cecilia spoke.

'The master may well read for himself, mun,' she said, as if he were not present. 'For he is a most learned gentleman, I will say that for him. And a kind gentleman also, who happen would not insist upon a reading when you have stood upon your feet in yon kitchen all day, mun.'

Then Nathaniel said, 'You are right, of course, my dear Cecilia, as you are right in many things except my learning and kindness, which you exaggerate greatly. It is for a separate reason that Clara has expressed a wish to read this evening, and I would not for the world have her tire herself after being in the kitchen all day if she would prefer to retire to her chamber. Can you keep a confidence, Cecilia?'

'Yes, sir,' she said.

'Thank you, my dear,' said Nathaniel. 'Then I may tell you that, for a reason unknown to my wife, she has begun to remember that some accident befell her a number of years ago, although she does not know what it was. And because words are gentler written than spoken, for they may be read at leisure, I am telling her that story in writing, and slowly, and asking her to make sure that I stop if she wishes to hear no more.'

During all of which speech I watched the frowns and puckers chase one another across Cecilia's brow, though she said nothing and made to leave the room.

'I pray you speak, Cecilia,' said Nathaniel, 'for it is not in you to keep silence, and now you do.'

'Well, sir,' said Cecilia, closing the door which she was half way through, 'I was minded to do as you do, saving your presence, and write down what I would say to you, as you do to your good lady wife. Yet since you have asked it, I will speak it. To my mind 'tis a tale better told to the mistress by a woman of her own gender, and to my mind also you are playing with fire, sir, pardon my expression at the present time, sir; for this is the soul of your dear lady wife which you have in your safe keeping, which you have promised to do before the Lord in heaven, and you know not what will befall her when that what is buried an' forgotten is brought to the surface, pardon my expression again at this present time, sir. If it must be said, it is best you ask Mrs Tregowan to do so, for she means well, sir, or that you find a physician, though you will be hard pressed to find a physician in Durham.'

After saying which Cecilia went out, leaving Nathaniel in a state of deep mortification, so that the tears stood in his eyes and he could not look at me.

'Forgive me, darling,' he said. 'I did not know.'

Then, in spite of the doldrums we were in, it came to me that, uninvited, there had arrived in the lexicon of sayings from Nathaniel's household, one more, "I did not know."

And I did what I had not dreamt of doing. I kissed my husband, and he me; and there came to me uninvited also another saying, for my head was suddenly full of sayings, 'We shall be happy, shall we not, my dear?' And in the instant his saying and my kiss fled as if they had been a dream, leaving us alone together with Cecilia's scolding echoing round the room.

'Cecilia is right, of course, darling,' he said. 'We must think how it is best that we are to proceed in this matter, for it cannot be left. It is not heaven weeping for a sinner,' he added presently, going to the window, 'though it might well be. I believe the thaw has come.'

And, indeed, a soft rain was falling, and my husband threw open the casements of the drawing room to let in the night music of the melting garden.

"Naught but Sacking to Lie Abed On"

This is the first equinox of the year, when day and night are equal and the whole luminous heaven should rightly rejoice in the awakening of the earth, but Cecilia has said that those who come into Durham from outside speak of the snow still lying in hollows waiting for a fresh fall to take it away.

And although the heavens might be said to rejoice, there is less of rejoicing in the household of the coal master, for it seems that we have all of sunk into our separate secrecies, not least concerning the mine at Shackleton. For, although the winch is freed and the men are back, and Cecilia has brought word that the closed up part of the pit is to be opened again, there remain seethings of discontent abroad, and a perpetual presence of men at our gate, largely from outside the city who make it their business, though it is not, to offer up the discontent of the colliers, whether they wish it or not.

All this I have from Cecilia, for there is nothing from my husband, as if in discontinuing the story he was telling he has discontinued all other discourse. And I could even think that, having wed, we are now unwed.

'The candymen are at the gates of Shackleton you know, mun,' Cecilia said, which I did not know, for

Shackleton has no gates. 'Happen the master don't know neither, for they down there won't say, not until they've given up all their goods and there is naught but sacking to lie abed on. 'Tis on account that they've been on half pay this last quarter gone. The master has asked of Bertie-mun to take for dispatch in the night coach a letter addressed to York, mun,' she added. 'But 'tis not for me to draw conclusions.'

Yet in spite of the silence and unease I am unaccountably freed from the malign presence I have sensed in the house for these weeks past. Whether it is that some visitor to the house now no longer visits, or whether the imagining of such a visitor has gone, I don't know. For such other visitors to the house I know, being Mr Higgs and Mr Thorley who come to discuss matters relating to the mine, whose acquaintance I have made at the chapel and who cause me no alarm. Mr Higgs being tall and pale of face and so near-sighted that he is obliged to stoop to bring anyone to whom he is speaking within his range of vision, and Mr Thorley being his opposite, level with me in height, and with a brush of white hair framing a circular face; and both cheery and merry despite the troubled times and the pervading gloom of the dissenting chapel.

Which brings me back always to Nathaniel my husband, who, contrary to his habit of being much recovered, has shown no signs of recovery of spirits since Cecilia's intervention in the matter of the letters. Yet in the matter of his wound, it is true that he is much recovered, but for a cough that echoes through the quiet house at nights; though I do not know if it belongs to Bertie-mun or Nathaniel or both, for both have breathed the black breath of the mines.

So to Bertie-mun, who, when we were returning from the kitchen, indicated that he was to enquire at the sign of the Fox for any letters from the York coach.

And as I waited outside a voice which I knew, but did not know, broke into the reverie I was sunk in, saying, 'Mrs Chark, at your service, ma'am,' and passed on. And, although I saw no one, a hot shame flooded over me, which I thought had gone. For the presence of the speaker lingered, although the voice, which was slurred with strong liquor, had moved away into the crowded twilight.

Render unto Caesar

It being the Lord's day, which only serves to confirm my early supposition that life in Nathaniel's household would proceed in Sabbath days, and Mr Tregowan preached on, "Render unto Caesar the things that are Caesar's". Yet not a soul knew, and I suspect that Mr Tregowan did not know himself, who might be Caesar and what it was to be rendered on this, the twenty-second day of March in the year of our Lord 1812.

'I do not know if Patrick was wise in his choice of text, my dear Claribell,' said Mrs Tregowan, 'for the poor souls in Shackleton are many of them in arrears,' this last word she said in a whisper, 'on account of the half time pay, which is no one's fault, though there are many trying to lay the blame. And some say the candymen are at their doors, who are rough, unclean fellows if ever there were, my dear, though I have not in my life set eyes on such a one. For which reason, and because the dear Lord has taken away the snow and ice, I propose that we try to make our mission to the family I have told you of if you are in agreement, which task is not in addition to attendance in the kitchen, for a body can only do so much. I have it on good authority that the kitchen will cease to run when the men are back on full time, dear.'

All of which talk made me think that Mrs Tregowan, though she is a woman, might have made a coal master herself, had the Lord fashioned her as a man.

'You will think that I talk as if I were a coal master myself, my dear Claribell,' she said, 'and if I were, no man would be on half pay.'

Then a fierce blush spread over her face, and I believe she would have reeled in her words as any fisherman on the Wear reels in his catch, but that she could not.

'Darling, forgive me,' she said. 'I meant no criticism of dear Nathaniel, for though they in Durham would heap fire and brimstone on his head, yet I know it for a fact that the gentry who have ownership of the land set down the laws and the rents, and the coal master is, as it were, caught between the colliers and the landlords and cannot do right whichever way he turns, neither in the matter of rents nor in the matter of wages. If you are wondering how this knowledge has been given to me, Claribell, so also do I, save that I came down in my station in life on marrying dear Patrick, he being a dissenter, you know, or I might well be housed in some castle on the borderland as my kindred are. You did not hear that latter, did you, my dear?'

So I told Mrs Tregowan that I had not heard, for the question was her way of asking me to hold my peace on the matter, without saying in so many words, as she did not wish me to think she doubted my prudence.

'And I might say also, my darling,' she continued, for she had not yet finished with her observations on the rents payable in Shackleton, 'dear Nathaniel could make his situation more amenable by letting it be known to the colliers that he does not set the rents, but he is an obdurate gentleman, darling, for all his kindness, and if

141

he could go abroad in a downpour of fire and brimstone he would. And I have to say he is worse in that respect since poor Arabella's passing, as if he would be always imposing a penance on himself. Dear me, Claribell, you did not hear that latter, did you?'

So I said to Mrs Tregowan no, I had not heard it, which did not pacify her in the least, and she became even more flustered, which I understood was because she had said Arabella's name.

In the afternoon there were at the Sabbath school, as I thought, the same scholars who had attended first of all, whose names as always were given as William Darbyshire, Frederick Pennell, James Sowerby, Alfred Baines, Amos Frost, Bartholomew, and Gregory Parrish. And I was about to say farewell to them at the end of the lesson and see them away, each with a heel of bread, when the scholar who gave his name as Frederick Pennell approached me, as had a scholar of that name previously, with a rough piece of paper, as if torn from a book, and said, 'Asking your kindness, mun, we would study this.'

And as before, all the scholars fell into a silence, watching me as I read, the words being these: "Several laws are in existence for regulating and limiting work-men's wages. Why not leave them as free to make their own bargains, as the law-makers are to let their farms and houses? Personal labour is all the property they have. Why is that little, and the little freedom they enjoy, to be infringed?"

'It is a passage of some length and complexity,' I said. 'Which is the part you would study?'

'We know not, mun,' said Frederick Pennell. 'Yet we would know the meaning of it.' Then I asked, as I

142

had asked before, how the passage came into their possession, to which Frederick Pennell answered as he had answered previously, 'It came to us, mun.'

Afterwards, when we were all of us at the table, for despite the constraint in Nathaniel's household we still have high tea together on the Sabbath day, Cecilia said, 'Them candymen's at the gates of Shackleton, sir, on account of areas in rent, though I know not what areas is, sir. 'Tis not in Mr Johnson, leastways not as makes any sense. Yet there is areas in rent, sir.'

And I watched the colour rise in my husband's face, and a dark frown gather on his brow, thinking he was about to vent his anger on Cecilia. Yet he did not.

'I did not know,' he said. 'How come you to know this, Cecilia?'

'Bodies is talking, sir,' she said.

Not a Breath of Wind nor a Gleam of Sun

The mines of Shackleton, Thayne and Blennowe are closed, as it is holy Friday. And Durham generally is closed, for few are abroad except the perpetual presences at our gate; "presence" being the word I find myself adopting, lacking a better, for any malign or unwished for incursion into my consciousness. And even they, the presences at our gate, are without the sustenance of strong liquor in deference to the day's observance. And it is as if the world itself is closed also, for there is not a breath of wind nor a gleam of sun, but only a grey sea fret.

Yet today, for all that everywhere else is closed, Mrs Tregowan said that we should accomplish our mission of mercy and visit a collier's family, which she has had in her mind 'for weeks, my dear Claribell, and holy Friday is a good enough day, when we shall find them all together under their roof,' without saying if we would be welcome on a day when the mine is closed and they might otherwise lie late in their beds.

'We must appear plain in our dress, my dear, for we wish not to arrive on their threshold as ladies. And I do not like to say this, my dear Claribell, but poor Enid had a brown stuff cloak for the purpose, which I am sure still resides in a closet somewhere, for Nathaniel could not deal with those matters, you know, my dear, and I fear those matters are not dealt with to this day.'

Yet I didn't know how I could ask of Nathaniel such a thing as the loan of his deceased wife's cloak. And I confided in Mrs Tregowan that I could not ask. So she said she would ask him herself, making the request look as if it had come solely from herself, as indeed it had, and that I was ignorant of it. Which request must have been made already, before her discourse with me, for Nathaniel joined us presently and asked us to go with him to the room which had formerly been mine. And, as if he needed witnesses to such an act of violation, he quickly unlocked the closet door, retrieved the brown cloak of which Mrs Tregowan had spoken, and placed it in my hands, kissing my hair as he did so.

All of this was accomplished in a silence which inhibited even Mrs Tregowan's speech until we had left the room and Nathaniel had gone.

'You will think I am a cruel woman for forcing on dear Nathaniel such an act of sacrilege, my dear,' she said, and I told her that I did not think any such thing of her.

Yet she insisted on remaining a cruel woman all the way to Shackleton, reiterating her low opinion of herself from time to time in a low voice, for the thoroughfares were empty and quiet, and there was nothing to be heard but the occasional echo of clogs on the stones and the song of birds.

'We will not outlast our welcome, my dear Claribell,' she said, 'which is no more than an expression for there may not be any welcome at all, on account of this family being lowly and despised even among those in Shackleton. Yet we must be of good

145

cheer and take their ill will not upon ourselves, but offer our discomfiture up to the dear Lord.'

And it came to me that Mrs Tregowan orders her life in this way, so that I wondered for a split moment in time if I might have done the same myself. But I had not, and it was too late now. And the vision came to me of a garret room and of a malignancy, as of a great incubus weighing on me, and an overpowering breath of strong liquor. Yet the vision fled as soon as it arrived, leaving behind only the sour air around us, and in front of us a poor dwelling, no different from the rest, but that the curtains, such as they were for they fell in grimy tatters, were closed.

'You will discover now that I am not only a cruel woman but rude also, my dear Claribell,' said Mrs Tregowan, 'for it will serve no purpose to wait for an answer because none will come.'

Having said which, she knocked once and entered hastily before the door could be barred from within. And, indeed, those inside might have done so, had they had any choice in the matter, for when my eyes became used to the darkness I saw that the man of the house, who was much dishevelled and beaten about the face, lay in bed, and the woman was in a state of near undress, holding a bairn to her breast with one hand, and with the other attempting to wash herself using a thin rag. And ill-concealed in a corner of the room was an uncovered pot, the aroma from which stood in the room, though the longer we were there, which was not long, the more I became accustomed to it.

Then seeing they had company the man and woman gathered themselves, the woman placing the bairn in a cot and the man rising from his couch.

This is Clara, my dear,' said Mrs Tregowan, 'and, Clara, this is Hilda,' introducing the man; 'and this is Charles,' introducing the woman. Whereupon they glanced at each other and smiled wanly.

'Thou hast it wrong way roond, mun,' said the man. 'I be Charles Spence and she be Hilda Spence, an' we would offer ye to drink but we have naught but the dregs o' sour ale.'

To which Mrs Tregowan replied, thanking him, that we had recently broken our fast, and moreover she did not like to take beverages on account of needing the privy so often.

'So we'll be thanking ye to go now,' said the man, 'for we didna invite ye.'

'No you did not, Charles,' said Mrs Tregowan, 'and so long as you hold yourselves aloof you will remain in this plight,' taking from her reticule as she spoke a brown paper parcel tied with string in which was my pitiful attempt at making a straight hem on a bairn's smock. And fearing that the woman would take offence at being given such inferior needlework I told her that I was the perpetrator of such a dismal effort, watching her hold up the garment and examine closely the hem.

'I can do no better myself, mun,' she said, and straight away put the smock on the unprotesting little bairn, who looked bonny enough. Yet I wondered how any could thrive in such a dark place.

'That went better than we could have expected,' said Mrs Tregowan. 'It is because you were there, my dear Claribell, for they are used to me and they know they may say what they please. You realise, my dear, that they are the kindred of poor Tessa, her brother and his wife. I would not have said, but that Charles gave his name. I do not know if they are avoided by their neighbours or whether they hold themselves aloof out of shame. Yet there is no shame in being with child, my dear Claribell,' she added quickly, 'even though it be outside wedlock. You did not hear that latter, did you, my dear? No, I know that you did not. We are going now to call upon Felicity, who will allow us to use her privy. And we may wash our hands and faces, for it is best, you know, my dear, and I need not tell you why.'

And if I had recently seen a martyr in the figure of Hilda Spence, I encountered another in Felicity Walsh, who, seeing that Mrs Tregowan was accompanied, blushed and busied herself with making tea. For, to my mortification, it was not Mrs Tregowan on whose account she was discomfited, but mine. Nor could I say anything to take away her unease, but rather her agitation increased the more I tried to pacify her. And that state of affairs continued until Mr Walsh entered, for he was soon engaged in conversation with Mrs Tregowan on the matter of indemnity.

'My dear Barbara,' he said, 'I agree wi' thee that some manner of assistance should be put in the way of the unfortunate fellow, for he may not go down pit when the drink is on him, and no doubt the recent tragedy has not inclined him towards society neither. Yet indemnity in these cases is for spouses an' offspring, and I know not of a case where a brother has been granted indemnity.'

'My dear Jack,' said Mrs Tregowan in reply, 'perhaps you could plead with Nathaniel to make an exception in this case.'

At which point in the conversation I glanced across at Felicity, though I do not know why I did so, and observed a deep blush rising in her face. And seeing that I had noticed it she rose quickly from her chair, excused herself, and left the room, without, however, quite closing the door, so that painful sobs were to be heard retreating down the passageway, until another door closed deep within the recesses of the house and all was silent.

'Do not go after her, I pray you, Barbara,' said Jack Walsh, for Mrs Tregowan was making to follow. 'Poor Felicity has been in such a way lately, and I am told that it is the manner of women approaching the middle of their pilgrimage on this earth.'

'Nonsense, Jack,' said Mrs Tregowan, resuming her seat. 'Felicity is only a young woman, and fair of face also, though you do not see it, being her brother. her sensibilities have been upset by our discourse relating to poor Tessa's kindred, to be sure. What do you think, Clara, my dear?'

I agreed that could be the case, though I had seen, which Jack Walsh and Mrs Tregowan had not, so involved were they in their discussion, that it was the mention of Nathaniel which had distressed Felicity. Not only that, but my very presence under her roof surely served to have deepened her anguish. And also, were she in my place, for my mind travelled on apace as a silent counterpoint to the continued talk on indemnities, Felicity would have been modest, yet not terrified, and a wife to Nathaniel, which I am not. And furthermore, I could hear in my mind his voice, if he were ever to discover the secret that lay buried in Felicity's heart, 'May the Lord forgive me. I did not know.'

So we left presently, with, as I understand, for I had lost the thread of the conversation between Mrs Tregowan and Mr Walsh, the question of indemnity for Charles Spence as yet unsettled. And Felicity, appearing composed, did her utmost to help me on with my cloak, which was not mine but borrowed from Arabella Chark, as she would have perceived; and she offered her perpetual friendship, whispering to me, for Mrs Tregowan and her brother continued to talk of indemnities as if the matter would never end, that she had always suffered in this way with the changes of the moon, knowing that I would understand what she wished me to believe.

"Personal Labour Is All the Property They Have"

The sea fret continues, covering like a heavy grey pall the whole city of Durham, muffling all sound and subduing all mirth. And it seems, as it often does, that even the trees are weeping, shedding silver tears from every twig and filling bud. And all that today, on what should be the most festive of days, though I don't believe that those who go into the dissenting chapel ever feel festive on coming out of it, even though they might have been festive going in. Nor indeed am I festive today, for my thoughts return all the time to poor Felicity Walsh and her outburst of grief, and I return also to the opinion that Nathaniel would have been more blessed in Felicity as his wife than in me.

Such thoughts were jostling in my mind when there was a knock on my room door, which I did not answer, thinking it to be Willow or Cecilia, who would let themselves in. Yet neither came in, and going to the door I found my husband waiting there with my cloak and bonnet in his hand, which he proceeded tenderly to put on me, arranging the bow under my chin and settling the cloak across my shoulders, and then brushing away the tears which I did not know were there.

'You are in the doldrums, my darling,' he said, 'and I fear attendance at chapel will not raise your spirits, nor mine either, yet we must go, for Barbara will be singing an aria of Mr Handel and we cannot hurt her feelings.'

We set off for the dissenting chapel as is our habit, with Nathaniel and I in front, followed by Cecilia, Willow and Bertie-mun in a line at the back of us, arriving when the chapel was already full; only for the reason that my husband had need, as he thought, to dress me, though I could have accomplished the deed more quickly, though with less of precision, myself.

So we placed ourselves all together on a form at the back which had been brought in for late-comers, most of whom were from the hamlet of Shackleton. And to be placed at the back, though not out of the sight of God, as Nathaniel said later, was as well, for no sooner had Mrs Tregowan begun to sing "I know that my redeemer liveth" than the bench began to shake with the stifled laughter of Willow, who transmitted the same to Cecilia, and so to Bertie-mun as if it were a fever. Nor would they be pacified even after Mrs Tregowan had finished, but continued until the end of holy service. And it came to me that Nathaniel had deliberately made us late, so that we might take up a seat at the back and not show ourselves up as a public example.

Then leaving Willow and Cecilia to attend scripture, and Bertie-mun to go to his kindred in Thayne, though I did not know he had any kindred, we stood ready to go home, which would have been as well, given the disgrace we had made of ourselves, and also would have spared Felicity the anguish of meeting me with Nathaniel. Yet Felicity would not be spared, and followed after us, greeting us with great kindness and cordiality, and wishing us the joy of the season. And I said, for I could see that Nathaniel did not know how to account for our abrupt departure from the chapel, that our household had caught a fit of mirth and we left precipitately as we felt ashamed of ourselves. All of this Felicity heard with great good humour, relating the same to her brother Jack who presently joined us.

'And what gave them a fit of mirth?' he said.

Nathaniel replied that Willow was always of that habit for she could not express her praise of the Lord in any other way, being without speech and hearing; which dereliction of the truth pleased Jack Walsh greatly, and he said he would call upon Nathaniel to plead for him at the day of judgement, so persuasive was his talk.

At which point Felicity bade us farewell for, as she said, she had laughed so much as to provoke a cough, and she was thankful it had not come on in the service; although to my mind she need not have concerned herself for the dissenting chapel is always filled with the coughings and wheezings of the colliers, and one more would not have been noticed. And between us we had told several half-truths, yet it did not matter.

Although the scholars might have been expected to give themselves a vacation on this day, the Sabbath school took place nevertheless. And besides those who had given their names before, being William Darbyshire, Frederick Pennell, James Sowerby, Alfred Baines, Amos Frost, Bartholomew and Gregory Parrish, there was one more scholar, who gave his name as Colin Beech, besides Willow and Cecilia, making ten in all.

'We would study this, mun, if you please,' said Frederick Pennell, handing to me the same tract, as I thought, that he had brought with him before. ''Tis more of it, mun, if you please,' he added, no doubt seeing my perplexity. So I read: "Several laws are in existence for regulating and limiting work-men's wages. Why not leave them as free to make their own bargains, as the law-makers are to let their farms and houses? Personal labour is all the property they have ... When wages are fixed by what is called a law, the legal wages remain stationary, while everything else is in progression; and as those who make that law still continue to lay on new taxes by other laws, they increase the expense of living by one law, and take away the means by another."

'Happen it doon't mek a deal o' sense to ye,' said the scholar who had introduced himself as Colin Beech. 'But it do to us, leastways it will when all have done studying it. It means, mun, that the pay was half during yon closure, an' candymen be at our doors an' yon landlords have gone put up rent the moore. An' it done mean moorovver that all we have in our possession is yon labour. An in addition, mun, yon Act stipulates men may not gang up to approach masters for pay. Therefore 'tis my conclusion, mun, that our only recourse be to withdraw our labour, for the mine willna run if there baint none labour. Yet far be it from us to ever say you tot us yon tract, mun.' And I could see the eyes of all fixed on me, waiting for an answer.

Then I heard a voice, though I do not know if it was mine, say, 'We may study this.'

Until the Ewes and Lambs Were No More Than Dim White Lights

And, much like the sea fret that has descended on the city of Durham, a grey gloom has fallen on me, which, though it is no new thing, would scarcely permit me to dress and get ready for the day; a state of which Nathaniel must have been aware, for Cecilia came knocking on my door at the half hour after eight, saying the master would see me at a time to my liking.

'You need not call him the master, Cecilia,' I said, which querulous retort she hardly deserved, for she means well.

'Happen I call him the master when he is behaving like a master,' she said, 'begging your pardon, mun, for he is your wedded husband. Happen it is not to your liking to be put about at this hour in the day, mun, though you do not say so. The master asks that you let me know when you may see him so that I may tell him. There has something bitten him, mun, if you'll excuse my plain speech. An' for that reason I would gladly go with you yet I know I may not.'

So I told Cecilia that I would be ready in half an hour, asking her to send in my maid Willow, for I could hardly summon up the will to stir myself. And Willow, seeing how I was, followed me into the drawing room, where my husband was seated at his desk with a slender volume in front of him.

'Willow may stay,' he said, rising from his chair as we entered. 'You are not well, darling. Pray sit down. Willow, make yourself comfortable by the fireside, my dear,' he added, which Willow promptly did, although she has no hearing. 'You are not well, darling,' he said again.

I told Nathaniel that the sea fret has a lowering influence on my spirits, asking him then what was the volume placed on the desk between us.

'We need not trouble ourselves with the volume at the moment,' he said, picking it up and putting it in his pocket. 'It is of no matter. It is an inflammatory work that has come into the hands of certain of the colliers, that is all. Such tracts have appeared from time to time since the rebellion in France. But there will be no rebellion in England. Forgive me, darling, I have spoken out of turn at a time when you are in the doldrums.'

'And so are you, Nathaniel,' I said, for the colour had fled from my husband's face as he spoke of the rebellious tract. Then he asked me to sit down at the desk, taking the chair opposite.

'You are lovely this morning, darling,' he said presently, and his colour flooded back.

'And you also, sir,' I said, and he leaned across the desk and kissed me, and I him, for Willow had fallen into a slumber in the fireside chair. And for that slender moment all thoughts of Felicity Walsh, who is more lovely, and more deserving, and more innocent than I, had gone far away.

'Bertie-mun has brought a letter from the York coach. It is an invitation of sorts,' my husband continued, taking a much-folded sheet of foolscap from the same pocket in which he had deposited the inflammatory tract. 'Pray read it, darling. It puts my untidy script to shame.' And, indeed, the letter was exquisitely written, and had about it the sweet scent of medicinal lavender and rosemary, over and above the dark aroma of the ink.

'It is a work of beauty,' I said. 'But it is addressed to you, Nathaniel,' and I handed it back to him unread.

'It is addressed to me but it concerns my beloved wife,' he said.

'Enid?'

'No. Clara who is my wife, whom I love with all my heart. Forgive me, darling. This talk sends you deeper into the doldrums, for you have always felt yourself to be undeserving, as indeed I do of you, and with more reason. The letter is from a physician practising in York.'

Then the words of Cecilia came back to me, that what must be said should be said in the presence of a physician or … I had forgotten her expression, but the thought of Mrs Tregowan came to me, followed closely by Cecilia's words … "a woman of her own gender".

'From a physician?'

'A physician practising in York. The letter invites us to go and see him in York.'

'Why York?'

'He is a man of integrity and has a fine reputation.'

'And are there no others nearer to Durham with integrity and a fine reputation?' I said, for the sudden prospect of a day's journey in a dark, malodorous coach troubled me exceedingly.

Nathaniel drew a breath and took my hand. 'The physician is a Frenchman,' he said at length. 'Although I will, if you permit me, be with you, darling, you may say to him what you please and I shall not understand a word that passes.'

Which observation put me in mind, inconsequentially, of Willow, who had slept through our conversation, yet had she been wide awake she would not have known a word of what we said.

'Does the letter say anything else?' I said.

'He gives his name, and as it is a French name, tells us how to enunciate the word. He tells us how to find the dispensary close by the Monk-bar.'

'Is he a good man, Nathaniel? We are to entrust him with our souls.'

'I cannot answer that, darling. Only to say that he is between sinner and saint, which is how we all are on this life's pilgrimage.'

'I will go,' I said, for our deliberations looked likely to last out the day and Willow had begun to stir.

'We will write then with our acceptance,' said my husband, 'and try not to make it look as if we pay this good physician a compliment by condescending to see him, rather than the truth of the matter, which is that he pays us a compliment by seeing us,' during which convoluted speech Willow, who was now fully awake, looked from one to another of us in perplexity. And if she had hearing I would have been asking myself which word had brought on her perplexity. Yet she had not heard any part of our discourse. And when Nathaniel had gone from the room she took from her pocket a volume looking so much like that which my husband had put in his pocket that it could have been the same one.

'What book is that, Willow?' I said, and she handed me the volume, which was slight and roughly bound, with plain board covers. I opened it and turned the pages. 'What is this, Willow?' I said again.

She took the volume from me, turned to a page with a marker, and handed it back. "Several laws are in existence ..." I read on, horrified and fascinated in equal measure. Then I turned to the front of the book to see who might be the perpetrator of this so-called "inflammatory text", a copy of which resided even then in Nathaniel's pocket, and which he would no doubt have forgotten about and carried on his person to Shackleton mine. I gave the book back to Willow, who returned it to her pocket. Then I asked myself how Nathaniel had come by his copy. Then I asked of my maid Willow the same thing, though she has no hearing or speech.

And it came to me that the doldrums fell on me as a consequence of what I took to be my part in inciting the colliers to rebellion against their lot, if that indeed is what I had done. And Nathaniel's reluctance to discuss the contents of the insurrectionary document with me was on account of my low spirits. And always at the back of my mind was the angelic presence of Felicity Walsh, who would have been a good wife and yet supportive of the interests of the colliers, as I have no doubt Arabella Chark had been.

The day passed on, until, with the first gleams of sun after mid-day my low spirits began to drift away, and Nathaniel returned from Shackleton early, saying we might go for a walk and see the first lambs of the season, which I supposed was on account of his supposing that I was still in the doldrums and wishing to divert me. So, setting off at 4 o'clock, we walked along the Wear pathway into the fields. And there we saw, early in the season, a flock of ewes with bright white lambs flecking the hillside, yet near enough and fearless enough, for they were still new to the world and its disorder, to crowd together and look at us.

'Those who work in the mines, do they see the lambs?' I said.

Yet my husband did not hear, and I said no more, thinking that the question was likely to be deemed inflammatory, after the same manner of the volume entitled *The Rights of Man*, which for all I knew still resided in his pocket, and for all that I knew also, would remain forgotten about until Cecilia took away the coat to brush it.

Then we walked on as far as the place where the river runs into woodland, and as the sun was going down we retraced our steps, meeting on the way the one-time visitor to our scullery, whom I thought I knew as Brim Salter, but now sober and in his right mind, and quiet of speech and manner.

Yet, for some reason of which I was unaware, my husband, who is never at a loss for words, had little to say for himself. And believing myself to be a constraint on their conversation I lingered to look at the lambs again so that they might walk on ahead, not knowing how long I was there watching the little creatures with their mothers. And as I stood at the foot of the hill the mist came down, thick as a blanket, until the ewes and lambs were no more than dim white lights glimmering through it, and then nothing of them at all but their plaintive voices.

When I made to join my husband and Mr Salter I could not see in any direction, neither towards Blennowe wood one way, nor the city of Durham the other way. And, by that time being drenched through and chilled, I set off to walk, covering, as I imagined, some three furlongs' distance, but seeing no landmark, not even the trees of Blennowe wood, except that on the way the sky swam red, which surely indicated the last of the sun sinking outside the drift of mist.

Then following the sunset up a narrow bridle-way, I came into yet more mist, as if all the angels in heaven were covering up the new lambs with blankets for the night, for the day was fast declining into twilight. Nor did I know how long it was since I had stood at the foot of the hill with my husband, except that it seemed in a different life, and one which would never come back. And I was striving to hold on to the innocent scene of the ewes with their lambs, yet there was at my back the cold terror gaining on me, that I had lost myself in the mist and that I would emerge from it not into my own life but into another life of someone else's making. And the terror, as if it were a wild beast, had nearly caught up with me, and was even then reaching out to grasp at my cloak when I became aware of a voice calling,

'Clara!

'Clara!' which should have been that of my husband, but was not. And another thought came to me of a Sabbath day school, yet not the school in the house on the Rose Pavement, but an earlier school.

And I called out, 'Adsum!' as I had taught the scholars in the other school, until the Latin word, far from meaning, "I am here", became corrupted into its opposite, "absent".

'Adsum!' I shouted again.

And the words came back, 'Stay where you are,' until I heard presently on the bridle path the sound of boots. Yet I saw no one until Brim Salter stood by me in the mist.

'Your husband went one way and I went the other, Mrs Chark,' he said. 'And we have found you, thank God. If I may humbly offer you my arm I shall take you back, for we are not far off.' Having said which Brim Salter fell silent, and he would not accept my gratitude or that of my husband, saying that it was but a small thing he did, and that any other would have done the same.

Where We Would Not Be
Welcome

It is thirty days since the last entry, for I had no will to write. And I have been waiting all this time for my husband to suggest anything for a diversion, but he has not done so. And I don't know why it is, whether I am perpetually lost in the mist, or because we met Brim Salter on the way, but he has not said that we should walk to see the lambs again. Which, to be truthful, made my heart ready to break, and I think Nathaniel's also. For there is no sight sweeter than placid ewes, who, for all that they are considered to be witless, bring their bairns easily into the world and nudge them into life and merriment.

And in the wanderings of my mind I have gone back many times to the dwelling of Hilda Spence and her little bairn, who, contrary to all expectations, survives. After which my thoughts return to the house on the Rose Pavement, and to the coal master, whose little bairn took one look at the dazzling world and followed his poor mother out of it; and I could believe that he and I, for our different reasons, will always be sunk in gloom and self-recrimination. Yet today was a day of blue skies and high, chasing clouds, with a warm breeze blowing in from the west, and my husband sent Cecilia early to ask for my assistance with his correspondence.

'You are fair recovered, mun,' she said. 'The master requires you to write a letter, though he can do the deed well enough himself, an' I tell him so, but he is an obdurate gentleman.'

'We have a reply from York,' said Nathaniel, and handed me the letter. 'It is addressed to you as well, darling, for I wrote to say that you were laid low after becoming chilled through in the sea fret. I do not know if I said the truth, but it is near enough the truth, which is the best we can do at the present time. You look lovely this morning, darling.'

'And you also, sir,' I said. For indeed he did, and if everything were otherwise, though I do not know in what way otherwise, I would be in love with my husband. 'I am recovered today, Nathaniel. Please tell me what is in the letter.'

'It expresses concern regarding your recent malady, and suggests a Wednesday for our visit, being quiet in the town of York more than on other days, and also few are travelling at the beginning of the week. Far be it from me to tell you what you should do, my dear Clara, but I feel it would be a more gracious reply if it were written in your own fair hand.'

Then I suddenly saw that the deed had to be done and that we must go to York. For Nathaniel, as Cecilia is ever ready to point out, is an obdurate gentleman, and once he has a thought in his head he is not likely to let it go.

'We will go next Wednesday, Nathaniel,' I said. 'If I write now, Bertie-mun will kindly see that the letter goes off with the night coach.'

My husband looked at me in some surprise, and placed in front of me a sheet of foolscap. Then, when the letter was done and sanded, I gave it to him before I could begin to think what I had agreed to, and he summoned Bertie-mun straight away, no doubt fearing I might retract what I had written, which was in the French tongue, albeit for a reason I did not know myself. So the letter went off.

And when Willow was about my room restoring it to order, though there was no disorder, I told her where we are bound next Wednesday, and for what reason, and that which I fear, for she has no hearing. And Willow stopped what she was engaged in, which was arranging the curtains in neat folds, and she looked at me, listening intently, for all that she could hear nothing, as I spoke to her in the bright sunlight of my fear of the journey in the night coach, and of my fear of my soul and body becoming the property of another, and of my fear of what that other would think of me.

Then I said to my maid, 'Dear Willow, I am a fallen woman,' and the good soul made to kiss my hand, and we both of us wept like silly girls.

Later on, Mrs Tregowan came, saying that we might go again to see the family of Tessa Spence, where we would not be welcome. 'But that is no reason for staying away, is it, Claribell, my dear?' she said.

To which I agreed readily, though to be considered an intruder under the roof of Charles and Hilda Spence seemed to me more than reason for staying away.

'I have spoken with Jack Walsh again,' Mrs Tregowan went on. 'Indemnity, you know, my dear. And I believe that we may yet talk him round, Claribell, for all that he says it is not for him to decide on the matter.

Yet if not to Jack Walsh, who holds the purse strings, as it were, I know not where else to turn, or indeed if anyone will own up to overseeing the matter of indemnities. For, Claribell, my dear, there are certain folks abroad and not least in the dissenting chapel, for we are not all of us saints by any means, dear, who believe that were Charles Spence to be given his due indemnity it would all go on strong liquor. And thereby I defeat myself in my own argument. Let us go, darling.'

So we set off for the dwelling of Charles and Hilda Spence in Shackleton, finding Jack Walsh already there, and his sister Felicity, who was busying herself tidying the room while Jack held forth to Charles Spence on the subject of which Mrs Tregowan had recently spoken, namely that even if he were to merit indemnity by virtue of being brother to Tessa Spence, yet because of his habit of strong liquor and his propensity to convert all payment that came his way into strong liquor he was undeserving.

Charles Spence listened in silence, and at the end of the discourse said, 'Now thou has had thy say, Jack Walsh, an we'll be thanking ye to go, all of ye. For we didna invite ye, Hilda an' me, an' likely we dunna welcome folks barging into the house wi'out so much as a knock, Miss Walsh.'

At which Felicity blushed and offered the apologies of her brother and herself for arriving in such a peremptory manner, and I believe her gentle words would have pacified Charles Spence, but that she was overtaken by a racking cough; that being the second time I had seen her so affected. And, indeed, whether it was Felicity's apologies, or her affliction, the ill manner of Charles Spence evaporated somewhat, and his wife offered Felicity a thimbleful of water, after which we took our leave, giving Hilda a new baked loaf before we went.

'You didna drink it, did you?' Jack Walsh asked of his sister when we were out of Shackleton. To which Felicity replied that she could do no other, and that indeed Hilda's draught of water was the gift of the angels in heaven, who would surely keep Hilda and herself safe.

Yet Felicity continued to cough painfully, and Mrs Tregowan said, after we had bid good-bye to her on her threshold, that she did not like the hectic red in her cheeks, 'for all that she is fair of complexion and has always coloured up on the least provocation,' Mrs Tregowan said. 'And there are certain others around here who look the same,' she added.

So I resolved to ask Willow to go with me to Felicity's house with a remedy for the lungs, or if not that, to see her after the holy service; that all being a great lexicon of words to impose on a soul who has no hearing, to which nevertheless Willow nodded assent. And Mrs Tregowan said also, on our journey home from Shackleton, that she had asked a certain one of her kindred, without mentioning any particular person, for a relief in rent for the miners.

'Until they have caught up, you know, my dear Claribell,' she said. 'But there has been no reply as yet. And I do not know that there will be, for I lowered myself in being wed to a dissenter, my dear,' she added. 'See the blackthorn, Claribell. That is surely a sign of a fine summer. We say in these parts that the blackthorn is the Lord's bounty, for even the smuts from the mines cannot sully it.'

And, indeed, clouds of white flowers decked the hedges, as if it were only humankind with their mines who disfigure and blacken creation, and see no ill in doing so.

Little Choice in Anything

It is the Lord's day, and if every other day in this account is the Lord's day, and not one in seven, it is surely because they are more crowded, as if the Lord would throw all the dissenters of Durham together.

Today Willow took with her to the chapel the remedy of *Pulmonaria* for the lung to give to Felicity Walsh, who received it graciously, thanking Willow profusely, and saying that her cough would be better in no time, or if not better, very much relieved. Then after the service Nathaniel and I went to see the maypole in the city square. Yet the sight of the bairns made me low rather than merry, and I think Nathaniel also and with more reason, though he did not say, and we left soon. For few were there without bairns, and we found ourselves onlookers while the whole world danced.

And in the afternoon the scholars attended, being as I thought different, yet with the names as they always are, namely William Darbyshire, Frederick Pennell, James Sowerby, Alfred Baines, Amos Frost, Bartholomew, Gregory Parrish and Colin Beech, as well as Cecilia, Willow and Bertie-mun; the text for study also being the same, beginning "... Several laws are in existence for regulating and limiting work-men's wages ..."

And it came to me that I had little choice but to instruct the scholars in the text of their liking; and, indeed, little choice in anything in my life; that I must visit poor Tessa's kindred whether they wish it or not, that I must sew a straight hem whether I can do so or not, that I must write my husband's correspondence, and so on. There being but one matter left to me and that is when, and indeed if ever, I should become Nathaniel's wife, for he is an angel of grace and patience towards me and does not show by so much as a word or a glance that anything is amiss.

And as these reflections ran on in my mind, so also the lesson ran on to its end, and each scholar left with the inflammatory text in his heart, a heel of bread in his hands, and with his customary expressions of gratitude, 'Thanking ye, mun; thanking ye kindly, mun.'

And as the Sabbath day instruction ran to its end, having no means by which its onward progress might be halted, so also the intentions of the colliers, which I do not fully know and cannot ask, run on to their end; and I can do nothing but wait for Cecilia to tell me, as she is sure to do by and by. Though it was not today that she told me the intentions of the colliers, for all she said in the evening was that the master requested my presence, looking at me with some suspicion.

'It will be about the journey to York, Cecilia,' I said, hearing which she huffed, being some way pacified, yet not all, and neither was I pacified.

For this also has its own necessity, that we must travel night and day, setting off tomorrow in order to present ourselves at the dispensary in the shadow of the Monk-bar on Wednesday morning, and then to entrust our souls to someone whom we do not know. As, indeed, I travel with a man I do not know, he being my husband, and as he travels with a woman I do not know, that being Clara Chark, his wife, who is strange to me.

"3 Lifes on Thy Concsence"

Now I find that the fear I have of travelling enclosed in the night coach to York is unfounded. We will not be making the journey to the coach stage after all; only Bertie-mun on his own, who is to take a letter addressed to the French physician, expressing our most profound regret.

'What will the gentleman think of us?' I said to my husband.

'I have told him as well as I might how matters stand regarding Shackleton,' Nathaniel said, 'as much as I know myself. Those who beleaguer us at our gates again are incomers. Who are the men who come to the Sabbath day school?' he said then. 'Do we know them?'

I told my husband their names, being William Darbyshire, Frederick Pennell, James Sowerby, Alfred Baines, Amos Frost, Bartholomew and Gregory Parrish, omitting, and I do not know why, the latest scholar, Colin Beech.

'They are mine,' said Nathaniel, as if they were his kindred and not the workers who harbour ill feelings towards him. 'We never did know Bartholomew's second name. He does not know it himself. What a pitiful world this is that a man should dwell in it with no brethren.'

'But you never talk of brethren of your own, Nathaniel,' I said.

'Why, they are all my brethren,' said Nathaniel. 'No one ever said that brethren have to agree.'

'It has occurred to me that certain of the brethren might sometimes be lady scholars,' I said.

'How so, darling?' said Nathaniel.

'For the reason that some of them gentlemen wear bosoms under their blouses,' said Cecilia, who had just then come into the drawing room. I watched the colour rise in my husband's face.

'Cecilia, remember that you speak in front of my wife,' he said.

'Happen the mistress has heard the word before,' said Cecilia. 'She being a lady also,' she added.

I told Nathaniel that indeed I know the word well, and had myself remarked on the phenomenon of the gentleman scholars to Cecilia, before she mentioned it herself.

'It was so in Enid's time,' he said presently.

'Enid knew the word likewise, sir,' said Cecilia, 'for she remarked also on the fonamy to me, though happen not to you, sir. 'Tis as it is, sir. Them at the gate offered ribaldry to Bertie-mun when he took the letter, sir,' she continued. 'An' I begged him to go out t'other road but he would not for he is an obdurate gentleman.'

'Then that is two of us who are so afflicted, Cecilia, my dear,' said Nathaniel.

'Them as wait outside, sir, they say there has been evictions on account of areas, which I know from my kindred also, sir, and no folks are privy to where they have took theirselves. Leastways, none is saying. I know there's naught you can do about it, sir, for there's others that is the landlords, but 'tis just to inform you, sir.'

'Thank you, Cecilia, I have been informed already,' my husband said. 'And before you give yourself the trouble of telling me the names of those who have been evicted, I know that also.'

'An' there are some, sir, who says them as are evicted have done as Mistress Spence did when she discovered herself shunned and outcasted by her kindred. For there are none in Shackleton as would take them in on account of you know what, sir. If you'll excuse me, sir.'

'There is little we can do about those around our gate,' said my husband when Cecilia had gone. 'Yet to go to York and abandon Bertie-mun to their ribaldry, that would not be right. Pray sit down. You are lovely this morning, darling.'

'And you, sir,' I said.

'Cecilia's tongue runs away with her at times,' he said, 'yet she means well. It is no little thing to remain steadfast in times such as these. She concerns herself overmuch with the matters of the colliery, which I do not like. Please forgive me for talking of Enid in your presence, Clara, darling. It is nearly three years since she passed out of this world, and I would, if I could, let her rest in peace.'

'I would wish that you talked of her, Nathaniel,' I said. 'You don't talk of her at all.'

'Is that so, darling?' he said. 'I did not know.'

'Cecilia said Enid remarked also that some of the gentlemen scholars at the Sabbath day school were not gentlemen but ladies. For they were lighter in speech than the gentlemen,' I added, seeing that the colour was about to rise in my husband's complexion again. Then, recovering himself in the face of what might have been an expression he deemed unfit for a lady, Nathaniel said

173

that Enid had entertained the notion that different scholars each week attended the Sabbath day school, so that all might in turn take home a heel of bread.

'We argued vehemently about the matter until her end, may the Lord forgive me. She drew the inference that the colliers had insufficient remuneration, to which I would always reply that they had sufficient in remuneration, so adequate a sufficiency in fact that those among them who were so inclined attended the sign of the Spikenard on a Saturday night.'

At which point, and before Nathaniel could ask me why I thought different scholars attend the Sabbath day school each week, my maid Willow entered the drawing room with merriment sparkling in her eyes, such that I had no doubt that Cecilia had related to her the recent conversation on "bosoms", although she has no hearing.

'And supposing they were to plead for more pay?' I said.

'There is no "they" about it,' said my husband. 'The law forbids that "they" combine. While trade is yet satisfactory, and, indeed, we will soon recover the lack of output we suffered on account of the disaster, and while prices are stable, they need not more nor less in pay.'

Willow was looking intently from one to the other of us, for all that she could hear nothing.

'Willow, my dear,' said my husband. 'What is it?'

Willow gave to him the day's correspondence and took her leave, still with the laughter upon her, to the extent that I was certain I saw her sweet mouth form the word "bosoms" as she turned to draw the door closed behind her.

Seeing she had gone, Nathaniel kissed me, for it is ever thus when there has been a difference of opinion on the mine. Then, passing his hand over my hair, he said, 'I do not ask you to agree with me, Clara. It is enough that I am able to tell you of these matters. We must to the matter in hand. There is nothing I would hide from you, darling.'

And while my husband was opening the correspondence I found myself wondering if there was anything I would keep from him, coming quickly to the conclusion that indeed there was, not least the nature of the instruction the scholars had asked for: "We would study this, mun."

'You had in your pocket something you said was an inflammatory text, Nathaniel. Did you examine it?' He looked up with surprise.

'Why, yes, darling,' he said. 'I make it my business to read everything that comes into this house. Why do you suppose we exchanged Mr Richardson for a more amiable novel? I was afraid for your happiness if you continued with Mr Richardson's work. This is from Jack Walsh,' he continued, passing a letter across the desk to me. 'Pray read it and see what you think, darling.'

'I don't understand the principle of indemnities very well, Nathaniel,' I said. 'Yet I believe Mr Walsh is proposing that any indemnity due to Charles Spence for the loss of his poor sister may be devoted to paying off his arrears of rent, for he and his wife have been evicted.'

'Do we do this, darling, knowing that the next quarter will see him in the same plight, or do we let him go on his way and pray that the good Lord will have mercy on him?'

'He has a bairn,' I said. Nathaniel frowned.

'May the Lord forgive me,' he said. 'I did not know, yet my dear wife knows. We will lay that aside and come back to it when we have dealt with this next.' Yet suddenly he was at the door calling for Willow.

Cecilia appeared, running up the stairs.

''Tis no use hollering for Willow,' she said.

'Who brought this?' said Nathaniel, waving the letter before her.

'I cannot see, sir, with it wafting before my eyes in that manner,' said Cecilia. 'If it was with them other letters it was in the box, sir.'

Then, in handing the letter to Cecilia, Nathaniel let it go and the page fluttered down to the desk, coming to rest with the written side upwards.

"CHARKE THOW HAST 3 LIFES ON THY CONCSENCE," it read.

No Authority over the Landlords

Nathaniel swept up the letter from the desk and threw it into the grate, where a low fire had been lit on account of a May frost. The letter flared briefly, and subsided into an agonised writhing and crumpling as if it were a living thing. Then, taking the poker, my husband thrashed at it until it died. He said nothing, nor did he look at Cecilia and me, but left the drawing room to answer the front door bell. We listened to his footsteps descending the staircase and going the length of the hall. We listened then to his voice at the door, though we did not hear what he said. Cecilia brushed the charred remains of the letter back into the grate, and was engaged in doing so when Nathaniel ushered Mrs Tregowan into the room.

'We are all of us gathered here, as you see, Barbara, having recently been occupied with our correspondence,' he said.

'I importune you, Nathaniel dear,' said Mrs Tregowan, 'which I would not do for the world, but that Charles and Hilda Spence have been turned out from their dwelling, and a padlock is on the door.'

My husband asked Mrs Tregowan to be seated. Cecilia continued to sweep the hearth, although there was nothing to sweep but the space where the charred remains of the letter had been.

'You may speak in front of Cecilia,' Nathaniel said. 'I believe she knows of the eviction of Charles and Hilda, as does my wife. You may speak freely, Barbara.'

'We all of us in this room know that it is none of the doing of the coal master,' said Mrs Tregowan, 'for the coal master has no authority over the landlords and it is they who have called in the candymen. Yet I am afraid that those at your gate nevertheless hold you responsible, or otherwise wish to impute this evil to you, my dear. I heard words on my arrival that would make even the ears of Lucifer burn with shame, not to mention your good servants.'

'Willow has no hearing, mun,' said Cecilia.

'No, dear, forgive me, I quite forgot,' said Mrs Tregowan.

'Yet you have something other than Lucifer on your mind, Barbara,' said my husband.

'Indeed I have, dear,' said Mrs Tregowan. 'It is the matter of what to do with Moses.'

'I do not know of a Moses, Barbara,' said my husband.

'Then if you do not, Nathaniel, we must ask of your good servant Cecilia.'

'Me, mun?' Cecilia looked up from the hearth.

'Tell your master the story of Moses from the Old Testament book of the Exodus, my dear.'

'He was hid in them bulrushes, sir,' said Cecilia. 'Then Pharaoh's daughter, she comes along for to bathe herself an finds him an takes him to yon palace. Happen the master knows that, mun.'

'Yet he does not know that a bairn was discovered in the cover of reeds by the tributary, having been placed there, warmly swaddled, shortly before certain colliers went that way to their labours,' said Mrs Tregowan. 'It is the bairn of Charles and Hilda Spence, for I know him by his six toes.'

'And where is this little bairn now?' said Nathaniel.

'With Pharaoh's daughter, of course,' said Mrs Tregowan, 'who has naturally sought out a nurse from among the mining women. She had not to look far before she found a poor soul whose bairn has lately passed out of this world. You are silent, Claribell, my dear. I fear this news troubles you greatly. The bairn looks little likely to thrive, for all that poor Hilda was a good mother, and he is bonny enough. But the poor mite does not stir, and it is in the nature of bairns to protest. Patrick will baptise him, which is at present the little one's greatest need.'

'Happen the bairn stands in great need of a physician also, mun,' said Cecilia.

'There is no physician in the city of Durham,' said Mrs Tregowan. 'The Lord Jesus will be the little bairn's physician. He also needs a godfather, Nathaniel, my dear.'

My husband said nothing.

'It is a hard question to ask, but nevertheless I am asking you, my dear,' Mrs Tregowan continued. Still my husband said nothing. 'I am asking you, Nathaniel, my dear,' Mrs Tregowan said again. 'Claribell, my dear, perhaps your husband will hear you whereas he does not hear me.'

'We will accompany you to the palace of Pharaoh's daughter, and my husband will consider the matter on the way,' I said.

So we set off muffled in our heavy cloaks, for the frost had not yet gone from the shaded sides of the

179

thoroughfares, and our breath rose like clouds of smoke into the May morning. Nor did we know where we were going, only that we went down the hill towards what is called the Shackleton basin, where the fair city of Durham ends and a dark tributary creeps towards the River Wear.

'I must needs call on dear Felicity while we are on her doorstep,' said Mrs Tregowan, knocking and letting herself in.

And I would have observed to my husband that she had need of the privy, but that I was afraid he would be offended by the word, as greatly as if it were spoken by Lucifer and not by his own wife, so I said nothing. Then my mind drifted towards that whole lexicon of words Nathaniel could not hear from the lips of a woman, though I do not know what manner of words he uses with the miners.

'You are suddenly of good cheer, darling,' he said, 'which makes me think you have had a merry thought. Here comes Barbara.'

But it was not. Instead, Jack Walsh presented himself at the door and ushered us into the parlour, which was chilly, and the furnishing covered with drapes. And although I have been under the roof of Felicity and Jack Walsh before, I felt suddenly disquieted for a reason I didn't know.

'Forgive us, Mrs Chark,' Jack Walsh said. 'It is a bitter cold place and seldom used.'

Then he continued to talk to my husband about colliery matters, pacing backwards and forwards across the room, until the sound of steps could be heard in the hallway and the front door opening and closing. Jack Walsh put his head round the door.

'Is the coast clear, Felicity?' he shouted.

'You always did like an intrigue, Jack, my friend,' said Nathaniel. 'What is afoot?'

'All will become known, Nat,' said Jack Walsh. 'Felicity and I are of a sudden no longer on our own. It is a sorry business, and I see no good outcome.'

He preceded us along the passageway to the back living quarters and opened the door, standing aside to let us enter, which, had he known of Felicity's sensibilities, he might not have done; yet he did not know and let us enter the room, so that his sister was without warning confronted in her own house by my husband, Nathaniel.

'I am become Pharaoh's daughter,' she said, blushing. 'See.'

A little bairn lay swaddled in a basket in the ingle, with Mrs Tregowan seated by him. On the other side of the hearth sat a young woman who, though of rare beauty, was, as I supposed, from the hamlet of Shackleton.

'This lady is called Julia. It is a pretty name, is it not?' said Felicity. The young woman rose and curtsied.

'The bairn was found by colliers on their way to the pit. It is Hilda's little bairn, whom I know by his six toes, and Barbara is in agreement.'

The hectic colour mounted in Felicity's face and she began to cough. 'The physician will look to this cough,' she began, but then stopped her talk suddenly as if she had spoken out of turn.

'There is no physician in Durham,' said Mrs Tregowan.

'That there is not,' said Jack Walsh. 'Happen they who need a physician must look abroad and in the meantime rely upon your maid, Willow, Mrs Chark.'

'Poor Julia's bairn passed out of this world,' Felicity continued, in an effort, as I thought, to cover her confusion; whether on account of Nathaniel being present, or on account of her cough, or because she had spoken of a physician in whose existence in the city of Durham none of those present believed, I do not know.

'Felicity, my dear, I fear you are not well,' said Nathaniel, taking her hand, which act of gentleness made her confusion the greater. 'You suffer with a collier's cough. Clara will ask Willow to bring you *Pulmonaria* from the apothecary cupboard, for it has made many a collier sound in health again.'

'Your dear wife has already asked Willow,' said Felicity.

'Yes, yes,' said Jack Walsh. 'That is without a doubt very good of Miss Willow. Yet there is another matter of more immediate concern, for Barbara informs me that Patrick will be here directly, and that you have agreed to stand godfather to this likely young gentleman, Nat. Since, for all that I attend the chapel for Felicity's sake, I am an unbeliever, may the Lord forgive me if he is up there.'

'That is the first I knew of it, Jack,' said Nathaniel.

'My brother's unbelief comes and goes,' said Felicity. 'For the moment he is an unbeliever as he is of the opinion that those in the pit have scant regard for their masters and for that reason will not align himself with a pit family but the truth is that all in Shackleton have scant regard for Charles and Hilda Spence on account of poor Tessa and the little bairn must needs be baptised.' All of which speech, delivered with great rapidity and without punctuation, provoked a painful fit of coughing.

And at this point also Mr Tregowan arrived, bringing with him Bertie-mun, who carried in his hand a letter for Jack Walsh from my husband. The outcome of which arrival, for I have forgotten the middle and remember only the end, was that Bertie-mun agreed to stand godfather to the little bairn. And we didn't know whether he was pleased or perplexed by the request for his poor scarred face registers nothing.

Then my husband, not wishing to leave Bertie-mun alone with the weal of the little one to bear through life, said that he and I would also be godparents if I were in agreement. So within the space of half an hour we travelled from our chaste lives to having in our care the soul of Moses, for so he was baptised, everyone having forgotten his name if they ever knew it, and indeed if he had one. And Mr Tregowan read from the testament the story of the bulrushes which Cecilia had been asked by Mrs Tregowan to relate. Yet there was not one there among us, looking at Moses, who believed he would live and thrive, unless it was Julia Beech, who throughout the clatter of conversation remained silent, as indeed did the little bairn.

'I don't like that high colour in Felicity's face,' said Nathaniel as we walked home, for we had left Mr and Mrs Tregowan with Pharaoh's daughter, and Bertie-mun had gone to the coach stage to see if there might be any letters. 'She has ever been ready to blush when so much as a word is spoken to her, yet I don't like to see that hectic colour and hear her cough,' he continued, knowing well that I would follow his unspoken thoughts. 'And I fear that Jack sees nothing but the idiosyncrasies of womankind. We must look to poor Felicity's welfare, darling.'

'We will no doubt be calling on her often, for we have to look to our little bairn,' I said.

'Indeed, our little bairn,' said my husband, and I looked up and saw his face cast in melancholy, the same as when I was brought to the house on the Rose Pavement, and he had said, 'We will be happy, will we not?' as if the saying of it would accomplish the fact.

We continued on to the Rose Pavement in silence, finding men still at our gate and the odour of strong liquor present, as if some other person had recently been there and gone, leaving behind a fragment of himself. And, passing by in silence, we had scarcely come to the front door when a piece of stone was thrown in our direction, for the fabric of the front wall is loosened by many seasons' frosts; and around the stone was wrapped a scrap of paper. My husband picked it up, keeping it in his hand; and, standing back to let me enter the house before him, he went into the house, letting his cloak fall to the floor, and promptly disappeared.

While I was still hanging up our cloaks in the closet, Cecilia came down the stairs.

'The master is in the drawing room, mun,' she said. 'An' I did not know if it were better to stay or leave for he has the looks of the apoplexy coming on him and can scarce speak for fury, mun, which I have not seen on him before, he being a quiet mannered gentleman, as you know, miss. With your leave, I will come with you to the drawing room, for as it is the Lord's truth, mun, I dunna like the look of him.'

We went to the drawing room and found my husband there standing by the hearth, and with the poker in his hand, inciting the fire to life, which occupation so absorbed him that he did not hear our entry. He continued to thrash at the fire while we stood there, furiously, as if he saw before him the serpent from the Garden of Eden lying coiled in the grate, in his house in the city of Durham.

'I'll get Bertie-mun, miss,' said Cecilia.

And, whether it was the closing of the door behind her, or because Nathaniel was satisfied that the serpent was quite extinguished, he turned round, and noticing me at the door his fury left him and he took my hand.

'It is gone,' he said, glancing over his shoulder as if to make certain that the serpent with which he had been attempting to do battle was quite slain. 'I know not why, whether the page was dampened with the frost or for some other cause, that it would not burn. But it is burnt now.'

And letting go of my hand he belaboured the fire again, which, had he not done so, would have kept its secret. Yet in doing so a part of the page which had not been consumed by fire flared into life and I saw written there two letters, as if of the ending of a word, the letters being ... RE ... though my husband did not know that I had seen, and understood. For the word has been a familiar one to me.

Then Willow came in, as Cecilia was still looking for Bertie-mun, who, for all that we knew, had gone on from the coach stage to see his kindred in Thayne.

'Do you know who threw this, Willow, my dear?' said my husband, handing to Willow the stone around which the paper had been wrapped. Willow then took him to the side window from which the front gate is visible, shaking her head and opening her hands to demonstrate their emptiness. And, indeed, those who had been at the gate had dispersed as if they had never been there. And Willow swept the hearth, putting back into the fire the word it had spewed out, and I had no doubt she also knew what the word was.

For Strangers to Find

The lilacs and horse chestnuts, which were tightly in bud on the day Charles and Hilda Spence were evicted, are out in the garden on the Rose Pavement. But the dwellinghouse of Charles and Hilda stands as it did then, on the fourth day of May after the candymen had left, with the lock still on the door and the curtains, which Felicity had tried to put right, hanging loose and in tatters, so that anyone passing by may look in and see that the place has been emptied of every last possession they had. And there is no news of Charles and Hilda Spence, or where they went, for no one saw them leave to notice what direction they might have taken, and none, if they did see, will own up to having seen them.

And, for all that they have gone without a trace, and even though they left their bairn for strangers to find, which in the polite thoroughfares of Durham would be a matter of outrage, yet it is not in Shackleton, for little else is expected of the colliers by the citizens of Durham. And, indeed, there are many who consider the little bairn to be fortunate.

So Moses continues to dwell in his basket in the palace of Pharaoh's daughter, neither thriving nor failing to thrive, but accepting without complaint the attentions of the good woman Julia Beech, whose own bairn passed out of this world. For, in spite of having as near as not declined the office of godfather, my husband insists that we fulfil our duties to the last degree. And I do not know how it is for Felicity that she sees Nathaniel forever under her roof, but she suffers his presence with a good grace, and with painful blushes, which he takes to be the malign consequences of the cough she suffers.

Nor do I know how it is for the little bairn to see from his place on the floor of the world his towering, black-clad, dissenting godparents, Nathaniel and I. For Bertie-mun, his other godfather, is humble of spirit and does not think his presence worthy, yet he has sent to the bairn Moses a small testament which was his mother's, which affected Felicity greatly.

And although I have begged her to call me Clara, and she has said she would, she insists on calling Nathaniel and I "Mr and Mrs Chark". Only today, as we were leaving the dissenting chapel, and Nathaniel was deep in conversation with Jack Walsh, Felicity called me by the name Clara, and asked if we might sit a while on the seat under the oak, which is just now coming into leaf, from where Mr Chark and Jack, her brother, would readily see us once their conversation was done, she said – if it was not an imposition on me. To which I answered that I felt honoured to be in her company, and indeed unworthy, which was true. And Felicity laughed and said either it was the lowering influence of the dissenting chapel or that I had caught some of Bertie-mun's humility to make me feel that way.

'Yet we are not here to discuss humility or we will never be done,' she said. 'I would ask you, dear Clara, to come on a visit with me. You may refuse if you wish, for I can't say in this open place who it is we are going to visit. Though no one is listening,' she added, looking towards the chapel, where the doors were being closed.

'It is but a short walk, and I have asked Bertie-mun to come with us; forgive me for taking such a liberty, Clara. Jack could well have ensured that indemnity had he so wished,' she added. 'For though he is my brother and we have no other kin in this world but each other we do not always agree together on the matters of the mine. I sometimes think he regards me as a woman fast approaching my dotage, though he is the older by five years.'

At which point in our conversation we noticed Jack Walsh approaching, who remarked that we had been so preoccupied in our discourse that it must surely have been relating to the conduct of Shackleton mine. And Felicity said to her brother it was exactly that, telling him in no uncertain terms that he might have arranged that the indemnity due to Charles Spence, as was right and proper, should have cleared off his arrears of rent and so prevented the eviction.

'Then I should not as a consequence be Pharaoh's daughter nor Mr and Mrs Chark and their good man Bertie-mun be godparents with no time of grace to prepare themselves for such an undertaking,' she said.

And Felicity spoke as someone who has nothing in this life to lose, and who might say whatever it pleases her to say, which she continued to do, rapidly and without punctuation as is her way, until I caught my husband's eye and wondered if her high colour might after all, be not so much maidenly modesty as sickness, as indeed he had said.

'I have not heard Felicity so unguarded before,' said Nathaniel after she and Jack had left us, 'though I do not know that her plain speech was not made deliberately to provoke Jack.'

'No, Nathaniel,' I said.

'Meaning that you do not know, or you do not agree, or that you will not say,' he said.

'Yes, Nathaniel,' I said.

'All?'

'All, for I did not understand your sentence, Nathaniel,' I said. 'There were too many "nots" in it and I could not unravel them.'

Nor did the day's unexpectedness end with Felicity's plain speech, for when I went into the school room in the afternoon I saw that Cecilia and Bertie-mun had brought into use the three spare benches which customarily rested against the wall. 'On account of all those being present, mun,' Cecilia said.

'There are but seven, Cecilia,' I said.

'Happen there are seventy times seven today, mun,' she said, 'for I know not the number exactly but 'tis more than seven. They won't importune you, mun, be they never so many.'

Which many, when they came through the door into the school room, seemed to me a number without end, until there were twenty-one present; and not clad as it was their habit to be as if they had lately risen from the mine, so that I did not know men from women, but as if they were in the chapel, brushed and clean. I asked them to be seated, but they would not, remaining standing in a cluster behind the collier who had first given his name as Colin Beech, who stepped forward with a paper in his hand.

'We are come today, mun,' he said, 'all of us, for happen you know that though there be few names there are many scholars.

'Happen you know also, mun, that certain of the scholars be not men but women, our sisters and spouses who must needs go down pit to mek up wages.

'Happen you know moreover, mun, that they must needs be down pit when they are far gone wi' child and when nursing their bairns also, to mek up wages, an' pay off arrears of rent.

'Happen you know, mun, an' I believe you do, for I have it on good authority that you do know, there be bairns of the colliery folks tha' come inta this fair world so tired an' wan that they are ready to leave it again directly an' return to their rest. An' if they were to thrive as soon as may be they are put down pit to mek up wages.

''Tis a severe life down them pits, mun, for them bairns who mus' needs traipse them low roads on account o' their being little in stature, an' thrust an' heave though they be little.

''Tis a severe life down them pits, mun, for women, whom the Lord God made not to be clad as men an' heave an' haul an' bring forth maimed bairns. An', mun, saving your honour, be in them roads when they are after the manner of women, if you tek my meaning; 'tis an indecency, mun.'

Colin Beech handed me the paper on which was written the part of the lesson we had lately studied: "Why not leave them as free to make their own bargains".

'An' we understand, mun,' he continued, 'that there text you hold in your fair hand sez we may ask them masters. But we may not, mun, for them laws forbid that we go the whole lot of us unto our masters an ask. Therefore what the text bids us do we cannot, mun. An' we mus' needs see them bairns an' our spouses an all down pit merely to mek up wages, saving your honour, mun.'

After saying which, Colin Beech fell silent, and I looked into his face, which though of a different cast and worn down with many years of labour could well have been Nathaniel's, in that the same sorrow was written there.

'You do not tell me that your own little bairn passed out of this world, Mr Beech,' I said. 'Why do you not say that?'

Colin Beech looked at me in puzzlement.

'Why, mun,' he said. 'I know not the word for it but such a tale would be to gain advantage by appealing to a woman's tender nature, an' I wouldna do that.'

'What will you have me to do?' I said.

Colin Beech continued to look at me, but said nothing.

'If Colin willna tell thee, mun, since he has lost his tongue, another fellow will,' said the man who had first given his name as James Sowerby. 'We would that you carry our woes unto the master, you being his dearly beloved wife, for he is like to hear thee, mun.'

'Only so as ye willna tell him o' the loss of our little bairn, if you please, mun,' said Colin Beech, 'for the reason I ha' just now rehearsed, an' the master having been in a like plight.'

And it came to me that I had not told my husband that one called Colin Beech was among the scholars, though only then did I know the reason why.

'I will carry your woes to the master,' I said.

Yet how or when I would carry their woes to the master I did not know. For all together their troubles seemed too heavy to be borne, as if I were on my own carrying every one of them now that they had been told to me. And my husband, knowing none of this, and having a new and amiable topic of conversation at his disposal, talked at the tea table of the bairn Moses, relating again how the little fellow had been left in the reeds by the side of the tributary awaiting whatever stranger might pass by and find him; which tale Cecilia knew well enough after Mrs Tregowan's request to her to remind the master of the passage in scripture, and she huffed quietly to herself.

'Happen we know of the baby Moses in them bulrushes, begging your pardon, sir,' she said, 'for we have oft heard of it in holy scripture, to the extent that we would wish Mrs Tregowan to permit the baby Moses to be grown so as we might all of us flee the land of Egypt. 'Tis Mistress Beech who is nurse to the little bairn, is it not, sir?'

'I believe so, Cecilia, my dear,' said Nathaniel. 'Clara knows more of these matters than I, and you may ask her in the privacy of her room.'

'An' the bairn of Mistress Beech passed out of this world,' Cecilia continued doggedly, until I feared that she also had taken the woes of the colliers upon herself and was about to set them before the master as we sat at the table. Which she might well have done had not my husband, fearing no doubt some new and unsettling female word in the lexicon, offered his gratitude to Bertie-mun for sending his mother's testament to the little bairn, thus bringing Cecilia's speech to a halt as poor Bertie-mun strove to find a response.

Then later, in the drawing room, Nathaniel returned to the matter, saying he must ensure that Bertie-mun has a testament to replace that one he had given away. And Cecilia was called, and asked to find out if Bertie-mun has a testament or not; all of which confirmed my supposition that the office of godparent has disquieted

Nathaniel exceedingly, the more so in that it is an office he did not wish for, but took on rather than leave Bertie-mun alone with the heaviness of it.

'If you please, sir,' said Cecilia on her return, 'Bertie-mun has a testament given to him by Mrs Tregowan, for Mistress Walsh told her what had passed.'

'Thank you, Cecilia,' my husband said. 'I am sorry for calling on you this late on the Sabbath day.'

''Tis no matter, sir,' said Cecilia; then reaching the door of the drawing room she turned round. 'Sir?'

'Cecilia?'

'Happen Mistress Beech nurses the bairn on account of her own bairn having passed out of this world, sir.'

'I believe so,' said Nathaniel.

'An' happen Mistress Beech laboured down pit,' said Cecilia.

'Mistress Beech was born to it,' said Nathaniel, 'and the rest of Shackleton with her, and her forebears also. It is the work the Lord God has ordained for them on their earthly pilgrimage.'

'If that is thy opinion I can say no more, sir,' said Cecilia.

'It is not an opinion. It is the truth,' said Nathaniel.

'Then the Lord sez that them wi' child mus' toil in them mines hauling an heaving an' give birth untimely to mek up them wages, sir,' said Cecilia.

Nathaniel rose from his chair, white of face and towering as it seemed a league's height above Cecilia, who stood as she was, in the door way, her hand on the knob.

'I am not afeared of you, sir,' she said.

'No, I believe you are not, my dear,' said Nathaniel, and sat down again. 'You know that I find it disagreeable when you interfere in the matters of the colliery. Now go in peace, my dear.'

'Cecilia means well,' said my husband when she had gone, 'but she does not know what she is talking about. Say something, darling,' he said presently. 'Don't leave me to have this conversation with myself.'

'Neither do I know what I'm talking about,' I said. 'Cecilia thinks that the women with child who work in the pit as a consequence give birth untimely, for it is heavy work.'

My husband winced, whether on account of the matter itself, or because his wife was talking of such things alone in his presence, I could not tell.

'That should not be so,' he said at length. 'Such a state of affairs must not be allowed in Shackleton. It cannot be. It must needs be brought to a halt.'

'She said the women are obliged to go down the pit, even when they are with child, to make up the wage,' I said.

'Nevertheless, the practice must needs be put an end to regardless of the extra wage coming in,' Nathaniel said. 'I will call upon Mr Higgs and Mr Thorley to discuss the matter.'

By which I understood with dismay that rather than alleviate the plight of the colliers, Cecilia and I had increased it, for if every woman with child could not work the wage would fall greatly.

'The wage will be curtailed, Nathaniel, unless the colliers are given a rise to make up their pay,' I said.

'Indeed not, darling,' he said. 'The wage will remain as it is, which is the rate for colliers. But they in such a situation as Mistress Beech found herself shall not labour in the mine.'

'Which surely means that for those households where the mistress is with child there will be less incoming.'

'The wage remains the same, which is the rate for colliers,' said my husband. 'Now the matter is closed, darling.'

'No matter, mun,' said Cecilia, for she had not yet gone to her rest when I left the drawing room, 'for if you an' I know not which are women an' which are men when they come to the Sabbath school, neither more will Mr Higgs an' Mr Thorley.'

Which perfect reasoning from Cecilia did nothing to pacify me.

The Looks of a Woman
Who Has Taken Strong
Liquor

I find I am without employment as the little bairn Moses
has now no need of my dubious hemming, having found
himself in the palace of Pharaoh's daughter where he
lacks for nothing unless it is his parents, who are
nowhere to be found.

And always in my mind is the letter sent to Nathaniel
charging him with the taking of three lives, the meaning
of which I dare not contemplate; Mondays being those
days when I am invariably in the doldrums, for my
husband has always gone down early to Shackleton, and
I wander around the house like a lost soul, seeing
Willow and Cecilia occupied with the wash and Bertie-
mun with the mangle. And today was to be no different
from any other Monday, I thought, until Felicity Walsh
came, bringing only herself.

''Tis Mistress Walsh, mun,' said Cecilia, 'an' I do
not like the looks of her, not that she is not fair of face
an' with a nature to match, mun, but a high colour sits
upon her countenance an' that I do not like. She said to
tell you she wishes not to importune you if the master is
in, mun, so I tells her he is gone to Shackleton. She waits
your presence in the drawing room, mun, for the parlour

is chill an' as I say I like not the looks of her with that colour on her face.'

And, indeed, Felicity's countenance had not only a high colour, but was on fire.

'It is the climb up to the Rose Pavement,' she said, for I gathered that Cecilia, who means well, had mentioned her heightened colour. 'Those of us who live at the foot of Durham are not accustomed to such exertion. Jack is never tired of telling me that I have the looks of a woman who has taken to strong liquor. But it is not so. My brother has always been a harsh critic though no one would know it as he masks his comments in merriment. Please forgive me, Clara. I am a poor companion this morning.'

After saying which Felicity fell silent, and I didn't know why she had come here, for I have no doubt that she occupies herself daily in avoiding Nathaniel, and had Cecilia told her he was at home she would have taken her leave immediately.

'You will be enquiring of yourself why I am here, Clara,' she said presently. 'I have been asked to give this to your maid, Willow, and I do not know what the word is.'

Felicity took from her reticule a scrap of paper and handed it to me. On it I read the ill-formed word, *Pulmonaria*, written as if with the wrong hand.

'It is in the apothecary cupboard,' I said. 'Willow knows what the word is. Is it for the little bairn?'

'It is for the cough I have,' said Felicity. 'Thank God, the little bairn, though he does not thrive, does not ail either.'

'Willow has no speech or hearing, yet we need not look far for her on wash day,' I said.

I took Felicity to the scullery, wishing all the while to ask, though I could not, who might have written the word on the rough prescription she brought with her. I gave Willow the paper, which she studied briefly and then went to the apothecary cupboard.

'It is for Mistress Walsh, Willow,' I said.

Willow gave the remedy to Felicity, scrutinising her face as she did so.

'Clara, could you tell Willow how grateful I am?' said Felicity.

I told Felicity that she might say that to Willow herself, for though she has no speech or hearing, she understands what is said. And Felicity did so, saying to Willow also that, although the remedy with the indecipherable name would not quite take away the malady it would give her some respite from the cough which sorely troubled her.

'I must get better, for we have not yet made the visit I told you of, Clara,' Felicity continued, 'and it must be done while there is still time.'

And I did not understand the meaning of the words, "while there is still time", but I couldn't ask Felicity the meaning, any more than I could ask her who had written the prescription of *Pulmonaria* for her, there being no physician in Durham.

'If it pleases you, dear Clara, we may go this very day,' Felicity said. 'If Bertie-mun were to accompany us he might also see the little bairn.'

So it was settled that Bertie-mun and I were to call at Felicity's house at two hours after mid-day. And, indeed, he would have accompanied Felicity back home there and then, seeing her fiery complexion and hearing her cough, but that she declined, saying that she knew he had the mangle to attend to.

'It is also down the hill,' she said.

And it came to me that Felicity Walsh might pass through the most dismal streets of the city of Durham on her own and unmolested, for even those few men who had assembled again at our gate, and might have been expected to offer ribaldry, stood away to let her go by.

Cecilia came into the drawing presently with Bertie-mun, saying that he had done with the mangle and was free to accompany us when he had dined, which I gathered was more her own wish than Bertie-mun's for he would never hesitate to leave whatever he was doing if he saw a greater call on his assistance elsewhere.

'For he has been at them mangles, mun,' Cecilia said, 'and I know not where you be going but 'tis a fair walk on foot for them as has no repast inside of them.'

By which I understood that Cecilia knew not only of our visit but knew also where the visit would take us, which I did not.

'An' happen Mistress Walsh knows not,' she continued, 'or like as not she would not take you there, though I know not where you are bound, but just to say that Bertie-mun will bring ye safe back home. An' happen the master knows not neither, mun, an' I will not tell him for doubtless he would not wish it neither,' she added.

So Bertie-mun and I set out at an hour and a half after mid-day for Felicity's house, Bertie-mun having presented himself in the drawing room dressed as for a Sunday and holding in his hand a small brown paper parcel tied with string, and I taking in my reticule for Felicity from my maid Willow the remedy called *Centaurium* for the breathing, together with her note of the morning on which was written the word *"Pulmonaria"* and more of the remedy of that name. For

199

I wished the script to be gone before my husband came home, knowing that he reads everything that comes into this house.

And I gathered, when we arrived at Felicity's house on the Lower Culvert, that she had recently suffered a fit of coughing, for she could scarcely get her breath, and was seated upright in the ingle with her hands opening and closing as if she would grasp at the air around her.

'You are not well, Felicity,' I said. 'Today's visit may be done tomorrow or on any other day, as soon as you are recovered. Willow has sent you the remedy called *Centaurium* for your breathing, and I have brought back the paper with the word *Pulmonaria* and more of the remedy.'

'Willow is more clever than I, for she could read the script,' said Felicity.

'It is as if the writer used the other hand,' I said. Felicity turned the paper this way and that, studying the word.

'You are right, Clara,' she said. 'How strange.'

And while she was contemplating the mystery of the word *Pulmonaria*, studying it from all angles, her breathing quieted, as if the sight of the word effected a cure. She rose to her feet.

'We will go now,' she said. 'It is only half a league by the river path. If we may, we will ask Bertie-mun to lead us, for the first part of the journey is desolate, and not many go that way.'

For all that I live in the city of Durham, I didn't know that a place of such desolation existed close to its crowded streets and shining river, for the glittering waters of the Wear became suddenly dark and foul, creeping past reeds choked and blackened with coal dust, and under our feet were thick clods of mud. And the sky itself became dark as if, and against the laws of nature, it reflected the dour river, rather than the opposite.

'It is only a few steps before we are back on the road,' Felicity said, then to Bertie-mun, 'You saw the little bairn?' which question Bertie-mun answered as well as he might, that he had seen the little bairn.

And, noticing that he was now without the brown paper parcel, Felicity thanked him for his kindness. For, having embarked on her journey, she had recovered so far as to be able to talk as well as walk, which, in spite of her illness, she did rapidly, and as was her habit without pausing for breath.

'It is not far now,' she continued, as we entered a thoroughfare of poor tenements with the Monday wash strewn greyly between them.

Felicity stopped in front of a tenement much like the others, but for the bell above the door, and a plain plaque bearing the title, "Sainte Agathe". She knocked at the door. We waited.

Which I Could Only Think of as Despair

And suddenly it was as if it were not Felicity standing by my side at the door of the house of Sainte Agathe, but someone else, whom I had come to know well, but could not place. And in my mind I went back to that earlier arrival, and remembered being taken in and placed in a dormitory with other women, where I must have remained until one day, finding myself in a room on my own, I was told that the lady and gentleman visitors had requested it.

As Felicity and I were waiting I remembered also that on the occasion of my first arrival the lady with me, whom I could not place, had said, 'The sister who keeps the keys is infirm, and takes a long time in reaching the door, my dear.'

'The sister who keeps the keys is infirm and takes a long time in reaching the door,' I said. Felicity looked at me in surprise.

'Yes, that must be so,' she said. 'The holy sisters have been told that we are of the dissenting persuasion, yet they do not mind. I dare not think how my brother would be if such a one as he calls a papist came knocking on our door.' Presently the door opened.

'*Clara, ma chère!*'

'I have come with my friend, Felicity, Sister Joseph,' I said, for Bertie-mun, seeing that we were well met, had gone away.

'*Comment vas-tu, ma chère?*'

'*Bien, merci, et vous-même?*'

'*Tres bien, merci, ma chère. Felicity, ma chèrie, bonjour.*'

The house of Sainte Agathe was as it had been, only that the plaster peeled more, and the paint was dulled. Yet the same aroma lingered there, compounded of the mid-day meal, beeswax, and something other and indefinable, which I could only think of as despair. We were led along the passage to the door giving onto the cloistered walk, and beyond that to another door opening onto the public ward.

'We have brought her into the company of others for her spirit was melancholy.'

'*Merci, madame.*'

Felicity's gaze wandered round the ward and returned to where the holy sister had recently stood.

'I do not see her,' she said, 'for all the poor souls look alike and since I have had the malady I do not see well, which Jack says is on account of my time of life,' she added, without saying what she was surely thinking, that the poor souls were all of a likeness because their hair had been shorn and each one of them wore a linen cap. 'We have come to see Hilda,' she said to the nearest of the women. 'Hilda Spence from the place named Shackleton. Is she in here, pray?'

'Happen Hilda Spence was the one who brought in them parasites,' the woman replied, 'for we had all of us our own hair afore she came. But happen it were some other. She is at yon end, mun. She were drawn out o'

Wear as far as I know, an' I might as well tell ye for tha' willna get her talking.'

Then Felicity thanked her informant and made for the end of the ward, where there lay a woman who was hardly recognisable as such, so pitifully bruised was her poor face, and her arms also, which lay quietly on the coverlet.

'I have brought Clara to see you, my dear Hilda,' said Felicity. 'She made the hem on your bairn's smock.'

Hilda Spence lifted an arm and attempted to turn her head towards us. Then, for all that her face was badly damaged, she spoke.

'The bairn?'

'Your bairn is doing well, Hilda,' said Felicity. 'He is being nursed by a good woman from Shackleton and will be returned to you whenever you are able to take him back. He is a fine young man, is he not, Clara?'

I agreed, for I could do no other, although the little bairn is not doing well. Yet I had no doubt that Felicity had her own good reasons for spinning such a tale.

'And Charles, is he with thee?'

'No, Hilda, he has not come here today,' said Felicity.

'Then he will come tomorrow?'

'I do not know, Hilda,' said Felicity. 'If you will tell me where he is I will send a message to him to say that you are asking for him.'

'They drew me forth out o' the Wear, an' happen they drew Charles forth as well, if indeed he were in the Wear, for it was dark an I saw not nor heard nothing of him.'

'Clara and I will surely find him, Hilda, my dear,' said Felicity. 'All will be well, I promise.' And with

204

those improbable words Felicity motioned to me to follow her out of the ward.

'They have told me that poor Hilda is so much hurt inside that she is likely to pass out of this world,' she said, without saying who her informants were, merely calling them "they". 'And she is as well to go forth on her journey believing her little bairn to be in health and her husband yet in the land of the living, although it was an untruth I told. Clara, my dear, it is incumbent upon the whole to look to the weal of one of their brethren, although he is a taker of strong liquor.'

By which I understood that Felicity, who, on account of her modesty, would not say my husband's name, meant that I should ask Nathaniel to put the matter in hand, and seek out Charles Spence if he were to be found.

'Willow may stay if she pleases,' said Nathaniel, for Cecilia had made it known that I was not myself after being out with Felicity Walsh, and Willow had followed me to the drawing room. 'She may sit by the fire,' he added, for although it is May there was a low fire in the grate. 'What is it, my darling?'

'Felicity has found Hilda Spence, Nathaniel,' I said. My husband rose from his chair, as if he would set out for her that very minute.

'Indeed?' he said. 'Where is she? We must bring her back.'

'She is at the refuge of Sainte Agathe with her poor face so wounded that no one would know her, and every hair on her head has been shorn off so that she needs to wear a linen cap.'

'Darling,' said Nathaniel, 'how do you know this?' He sat down again.

205

'I have seen her,' I said. 'I went with Felicity to call on her.'

'Then you have been to Sainte Agathe, darling?'

'Yes, but it is no matter.'

'Have you eaten, darling?'

'Yes. No. Somewhat.'

'Which is yes or no?'

'Yes and no. She asked about the little bairn then she asked about Charles. Felicity told her that the little bairn thrives and that we will find Charles, which things are not the truth, but Hilda is much hurt internally and will not live long.'

'And?' Nathaniel took my hand and kissed it, for Willow had fallen into a slumber in front of the fire after the labours of Monday wash day.

'Felicity told Hilda that she and I would find her husband.'

'And where will you look, darling, when there is not one in Shackleton or in the city of Durham who knows where he might be?'

'Hilda told us she had been drawn out of the Wear,' I said, 'and she didn't know or not if Charles had been in the river as well, because it was dark and she couldn't see.'

Nathaniel said nothing, but poked the fire as if to consign another serpent to the flames.

'We will gather together a band of men to follow the Wear down as far as we are able,' he said. 'All this might have been avoided had we settled the indemnity, but we did not and this is the consequence, may the Lord forgive us. I will seek the advice of Patrick. Do not be dismayed, my darling.'

Then, as Willow continued to slumber, he kissed me, and I him.

'You are lovely tonight, darling,' he said.

'And you, sir,' I said.

'That is not so, darling,' he said, 'that is never so.'

On the Bank of the Wear in the Days of her Youth

Mrs Tregowan came early today, this being as I think the one hundredth and thirty-eighth day I have lived in Nathaniel's household, and revealed that she knew the whereabouts of Hilda Spence, having been told by a member of the dissenting chapel who lives in Thayne.

'They say she has been taken in by folks in Blennowe, Claribell, my dear, though I am not supposed to know that, and I would advise you not to know it either, my dear, for none have seen her or Charles, and it is not seemly to spread rumours. Your husband is at present in conversation with Patrick, and I would advise you not to know that either, for word has gone around that Charles was last seen standing by the Wear and none too steady in his balance. But if I were to tell you what I think, Claribell, which I will not for it is idle supposition, I would say that poor Hilda and Charles, yet less Charles for he is not in charge of his decisions, being far gone in strong liquor, left the little bairn to be found by any stranger passing by and took themselves out of this world. Which I will not say, for besides that it is idle speculation, it is a wicked charge to lay on any soul. Though, my dear, I have always in my heart a tender place for poor Judas Iscariot, have you not,

Claribell, if you call to mind the passage in the scripture, darling.'

And Mrs Tregowan went on to say that she had likewise stood on the bank of the Wear in the days of her youth when she had married beneath herself and been cast off by her kindred.

'For indeed, marrying beneath my station was somewhat of a shock, Claribell, Patrick being of slender means, and I so dreadfully spoilt.'

Then I told Mrs Tregowan that I could not think she had been spoilt, which pleased her very much, for, if she gives herself any thought at all, it is to think poorly of herself.

'What was I saying, my dear?'

'Judas Iscariot,' I said.

'Alas, poor Charles,' she said, 'for he betrayed no one, only himself and his poor wife Hilda by his liking for strong liquor. They will get up a party, of course. Mr Priest and Mr Salter will go, and I've no doubt dear Nathaniel, and I know not who else, for the men who work in the colliery are not at liberty, besides which Charles and Hilda still carry their stigma. And you will be wondering why I am here, Claribell. I am here to tell you that you must do your utmost to prevent your husband in such an undertaking. More than that I cannot say, for it is but an angel's whisper, or, as most would say, a hunch that something is afoot. Suffice to say that the Wear path travelling towards Blennowe crag is but narrow, and has a steep declivity down to the river, and not a few have come to grief there, by accident or not.'

So I resolved to discuss the matter with my husband when he came home, as he would surely do by the fourth hour after mid-day, it being Wednesday; but not, I have to say, with any expectation of altering his mind which can never be done, as, in Cecilia's words, he is a most obdurate gentleman, and having once resolved will carry through his resolve whatever the consequences, even more so if he believes those consequences to be to his detriment.

Yet Nathaniel did not return by the fourth hour after the mid-day, and had not done so a half hour later, when Cecilia announced that Mrs Tregowan begged the pleasure of my company in the drawing room.

'There is some mischief, mun,' Cecilia said, 'for the master is not come home an' Bertie-mun neither. An Mrs Tregowan is full of words, though she has not said aught to me, if you take my meaning, mun. She has on her heavy cloak, mun.'

'You have not seen Nathaniel, Claribell, my dear?' Mrs Tregowan said as soon as Cecilia had left the drawing room.

I told her I had not.

'No,' she said, 'you will not have seen Nathaniel for the party has already set off. We must waylay them, my dear. There is something wrong, and I do not know what it is.'

And it came to me instantly that Mrs Tregowan spoke the truth though neither of us knew what the truth was, yet had she said an angel had told her in a dream I would have believed her.

'I have behaved out of turn and have enlisted the help of Bertie-mun, my dear,' she said. 'We will board the stage as far as Blennowe crag and trust to the Lord, for we can do no more. Bertie-mun is holding the coach for us, Claribell. We must needs go now.'

And Mrs Tregowan was already at the door looking for Cecilia to bring me my heavy cloak.

'For the sea fret may well be in, my dear,' she said. 'With the Lord's help we will be done while it is still light. I might as well tell you, my dear, that a certain one was unduly eager to be in the search party, which I did not like, though I would not wish to pass on ill tidings of another. You have not heard this, my dear, for I may be mistaken and it would please me if I were. Indeed it would. For many a good soul has erred and strayed.'

We set out, finding Bertie-mun holding the Doncaster coach at the sign of the Cross Keys, and the coachman walking back and forth as if he would have gladly been on the road a half hour ago. And we found that there was one other traveller inside, also muffled against the sea fret, who did not speak a word, not so much as to pass the time of day, but rather receded into a corner as we boarded; and whether it was a man or woman who travelled with us we could not tell.

We rode then to the edge of the city of Durham, seeing on our right side the three mines of Shackleton, Thayne and Blennowe, gilded each one by the evening sun, which reminded me of the first morning I had looked out of the window in Nathaniel's house on the Rose Pavement and had been shown the fair city of Durham and her collieries lying across the valley of the Wear. To our left, on the seaward side, which, although the sea is many leagues distant, the fret was rolling in as a great carpet might be rolled out across the floor, increasing the farther we went out of the city until by the time we disembarked at Blennowe crag it seemed only a few furlongs away.

Then the coachman, saying good-day, cracked the whip, leaving us standing in the shadow of the inn called the Blennowe Carr, out of which shadow Mrs Tregowan quickly moved.

'For I do not like to be anywhere near strong liquor,' she said to me, then addressing the other passenger, who had disembarked with us, 'Where are you bound, my dear? For you travel alone and the sea fret is coming on.'

'I wished to come with you,' the other said, uncovering her head. 'My brother was talking at the door with someone he did not let into the house on account of his insobriety but who was enough in charge of himself to put himself forward for the search party for Charles Spence which in itself is praiseworthy but I am afraid the motives of some are not.'

A fit of coughing seized Felicity, who turned away swallowing hard, as if she would swallow her malady.

'We will go,' she said. 'The search party will follow the Wear to Blennowe crag coming from Durham and we will meet them. I know the way, for Jack and I came here as bairns, though he always suffered from my presence. The sea fret will be a long time coming in. It has still to roll down into Blennowe vale and climb out again and it has a habit of lingering in the valley before it climbs.'

All this speech was delivered in Felicity's customary headlong manner, as if she would have her say before the cough overtook her. After she finished speaking she stepped ahead of Mrs Tregowan and I onto the Wear path and in no time was half a furlong ahead, walking rapidly as if nothing ailed her.

'I do not like the look of her,' Mrs Tregowan said, and, indeed, I had also noticed her colour and the shine in her eyes. 'She has the looks of a young woman bound on keeping a tryst with her sweetheart, yet in my opinion it is her ailment that makes her so. Claribell, my dear, you need not stay back for me, but do mind the crag, darling, for it is a long drop down to the Wear should a body lose their footing, which they are apt to do with rabbit burrows all over.'

And I was even then deliberating in my mind whether to follow Felicity or stay with Mrs Tregowan, who laboured in her walking and had no less colour on her face than Felicity, when the search party appeared round a bend in the path at some distance ahead of us, whom Felicity had seen in the same moment, and made as if to run towards them. But she had gone no farther than a few steps when she tripped and fell, flailing with her poor arms in the last of the evening sunlight. And neither the search party ahead nor Mrs Tregowan and I coming on behind could save her.

And we all, the search party ahead, and Mrs Tregowan and I coming on behind, ran to where we had last seen her, all of us arriving at the same time, and no one was willing to look over the crag to see how far she had fallen. Until Mr Salter, who made up the search party along with Nathaniel, Bertie-mun and Mr Priest, lay face downwards and looked over the crag, saying that she was a long way down, yet not so far as the waters of the Wear might wash over her. Having said which, he scrambled to his feet and went over the edge, grasping at jags of rock and stumps of elder, with Nathaniel, who had already thrown off his cloak, about to follow, but that Mr Priest intervened.

'Saving your honour, sir,' he said. 'Them as have toiled down pit next. If you an' your man would kindly lower the ropes an' haul up, sir, thanking you, for that is the most needful at this time.'

Then Mr Priest went down, taking a sail cloth, and presently disappearing from sight under the crag, and Bertie-mun began to set out the ropes on the grass nearest the edge; yet finding there some obstacle, he set them down further off, returning presently to the same place to examine the hindrance.

So we waited, my husband pacing backwards and forwards, until, no doubt anxious that the call for ropes would come while Bertie-mun was still occupied, he stopped his pacing and went over to ask what the matter was. In answer to which Bertie-mun placed in Nathaniel's hand some object I could not make out, much muddied, which my husband transferred to the pocket of his coat, without looking at it and saying nothing. And I noticed that Mrs Tregowan, although she would have hidden her tears, was weeping silently.

'This way I am no use to poor Felicity, Claribell,' she said, 'yet it is a long time since Mr Priest and Mr Salter went down the crag, and I fear this silence bodes no good.'

Which silence, even as Mrs Tregowan spoke, was broken by the call of, 'Ropes!' echoing along the crag and repeating itself far off in Blennowe vale, where the mist settled over the homesteads and the peaceful smoke of evening fires rose up to meet it. Then came Mr Priest's voice.

'We will need more men, sir,' which cry similarly came back to us from across the vale, as if by itself it would summon help.

'Mrs Tregowan and I will go to the inn to ask if there are any who can help,' I said, wishing in my heart to reassure Nathaniel that we would come to no harm, for I could see in his eyes and in the frown that flickered across his brow that he would not willingly have his wife go into a house of strong liquor, and no doubt of ill repute also. Yet Mrs Tregowan, also seeing my husband's face, had no such qualms.

'I have been in such places before I was wed to Patrick, my dear Nathaniel,' she said, 'and they inside a hostelry are the same folk as those outside, is that not so? The dear Lord does not abandon us the moment we cross the threshold of a hostelry, nor does he abandon poor Felicity the moment she falls over the edge of the crag, whatever wounds she may suffer.'

Having said which, and fortified herself in doing so, Mrs Tregowan fell silent until we reached the sign of the Blennowe Carr, which she entered, announcing herself as the wife of the dissenting minister; at which announcement those inside put down their pots and stopped their talk in anticipation of a preaching. 'And this is my friend,' Mrs Tregowan continued, 'and we come for help as one of our number has fallen over the crag.'

'We are allus ready for such an event,' one of the men said presently, and opened up a press in the corner of the room. 'Have we need of winch?'

'Yes, if you please, sir,' said Mrs Tregowan.

'Salter were here earlier an we knew a certain party to be out on the crag,' another man said. ''Twas a fool's errand wi' the mist coming in.'

Then, as we set off once more along the path, which was now scarcely visible, for the fret had climbed out of Blennowe vale and wrapped us around on all sides, the same man said to me, 'We han naught to do wi' this, mun. 'Twas a ploy dreampt up by another, not mentioning no names. We will ha' thy husband up in no time.'

So I said to him that it was a lady who had gone over the edge, to which he replied, 'Good Lord, an' it should come to this,' asking then the name of the lady and if it might be anyone he knew, but he did not. And as we were approaching the place, which we knew by the voices of the search party rather than by the sight of them on account of the thick sea fret, the same man asked the ladies to please stand back.

'Poor Felicity lives,' said Mrs Tregowan when we had taken ourselves away, 'for they were talking to her, were they not? It is not that we are a hindrance that we have to stand away,' she went on, 'but because they who are brought up are often wounded so as to frighten womankind. For I remember when I was a girl seeing one such brought up from the crag and I have never forgotten.'

Yet Felicity, lying on the ground on a sheet with Nathaniel's cloak covering her, showed no visible wounds, only that the colour had left her face, and her eyes, which were open, appeared to see no one.

'Ye han needs talk to her, for they hear when tother senses han fled,' one of the men said. Which Brim Salter did, talking gently to her, though we could not hear his words, while she was being carried back to the inn. 'We will come back for winch an all,' said the same man. 'For 'tis but a short step an' fret will be ovver in morning. Go you inside, sirs, an' the ladies wi' you.'

We were ushered into a back room, and poor Felicity lowered onto the floor, where she lay unmoving and unseeing, with her eyes wide open, while talk ensued between Mr Salter and others outside the door. And not one of us in the room knew what to say, for all that we had been asked to talk to Felicity, until Mrs Tregowan eventually broke the silence.

'All will be well, Felicity, my dear,' she said. 'Can you hear me, darling? It is Barbara. I never did like that name, you know. It puts me in mind of he who was released in the place of our Saviour, Saint Matthew chapter twenty-eight, you know, dear.'

And whether Felicity heard or not, we did not know, for Mr Salter came back in, asking that she might be carried to an upper chamber, where a physician would attend her in the presence of a good woman from Blennowe; upon hearing which Nathaniel exchanged a glance with Mrs Tregowan, and Mr Priest cast down his eyes, Bertie-mun having absented himself, as we understood later, to return along the path and retrieve the winch before darkness quite fell, and the two other men also gone, and before a word of thanks could be said. Then Mrs Tregowan again glanced across at Nathaniel, and seeing that he answered her glance, rose to her feet and left the room, coming back some moments later to say that dear Felicity was in the care of a holy sister and had been pronounced able to withstand the journey home.

'Though not on the night coach,' she added, 'which is enough to shake up anybody's bones though they be in sound health before embarking.'

So a cart was brought and filled with as many bolsters as they could find at the inn, and Felicity was laid on it as she was, with her eyes wide open and her face bleached as the pillows on which she lay.

And a gentle mare was put in the traces, and a driver found, being one of those men who had helped on the crag, who said again to me, 'This were none of our doing, mun.'

Then we set off at a walking pace for the city of Durham, with Mrs Tregowan, Mr Priest, Bertie-mun, Nathaniel and I following, Nathaniel having been given back his cloak.

And at the end of the day there were two missing, being Mr Salter whom we had not seen since we entered the inn, and Charles Spence on whose behalf the party went out, but who was now forgotten.

A Single Case of Stythe

''Tis the cross I have to bear, mun,' said Cecilia. I asked her to which cross she was referring, for to my mind Cecilia has many crosses to bear, carrying, as she does on her slender shoulders, all the troubles of Nathaniel's household and those of the colliery at Shackleton also.

'Why, mun,' she said, 'I am for ever brushing out the master's pockets, which is a place I know I should not go, mun, but that they are every day inhabited by paraphernalias, mun,' and she opened her hand to reveal a much-muddied iron spike. 'An' if I did not know him to be present in the drawing room, mun, I could have thought him to have been present at yon crucifixion, for he has that look of melancholy upon his face the same as he has upon a holy Friday; an' he requests your company, mun, an' happen you will cheer his heart. An' happen you will not tell him about them paraphernalias, mun, which I know you will not.'

Yet Cecilia, following me into the drawing room, told Nathaniel herself. 'Begging your pardon, sir, an I will be gone directly,' she said, 'I have transgressed against you, sir.'

'You had best tell me about it, my dear, and I will then tell you whether you have transgressed against me or not,' said Nathaniel.

Cecilia opened her hand, in which lay the iron spike.

'I was brushing out your pocket, sir,' she said.

'You will find its companion on the desk, my dear,' said Nathaniel, 'and also a trip wire Bertie-mun found laid between the two devices. The one who has transgressed is the one who laid the trip wire, who has transgressed not against me but against himself and against Felicity. It is not you who have transgressed, Cecilia, my dear. You may go with a quiet mind.'

''Tis he who wrote them letters, sir,' said Cecilia. ''Twas intended for you.'

'We do not know who laid the wire or for whom it was intended, Cecilia, my dear,' said Nathaniel.

'Happen you don't, sir, but the rest o' Durham knows, saving your honour for you know best, sir,' said Cecilia, with which she was gone.

'Pray be seated, darling,' said Nathaniel. 'Bertie-mun found this laid across the pathway.'

'I saw him searching, Nathaniel,' I said. 'Felicity had a sense of something of the kind, and so did Mrs Tregowan. Felicity wished to warn those on the search party.'

'Rather me than poor Felicity,' said my husband, burying his head in his hands. 'I am asking myself why it was that the good Lord permitted such an accident to overtake Felicity and spared a sinner like me.'

'It was not the Lord who laid the trap, Nathaniel,' I said. 'Nor are you a sinner, only to the extent that Mr Tregowan would have us all believe we are sinners. You would chastise yourself for your own existence if you could.'

He looked up.

'So I would, darling,' he said. 'At the very moment I am inclined to think it would have been better if I had not set foot in this world, for I have on my conscience the passing of poor Enid as well as the hurt done to Felicity. Say something, darling,' he added presently, 'else I am talking to myself.'

'How can that be?' I said.

'How can it be?'

'How can it be that you lay the charge of Enid's passing and Felicity's hurt upon yourself, Nathaniel?' I said needlessly, for I knew well the drift of his thoughts.

'Forgive me for my plain speaking, darling,' he said, taking my hand. 'As to Enid, and to my lasting shame, she suffered greatly in the carrying of our bairn, and the bearing of the little one was too much for her. May the Lord forgive me, for I did not know it would be so. And as to poor Felicity, the trip wire was, of course, intended for the master of Shackleton mine.'

I saw that there was nothing to be gained in trying to persuade Nathaniel otherwise, and that he would carry these sufferings of conscience with him for the rest of his life.

'Say something, darling,' he said.

'I can't tell you that you are mistaken, Nathaniel,' I said, 'for though you will hear me you will never believe me. Yet I may carry half of your afflictions, as you carry half of mine, and have done so for a long time, for which I thank you with all my heart, sir.'

Nathaniel took my other hand, and we were seated thus, hand in hand across the desk in the drawing room, when Cecilia knocked and ushered in Mrs Tregowan.

'I may not stay, my dears,' she said, 'for I am much occupied with my girls this morning, but,' Mrs Tregowan took a handkerchief from her reticule and dabbed at her eyes, 'Jack has requested that Patrick calls upon Felicity, and I do not like the sound of that for he is not such a one as to welcome the dissenting minister under his roof. Perhaps you would like to attend as well, my dears, for I do not know how I will suffer Jack Walsh on my own. It is always in my mind that poor Felicity has been so worn down by his banter that she became susceptible to the coughing malady. You did not hear a thing of what I have just said, my dears. I must go now.'

'There is much I haven't heard of lately,' I said to my husband after Mrs Tregowan had taken her hasty leave. 'What does Mrs Tregowan mean by her girls?'

'Barbara is always occupied with acts of charity,' said Nathaniel. 'No doubt she was referring to something of the kind.'

'Acts of charity?'

'Yes, darling, of some kind.'

'Meaning you don't know, or you will not say?'

'I do know and I will say, darling,' he said presently, still holding my hands. 'Barbara looks towards those poor, innocent souls who have been found in the streets of Durham at night and have been taken in by the watch. Forgive me, darling. I would now be asking you to say something, but I cannot.'

'We will have to go to see Felicity,' I said, 'if only to protect Mrs Tregowan from Mr Walsh.'

'Indeed, darling,' Nathaniel said. 'We don't know at what time to call. Did Mrs Tregowan tell us?'

'I think she did not,' I said.

'Mr Higgs and Mr Thorley will be here presently, darling,' he said. 'I expect no good tidings.' I was about to rise from my chair, but he caught my hand. 'Sit down, my dear,' he said. 'I have taken much time in lamenting my own desolations and have not asked how you are this morning. Forgive me, darling.'

'I feel overwhelming anguish,' I said.

'And?'

'Of the three of us, poor dear Felicity, and dear Mrs Tregowan, and I, it would have been better if I had fallen.'

'And?'

'For I am fallen already, Nathaniel, and Felicity is like an angel.'

Then, taking my hands, he drew me towards himself and so we stayed, like broken, shipwrecked creatures, clinging to each other, until a knock on the door announced Cecilia.

'Mrs Tregowan said to tell you that Mr Tregowan will be with Mistress Walsh at three after mid-day, for she forgot to say. Mr Higgs and Mr Thorley await the honour of your presence, sir, and are in the parlour.'

'Perhaps you would send Mr Higgs and Mr Thorley up to the drawing room, Cecilia, my dear. They may speak in Clara's presence.'

'I will go, Nathaniel,' I said. 'It is likely that Mr Higgs and Mr Thorley will not say all they wish if they are to be overheard by an ignorant woman.'

'You will not go, darling,' said Nathaniel. 'I do not wish you to leave my sight.'

And we might well have continued in our dispute, but that the door was tentatively opened and Mr Higgs entered, followed by Mr Thorley, or the other way round, for I have always confused them one with another, whom my husband welcomed with a cordiality at odds with his low spirits.

'Come in, Dan. Come in, Percy. Pray make yourselves at home. You may speak freely in Clara's presence, for she knows well the intricacies of Shackleton.'

'Happen Mrs Chark would make a better go of ordering the colliery than ourselves,' said Mr Higgs, or Mr Thorley.

'Ah, there's many a true word spoken in jest,' said my husband. 'I have often thought the same, and I have no doubt, also, that Cecilia would order the workings of Shackleton to the approval of all.'

At which Cecilia appeared, as if by magic, with a flask of tea, as the gentlemen were caught up in the merriment of the moment.

'We have just now been hearing how you might well order the mine, Cecilia,' said Mr Higgs, or Mr Thorley, at which Cecilia blushed.

'Oh no, Mr Higgs,' she said, thus bringing to an end my confusion. And I remembered my first impression of Mr Higgs, as being the taller gentleman, and added to my private lexicon the word "high", having most letters in common with the name of Higgs.

'We must now to serious matters, gentlemen,' said my husband when Cecilia had gone.

'Indeed,' said Mr Higgs. 'A case of stythe as we think, sir. Not severe, but it needs attention.'

'A single case? Who?' said Nathaniel.

'Colin Beech, working the north pit,' said Mr Higgs, laying out on the desk a much-worn plan. 'Reported light headed and fatigued, sir.'

'But we understand the bairn passed out of this world,' said Mr Thorley, 'and that is likely to drive any man to sickness, saving your presence, sir.'

'Yet we must look to it,' said Nathaniel. 'Mr Beech is not a fellow to mistake the ills of the spirit for the ills of the temple.'

'Quite,' said Mr Thorley. 'No sign of Mr Spence, sir?'

'No, sir,' said Nathaniel. 'The search was curtailed by a sorry turn of events, as you may know.'

'We did not know,' said Mr Higgs. 'All talk is of Mistress Walsh and none of Mr Spence.'

'We failed to find Mr Spence,' said Nathaniel. 'What are they saying of Mistress Walsh?'

'That which she is saying herself, sir, namely that she missed her footing, for she came to herself somewhat and spoke, sir. That is the news abroad in Durham.'

My husband said nothing. Mr Higgs and Mr Thorley glanced at one another.

'Then we must go down with the men on the morning shift, sir, to see to the reported incidence of stythe,' Mr Thorley said. 'That we must do, sir, and in the meantime make sure the men do not go near to the reported source of the mischief. And check for the firedamp also, with the Spedding mill, sir.'

'It should not have been Felicity,' said Nathaniel again, as we made ready to leave the house after Mr Higgs and Mr Thorley had said their farewells. 'As long as I live I will have it on my conscience that poor Felicity fell over the trip wire that was intended for the master of Shackleton. Indeed, Cecilia, you were right when you said that all of Durham knows it to be so, and I've no doubt Percy Higgs and Dan Thorley also.'

'I would not have said such words if I knew you would take them to heart, sir,' said Cecilia. 'May the Lord forgive me for my plain speaking. I have caused you much grief and torment.'

Then my husband, seeing that Cecilia was in a state of dismay equal to his own, ceased his self-recriminations and told her to be comforted, saying that

225

her plain speaking was a blessing, as no other, even in the collieries of Shackleton, Thayne and Blennowe, would stand up to him, unless it was his darling wife; and even Clara did not so with the temerity of Cecilia, to whom he would always feel gratitude for reminding him every day that he was mortal.

'If you say so, sir,' said Cecilia, 'for I know not a word of what you talk about, but I see you mean well. Willow and Bertie-mun and me would convey our well wishings to mistress Walsh, for Mr Higgs said she has come to herself.' And Cecilia put into my hand a brown paper parcel.

''Tis but a cake of sugar, mun,' she said, 'for poor Mistress Walsh needs her strength. We knew not what other we could do for her or the bairn an' Mistress Beech. 'Tis from Thursday market, mun.'

'Cecilia, my dear,' said Nathaniel, 'you might better have looked for a cake of sugar in our own pantry than look in the Thursday market.'

'I liked not to ask, sir,' said Cecilia.

'No, I believe you did not, my dear,' said Nathaniel.

'Asking your pardon, sir, but Mrs Tregowan expects you to bear her company an I wish not to hinder you,' Cecilia said, no doubt seeing that my husband had it in his mind to prolong the discussion on the obtaining of sugar to any length in order to put off the visit to Felicity, as if by delaying it the obligation would go away all together.

On our arrival we found Mr Tregowan already inside the house, and Mrs Tregowan standing in the garden and suffering with a good grace Jack Walsh, who continued in his discourse, unaware of our presence.

'Felicity was always a one to get into situations,' he was saying. 'And a body would be hard pressed to

226

configure how such mayhem may reside in so meagre a frame, but there you are. Happen the fall over yon crag at Blennowe has knocked the cough out of her, for it fair rattles my peace, day and night; though I don't say she doesn't suffer with it, for she does, and at odd times I ha' seen her secreting a pillow tick into Monday wash tub. Come in, come in,' he said, noticing us. 'You will find Felicity nicely. There's many a one who went over Blennowe crag who came up worse, to be sure. With good fortune and a following wind Patrick will be done with her presently.'

Who, even as Jack finished speaking, came out of the downstairs room which had been set aside for Felicity. Yet it was not Patrick Tregowan of the dissenting chapel on the Sabbath day who came out of the room, but a man quite other, looking for all the world as if his face had been etched out of the stone of Blennowe crag, so grey was he.

'Patrick, my good man,' said Nathaniel, seeing what I had seen. 'You are not well.'

Mr Tregowan made no answer, but stood holding the door open for us, so that without any preamble we were in Felicity's room, finding there not only herself, but also my maid Willow, seated by the window.

'Mr Tregowan did not wish to see me without a companion,' said Felicity. 'I took the liberty of asking Barbara if she would kindly steal Willow from your household which she did yet not willingly for she has always in her mind that her name is like that of the malefactor who was released in the place of our Saviour. Dear, Clara, I make no sense. Please say something or else I will become as voluble as your husband, though even he is silent today. I fear I have caused you all a great deal of trouble.'

I told Felicity that indeed she had not, for I could see that Nathaniel had lost every word he ever knew, except those that hammered at his soul, and which he could not say in front of Felicity, being that the trip wire was intended for himself. I asked her then how she was, whereupon she got up from the sofa on which she was lying and walked over to the window.

'I am recovered, you see,' she said. 'I am told it was a minor concussion of the brain, which took me away from myself for a while. Yet all the while I could hear Barbara telling me that her name put her in mind of the malefactor who was released in the place of our Saviour whose story is told in St Matthew chapter twenty-eight. Yet the story of Barabbas is in chapter twenty-seven for Mr Tregowan had us study the passage not many weeks gone.'

'Indeed, I also heard Barbara say chapter twenty-eight,' said Nathaniel, 'and I did not like to contradict her. I am afraid you are tired, my dear Felicity.' Saying which, he took her by the hand and led her back to the sofa.

'We must not tell Barbara that it is chapter twenty-seven,' said Felicity, and we all of us made merry as best as we could; and Willow also, who was seated at the window convulsed in silent laughter, for any talk of holy scripture, although she has no hearing, diverts her greatly.

'You will wonder how I happened to fall when everyone else happened not to fall though we were all of us on the same path,' said Felicity. 'And I might ask the same of myself but for the fact that if ever there was so much as a feather in my path I would trip over it as Jack will tell you.'

Willow glanced across at my husband and I, as if she had heard Felicity's words.

'Come, come now, Felicity, that cannot be so,' said Nathaniel, 'for I never saw you trip yet until last evening and there were no feathers to be seen on Blennowe crag, or else I missed them.'

Felicity laughed and blushed, not with the painful blush of the coughing malady, but with the blush of a young maid. And the thought came to me, and I do not know why, that the greatest gift I could offer her would be that of my husband's presence, that she might be able to see him alone, if only once, and not as one of the general company.

Presently we took our leave, calling before we went into the back room, in which Julia Beech sat rocking the little bairn in his cradle. Yet neither my husband nor I had any words to say, apart from asking Julia how she fared, and also how the little bairn Moses fared, and I could not but think that we are the most unlikely of godparents a little bairn could ever be burdened with.

'The bairn does not thrive, nor yet does he pass out of this world,' said Julia Beech. 'An' he will do neither while his kindred are middle way between this world an' the next, for he knows not which way to go. As for myself, and thanking ye kindly, I fare well enough, though my husband not so, for he is afflicted by the stythe, sir. 'Tis not to complain, sir, saving your honour.'

Then Nathaniel told Julia Beech that Mr Higgs and Mr Thorley were going down with him the next day, and taking the Spedding mill, to see if anything was there in the way of firedamp and stythe; through all of which conversation the little bairn Moses slept, opening his eyes only once, to look up at Julia, whom I will never again think of without hearing at the same time the voice of Felicity saying, 'It is a pretty name, is it not?'

And I was still questioning in my mind how Felicity was to see Nathaniel on his own when I realised that we had not delivered Cecilia's gift of sugar, which was still in my reticule.

'We must go back with it,' said Nathaniel, then said that he would go back on his own, for he could cover the distance in no time. 'And Jack will deliver Cecilia's gift,' he added.

'It is better that you take it to Felicity yourself, Nathaniel,' I said.

'It is only a quarter of an hour since poor Felicity saw me,' he said. 'She will not wish to see me again, darling.'

'Please, Nathaniel,' I said.

Then, taking my face between his hands, he kissed me, for we were by the Wear and on our own, and said that he would do as I asked, and see to it that Willow should accompany me home.

'She is here, Nathaniel,' I said. For, indeed, Willow had appeared as her name was spoken, with the merriment of the holy scripture still on her, and, catching my eye, her sweet face made the words, 'Chapter twenty-eight.'

Arriving back at the Rose Pavement, we found Bertie-mun attending to the garden at the back of the house, where Willow also went, to look over the thyme and lavender, so that I entered the house alone. And I was still in the hallway when the front doorbell rang, which I answered, expecting I did not know whom, but not the visitor who stood on the threshold.

'I wish not to importune you, Mrs Chark,' he said. 'I am going away and have come to say farewell.'

'Then you wish to see my husband,' I said.

'It is you I wish to see, Mrs Chark,' he said. 'I beg your forgiveness. Farewell.'

Then he kissed my hand and was gone. And I turned, to find at my back Cecilia and Willow and Bertie-mun, not knowing how long they had been there, or what brought them into the hallway. Only that Nathaniel later questioned me as to what had happened, turning my face towards the last light of the spring day, as if he would read what was written there.

The Wings of the Morning

Today has been the anniversary of Bertie-mun's coming
to the household four years ago on the twenty-fourth day
of May, which Nathaniel regards also as Bertie-mun's
birthday, the date of which is unknown. And it is four
years since the great fire of Thayne from which Bertie-
mun was brought out alive after having been trapped for
two days in a pocket of clean air when the sides caved in
behind. And, although his fellows were winched up
before him, there was not one among those nineteen
souls who did not succumb to the stythe later, for all
that, as they were brought up, they looked as well and
youthful as if it had been their wedding day. Yet that day
Bertie-mun left in the pit the fair face of his youth and
emerged back into his life as a man for ever disfigured.

All this Cecilia told me, coming into my room early
when I was getting ready for holy service. And, when we
were gathered in the hallway and about to set off for the
dissenting chapel, my husband congratulated Bertie-mun
upon another anniversary in the household, offering him
his liberty for the day to do as he pleased, which Bertie-
mun declined, saying as well as he was able that to be in
the household with the master and mistress, and Willow
and Cecilia, was reward enough for him. Which
sentence, being the longest and most painstaking I have

yet heard from him, rendered him silent for the greater part of the Sabbath.

The morning was warm and sunlit, with lilac out in the garden and a mistle thrush building her nest above the lintel of the house. Yet, for all that the day was as lovely as the first day in the creation of the world, and the garden as untroubled as the garden of Eden, my husband's face was sunk in a melancholy which reminded me yet again my first morning in the household when I looked up and saw all joyfulness driven from his countenance.

'It is a lovely morning, darling,' he said as we walked to the chapel, with Cecilia, Willow and Bertie-mun following on behind us as is their habit.

'Yet you have the doldrums upon you, Nathaniel,' I said, for we were not near enough to our household to be overheard.

'Indeed, I have the doldrums,' he said, 'and you also, Clara, darling,' with which observation I agreed. 'We will no doubt leave chapel with our doldrums scattered, will we not, darling?' he continued.

'If you say so, sir,' I said.

'For it has never yet been the case that I have entered the chapel with a heavy heart and my dear friend Patrick, for all that he is a good and saintly man whom I love dearly, has not made it worse,' said Nathaniel.

And I was still trying to unravel my husband's sentence when I looked up at him in search of enlightenment and found his eyes sparkling and his face flushed as if he were convulsed with merriment.

'You must not let Willow see you like this, sir,' I said, which remark increased his mirth the more, so that we were obliged to take a turn round Chivenor Square before we went into the chapel.

And we arrived as the service was starting, taking a seat at the back with those others who habitually behave themselves improperly. So it was that Nathaniel and I were still settling ourselves at the back of the chapel and enduring the glances of those in front of us, who turned round to see what manner of latecomers we were to be arriving when Mr Tregowan already stood behind the lectern, when Jack Walsh arrived also, with Felicity on his arm. Then the interest of the congregation in the last bench of the chapel increased considerably as all turned round to see if it was indeed Felicity Walsh who was there, four short days after her fall over Blennowe crag. And such was the commotion that Mr Tregowan, having already announced the one hundred and thirty-ninth psalm, halted the service and greeted her.

'This is indeed the hand of the Lord that we see you in our midst, Felicity,' he said. 'We bid you welcome.'

Then all those around reached out to touch her, as if to make certain for themselves that she was indeed Felicity Walsh who was in their presence, and not her angel who had come back to Sunday service, and many wept.

'It is fitting that we take as our psalm today number one hundred and thirty-nine,' Mr Tregowan continued. 'For though we take the wings of the morning and fly to the uttermost ends of the earth the Lord is surely with each one of us.'

During which talk the blush on Felicity's face grew deeper, and I could see that she would gladly have flown to the uttermost parts of the earth rather than stayed in the dissenting chapel and suffered further attention. But at length, the service drew to a close, and she waylaid my husband and I as we were leaving, it being our habit to do so promptly as all know that we have the Sabbath day school to attend to.

'I had intended to creep in at the back,' she said. 'It was very hot in the chapel, was it not? I could not breathe.'

To which Nathaniel answered that he supposed it was, but being of greater stature than those around him he was generally able to breathe. Then, turning to Felicity, he took her hand.

'You are not quite recovered, Felicity, my dear,' he said. 'You will be different again tomorrow, and better again on Tuesday, and every day thereafter you will be better.' Yet Felicity merely looked up at my husband, with all her colour gone, and, indeed, with the same pallor on her face as she had when she was brought up from Blennowe crag.

'We must go to see poor Hilda again, Clara, my dear,' she said presently, coming back to herself somewhat. 'Pray forgive me, I did not know where I was for the moment, but it was not here with the sweet sound of the Wear and the scent of lilacs on the air.'

'It could be that you had taken the wings of the morning, Felicity, my dear,' said Nathaniel. 'We will accompany you home, if we may.'

And, he taking one arm and I taking the other arm, we set off for her house in the Lower Culvert, Jack having stayed behind, as it is his habit to do, for all that he has scant liking for the dissenting chapel.

'We were late also, Felicity,' I said. 'We arrived only the minute before you, for the reason that Nathaniel had a fit of merriment and we were obliged to take a turn round Chivenor Square until he had composed himself.'

Felicity laughed and her colour returned a little, seeing that we were by then almost on her threshold.

'And what was Nathaniel merry about, Clara?' she said. 'There is not much to be merry about in the dissenting chapel though I do not say the same of God's world outside the doors of the chapel. Forgive me I must hear this story later. I shall forget it if I hear it now. The headache I have seems to drive away my memory. Poor Julia has not only the little bairn to look to, but also Pharaoh's daughter.'

So saying, Felicity wished us farewell, and said that she would be sufficiently well to visit Hilda Spence the next morning, or failing that on Tuesday, for, as Nathaniel had said, she would recover more with every day that passed.

And my husband and I wended our way homewards, saying little until we arrived at the Rose Pavement, which is deserted now, since those who were gathered at our gate before have gone.

'I do not like the headache,' said Nathaniel, as if the thought had come to him out of nowhere. Then I asked him how long he had suffered a headache, to which he answered that he was not speaking of his own headache, but of Felicity's, for he had never known a headache in his life.

'It would be more to be marvelled at if Felicity did not complain of a headache after falling over Blennowe crag, Nathaniel,' I said.

'But it was not with her the day after her accident,' he said. And my husband could not let the matter go, until I said we should ask Willow to look in the apothecary cupboard, which pacified him a little but not greatly.

So to the Sabbath day school, where the scholars appeared, all of them dressed as if for chapel, giving their names, as was their custom, as William Darbyshire, Frederick Pennell, James Sowerby, Alfred Baines, Amos Frost, Bartholomew, Gregory Parrish, and also Colin Beech, who was but a shadow of the man who had stood in the schoolroom on the last Sabbath.

'I beg you all be seated,' I said, for I doubted that Colin Beech could stand long on his feet, and knew that he would not be seated while the other scholars stood.

'Do not mind me, mun,' he said. 'I have been sick of the stythe, but I am on the way to betterment, thanking ye. We heard what the master said o' the matter we rose last week, mun.'

Then I told the scholars what my husband had said, being that those women with child should not labour in the pit, which had not improved the lot of the colliers but rather made it worse, for the reason that the wage was to remain the same and as a consequence the incomings would diminish. After which Colin Beech begged me to take comfort, for I had done what I could and no more was to be expected from Nathaniel Chark.

'Asking your pardon, he being your wedded husband and the like. An' asking your pardon again, mun, for Mistress Enid met wi' the same in her day, may the Lord rest her sweet soul,' Colin Beech said. Then, handing me a paper, he added, 'We would study this, mun, saving your honour. 'Tis but a short text.'

'"Personal labour is all the property they have,"' I read.

'We would ask, mun, what is this property yon text speaks of?'

So I said to the scholars that, as I understood it, property meant something that is owned and is therefore a thing of value, and that the work that each man does is therefore a thing of value.

237

'Aye, as we thought,' said Colin Beech. 'Thanking ye, mun.'

And presently, after studying the text, which each committed readily to memory, the scholars went on their way, shedding their top coats as they left the house, for the day had become hot and the Rose Pavement was alight with the sun filtering through the new leaves of the limes. Yet, in spite of the shining afternoon, I remained desolate, which was how Nathaniel found me, still in the schoolroom as I had no will to embrace the spring, the loveliness of which was as torture to me.

'We will take a turn around the garden, darling, where we will see a miracle,' he said, leading me by the hand in the same way that he had led Felicity back to her sofa, until we came to the grass path and the briar hedge running along by the carriageway. Then, taking off his coat and placing it around my shoulders, Nathaniel asked me to keep still, but keep my eyes on the briar hedge; which I did, until presently a blackbird flew in and there rose from the hedge a cacophony of squawks as she fed her young. And turning away, he led me back to the house, asking me as we approached the door if I would keep him company in the drawing room to see a visitor, who would presently arrive, to which I agreed.

'Thank you, darling,' he said, then he asked me to hold in my mind, whatever might be the outcome of the forthcoming meeting, that we had recently stood in the garden in the presence of new and joyful life, which, whatever passed in the gloomy world of men, would continue the same year after year in the garden, and wherever else the Lord's creation was to be found.

And we found, already waiting in the drawing room, Mr Priest, who said that Cecilia had let him in and offered him refreshment, which he had declined on account of the nature of his mission, saying also to me that he was kindred to Colin Beech by virtue of their having the same mother, for he did not like to go straight into the tale he had to tell. And I said to him that, had he not told me of their kinship, I might have known from their same pleasant features and grey eyes.

'You may speak in front of my wife, Roger,' said my husband. 'We thank you for breaking into your Sabbath day.'

'I cannot say such things in the presence of a lady, sir,' said Mr Priest. Then I said to Mr Priest, seeing him still unable to deliver his message, that I believed I knew the nature of his tidings, for my husband had prepared me.

'If you wish then, mun,' said Roger Priest. ''Tis concerning Mr Spence. When we was down yon Blennowe crag for to bring up Mistress Walsh there were as it seemed somewhat like rags at foot o' crag, thas all I han to say, mun, saving your honour, sir, an' begging your pardon, Mrs Chark.'

'Did not Mr Salter also see that there was something like rags at the foot of the crag?' said Nathaniel.

'I know not, sir,' said Roger Priest, 'for he an' I does not communicate over much, an' moreover I thinks he is gone, sir. 'Tis to say, sir, I'm willing for search party again.'

'Thank you, Roger,' said Nathaniel, persuading him also, but with much difficulty, to take refreshment before he left.

So Cecilia brought in tea and toast and my husband told Mr Priest at length about the little bairn Moses, although Mr Priest knew the tale well, being kinsman to Mr Beech, only so that he might not carry back to his own dwellinghouse the heavy tidings he had carried to

239

ours. After which I looked for Willow to tell her of Felicity's headache, although Willow has no hearing, and she brought from the apothecary cupboard preparations of nutmeg and betony, which she and I will take to poor Felicity.

For there is no one who thinks of Felicity Walsh other than as "poor Felicity".

The Tail of a Rope

'The master says to tell you he is gone to Shackleton, mun,' said Cecilia, 'an' I would say it to no other than your good self, mun, but it was the talk of the chapel after you an' the master had taken your leave. Though I don't know if I should be repeating such matters. Yet I will, mun, the master being your wedded husband. 'Tis said Spedding's faulty, mun and they know not what mischief resides in pit, for yon machine is not telling them rightly. Therefore the master is gone early down to Shackleton.' But even as Cecilia finished speaking we heard the front door open and Nathaniel returning, with company. ''Tis Mr Higgs and Mr Thorley,' she said.

'I was always mistaking those two gentlemen one for another,' I said.

''Tis easy, mun,' said Cecilia, 'for Mr Higgs is lame in his walk whereas Mr Thorley is not, an' Mr Higgs is the taller, mun.'

'But if they are both of them seated I am none the wiser,' I said.

'That is true, mun,' said Cecilia, then, the door of the room opening, she greeted Mr Higgs, who entered first. 'You have brought a fine day with you, Mr Higgs.'

''Tis all the finer for seeing you, my dear Cecilia,' said Mr Higgs, at which Cecilia, seeing the frown that flickered across Nathaniel's brow, took her leave. 'No harm is done, sir,' said Mr Higgs.

'Only so long as she does not leave my household and go to yours, Percy,' said Nathaniel.

'Come, come, sir,' said Mr Higgs, 'she dwells in the household of the most handsome man in Durham,' which riposte was not to my husband's liking either.

'We must to the matter in hand, gentlemen,' he said. 'The Spedding mill brought up from Thayne is not effective. We do not know why, but it is not. It will not tell us whether or not there is firedamp present. Come in.'

The door opened and Willow entered with a tea trolley, which Mr Higgs hastened to take from her.

'You see, you have frightened Cecilia away, Percy,' said Mr Thorley. 'Happen you were too free with your speech, for she is a good, chapel going young woman.'

'We may talk in the presence of Willow,' said Nathaniel before Mr Higgs could speak further, then, turning to me, he asked if I would stay also. 'The Spedding mill is not effective and we cannot therefore investigate with any safety the presence or otherwise of firedamp,' he said, as if I had not heard him the first time.

''Tis only Mr Beech complained of effects of stythe,' said Mr Higgs, 'and his ills could well be of another cause, for the poor fellow has not had life gentle of late. An' no one can find yon fellow who supposes himself to be a physician.'

'There is no physician,' said Nathaniel.

'Therefore, we cannot be certain Mr Beech is badly of the stythe,' said Mr Thorley. 'An' were it not for suspicion of stythe, which suspicion may be unfounded, we would not ha' contemplated testing for firedamp also. Mistress Willow brews a fine cup of tea, sir.'

'Then I must take it that you advise that Shackleton remains open, sirs,' said Nathaniel. Mr Higgs and Mr Thorley exchanged a glance one with the other.

'Wi' caution, sir,' said Mr Thorley.

'Pray explain what you understand by the word caution, Dan, my good fellow,' said Nathaniel.

''Twas but a manner of speaking, sir,' said Mr Thorley. 'Mr Higgs an myself advise that Shackleton be kep open.'

Then Mr Higgs and Mr Thorley sought out Willow who was seated at the window and thanked her for the tea, although she has no hearing, after which they went on their way.

'We must trust to the Lord that all will be well,' said Nathaniel after they had gone, and while Willow, who had appeared to be slumbering during the talk about the Spedding mill, busied herself with clearing away the tea cups. 'Did Willow find a remedy for Felicity's headache, my dear?'

I said that Willow had found in the apothecary cupboard the remedies of nutmeg and betony, whereupon Willow produced the remedies from her apron pocket, giving them to Nathaniel so that he might read the labels.

'Felicity may try them,' he said, 'but I doubt if they will help her now. Thank you, Willow, my dear.' And I gathered that the visit of Mr Higgs and Mr Thorley had plunged my husband again into the doldrums, in which state he would have likely remained all day, had not Mrs Tregowan just then knocked and showed herself in.

'I did not wish to impose any longer on dear Cecilia on wash day, my dears,' she said. 'Claribell, how lovely you look this morning.'

'I tell her the same every day yet she does not believe me,' said Nathaniel. 'You must have encountered Percy Higgs and Dan Thorley, Barbara. They have just this minute gone on their way.'

'I might have done so, but that I was in the scullery conversing with Cecilia,' said Mrs Tregowan. 'It is all about that poor Charles Spence has been discovered at the foot of Blennowe crag. He was sighted by Mr Priest when he went down for poor Felicity, though it was not Mr Priest who told me nor yet the other gentleman, who has not been seen since the mishap.'

'We have already heard, have we not, Clara?' said Nathaniel. 'Ill tidings travel fast.'

'Patrick is determined to go down and read the office,' Mrs Tregowan continued, 'but I do not know how he will accomplish that, for he suffers from the vertigo merely looking out from our garret window.'

'We must establish first that it is Mr Spence,' said my husband.

'That is of no matter, dear Nathaniel,' said Mrs Tregowan, 'for Patrick is still minded to go down and read the office, whoever it is at the foot of Blennowe crag.'

'Patrick is right, of course,' said Nathaniel. 'Whoever lies at the foot of Blennowe crag must be committed to the dear Lord's keeping. May he not read the office from the pathway, Barbara?'

'That is exactly what I suggested,' said Mrs Tregowan, 'but he will not.'

'Then we must see that Patrick comes to no harm,' said Nathaniel, unaware that the door of the drawing room had opened and that Mr Tregowan was standing in our midst. 'He must be winched down and we must go with him to see that he comes to no harm. It may be that Willow has something in the apothecary cupboard for the alleviation of dizziness.'

'The remedy is known by the popular name of Feverfew,' said Mr Tregowan. '*Tanacetum parthenium* to those of us who know our Latin.' Which included only Mr Tregowan himself, there being present Nathaniel and I, Mrs Tregowan, and Cecilia, who had come in with Mr Tregowan, and none of us would own up to any Latin. 'No Latin among us?' said Mr Tregowan, 'which is not to belittle our collective learning, for I myself know only those two words, and for the life of me I cannot remember how to spell them. I apologise for my peremptory arrival. How is Mr Richardson these days, Mrs Chark?'

Then, seeing that Mr Tregowan would willingly think of anything but the descent of Blennowe crag, I told him that I had abandoned Mr Richardson in favour a work entitled *Sense and Sensibility* by an unnamed lady.

'You see I am a fickle woman, Mr Tregowan,' I said.

'Ah, I will tell you a secret, Mrs Chark,' he said. 'The unnamed lady is a Miss Austen. She has a lightness of touch one does not find in Mr Richardson, is that not so?'

'We have all of us decided to winch you down, Patrick,' said Nathaniel, although only he had decided. 'Mr Priest and Bertie-mun will accompany you, as shall I, for we are each one of us fellows of the mines. It is best done as soon as we may, so that the good soul, whoever lies there, shall be at rest.'

'Poor Felicity told me,' said Mrs Tregowan. 'For though she had suffered a concussion to the brain she was aware in her mind and perceived that she was not alone on Blennowe crag. But you have not heard that latter,' she added. 'Poor Felicity bade Patrick to say nothing for fear the tidings would be given to Hilda in an untoward way. Yet all of Durham knows.'

Then it was decided once more that the office should be read as soon as possible and we set off, Mrs Tregowan and I in the day coach bound for Doncaster, and Nathaniel and Mr Tregowan on foot, while Bertie-mun was despatched to call on Mr Priest, and also summon the help of Mr Carson and Mr Daunt, being the two gentlemen from the Blennowe Carr who had brought the winch on the previous occasion; this taking upwards of two hours, for when we arrived the sun was high and the day warm and placid, and filled with the scent of hawthorn and the song of larks.

As I waited on the pathway fear gripped me, no less than if it had been myself about to be winched down. And I believe Mrs Tregowan was the same, for her eyes were tight shut, and her face became as white as the stone of the crag as the winch arrived, I have to say amid oaths from Mr Daunt and Mr Carson as they tried to carry it along the grass path which was deeply rutted with rabbit burrows.

'I think I do not need this, my good men,' said Mr Tregowan surveying the winch, which indeed looked in the daylight like an instrument of terror, worse than the crag itself; having said which he disappeared over the edge with the other gentlemen following.

And we could hear his voice reading the office for the dead, the gentle words of which travelled far and wide across Blennowe vale, and echoed around the green hills under the sunlit sky. Yet neither Mrs Tregowan nor I thought to ask if it was Charles Spence at the foot of the crag, or some other unhappy soul who had lost their footing in the mist, or indeed lost their footing on the path of their life.

Then Mr Daunt and Mr Carson, who both had the Christian name of Ben, took the winch back to the inn, saying as they went, though all others remained silent, that the fellow Brim Salter had last been seen at the sign of the Blennowe Carr some day or two following the incident of Mistress Walsh, and one at the inn, far gone in liquor, supposed him to have passed through the door leading to the garret stairway with a brown paper parcel under his arm; all of which conversation was so punctuated with oaths that Mrs Tregowan intervened and begged them to remember the occasion they had lately witnessed.

'Saving your honour, mun,' said Ben Daunt, 'but the reverend gentleman is taken badly.'

Which, indeed, Mr Tregowan was, for having accomplished the descent and ascent of Blennowe crag he could now scarcely place one foot in front of the other, and Bertie-mun and Nathaniel were helping him, one on either side, to reach the inn, where he was taken, as I thought, to the room where Felicity had been taken.

'Wi' the difference thas no physician,' Mr Daunt was saying from the adjoining room. Then I remembered the Feverfew which Willow had given for Mr Tregowan's dizziness, and gave it to Nathaniel so that he could take it into the back room where Mrs Tregowan sat with her husband.

With the departure of Nathaniel and Mrs Tregowan we fell into silence, so that the voices of Mr Daunt and Mr Carson could be heard, the doors being open, continuing their discourse begun on Blennowe crag concerning Mr Salter, to the effect that he had last been seen going through the door that lead to the garret carrying a brown paper parcel, 'wi' the tail of a rope hanging out of un,' it had been reported. Until the conclusion was reached that the very door led out from the room they were seated in, and an application was made to the innkeeper to open up the door so that the garret might be searched. To which request the innkeeper delivered a firm refusal, saying that the door had not been opened this many a year for the reason that the key was lost, and hearing which Mr Priest exchanged a glance with Bertie-mun. And still Nathaniel did not come back.

Presently a jug of water was brought in by the innkeeper's wife, with glasses, for it was known that all the party were dissenters. And I could readily have drifted off into a sleep in the warm sun that slipped in and out of the dust in the room, hearing nothing but the silence and a bluebottle banging against the windows and the continued voices of Mr Daunt and Mr Carson as if from some other world. Until the innkeeper returned and said that the good minister, who was much recovered, advised that the ladies should return to Durham in the afternoon coach, and that he and Mr Chark would follow.

'They will come on later, Claribell, my dear,' said Mrs Tregowan, who had followed the innkeeper into the room in which we were seated; and the innkeeper then made to leave, indicating that Bertie-mun and Mr Priest should accompany him.

'There is some matter they are concerned with, which is surely to do with poor Mr Spence or whoever it may be who lies at the foot of Blennowe crag,' said Mrs Tregowan. 'For, as Patrick said to the innkeeper, it is strictly speaking the established church of Durham which has the care of all souls for far around, yet it escapes my memory how far, though I once did know, my family being Church, you know, Claribell, my dear. Which is how I come to be acquainted with Mr Handel's airs, and I would that dear Nathaniel might cast an eye over a work of Mr Handel, for he has a fine tenor voice. But he will not, for all that I tell him that Mr Handel, being from foreign parts, was not Church, as far as I know, though none can ask him now. And I fear also, my dear Claribell,' she added, 'it was Enid's passing that took away Nathaniel's inclination for Mr Handel, for Enid played the fortepiano, you know, dear.'

Mrs Tregowan fell silent as we walked from the coach stage up the steep thoroughfares to the Rose Pavement, then, finding herself once more on level ground, she continued her speech. 'And I do not know if I told you, Claribell, but my kindred cast me off after I married Patrick, saying that I had made my bed and I must now lie on it.'

"Matthew, Mark, Luke and John, bless the bed that I lie on," I thought, though I said nothing.

'Indeed, Claribell, continued Mrs Tregowan, 'I have said the childhood prayer many a time, which you surely know, and it came into my mind when poor Tessa was discovered in the north pit.'

I told Mrs Tregowan that the same thought of Tessa Spence had visited me, and so we passed the journey back, arriving when the afternoon heat was beginning to wane.

'Were we to have seen Felicity today?' said Mrs Tregowan. 'All days seem like one another to me, and I can hardly believe it is still Monday. It is always the way with me when a soul passes out of this world, for I am hard pressed to believe that I am still alive, which indeed

I am, dear Claribell, for there is the household linen blowing on the line, and it is still wash day. If I might use the privy, darling, for Bertie-mun keeps it very clean and I dared not ask the good folk at the inn, for heaven knows what I might have found there.'

Then Cecilia, finding Mrs Tregowan with me, brought tea and currant loaf to the drawing room, not leaving, but hovering in the doorway.

'Pardon my plain speaking, Mrs Tregowan, for I see you and the mistress returned home, yet not the master and the Reverend Tregowan, and it has come to me that there has been a mishap. Yet you need not to tell me.'

'The master and the Reverend Tregowan are delayed, Cecilia,' I said. 'We do not know the reason. But we know that they are safe and sound, for we were all taken to the inn at Blennowe crag, and the good people gave us water to drink, knowing that we are dissenters.'

'Which I would have known from your toggery, mun, for the aroma of the ale house came in with you. I will have your cloak out to air when you have done with it. Mr Walsh was here, mun.'

'Sit down, dear Cecilia,' said Mrs Tregowan. 'It is not right that we are seated and you remain standing after the ardours of Monday wash day.' But Cecilia would not, and it came to me that I have never seen her seated at any time other than at the tea table on the Sabbath.

'Mr Walsh said that Mistress Walsh wanders in her mind,' she said, 'yet saving your honour, mun, I have heard him say such things about her after Sunday service these years past, and I know not how she keeps her temper.'

'You may speak freely in my presence, dear Cecilia,' said Mrs Tregowan. 'I did not hear the latter.'

'That is all I have to say, Mrs Tregowan,' said Cecilia, 'begging your pardon, for I know holy scripture bids us not to speak ill of one another.'

'It was not very ill, my dear,' said Mrs Tregowan. 'Did Mr Walsh ask us to go and see poor Felicity today?'

'Not in so many words, mun, but I surmised that was the purpose of his visitation, for it is not in his habit to toil up yon hill to Mr Chark's house.'

'Claribell, my dear,' said Mrs Tregowan, 'I know you will tell me truthfully what is in your thoughts.'

'My thoughts are that we have not the inclination to go to Felicity's house for we are fatigued after this morning, yet we must go,' I said.

'Indeed, Claribell, my dear,' said Mrs Tregowan. 'We must go. When was it that you saw Mr Walsh, Cecilia, darling?'

'Why, mun, you had shortly left when he came ringing on the bell,' said Cecilia. 'And not having darkened the door once this twelve month it is of a sudden such a matter that he must be let in immediate. Asking your pardon for my plain speaking, but Mr Walsh says you must needs go. I am only conveying the message, mun; 'tis not me telling you. Bertie-mun is now back and is at liberty to go with you for it would please him to pass the time o' day wi' the little bairn,' she added.

Then seeing that Cecilia had our visit to Felicity already in hand we set off, Bertie-mun taking with him a brown paper parcel, and I the preparations of nutmeg and betony for Felicity's bad head. And we were still a distance away when we saw Mr Walsh wandering around, as if he were searching for something, though he did not see us for he is near of sight.

'Jack,' said Mrs Tregowan. 'Jack Walsh, we are finally come to see dear Felicity, and indeed your good self. How do you fare, Jack?'

'I fare well enough,' he said. 'But Felicity wanders in her mind. You will find her absent from herself, an I canna bring her back this time, though I have tried. Come in, come in, how do you do, Mrs Chark? Come in. Will ye have tea?'

'Thank you, Jack, we have taken tea,' said Mrs Tregowan.

'Then ye will come an' see her,' said Jack Walsh, leading us to the drawing room, where we found Felicity not absent but present, and looking not different from her usual self although she was supposedly absent. 'Happen you will get more sense out o' her than I do,' Jack Walsh continued, speaking as if Felicity was not there in front of him. 'For she an I never did enjoy a meeting o' minds, so to speak.'

'Now then, Felicity, my dear,' said Mrs Tregowan, closing the door which Mr Walsh had left standing open. 'How do you fare?'

'I believe I was never better,' said Felicity. 'I had best be recovered for there is work awaiting me. I will be better as soon as ever the pain in my head is gone, which it will be presently, for the coughing malady is over and gone.'

'Barbara and I might see Hilda Spence in your place until you are rid of the headache,' I said.

'Poor Hilda has no need of a visit for she now has company in plenty,' said Felicity.

'Yes, my dear, they are good souls at the house of Sainte Agathe, even though they are of the opposite persuasion,' said Mrs Tregowan. 'They have offered solace to my girls many a time, albeit that it is a rough kind of solace, but they mean well.'

'Hilda has gone away from the house of Sainte Agathe,' said Felicity.

'Indeed?' said Mrs Tregowan. 'Happen your brother heard of it. There are all kinds of tales flying around Durham.'

Then I gave Felicity the preparations of nutmeg and betony which Willow had sent for the pain in her head, and she asked me to make sure that I thanked sweet Willow, asking the same again and again until Mrs Tregowan stopped her. 'Now that will do, dear Felicity. Claribell will not forget. Presently your headache will drift off, my dear, if you will only rest a while and let the medicine help your recovery.'

'I have work and I cannot rest,' said Felicity. 'There are too many bairns.' Then I asked Felicity how the little bairn Moses was. 'Oh,' she said, 'Moses is with Pharaoh's daughter,' and directed us to the passage in the scripture, which she said she could not remember exactly, but it would come back to her as soon as the ache in her head went off; after saying which she fell into a deep and uneasy sleep, and Mrs Tregowan indicated that we should leave.

'For poor Felicity will likely not recollect that we have been here,' she said when we were out of the door. 'We must not forget Bertie-mun, Claribell.'

We found him seated in the nursery room with the bairn Moses on his knee, and with merriment at the corners of his eyes, being the only parts of his face which register expression, and Julia Beech, who had lately been downcast, was merry in equal measure. And seeing Bertie-mun so diverted, and happiness brought to the sweet face of Julia Beech, I said to Bertie-mun that Mrs Tregowan and I would find our own way home. So we sought out Jack Walsh to tell him that we were leaving, finding him wandering disconsolately in the garden.

'Did ye get any sense out o' her?' he said.

'We fared no better nor worse than you, Jack,' said Mrs Tregowan.

'Aye, then 'tis not just me,' said Jack Walsh.

'Happen she will awake with a clearer mind, for Willow has sent to her preparations of nutmeg and betony from the apothecary cupboard,' said Mrs Tregowan.

'I know yon betony of old,' said Jack Walsh. ''Tis for madness, as sure as I stand here on God's earth.'

'In a small dose it is for the headache,' I said. 'In a larger dose it is for the relief of madness. Felicity has been given a small dose, for that is what I was given by Willow to bring to her,' not knowing if what I said was the truth, but it nevertheless pacified Mr Walsh, who said,

'Aye, thanking ye, Mrs Chark, and Mistress Willow,' and wished us farewell.

'Dear Bertie-mun dotes on the little bairn,' said Mrs Tregowan as we went through the town, slowly enough for she does not well with her walking, and I told her that Bertie-mun never visits the little bairn without taking with him a brown paper parcel.

'He is wed, you know, Claribell,' she said, 'or leastways you may not know for dear Nathaniel will not spread talk of others if it is of a personal nature. Bertie-mun was a handsome man before the fire in the mine stole from him his good looks, with a fine tenor voice. Indeed, there was no partiality in the gifts God had bestowed on the miner Herbert Tull and the master Nathaniel Chark. Yet after the fire, Bertie-mun's wedded wife returned to her kindred taking the bairn also and Bertie-mun had little inclination for the mine, which state of affairs would have cast him out of Thayne, for they cannot dwell there and not labour in the pit, but that Nathaniel took him in. And I might say also, my dear Claribell, that Nathaniel was likely to go the same way after poor Enid passed out of this world but that you came into his life. I suggest, my dear, that since we are heading in the direction of Sainte Agathe we should go in there and see poor Hilda, for though we are fatigued we shall be more so tomorrow.'

Yet we arrived at the house of Sainte Agathe as Hilda Spence was being dressed for her final journey in this world, which, they said, was to be expected, for she had sunk into a deep despair, saying that her husband would not come to her so she must go and seek him out, in the same way, as I imagined, that she had gone out many a night in her life to bring him back home when the strong liquor was on him.

And I stayed until Hilda was made ready, looking, as she did, like an angel from heaven who had cast off the cares of the world, for death had taken away from her the wounds we had recently seen and restored to her the face she might well have worn as a young girl. And I wondered if the same had happened to her husband Charles, that he looked as if he had cast off his cares. But I knew that no one would tell me, even if I should ask, which I will not.

Then Mrs Tregowan returned, as I thought, from the privy, though she said she had been seeing to the welfare of her girls, an expression I have heard from her on occasions, yet she has not thought fit to say more to me on the matter, and, indeed, would have reeled back the word as soon as she had said it, 'You did not hear that latter, my dear.'

And still Nathaniel was away from home, and did not return until the last flare of the sun was in the west. And hearing the front door opening I saw him from the window coming in, caught in the sun as if he passed through fire. Then finding me in the drawing room he kissed me, looking into my eyes in bewilderment, and said, 'You are alive, my darling,' then left the house again.

In a Place of Darkness

The watchman had called the midnight hour when my husband returned, letting himself in by the garden gate and coming up by the back staircase so as not to make any noise. Yet his footsteps set every dog in the city of Durham barking, and every owl calling, and I soon heard Bertie-mun laying a fire in the scullery and Cecilia setting a pan boiling; for after dark every slight sound travels through the house as if it is the whole army of Napoleon Bonaparte on the march. And so loud was the tramping and clattering that I went down to the scullery.

'The master said not to trouble you, mun,' said Cecilia, 'but seeing as you're here I'll be telling him.' And so saying, she filled a jug with hot water and went out with it, returning in a short while to say that the master would be down presently and telling me to be seated by the fire. 'He is not himself, mun, an' happen it will cheer him to have you by him, for the darkness is come on him again, pardon my plain speaking, but I was minded to warn you.'

Then Willow also appeared in the scullery and took a preparation from the apothecary cupboard. And I must have drifted into a doze seated in the chair beside the fire, for when I opened my eyes Nathaniel was there, looking at me with the same bewilderment in his eyes that I had seen earlier.

'I am half gone out of my mind, for I saw some other person seated there in your place, Clara, my darling,' he said. 'Pray forgive me.'

'It is likely because my hair is in disarray,' I said. 'What will you think of me, sir?'

'I will think you look lovely, darling,' he said.

'And I you, sir,' I said. 'What time is it?'

'Nigh on the dawn,' he said. 'You are shivering, darling. I will mend the fire, for Bertie-mun and Cecilia are long gone to their beds.'

'Then I shall make tea, sir,' I said, 'and we will be servants one to another. You will be Bertie-mun and I shall be Cecilia. You are not gone out of your mind, Nathaniel. Yet I think your mind has gone out of you and dwells in a place of darkness and melancholy.'

'That is so, darling,' he said, 'and I cannot tell you where in case you follow me into that same darkness.'

'I would follow you anywhere, sir,' I said presently. He looked up.

'I believe you would, darling,' he said. 'But I will not let you. It is enough that you are here by my side and the daylight is near at hand, which I was beginning to think I would never see again.'

I begged my husband to tell me what weighed so heavily on his mind, but he would not, and so we were, seated in front of the dying fire until by and by the first of the morning sun needled through a crack in the curtains and the voice of the blackbird called him back into the land of the living. Then he kissed me, and I him; and drawing back the curtains we looked out at the garden, where the dew was on the lawn and every blade and leaf shone with the early fire of the sun. And we did not hear Cecilia entering the scullery.

'Why, sir, you should be ashamed of yourself,' she said. 'I begged the master not to tell you, mun, for 'tis not a tale for the night.'

'The master has told me nothing, Cecilia,' I said. Cecilia scrutinised my face, then Nathaniel's.

'Happen that is so, mun,' she said, 'for I see it still writ upon his face an' not on yours. Neither did he tell me, yet it was all over the county of Durham and had entered this house before ever the master did. If you do not tell the mistress, sir, happen she will come by some ill report, an' not God's truth neither.'

Then Nathaniel said he would tell me in the presence of the Reverend Tregowan and Mrs Tregowan in the afternoon, and hearing that Cecilia was somewhat pacified.

So at two hours after mid-day Mr and Mrs Tregowan were shown into the drawing room by Cecilia, Mr Tregowan looking somewhat restored to himself after his journey down Blennowe crag the day before.

'Mrs Chark, my dear, I would wish that we were gathered together to discuss the work of Miss Austen,' he said, 'but we are not, though I may tell you while we are waiting for your husband that Barbara is now pursuing the fortunes of Pamela, is that not so, Barbara?'

'And trusting life deals with Pamela more gently than with poor Clarissa,' said Mrs Tregowan. 'Where is Nathaniel, my dear Claribell?'

'I do not know,' I said. 'This is the first time I have known him to be late.'

'Perhaps we should ask Bertie-mun to go out and look for him in case anything is amiss,' said Mrs Tregowan. 'Claribell, you have gone quite white. What is it, darling?'

Then I told Mrs Tregowan, as if Cecilia had not already done so, that Nathaniel came home after midnight deeply troubled, but that he came back to himself a little, though not greatly, with the light of the new day.

'Ah, the rosy-fingered dawn,' said Mr Tregowan. 'Tell me, Clara, is that from antiquity or from the bard?' Which talk, as I understood, was to divert my mind, for Mrs Tregowan had already left the room in search of Bertie-mun.

'I believe Mr Shakespeare may have borrowed it, Mr Tregowan,' I said.

'Yes, indeed. Beg, steal or borrow,' he said. 'The masters did not regard such theft as an infringement of the moral law. Rather, the theft of an idea was considered a compliment, was it not?'

'It was, Patrick,' said Mrs Tregowan, who was just then back in the room, 'and Mr Handel freely borrowed from his own works, which supposes him to have been given to self-congratulation, but I believe he was a man of humility, though I am not sure, but I do know him to have been much given to acts of charity. Ah, Nathaniel, my dear, we were beginning to despair of you. I must tell Bertie-mun you are found.'

'There is no need, Barbara,' said my husband. 'I have seen Bertie-mun.'

'And why are you late, dear?' said Mrs Tregowan.

'I was waylaid by Jack Walsh,' said Nathaniel. 'Please forgive me. We must now to the matter in hand.'

'With respect, Nathaniel, my dear,' said Mrs Tregowan, 'this is not Shackleton mine, that we must discuss "the matter in hand". You are here to talk to your darling wife, not to your viewer and overman, however worthy they may be.'

'Forgive me, darling,' Nathaniel said, taking my hand. 'I will leave the matter to you, Patrick, if I may. My darling wife sat with me in the scullery all night. I was in a place of darkness, and consequently I am good for nothing this morning.'

'Your darling wife fell asleep, Nathaniel,' I said.

'There is many a good soul who has fallen asleep on the night watch, dear Mrs Chark,' said Mr Tregowan. 'You need look no farther than the Garden of Gethsemane. I will say as gently as I am able what I must say, and may the sweet Lord help me. On the day just gone we were gathered together to commit to the Lord the soul of one of our brethren who was discovered at the foot of Blennowe crag. We believe the mortal remains to have been those of our brother Charles Spence, though we do not know for certain, and the matter now rests with the justice and the established church of Durham.

'After the committal we were given accommodation at the hostelry, and although I am a dissenter and do not hold with the consumption of strong liquor I have nothing but gratitude towards the innkeeper and his good lady, for the Lord sets his goodness in unlikely temples. And while we were there, I being in a room apart on account of an attack of vertigo, and my wife and Nathaniel with me, the good innkeeper, having been alerted by Mr Daunt and Mr Carson, bid us search the garret respecting the possible presence of a missing person. We found that person there, dear Mrs Chark, gone to the Lord and in his safe keeping regardless of the manner of his leaving this world. Then Mr Priest and Mr Tull were summoned, and together we brought down the mortal remains of our brother in Christ, Brim Salter, who had been the instrument of his own demise. And, for the reason that I am of the dissenting ministry and thus debarred from public duty, it has fallen to my friend Nathaniel to see to the summoning of the justice, and to inform those in authority in the established church at Durham. That is all, my dear Clara, and I see from your sweet face that you have heard all this with fortitude and grace, may the Lord bless you.'

Then I told Mr Tregowan how, having recently come back to the house one day not three weeks gone, though I could not remember when exactly, the doorbell rang and I answered it, finding there Mr Salter, sober and in his right mind, who said he had come to ask my forgiveness and bid me farewell for he was going away. Though I did not say that other, which I have not yet said, even in these pages, that after he had left I felt a great weight gone from my soul, which, rather than lifting my spirit, overwhelmed me with darkness, for a reason I did not then know. But, although I did not say it, my face must have said it as surely as if my voice had done so, and suddenly Cecilia and Willow were in the drawing room with a preparation from the apothecary cupboard.

And I remembered no more until I heard Cecilia, with a sharp scolding voice, ushering Nathaniel into the room, who, once she had gone, gathered me in his arms and stroked my hair until I had finished with my weeping.

'See, I come with gifts,' he said presently. 'From Willow a preparation of thyme, and from our dear friend Patrick a preparation of Mr Bunyan to cheer your soul, when you have summoned up the strength for such cheer, for he means well.'

'Did we say our thanks to Mr Tregowan?' I said.

'Yes, we did, darling,' said Nathaniel, 'though he would have none of it.'

'And did we give them refreshment?'

'Yes, we did, darling, though none had a taste for it.'

'Have they gone home?'

'Yes, darling.'

'Did I wish them farewell?'

'No, you did not, my darling, for you will be seeing them again.'

So saying, my husband took up my wrap which was lying on a chair and led me out into the garden, to the place where we had seen the blackbird feeding her young. 'They have flown now, darling,' he said.

'I saw them go,' I said. 'Bertie-mun was standing here one day as if in a state of catatonia, yet he was not absent from himself but was watching the fledglings one by one stand on the edge of the nest and topple down to earth.'

'I was late because Jack Walsh would have me go in and see Felicity,' Nathaniel said presently, though I had not asked the question. 'Poor Felicity ...' he hesitated, '... appears to be in a place apart from herself, yet not in the sense that she did not speak, for she did. She wished me farewell, darling. I believe the coughing malady has left her, which I feared was a consumption of the lungs for I have seen many go that way in Shackleton. She was wandering in her mind, darling, and although Jack said she had been asking for me, yet when I went in she thought I was someone other and not the untoward fellow that I am.'

And I understood from Nathaniel's words that Felicity had said those things to him which her goodness prevented her from saying in life, but which she could now say, being, as she surely thought, near the end of her journey; and I knew also that my husband understood the same, though he would not speak of such matters to me.

'It is not uncommon for a cough to leave a sufferer,' he continued, 'for the Lord is merciful, and I believe that all who pass out of this world do so in peace at the last moment.' Then he went on to talk of his father, who had passed away on just such a day of sun and new leaf, and the hawthorn on the hedge and bluebells round the bole of the sycamore; until we came again to the back door of the house.

And I resolved to go with Mrs Tregowan to see Felicity the next day, but let her know nothing of what had been said in the garden; certain that my husband and I would carry her secret to our graves, saying nothing of it to each other or to any living soul. For though the Lord is merciful in all matters, the world is not, and a passion smouldering in her heart would be remembered long after her sweet and blameless life had been forgotten.

"Gone While My Back Was Turned"

Yet I did not so much as pass the time of day with Felicity again, or ask her how she fared. For, hearing the sound of footsteps outside as night was gathering I went down, thinking it was Nathaniel. But I found there Bertie-mun, summoned as I was by a presence in the garden, which we discovered to be that of Mr Walsh, who had not rung the bell, but was wandering around in the expectation that he might be discovered.

"'Tis Felicity, Mrs Chark,' he said. 'An if Bertie-mun cares to attend also, ye are welcome, sir.'

So Bertie-mun and I set off, following Jack Walsh down the hill and across the Wear, where some women gathered on the bridge stood back for us, such was our haste. And I do not know why the thought came to me that they were those whom Mrs Tregowan called her "girls", except that I had a sudden wish for the company of Mrs Tregowan, for whom no happening on earth brings confusion, even though she has always misplaced my name. But she was not there, and there was nothing to be done but to follow Mr Walsh to the Lower Culvert, where we saw, from far off, that the windows were lit and figures were moving around inside the house.

Then Jack Walsh went to the room where Felicity lay, leaving the door open, so that we heard his great howl of grief, which, desolate though it was, did not last long for he was immediately in our company again.

'She was allus an' awkward one,' he said, 'an' she is gone while my back was turned.'

And we went in, Bertie-mun and I, finding there two holy sisters from the house of Sainte Agathe, as well as Julia Beech; and Felicity lying as if she were asleep, with her face washed and her light hair, which had hardly begun to show threads of silver, spread on the pillow round her head. And the little bairn was in his cradle, sleeping as peacefully as Felicity, but that one slept the sleep of this world and the other the sleep of eternity.

'Mistress Felicity begged me bring in the little bairn so that she might see him, mun,' said Julia Beech, 'which I said I would do presently for her sake, an' I returned to find her with a flux of the lungs an' already journeying out of this world. All o' which passed while Mr Walsh were out and about, mun.'

Then Jack Walsh came into the room, saying that he would keep the night vigil, being the last thing he could do for Felicity, having done little enough for her in her life.

'For she an' me didna share a meeting o' minds, may the Lord forgive me,' he added. And he asked if the holy sisters might stay with him, begging Julia Beech to take herself to her rest since she had watched over Felicity for many a night, and watched over the little bairn also. And, drawing me aside, he said that had Felicity not fallen on Blennowe crag she would still be alive in this world, for the coughing malady had passed, and that he who set the trip wire would likely face the charge of having deprived his sister of her life.

'An' what do you think, Mrs Chark? Is it manslaughter?' he said. 'Or happen I do you an' injustice in asking for your opinion at this present time. But mark my word, such as it is, for I have said many a rough word in my time, an' Felicity none, and she has been taken an I am spared. Mark my word, Mrs Chark, it will not rest here.'

Then I offered the condolences of my husband and myself, and also of our household, after which Jack Walsh wept a little and returned to the room where Felicity lay to keep the night watch. And Bertie-mun, speaking at greater length and with greater clarity than is his habit, and expressing an opinion, which also he is seldom heard to do, said that we would leave informing the master until the morning, for nothing could be done in the hours of darkness but pray for the sweet soul of Mistress Walsh.

Which tomorrow is this day, the twenty-seventh of May, in the year of our Lord 1812, and I awoke thinking I had not slept for the vision of Felicity was still with me, and the vision of her brother also keeping the night watch, although the sun would long ago have put out the light of the candles by Felicity's bed. Nor did I know what time it was, for all was quiet in the house, and it came to me that Nathaniel had already gone down to Shackleton, and that Cecilia, Willow and Bertie-mun were abroad in Durham, it being Wednesday.

And I was still casting about in my mind, wondering what the time was, when I drew back the curtains and saw Jack Walsh in the garden, as if by being there he would cancel the hours since his last presence and return to the day before, when Felicity was still alive in the

267

world. Even as I noticed him, I saw Bertie-mun and Cecilia also in the garden making as if to persuade him to come inside, and I knew that it would not be long before Cecilia was at my door.

'Begging your pardon, mun,' she said, 'for it is yet early, but Mr Walsh is in the drawing room an I know not what to do wi' him if you'll pardon my expression.'

'What hour is it, Cecilia?'

'It is early, mun, an' I like not to trouble the master neither, but I know not what to do wi' Mr Walsh for he is ever a contrary gentleman, yet not so much wi' you, mun. An I know not neither how sweet Mistress Walsh puts up wi' him.' From which I gathered that Cecilia did not know that Felicity was no longer alive, and that Bertie-mun had said last night the total of words at his disposal, having no more to say, even to Cecilia.

'Would you please call the master, Cecilia?' I said.

'If you say, mun, but you would be the better wi' Mr Walsh, saving your honour. He is seated in the drawing room, an' before you ask, for I know you are going to ask, he has been offered tea, an he says he has been partaking of tea all night, for he is ever contrary. It is nigh on six hours into the day, to answer your question, mun. I will bring you a jug of water.'

When I went into the drawing room there were already present Nathaniel and Bertie-mun, sitting in silence with Jack Walsh, all of whom rose to their feet when I entered.

''Tis not many hours since we were last in conversation, Mrs Chark,' said Jack Walsh. Nathaniel raised his eyebrow. 'I han not told your husband,' he added. 'Happen it were to come better from you for I am but a poor historian.'

So I related how I had heard footsteps in the garden late in the evening, thinking that Nathaniel had gone down but finding instead Bertie-mun, also summoned by the sound of footsteps, which were those of Mr Walsh who had come to tell us of poor Felicity's plight. Yet when we reached her dwelling she had already left this world, and good Julia Beech, as well as the two holy sisters from the house of Sainte Agathe, were in attendance upon her. Knowing as well, for all that he would not have me for ever asking his permission in what I do, my husband would have wished to be there also. Yet he did not look at me, but instead extended his hand to Jack Walsh, who wept a little, being much reduced by grief.

'I were a gruff fellow to her, Nat,' he said, 'an' we never did enjoy a meeting o' minds, so to speak, for she did so aggravate me wi' her incessant cough, begging your pardon, Mrs Chark.'

'Jack, my friend,' said Nathaniel, 'pray comfort yourself. The Lord looks not upon appearances but upon the heart within, and there was many a time Felicity said likewise. She knew you meant well by her.' To which comment Mr Walsh had no answer, and fell silent for a while.

'I have something to say in your presence, sir,' he continued by and by, 'for I ha' told Mrs Chark an' I think she has not told you, for ye knew not about tother. It come to me that Felicity would not ha' met her end had she not fallen on yon Blennowe crag, an' neither would she ha' fallen but for trip wire, for 'tis all ovver county of Durham that trip wire were laid on the Blennowe path for them as were coming out to search after Mr Spence. Not that I have aught against them gentlemen for it were none o' their doing. 'Tis merely to say that Felicity Walsh came up to trip wire in her innocence an' ha' forfeited her life on account of it. An' my proposal is, for I am near finished, that he who laid trip wire should be held accountable for Felicity's passing, for 'tis known, an' I need not say how 'tis known, that she suffered a concussion to the brain, for she were awandering all ovver in her mind. 'Tis me done, sirs. Mrs Chark, thanking ye.'

'And how do you suppose the matter is set in hand, Jack?' said Nathaniel, who indeed looked no less grief stricken than Jack Walsh, for he had always blamed himself, and here was poor Felicity's brother placing before him his own fault. 'I lay the whole to my charge, Jack, my dear fellow,' he continued, 'and I mind not to say so. No doubt it is all over Durham that the wire was laid for the master of Shackleton, which you liked not to say, Jack.'

'Saving your honour, sir,' said Cecilia, who had just then entered with a trolley of tea, ''tis no more your doing than the doing of the man in the moon, an' I trust Mr Walsh will agree.'

'I were not laying the charge at thy door, Nat,' said Jack Walsh. 'An' in answer to thy question, I propose we lodge the matter with the justice, an' that to do post haste before Felicity is laid to rest. 'Tis a fellow o' the name o' Morfew, sir. An' there be one other matter, namely that 'tis not meet for me to dwell in my house wi' a married woman an' a bairn, if you take my meaning, sir. An I see before me in this room the kindred in Christ o' the bairn, being yourself, sir, an' your good lady wife, an' your good man Bertie-mun. What's to do about that, may I ask, sir?'

Then my husband went over to the desk and took from the drawer three pages of foolscap, saying that the kindred in Christ of the bairn Moses should meet together with Jack Walsh in the same place on the next morning, with their three opinions arrived at independently and in private, to be placed in writing before him so that he himself might have the final opinion, which was only right, as his sister Felicity had of her goodness taken the bairn in.

'And if you will first take refreshment, Jack, we will seek out the justice,' Nathaniel said.

'Mr Walsh, I will with your leave tell Mrs Tregowan,' I said.

'Happen she has heard, Mrs Chark, but that would be good o' you,' he said.

I went out then with my husband and Mr Walsh as they were going that way in order to see the justice, and found Mr and Mrs Tregowan at home, having heard nothing, for those who lived near the dwelling of Felicity and Jack Walsh were accustomed to seeing the rooms lit up at night.

'Jack and Felicity were ever wanderers, my dear Claribell,' Mrs Tregowan said, 'and it was always one or another of them who would be pacing the house or the garden when all good folks are abed. And, may the Lord forgive me, though I speak the truth, it was when there had been a difference of opinion and the one could not abide the presence of the other.'

After saying which, Mrs Tregowan searched for a handkerchief up her sleeve, and not finding one, dried her eyes with her skirt while I was still looking in my reticule for a handkerchief of my own. 'Thank you, my dear Claribell,' she said. 'You will not hear this next, and I may tell you while Mr Tregowan is occupied with his sermon, that dear Felicity confided in him, both that she had known of the trip wire, and knowing it was

271

there, ran deliberately into it for she was aware that her pilgrimage in this world was nearing its end and she wished not to have the end that sufferers of the consumption have. But Patrick believes that she was even then wandering in her mind, and is neither believing nor disbelieving dear Felicity's words, but has placed the whole matter with the Lord, which is always the best thing to do. And Claribell, my dear, it is likely that Felicity said the same to Nathaniel, yet he will not tell it abroad, for any soul in the county of Durham may go to Nathaniel Chark with their secrets, which will remain secret. Now, my dear, tell me about poor Felicity.'

So I told Mrs Tregowan how Mr Walsh had been found by Bertie-mun in the garden and that we had gone down with him to his house, finding when we reached there that Felicity had already passed away into the next world; and how, at the last, she had asked Mrs Beech to let her see the little bairn Moses once more, but even as Mrs Beech was fetching him, for she did not do so immediately, being much occupied with her household duties, Felicity suffered a flux of the lungs and quietly slipped away.

'Do not weep, my dear Claribell,' said Mrs Tregowan, though I did not know I was weeping. 'We must look to poor Julia, for she will take it upon herself that dear Felicity did not see the little bairn at the last; yet Julia Beech had been watching over Felicity and the bairn for many a long day, and during the night also. Is there anything else you would like to say, darling?'

I told Mrs Tregowan what had been said by Jack Walsh, that he considered the person who laid the trip wire to be responsible for Felicity's passing, and that he wished the matter to be lodged with the justice.

'Who is James Morfew, and he is of my kindred,' Mrs Tregowan interjected. 'Anything else, my dear?'

And I told Mrs Tregowan then that Mr Walsh considered it not right for him to be in his dwelling with a married woman with a bairn, and had placed the matter before the bairn's kindred in Christ, being Nathaniel, Bertie-mun and myself. Then I told her also of Nathaniel's strategy for solving the question.

And I do not know if it was the effect of the hot sun streaming down through the high window onto me, giving me a headache, or the sorrowful events of the past days, but the thought came to me suddenly and with perfect clarity that Felicity had indeed fallen on the trip wire deliberately, not only because of her malady, but because in doing so she would save Nathaniel, even at the cost of her own life, which was likely to be but a short one. And as soon as the thought came to me I tried to banish it. Yet the more I tried to smother it, the more it sprang to life again, like some malign spirit hovering over me.

And I knew no more until I came to myself, not seated on a chair as I had been, but lying on Mrs Tregowan's sofa, and my husband's voice, as it seemed from far above me, saying, as I thought, 'There is no magician, Barbara.' Which he then repeated, 'There is no physician, Barbara.'

'She is awake, Nathaniel, my dear,' Mrs Tregowan then said. 'See, Claribell, we have magicked up your husband. Do you hear me, darling? She is not hearing us, Nathaniel, my dear, and the only one I know hereabouts who keeps a carriage and may take her home is James Morfew who is my kinsman, and I wish not to plead with him. I will go and ask Patrick what to do for the best, dear.'

273

Nathaniel sat on the sofa and took my hand, saying, 'Wake up, darling,' and looking into my eyes as if he could also read the thought I had had, which was still with me.

'She can't be going, can she, dear Nathaniel?' Mrs Tregowan's voice was in the room again. 'Heaven forbid that she is going, so soon after poor Felicity.' And I saw the expression in my husband's eyes turn from perplexity to dread, though I could say nothing.

'I cannot let her go,' he said. 'She is my life.'

Then Mr Tregowan's voice was in the room also, and I saw his careworn face as he stood at the end of the sofa.

'Clara, pray come back to us,' he said, 'for you have yet much to do with this world,' after which he was gone, as I thought to the scullery for a cup of water, for I heard the door open and close and his footsteps presently return.

'She is still with us, thank God,' said Nathaniel. 'I feel the grip in her hand. Pray speak to us, darling.'

'Will you take a sip of water, Claribell, my dear?' said Mrs Tregowan, to which I must have answered, yes, for Mrs Tregowan said, 'Thank God, she's back. We were worried about you, my dear, just for a minute,' she continued. 'Has Claribell broken her fast this morning, Nathaniel, my dear?'

'Cecilia brought in refreshment while Jack Walsh was with us, though none had the taste for it,' said Nathaniel.

'That will be it,' said Mrs Tregowan, then whispered in my ear some homely words, and I saw a frown flicker across Nathaniel's brow and his complexion darken, for he knew well enough that Mrs Tregowan was talking of women's matters, though he could not have heard her words. 'See, I have brought a smile to her sweet face, though I know not why,' said Mrs Tregowan. 'So you have lodged the matter with the justice, Nathaniel. What does he have to say?'

'That he will grant us a hearing, Barbara.'

'And when may that be, dear? For I fear I will not be at liberty to attend.'

'It will be at a time when you are at liberty to attend, Barbara,' said Nathaniel. 'We are all of us witnesses, and we are obliged to attend whether we wish to or no.'

'Of course, my dear,' said Mrs Tregowan, 'only that Mr Morfew is my kinsman, you know, though not of the branch that are landlords of Shackleton.'

'We will see to it that no insolence is offered to you, Barbara,' said my husband.

'I believe dear Cecilia is right when she tells me you are an obdurate gentleman, my dear,' said Mrs Tregowan. 'Patrick and I may attend, if it pleases Mr Morfew, on Friday next, only so long as Mr Morfew is prepared for our advent, and we do not have to read any untoward expression writ on his face.'

Then Mr Tregowan brought in tea and a currant loaf, for they keep no maid, and proceeded to slice and butter the loaf and pour out the tea, which I would readily have done myself, being somewhat recovered, but was not allowed to.

And by and by I came back to myself, and Mr Tregowan took me out to show me the kitchen garden, saying that as the spring was coming to the garden so also with dear Felicity, that she was in the spring of her eternal life, and, moreover, none need think her to be gone from this world for her good deeds would live for ever in the hearts of those who loved her.

Then Mr Tregowan showed me the pond, where a brown duck swam with her bairns, and, taking one in his hand, he showed me its tiny wings and feet, until its mother called for it to be put back.

Ependently and Unknown
to Each Other

"'Tis Mr Walsh, mun,' said Cecilia. 'He paces the garden like a lost soul and I know not what to do wi' him, for he will neither come in nor go away. Happen he may listen to you, mun.' So I went down and found Jack Walsh inspecting Bertie-mun's turnips.

"'Tis like to be a good year for un, Mrs Chark,' he said. 'I know I am come betimes but it sore troubles me to rest in the house where Felicity lies, though she be in her casket. We never did share a meeting o' minds, Mrs Chark, may the Lord forgive me.'

I invited Mr Walsh to come into the drawing room, saying that the occasion for which he was present, that of deciding the future of the little bairn Moses, might be brought forward since my husband and Bertie-mun were both at home.

'Thanking ye, Mrs Chark,' Jack Walsh said, 'for I like not to be in the dwellinghouse wi' a married woman wi' a bairn in tow, though heaven help me when they have gone and the women from Sainte Agathe also, for I shall be there wi' not a soul to bide wi' me.'

'We must needs think of that eventuality, Jack, my dear man,' said Nathaniel, who was now also in the garden. 'If you will, sir, we may look to the matter in hand without delay, for we have all of us written down our opinions, and we none of us knows what the others have written. Cecilia has gone to find Bertie-mun.'

'Thank you, Nat,' said Jack Walsh. 'I heard you were taken badly yesterday, Mrs Chark, an' I trust you are recovered.' Which I assured Mr Walsh that I was, for he wished to hear that, though the thought I had had still hung over me, like a dark curtain waiting to be drawn across my soul. 'I am pleased to hear that, Mrs Chark,' Jack Walsh said. 'You will have a fine crop here come July,' he added, nudging the soft black earth with the toe of his boot.'

For now he had been invited inside, Mr Walsh, in spite of his early arrival, seemed in no way anxious to go into the drawing room, and would willingly have continued his inspection of Bertie-mun's planting.

'Bertie-mun is in the drawing room, sir,' said Cecilia, who was now also in the garden.

'Then we should go there also, Jack,' Nathaniel said.

'There is a message from the justice, sir,' said Cecilia. And I did not know whether there was or not, but Cecilia's words prompted Jack Walsh to go inside and take his place at the table.

'Jack, we have each of us, my dear wife Clara, and Bertie-mun, and myself, being kindred in Christ to the bairn Moses, written down our opinions independently and unknown to each other on the folded pages you see before you,' Nathaniel said when all were seated. 'Pray, when you are ready, read them and ponder in the silence of your heart what each says, then, if you will, speak your mind, and may the Lord guide us in the right path.'

To which Bertie-mun alone answered , 'Amen'; and all of us sat with our eyes on Mr Walsh as he unfolded and read the papers one by one, taking each one up a second time and a third time, and reading again. Then he folded each one up again and placed them in front of him on the table as he had found them.

'Darling, I fear the sun is in your eyes,' said Nathaniel presently, getting up from his chair and going over to the window to pull the curtains across, and no doubt thinking some movement in the room might draw Mr Walsh towards a conclusion.

Yet we continued to sit there silently until the clock chimed the hour. Jack Walsh looked up. 'Dammee if they aren't the very same,' he said. 'All o' them.'

'And what do you understand from the words written there, Jack?' said Nathaniel.

'That yon bairn goes wi' Mrs Beech to her own dwellinghouse until such time as any kindred, if there be any, lay claim to him. An' if I'm not o' the same mind, Nat, what then?' Mr Walsh said.

'You are not of the same mind, Jack?' said Nathaniel. Mr Walsh took up the three papers and read them again.

'Aye,' he said presently. ''Tis for the best. The bairn goes wi' Mrs Beech. 'Tis for the best, Nat, 'tis for the best that the little bairn goes wi' Mistress Beech.' And he wept a little but not for long. 'Forgive me, Mrs Chark. I am not myself. For 'tis best done in the event I have second thoughts. Happen I were rare fond o' the little fellow.'

Then we went down with Jack Walsh to his house, Nathaniel, Bertie-mun and myself, to tell Julia Beech, finding her occupied with the flat iron in the scullery and the little bairn beside her in his cradle.

279

'Mrs Beech, we would ha' thy company,' said Jack Walsh. 'Mind ye not the flat iron, for 'twill wait for thee. Sit thee down.'

And we sat all of us at the scullery table and told Julia Beech the opinions of the bairn's kindred in Christ, namely Bertie-mun, Nathaniel and myself, watching as we did so a light brighten her eyes and a sweet smile come upon her face.

'An' thy rightfully wedded husband, what d'ye reckon he will say?' continued Jack Walsh. 'For happen we must be right wi' Mr Beech, being they husband.'

'Yes, Mr Walsh,' said Julia Beech.

'But what d'ye reckon he will say?' said Jack Walsh again.

'I will beg ye to write him a letter,' said Julia Beech eventually. Jack Walsh looked at my husband.

'Nat, you have a fair hand,' he said. 'Leastways, one o' these scripts is passing fair.'

'The fair hand is not mine,' said Nathaniel. 'It belongs to Bertie-mun. But to my mind a woman may write of such matters with a grace lacking in us fellows. What think you, Bertie-mun?' To which Bertie-mun agreed, for he could do no other. 'If you will write the letter, darling, we shall all of us add our names,' Nathaniel said.

So Jack Walsh went out for paper and ink, and I wrote a letter to Colin Beech, telling him of the decision of the kindred in Christ of the little bairn Moses, noticing that as I did so Bertie-mun could scarcely take his eyes from the little one, coaxing from him a tiny smile, which Julia Beech noticed also and said that the kindred in Christ of the little bairn would be welcome to see him at any time if they minded not to come into a Shackleton homestead.

'My husband will read it to me, mun,' she said as I handed her the letter to look over. 'He is a fair scholar, an' though I read I do not so well as he, for all that he tries to school me.'

'Then happen Mr Bertie-mun will go to thy dwelling an' summon Mr Beech here at a time o' his own choosing,' said Jack Walsh.

After which we took our leave, finding when we arrived home Mr Daunt and Mr Carson at our gate, seated on the ground with their backs against the railings, who, struggling to their feet, said they had heard about poor Mistress Walsh, and had somewhat to say to the master.

'You may do so in my wife's hearing,' said Nathaniel. 'Mr Daunt?'

'We be witnesses to the fact, sir,' he said.

'Mr Carson?'

'That is so, sir.'

Then Nathaniel told them of the hearing before the justice on the following day, being the twenty-ninth day of May, neither dismissing them nor encouraging them to linger for they had strong liquor about them.

'It is long since we talked,' said Nathaniel when we were indoors and had taken off our hats and coats. Then, taking my face between his hands, he said, 'You are lovely today, darling.'

'And you, sir,' I said.

'But you are not well, my darling,' he said.

'We none of us are well, Nathaniel,' I said.

'That is true, darling,' he said. 'We all of us feel this grief like a sickness of the soul, and I do not know what will be the end of it, for there is far to travel yet.'

'Mr Tregowan showed me the pond and the brown duck with her bairns,' I said. 'And he picked up a little one and showed me its tiny feet and wings, for he wished to show me that there is life still on earth as well as life in heaven.'

Then at the thought of the tiny innocent bairn with its bright eyes and tiny wings and feet I began to weep and could not stop, for all that Nathaniel held me in his arms and stroked my hair and tried to brush away my tears. Until he himself caught my affliction and we were both of us thus when Willow entered the drawing room, not knowing we were there, for she has no hearing. And she went out, presently to return with preparations from the apothecary cupboard, which we took as if we were both her bairns, while she waited until she saw that we were recovered.

'Willow, my dear, you have saved us,' Nathaniel said, 'for we might well have been here until nightfall, and I have to go down to Shackleton.'

Which place, with its dark pits and black soots and perpetual smoke and poisons, seemed to me all of a sudden the most comforting place, offering a haven when everything above ground was mystery and pain.

Then Nathaniel, before he went to Shackleton, told Willow about the hearing before the justice Mr Morfew in the morning, asking her attendance, for she had been present with Felicity at various times during her illness. I do not know if Willow understood or not, yet her eyes widened and she nodded as she looked up at my husband.

Knowing in Few Matters
and Ignorant in Many

'She will need to tell me her name, Mr Chark,' said Mr
Morfew.

'She has no speech or hearing, sir,' said Nathaniel,
'but you may address her if you look into her face.'

'Is she a defective, Mr Chark?' Mr Morfew said
then, leaning over the desk and peering down at Willow
who was dissolved in merriment.

'No, she is not a defective, sir,' said Nathaniel. 'She
is as we all are on this life's pilgrimage, knowing in few
matters and ignorant in many.'

'Saving your presence, sir,' then said Cecilia, rising
to her feet and clasping her hands in front of her as if she
were at Sunday service, 'but happen it is what you wear
upon your head, pardoning my plain speech, sir, for she
wouldna make light o' the solemn occasion, sir.'

Then Mr Morfew lifted from his head his periwig
and placed it on the desk before him, where it lay, a
sheeplike mound surrounded by rows of curls; which
gesture was too much for poor Willow, who then
laughed openly and could not stop, until Mr Morfew
rose to his feet and suggested an adjournment for the
space of half an hour, after which term the hearing

would assemble once more, only provided that Mr Chark's maidservant had composed herself.

And we were all of us gathered in the outer chamber, being Mr Walsh, Mr Daunt and Mr Carson, Mr and Mrs Tregowan, Mrs Beech, Mr Priest, Cecilia, Willow, Bertie-mun, Nathaniel, the clerk to the court, and myself; two holy sisters from the house of Sainte Agathe being excused on account of their calling, and a further person, unnamed, having passed away from this world. By which time Willow's laughter had fled and she sat next to my husband holding his hand in a state of tearful contrition, while Mr Daunt and Mr Carson talked between themselves.

'You will need to tell me your name, my dear,' said Mr Morfew leaning over the desk and looking down at Willow again, the periwig having been removed from sight.

'Marion Wellow, sir,' said Willow.

'What did she say, Mr Chark?' said Mr Morfew, for poor Willow's speech was hardly recognisable as such.

'Saving your honour, sir,' said Cecilia, rising to her feet and standing in the same prayerful attitude as before, 'I be her kinswoman, an' her name is Marion Wellow.'

'You will please to inform your servants that they are not to speak until requested to do so, Mr Chark,' said Mr Morfew, then to Cecilia, 'Thank you, my dear.'

'Marion Wellow?' said Mr Morfew, leaning over the desk and peering again at Willow, whose eyes were still on his head, where his hair, which was red and wiry, much like Mrs Tregowan's, had sprung into being once he removed his periwig.

''Tis like to last out a night in Russia when nights are longest there,' said Mr Daunt under his breath, though loud enough that all might hear; whereupon Mr Morfew tapped on the desk with his gavel and looked at Mr Daunt.

'Then we will begin, if the learned gentleman has done with Mr Shakespeare.' 'Your name is Marion Wellow, my dear?' he continued presently, to which Willow nodded.

'I would now beg all of those others present to state their names,' he went on, coming last to Mr Walsh. 'And you have called this hearing, sir? Pray state your case. I would that you step up to the desk so that you may stand facing Miss Wellow, sir.' Whereupon Mr Walsh rose from his seat and went to the desk, taking from his inner pocket an unfolded sheet of foolscap.

''Tis here, sir,' he said.

'Then pray read it, my good man,' said Mr Morfew.

'I be no scholar wi' words,' said Jack Walsh. ''Twas ever figures were my skill.'

'It is of no matter that you are not a scholar with words, sir,' said Mr Morfew. 'You are among friends, my good man.'

''Tis this, sir,' said Jack Walsh, folding the paper and returning it to his pocket. ''Twere my sister Felicity Walsh as died, sir.'

'Indeed,' said Mr Morfew, 'and you have my sincere condolences.'

'Thank you, sir,' said Jack Walsh. 'She had the coughing malady ...'

'Consumption, otherwise phthisis?' said Mr Morfew.

'I know not, sir, but she gone fell over trip wire on yon Blennowe path. An after that, sir, her mind went awandering, not that she was not ever one wi' a wandering mind, sir, an' the coughing malady, it ceased. Therefore 'tis my contention that he who laid yon trip

285

wire did cause the demise of my late sister Felicity Walsh.'

'There are here two different matters,' said Mr Morfew, 'one being that a trip wire was laid and the other being the cause of the demise of our dear sister, Felicity.'

'If you say so, sir,' said Jack Walsh, 'yet I contend 'twere trip wire, for the coughing malady had left her.'

'You may stand down, Mr Walsh,' said Mr Morfew. 'Mr Daunt and Mr Carson, if you please, gentlemen. Since you appear to be concerned about time, we may dispose of your evidence as soon as may be and give you your leave. You saw the trip wire being laid, gentlemen?'

'We did, sir,' said Mr Daunt.

'Kindly use the first person singular, Mr Daunt, that being the word "I", and let the other witness answer for himself.'

'I did likewise, sir,' said Mr Carson, 'being that I saw the trip wire being set, sir, though I knew not rightly the implications of the same, sir, else I should have likely apprehended the fellow.'

'And you knew by sight he who laid the trip wire?'

'We did, sir.'

'One at a time, gentlemen, if you please.'

'I did, sir.'

'And I also, sir.'

'Gentlemen, you will see on the table in front of you pen and paper. Kindly write down the name of the person you believe set the trip wire. Fold your papers and pass them forwards. We wish not to incriminate a fellow untimely by casting his name abroad for all to hear. Do these gentlemen write, does anyone know?'

'We do, your honour,' said Ben Daunt, which plural Mr Morfew appeared to overlook, and dismissed Mr Daunt and Mr Carson when they had done writing.

'Herbert Tull, please, stand forth, my good man. Pray tell us what you know.' Bertie-mun spoke with difficulty, but looked Mr Morfew in the eye, as if it were he who had no hearing.

'I removed trip wire,' he said, and stood down.

'Mr Chark,' said Mr Morfew, 'it appears that you give employ to personages with limitations. Pray get your man to write down his testimony. Does he write?'

'He does so, with a fairer hand than mine or thine, sir,' said Nathaniel. 'Bertie-mun, if you would please write down your testimony for Mr Morfew.'

Then my husband was called forth, for he was already on his feet, and told in few words of the search for Charles Spence on the Blennowe path in the company of Mr Priest and one other person who had since passed out of this world, which search party was later joined by Mr Tull; and of finding, on the path and approaching at a distance, his wife in the company of Mrs Tregowan and Mistress Walsh, the latter of whom ran forwards and tripped over the wire.

'You may stand down, Mr Chark,' said Mr Morfew. 'Would someone kindly hand Mr Chark a draught of water. We want no more folks passing out of this world than we have already. Thank you, Mr Tull. Mr Priest, have you anything to add to Mr Chark's testimony?'

''Tis supposed yon trip wire were laid for Mr Chark, sir,' said Mr Priest. Mr Morfew leaned over the desk.

'Supposed, my good man?'

'Aye, sir,' said Mr Priest. 'Supposed.'

'And who supposed, do you suppose?' said Mr Morfew.

'If I may unravel your riddles, sir, I would say Mistress Walsh, for she ran forrard to warn the search party. An' moreover 'tis well known in these parts tha' certain folks ha' gripes wi' Mr Chark on account of mine an' conditions o' labour an' pay, sir, though for mysen I mus' say tha' Nathaniel Chark is as good a man as any an' better than most.'

'And how would Mistress Walsh have been privy to these ill intentions towards Mr Chark, do you suppose?' said Mr Morfew.

'I know not how, sir,' said Mr Priest.

'You may stand down, Mr Priest,' said Mr Morfew. 'Mr Chark, bear up, my good man. Do you know anything of these ill intentions, do you suppose? I will ask you to write down the name of they you suppose to be responsible for the laying of the trip wire and pass it forwards, for the question of intent to take life is beyond the remit of this hearing.' Whereupon Mr Walsh was on his feet.

'Saving your honour, sir, but 'tis for this precise purpose I han referred matter to you, sir,' he said.

'A matter of the wilful taking of life is heard in a higher court, Mr Walsh,' said Mr Morfew. 'We are gathered here today to see if the testimonies of these good people are sufficient to have the matter proceed. Thank you, Mr Chark,' he added, for my husband had folded a paper and passed it forwards, yet I did not see that he wrote anything on it, nor did Mr Morfew unfold the paper. 'Mr Tregowan, reverend sir,' Mr Morfew continued, 'you attended Felicity Walsh when she was near her end. Did she say anything to you, sir?'

'She did,' said Mr Tregowan, 'by which I mean that we did not sit in silence, for dear Felicity was ever full of good will towards all save herself. Yet I may not say what passed, sir.'

'You may not or you will not, Mr Tregowan?' said Mr Morfew.

'I may not, sir, yet even if that were not the case I would not,' said Mr Tregowan.

'Is that so?' said Mr Morfew. 'I believe that Miss Wellow was companion to you during this converse with Mistress Walsh. If someone could convey to Miss Wellow that she is being spoken to. Thank you, Mrs Tregowan. Did you hear what passed in conversation between Felicity and the reverend gentleman, my dear? Write it down, dear, if you please. Does she read and write, Mr Chark?'

'She does, sir,' said Nathaniel. 'She has a fair hand.'

'Marion Wellow, sir,' said Willow, after which she wrote on the paper and passed it forwards. Mr Morfew scratched his head, which small gesture caused a tuft of red hair to stand up, a state of affairs which fascinated Willow greatly.

'If your servant is inclined to be merry again, Mr Chark, you had best bid someone escort her out of the chamber,' said Mr Morfew. 'Mrs Chark, you need not come forward. You saw Felicity in her illness. What did you observe of her condition?'

I told Mr Morfew that Felicity had suffered the coughing malady since I knew her, which was not half a year, and that after her fall her mind appeared to be wandering, which they said was on account of concussion to the brain.

'They said? Was that the opinion of a physician, Mrs Chark?' said Mr Morfew.

'There was no physician,' said Nathaniel.

'You may speak when you are spoken to, Mr Chark,' said Mr Morfew. 'The question was asked of Mrs Chark.'

'I do not know, sir,' I said.

'Thank you, Mrs Chark, you do not know,' said Mr Morfew. 'Mrs Tregowan, what did you observe of Felicity's condition?' he continued. 'I am sorry we have to renew our acquaintance under these mournful circumstances, Barbara. What did you observe?'

'As Mrs Chark told you, sir,' said Mrs Tregowan. 'I have nothing to add save that it pleases me to see you, James dear, for our difficulties were not according to my wishes.'

'Mrs Chark, if you please,' said Mr Morfew, 'if I might beg your attention.'

'Sir, can you not see that my wife isn't well?' said Nathaniel rising to his feet. 'She has answered already.'

'Pray compose yourself, Mr Chark,' said Mr Morfew. 'While your concern for your wife and your servants is laudable, we must to the matter in hand, sir. Mrs Chark, pray forgive me. You paid a visit to our sister Felicity and found that she had already passed out of this world. Tell the hearing about that visit, if you would, please.'

Then I told Mr Morfew how I had arrived to find Felicity laid upon her bed and her hair brushed and her face washed, looking as if she were sleeping, though she was not; and I told how I had found there also Mrs Beech, who was present in the household as nurse to the little bairn Moses, but who also nursed Felicity with great tenderness, finding also there two holy sisters from the house of Sainte Agathe.

'And pray, Mrs Chark, what did Mrs Beech say to you of the manner of Felicity's passing?'

'That she had suffered a flux of the lungs, sir,' I said.

'Which event mercifully carries many a sufferer of the consumption out of this world, though it is a sorry sight for those watching,' said Mr Morfew. 'Thanking you, Mrs Chark. Mrs Beech, pray.'

Mr Morfew leaned over the bench and peered at Julia Beech, who shrank before his inspection. 'Pray give your account, my dear,' he said.

Then Julia Beech said how Felicity had asked her to bring the bairn Moses that she might see him, and that she had been occupied with many household tasks, and arriving back in the room discovered Felicity to have suffered a flux of the lungs and passed out of this world, adding that she had seen many go that way in Shackleton. To which Mr Morfew said, 'Thanking you, my dear,' and begged Mrs Beech to be seated, for she was still on her feet with her hands clasped before as if, like Cecilia, she were at Sunday service in the dissenting chapel.

Then he opened the folded papers lying before him on the desk, and put on his periwig, at which point Mrs Tregowan leaned over and asked Willow to show her outside to the privy, for Willow's face was all merriment again to see the little curls arranged around Mr Morfew's head.

'I fear your servant does not know the gravity of the occasion, Mr Chark,' he said. 'Is she a defective?' To which my husband answered, for all that he had done so already, that Willow has no speech or hearing but is possessed of intelligence as much as any other.

And Mr Morfew said, 'Indeed?' raising one eyebrow, which facial gesture would have fascinated Willow the more, but that she was out of the chamber showing Mrs Tregowan to the privy.

And it came to me, all of a sudden, that it is Mrs Tregowan's face while she is singing which pleases Willow, rather than her voice, which she cannot hear. For I have always been mystified as to why Willow finds so diverting that which she cannot hear.

'We have here,' Mr Morfew said presently, 'certain papers on which have been written certain names. One paper has not been written upon, and one paper bears the script of the young lady who is Mr Chark's servant who did not understand what was asked of her and wrote down her own name. The other two also bear a name, which is that of one who has passed out of this world, he who is believed to have laid the trip wire.

'Therefore, ladies and gentlemen, I come to the following conclusion:

'Firstly, that while our sister Felicity Walsh, may the Lord have mercy on her soul, possibly died with,' he lay emphasis on that last word, 'the condition of concussion to the brain as a consequence of her fall on Blennowe crag, she died of, that is to say the immediate cause of her death was, a flux of the lungs, that being an end stage of the malady called consumption or phthisis.

'Secondly, we do not deny the fact of the trip wire, for Mr Tull removed it and we have here the evidence,' whereupon Mr Morfew produced the trip wire and two iron spikes from under the desk. 'We have, moreover, found caught upon this same trip wire a morsel of woollen fabric which corresponds to the cloak Miss Walsh was wearing that day.

'Ladies and gentlemen, I pronounce the cause of death to have been consumption, otherwise known as phthisis. He who laid the trip wire did so with intent to cause grievous harm, even death, not to Miss Walsh, but to certain of the search party for one Charles Spence,

292

which search party was simultaneously approaching the place in question from the opposite direction to that by which Miss Walsh, Mrs Chark and Mrs Tregowan approached that place. As I have said, he who is believed to have laid the trip wire has passed out of this world, and will be heard in the highest court a man may be heard in, namely that of heaven. It is probable that our sister Felicity knew of the trap, for the opinion is that she ran forwards to warn the search party. Felicity Walsh is not here to answer. Therefore, if all are in agreement, we will consider the case closed.

'Ladies and gentlemen, you may go in peace, for that which is done cannot be undone.'

Then Mr Morfew was gone, even as we were all of us rising to our feet; all of us but Mr Walsh, who remained seated with his head in his hands.

'Mr Tregowan, sir, ye will answer me this, being a learned man,' he said presently. 'Them as han passed out o' this world, sir, an' them as han left their misdemeanours in this world, be they not accountable in this world, sir? For yon justice, saving his presence, reckons they be not.'

'I know not, Jack, my friend,' said Mr Tregowan. 'I know not.'

At the Intersection of the Tonder and Wycliffe Roads

All night the words of Jack Walsh were in my mind and I couldn't be rid of them, being still awake when the sky began to lighten in the east and the first blackbird sang far off. Then every other bird began, until the air was full of merriment and, hearing a distant door open, I decided to go down also, expecting to find Bertie-mun out early, but finding instead my husband.

'Come, darling, I will show you a miracle,' he said, and taking me by the hand led me to the rose garden where one of the trees was covered, suddenly and early in the season, in yellow flowers. 'It did nothing last year,' Nathaniel continued. 'It was dead and now it is alive. You are lovely this morning, darling.'

'And you, sir,' I said. 'The tree is for Felicity. If Mr Tregowan were here he would say it is for eternal life.'

Nathaniel stopped, for we were walking round the rose garden. He took both my hands.

'I have begun to doubt of eternal life lately, darling,' he said. 'What will you think of me?'

'I will still think you are lovely this morning, sir,' I said.

'And tell me, darling, is there eternal life or no?' he said.

'There is eternal life, Nathaniel,' I said, not wishing to send him deeper into despair by saying anything other. And, indeed, as soon as the words were said his gloom lifted somewhat, and we continued to walk hand in hand around the garden.

'I fear Willow did not behave well yesterday, darling' he said presently. 'I do not know what there was at the hearing to divert her so much.'

'Why, Nathaniel,' I said, 'surely you realised that it was Mr Morfew's periwig.'

'Indeed, I did not,' he said, and I watched as the merriment, beginning in his eyes, spread to the whole of him, so that he was shaking with laughter yet making no sound. And thus we still were, walking around the garden, when we heard the sneck on the gate.

'Compose yourself, sir,' I said. 'It will be Mr Walsh and he cannot see us like this. I do not know if you have caught the laughter affliction from Willow, or she from you, for you are as merry as each other.' And the mirth would likely have redoubled its assault on my husband, but that Mr Walsh was there in front of us, coming through the rose garden, and much stooped and weighed down as if his pockets were full of stones.

'Begging your pardon, Mrs Chark,' he said, 'I wouldna impose on you at this early hour, for I had it in mind to bide my time in the garden.'

Then we took Mr Walsh to the yellow rose tree, and Nathaniel told him how he was about to ask Bertie-mun to dig it up as it didn't flower, yet this year it could scarcely lift its branches for flowers.

'Aye,' said Jack Walsh. 'I have oft noticed that life comes into a garden when a soul passes out of this world, an' I know not why it might be. I ha' summat to ask o' ye, Nat. For I were casting around in my mind so to speak, for a body to fulfil the task, an' it come to me that it would be Nathaniel Chark, being a fellow of understanding like. 'Tis all writ down, Nat, in the event I hadna the will to ask it of ye. 'Tis Sunday, following on from service, for Felicity would ha' wished it so. I'll bid ye good-day now, Mrs Chark.' And Mr Walsh took from his pocket a testament and gave it to Nathaniel, after which he left, taking a long time to sneck the garden gate, though it is easy enough.

'You were in the garden early, Nathaniel,' I said when Jack Walsh had left us.

'And you, darling,' he said.

'I could not sleep. I was all night thinking of what Jack Walsh said yesterday after the hearing.'

'He was full of words,' said Nathaniel. 'Which in particular?'

'He asked Mr Tregowan something about those who pass out of this world and leave their ill deeds behind. I cannot remember his exact words.'

'He asked if they are accountable, if they left this world before answering for their misdemeanours, as I understand it,' said Nathaniel. 'Patrick said he did not know.'

'The justice asked Mr Daunt and Mr Carson to write down the name of the one who had laid the trip wire.'

'He did,' said Nathaniel, 'and they wrote it down.'

'And he did not say then whose name it was. He said it was beyond the remit of the hearing. And he asked you to write down the name of the one who bore a grudge against you, and you passed forwards a blank page.'

'Let him who is without sin cast the first stone,' said Nathaniel. 'I could not write down any fellow's name, darling, which is not to say that I consider Mr Daunt and Mr Carson at fault for doing so. But I am as full of fault

296

as any man and I found it could not be done, which did not trouble Mr Morfew in the least for he considers our household to be all slow of understanding. I cannot remember his word.'

'Defective,' I said.

'A fine word,' said Nathaniel. 'I must remember it.' And the merriment sparkled briefly in his eyes then went out again. 'I could not sleep either, darling,' he said. 'And since you have told me why you could not sleep, I must also tell you why I could not.' Yet he said nothing.

'I'm coming with you, Nathaniel,' I said. He stopped, for we had resumed our walk round the garden.

'I did not say I was going anywhere, darling,' he said.

'But you are, Nathaniel, and I will come with you.'

'It is a place near Thayne at the intersection of the Tonder and Wycliffe roads,' he said presently.

'I am still coming with you, Nathaniel,' I said.

He turned me towards him and looked into my eyes, and I into his, reading there bewilderment and kindness, for even when he is sharp with Cecilia he cannot extinguish the kindness in his eyes, that being no doubt the reason she takes little heed of his admonishments.

'I can't tell you that you should not come with me, darling,' he said. 'There will be few enough, for few enough know of what is to take place. It is a matter only of furlongs if we take the path across the fields.'

Then, even as if I had conjured her up by thinking about her, Cecilia's voice was in the garden also, asking Nathaniel if he was going to break his fast or not, and scolding him for detaining me out of doors while the dew was still on the grass.

'And the mistress not having broken her fast either, sir, shame on you,' she added.

'We are taking a walk across the fields later, Cecilia, my dear,' said Nathaniel. Cecilia's eyes opened wide.

'If 'tis Thayne way, sir, the mistress ought not be going wi' you,' she said.

'It is her wish to go, Cecilia, my dear. I did not ask her,' said Nathaniel. 'I will take care of her.'

'Happen you will, sir,' said Cecilia. 'For that I do say of you, that you care for folks. But tha' does not make it right what you do. Only as long as she breaks her fast, and you also, sir, for I do believe you mean well.'

'You are not wearing your hat, Nathaniel,' I said, for he had been waiting at the front door for a quarter of an hour, and supposing him still to get ready I had not joined him.

'I will do without it for it is a hot day,' he said, 'but I speak only for myself.'

'So am I to wear a bonnet, sir?' I said.

'Yes, darling,' he said.

Then we went down through the town of Durham early, while they were still setting up for the market, and then over the Wear bridge, following the path of the river until we came to the gate leading into Thayne meadows, where Nathaniel took off his coat and threw it over his shoulder, removing also my bonnet. And we walked down through the meadows of Thayne, which were still white with cow parsley and dressed in buttercups, and where every blade of grass shone silver in the morning light. And before us rose up the dark mass of Thayne colliery washed in sun, as if nothing in the whole of creation was amiss.

'We are going to the colliery, Nathaniel?' I said, for the thought of the Spedding mill with its blood red sparks had drifted into my mind.

'No, darling,' he said.

And, indeed, when we came to the road lying below us we went not towards Thayne but towards the hamlet of Tonder, which was little but a tiny church looking like a kerchief dropped in a field, and a cluster of dwellinghouses.

'We will stop here, darling,' said Nathaniel presently, putting on his coat. Then he put on my bonnet, tying the ribbons under my chin and arranging the bonnet on my head with the same carefulness with which he might draw a plan of the roads in the colliery. And I settled his coat around his shoulders, and he tucked in a wisp of my hair; and we carried on to the signpost for Wycliffe, making our way to the back of a copse and to a rough field, yet not so rough that buttercups and cow parsley did not pour their gold and silver light on it. And we found there also Mr and Mrs Tregowan, and Mr Daunt and Mr Carson, who shook hands but said nothing, as if the whole of the created world would have stood in quietness, were it not for a lark high above us.

So we were, until out of the silence there came the sound of a horse and cart, and Mr Morfew leading it for it was his own dappled grey, and on the cart a black casket, rough and unadorned; and behind the cart a minister in the black robes of the established church, the voice of whom went out far over the meadows decked with cow parsley and buttercups, and lifted up to the sky, where the lark continued to sing: "I am the resurrection and the life, said the Lord: he that believeth in me, though he were dead, yet shall he live; and whosoever liveth and believeth in me shall never die."

Then Mr Tregowan read that psalm which talks of the valley of the shadow of death. And I looked around us and there were no shadows, not even our own, for the sun was at the top of his climb and all was summer.

'You may complete your office, gentlemen, thanking you,' the minister said to Mr Daunt and Mr Carson, for they had already taken up their spades. And he then shook them by the hand, and afterwards turned to each of us, though we are dissenters, thanking us also, and bidding us go back to our lives with peace in our hearts. And no one said any other word, for there was nothing to say.

The World Beyond the Chapel Door

'I had best sit with Willow, darling,' said my husband. 'If Barbara sings she cannot contain her merriment.'

'We had best be seated behind those tall enough to obscure Mrs Tregowan from Willow's view,' I said.

'It would make little difference, darling,' said Nathaniel. And he took a testament out of his pocket, which I recognised as that Mr Walsh had given him the day before, and which he placed in Willow's hands as she appeared with Cecilia and Bertie-mun in the hallway, asking her to keep it for him until he requested it of her.

Then we walked down through the lanes of Durham, where all the dwellings, and the hostelries also, had their shutters closed. And there was no sound but the song of blackbirds from the rooftops and the chatter of sparrows in the hedges, so that we could hear our own footsteps and the rustle of our wraps.

We found the dissenting chapel full, as they said it had been for an hour past, and as many waiting outside as were inside it, with the doors open so that those who stood outside might hear the service. For the service had already begun, it being always our habit to be just on time or late; which habit I have come to see as deliberate

301

on the part of my husband, for he never knows who in the household is going to shame him by their mirth.

'Happen all o' Durham an' Shackleton honoured Felicity more than did her own brother,' said Jack Walsh, who was all of a sudden by our side. 'I could ha' thought you weren't coming,' he continued, 'but that I asked of your husband a favour, Mrs Chark.'

'We will be outside, Jack,' said Nathaniel.

'Happen ye will not,' said Mr Walsh, 'for else ye will miss your cue, sir. What do you say, Mrs Chark?'

'My wife knows nothing of this, Jack,' said Nathaniel. 'I wished not to cause her concern for she will suffer more for me than if she herself were standing in front of the congregation.'

And the conversation would likely have gone on, but that Mr Tregowan was saying the service; which was but a short one, for he was soon at the chapel door bringing Jack Walsh in and saying to those outside that the gallery was to be opened up if they did not mind the dust and cobwebs there. At which many who were seated downstairs clattered up and we sat in our customary place at the back, Nathaniel with Willow on the bench behind Cecilia, Bertie-mun and myself.

Then Mr Tregowan asked all those present to consider the world beyond the chapel door, with its glittering sun and new leaves and dazzling flowers, saying that our sisters Felicity and Hilda, and our brother Charles, whose passing we were also commemorating that day, were at rest in just such a heaven, and that none should mourn, but rather rejoice for them, for they had stepped out of this vale of tears into glorious light.

And I could not see, on account of those who sat in front, but I could hear, rising out of the silence, the words of the book of the Revelation:

"'And I saw a new heaven and a new earth for the first heaven and the first earth were passed away; and there was no more sun, And I saw the holy city, new Jerusalem, coming down from God out of heaven, prepared as a bride adorned for her husband,

"'And I heard a great voice out of heaven saying, Behold, the tabernacle of God is with men, and he will dwell with them, and they shall be his people, and God himself shall be with them and be their God.

"'And God shall wipe away all tears from their eyes; and there shall be no more death, neither sorrow, nor crying, neither shall there be any more pain; for the former things are passed away.'"

And the speaker finished, who, though I could not see with my eyes, I saw in my heart, a man blessed with grace of spirit and beauty of person. And, having finished, he walked back to his place in silence, for those there knew that Nathaniel Chark, for all that he was the coal master and despised by many for his station in life, had known enough of sorrow himself.

Then we left the chapel and followed after the cart carrying Felicity Walsh and Hilda Spence to their final rest, where they were laid side by side. And it was only then that I noticed Julia Beech, standing afar off, holding in her arms the little bairn Moses. Mrs Tregowan had also seen her, and we both of us attempted to go and speak to her, but the crowd was such that she had gone away before we could reach her.

'Claribell, my dear,' said Mrs Tregowan, 'it is long since we have had a nice talk about the works of Mr Richardson and Miss Austen, for that is who Patrick says the lady author is. And I speak in this way, my dear, not to make light of what has passed but because I have seen you fading before my eyes these many days past. Say

303

something, my dear, for otherwise I will begin to fear that you cannot speak on account of the great gloom that has settled on you.'

Then I told Mrs Tregowan how I believed that Willow had been laughing at Mr Morfew's periwig and could not help herself, for we were by then well away from any who could hear us.

'Yes, indeed, dear,' said Mrs Tregowan. 'Although dear Cecilia said as much, I myself feared it was the hysteria, for young women are sometimes taken so. Patrick was anxious to invite poor Jack to our home, but he informs us that he has already invited himself elsewhere.' So Mrs Tregowan continued, talking then about Jack Walsh and how he would fare now that dear Felicity had passed out of this world, and about poor Charles and Hilda and the little bairn Moses, who had been orphaned thrice in his young life, until the hot mid-day sun clanged around my head and the scene swam before my eyes, and all I could think of was Felicity asleep under the dark, smothering earth.

When I came to myself I was seated in a chair in the drawing room at home listening to a curtain blowing in the breeze that came in at the open window, and the distant voices of Jack Walsh and my husband as they sat at the table and conversed.

'I could well ha' asked o' myself, Nat,' Jack Walsh was saying, 'if all o' this were inevitable, or could ha' been averted like. Beginning wi' mysen, sir; if I had settled indemnity on Charles Spence then likely he would ha paid yon rent an' not gone Blennowe crag way, an' then no search party an' no trip wire. An' likewise they in rent arrears after stoppage on account o' fire last winter, Nat, an likes o' wimmin wi' child tha' needs

304

mus' go down pit, sir; an likes o' one who shall be nameless tekking upon himself to lay trip wire, for int end all comes down to yon master whether he be blameworthy or no; for all on us know them as owns land exact them rents, being yon Morfew's kin.'

''Tis so, Jack, 'tis so,' said Nathaniel.

'An' I'll tell ye aught else, Nat,' Jack Walsh continued. 'They be griping down Shackleton way on account o' Spedding mill for she is broke, an' whether there be firedamp down yon pit no man knows for sure.'

'It is out of our hands, Jack, for Mr Higgs and Mr Thorley have been down and are of the opinion that the Spedding mill may wait,' said Nathaniel.

'Aye,' said Jack Walsh, 'may wait.'

Then I must have fallen into a sleep, for I thought I was by Shackleton mine and the air was choked with smoke and soots on account of a fire in the north pit. And I was watching the colliers being brought up out of the mine, for all the townspeople of Durham, being alerted to the fire in the pit, had sent down ropes to Shackleton. And of those coming up out of the pit not all were men, but some were women, and some were bairns. Then I was in the dwellinghouse of Charles and Hilda Spence, where Charles lay in a torpor from strong liquor, and Felicity and another, who was like myself, but was not myself but Arabella Chark, who called herself Enid, preferring to go by a plain and unremarkable name, were arranging the drapes at the window. Then a young woman came into the dwellinghouse, much blackened from the pit, whom I saw immediately was with child, and whom I knew to be Tessa Spence. And the door being left open a terrible word followed her in, hurled at her back by someone outside and echoed by he whom I thought to have been in a torpor; and there was also

305

another voice, much like my own, crying out, 'It cannot be!' which awoke me. And I opened my eyes to find Nathaniel looking down at me and stroking my hair, while the voice of Jack Walsh was elsewhere in the room saying,

'Happen I will ring for Mistress Willow, Nat, wi' your leave, sir.'

'What was it, darling?' said Nathaniel presently, for I was suddenly awake and back in the drawing room.

'I dreamt the pit was on fire,' I said.

'For which I blame mysen fairly an' squarely, Mrs Chark,' said Jack Walsh, coming also into my vision. 'We were discoursing about yon Spedding mill an' happen tha set off your dream.'

Then Willow, my maid, was in the room, and Cecilia also, who looked accusingly at my husband but said nothing.

'I'd best be going, Nat,' said Jack Walsh, 'for happen I han caused more an enough trouble wi' my unruly speech.'

'You must stay as long as you wish, Mr Walsh,' I said. 'It is I who should be apologising for falling asleep in the company of gentlemen.'

And seeing that Mr Walsh did not know then whether to be solemn or merry, hearing himself referred to as a gentleman, Nathaniel asked him to stay at least for a cup of tea; which he did, taking his leave shortly afterwards, but lingering for some time in the garden like a lost soul.

'He will be by the yellow rose tree,' said Nathaniel.

'I was dreaming of Tessa Spence, Nathaniel,' I said. 'Did I call out?'

'No, darling,' he said. 'We should not have been conversing between ourselves on matters of the mine instead of addressing our converse also to you. It was untoward of us.'

'I believe you carried on the talk of the mine with Mr Walsh seeing that it diverted his mind, Nathaniel. I heard mention of the Spedding mill.'

'My hands are tied, darling,' he said. 'Mr Higgs and Mr Thorley are of the opinion that we may well keep the mine working until such time as we have a viable Spedding.'

'And if your hands were not tied, Nathaniel?'

'My hands are tied, darling.'

Then Cecilia's plain words, as she calls them, came uninvited into my mind.

'You are a most obdurate gentleman, sir,' I said.

'Am I, darling?' Nathaniel said. 'May the Lord forgive me, I did not know.'

And I believe we did not know, either of us, whether we were merry or solemn.

"He Likes Not Women's Matters"

'How is she, my dear?' The voice of Mrs Tregowan was in the drawing room.

'As you see, mun,' said Cecilia.

'She looks peaky,' said Mrs Tregowan, whose voice was now within an arm's length of me though I could do nothing to let her know that I was conscious of her presence.

'Is it ... Cecilia, my dear?' Mrs Tregowan whispered, as if Nathaniel were also in the room.

'I do not know, mun,' said Cecilia. 'The mistress does always keep such matters to herself.'

'Perhaps she is not taken that way after her ... adversity,' said Mrs Tregowan.

'I do not know, mun,' said Cecilia. ''Tis not a matter I hear discussed under this roof, saving your honour, mun.'

'Quite, my dear,' said Mrs Tregowan.

'Begging your pardon, mun,' continued Cecilia, 'for I do believe you mean well, yet I do not know the answer to your question.'

'Perhaps dear Nathaniel ...' began Mrs Tregowan.

'The master may not be asked, saving your honour, mun, for he likes not women's matters,' said Cecilia.

'Dear, dear, dear,' said Mrs Tregowan. 'That should not be so.'

'No, mun,' said Cecilia.

Then it came to me that Nathaniel's household, each one of them, knows well how it is between he and me, that we are as brother and sister to each other, and not as husband and wife.

'Claribell, my dear, wake up,' said Mrs Tregowan, taking my hand. 'It's Barbara. Pray talk to us, darling.' But I could not, for no part of me would move, neither could I open my eyes.

'I will call Nathaniel,' said Mrs Tregowan.

'Begging your pardon, mun, but he is gone to Shackleton,' said Cecilia.

'Then I will ask dear Bertie-mun to go down to Shackleton and bring him home,' said Mrs Tregowan. 'This should not be, my dear.'

'No, mun,' said Cecilia.

Then Nathaniel's voice was in the room, and Cecilia's also.

'You need not go, my dear,' Nathaniel was saying, and I heard the door opening.

'Saving your honour, sir, but I am much occupied with the household, sir,' said Cecilia.

And I thought Nathaniel had also gone out of the room, for the door closed and all was silence, but for the birdsong coming in through the open window and the tap of a twig on the glass, and the sound of the curtain blowing into the room. Yet I was suddenly aware of his presence by my side, and the touch of a hand on mine.

'What will you think of me, sir?' I said, though no sound came.

'I fear Barbara is cross with me, and Cecilia also,' said Nathaniel.

'They say you do not like women's matters, sir,' I said, though still no sound came. And thus we were for I know not how long until the shutter, protesting in the breeze, flew off its moorings, and I opened my eyes to find Nathaniel seated on the chair arm.

'It is only the shutter, darling,' he said. 'Bertie-mun will secure it.'

'I fear I have spoken unguardedly, Nathaniel,' I said.

'You did not say a word, darling. Barbara had Bertie-mun call me back from Shackleton.'

'Did I not say anything, Nathaniel?'

'No, darling.'

'You would not say if I had.'

'But you did not, darling. Do not weep.' But I could not stop, and I was in my husband's arms, who, in the estimation of Cecilia, does not like women's matters.

'What will you think of me, sir?' I said eventually.

'I will think you are lovely this morning, darling,' he said. And I could not make my customary reply for weeping. Then Mrs Tregowan's voice was again in the room.

'Claribell must needs see a physician, dear Nathaniel.'

'There is no physician, Barbara,' said Nathaniel.

'Not in Durham, dear. Claribell must see a physician elsewhere,' said Mrs Tregowan. 'Until such time as another appointment is made, which I will see dear James about since we are kindred again. I'm supposing the consideration to the previous incumbent has been stopped and we may now appoint, Nathaniel?'

'It will stop as from next quarter day, Barbara,' said Nathaniel.

'Then we may reappoint,' said Mrs Tregowan. 'Now, how are you, Claribell, my dear?'

310

'I am much recovered,' I said, though still I did not hear any words.

'She can hear but she cannot speak,' said Mrs Tregowan. 'Did she say anything to you, Nathaniel, dear?'

Nathaniel did not answer.

'Forgive me, dear, it was not my intention to be inquisitive,' said Mrs Tregowan. 'Dear Claribell has suffered much.' Still my husband said nothing, until Mrs Tregowan, finding that she had only the four walls of the drawing room to hear her, took her leave.

'I do believe Barbara means well,' said Nathaniel. 'Was I offhanded with her, darling?'

'Only a little,' I said. 'She is accustomed to your words more than your silence.'

Then I must have fallen into a slumber, for I was no longer in the drawing room of the house on the Rose Pavement but out in the streets of Durham at twilight with the sounds of footsteps following me; which came no nearer yet neither did they recede, but were always the same distance behind me. Until, taking a short way, as I thought, through a dark and narrow thoroughfare near the Wear basin, I found myself roughly accosted and taken to some kind of tenement; for I suddenly saw myself lying on a pallet in what seemed a garret room, hurt and powerless to move or cry out, and looking, far above me, at the square of a skylight darkening into violet. And as I lay there I could hear voices on the stairs, knowing well though I could not tell how, that he who had caused the hurt was coming back to save me.

'We are accustomed to your words more than your silence,' a voice said. 'An' if you was to take my advice, sir, for what it is worth, you would maintain your silence. We will give the lady a draught and see her off.

311

There's many a one who has fared worse, if you take my meaning, sir.'

'It is not she whom I thought it to have been,' the other said. 'What have I done to her?'

''Tis nigh on late for them sentiments, sir, saving your honour,' the first voice said. 'Happen the good Lord, if he be out in the lanes of a winter's night before the lamplighter is abroad, will ha' seen thy contrite heart an will give thee time for amendment of life.'

When I awoke the sun had moved round to the west window and Nathaniel was seated again on the arm of the chair. And I knew that the sickness had passed and I was recovered, which my husband knew also, and reaching over to the desk for a cup of water held it, with the tenderness of any nurse, while I drank, even though he does not like women's matters.

'You are lovely this morning, sir,' I said.

'But it is afternoon, darling,' he said, and his eyes twinkled with merriment.

'I know that, Nathaniel,' I said. 'The sun is looking in through the west window, but I don't know if I told you this morning. Was Mrs Tregowan here?'

Then the sparkle in his eyes went out and he took my hand.

'Barbara is of the opinion that you should see the physician in York, darling,' he said, 'which we had considered and did not carry through, for which I blame myself, may the Lord forgive me.'

And seeing that Nathaniel was about to sink into the doldrums I kissed him, and he me, for all that he does not like women's matters.

'If it pleases you, I will write to the physician in York now, and Bertie-mun may take the letter for the night coach.'

So we sat down at the desk and I watched as Nathaniel wrote the letter with his left hand, and laboriously enough, for his arm has not yet regained its full strength following the assault inflicted on him earlier in the year. And I watched until it was done and sanded. Then my husband rang for Bertie-mun.

'He will be with the little bairn, Nathaniel,' I said, for Bertie-mun did not answer.

'Then I will take the letter myself, darling.'

'And I will come with you, Nathaniel,' I said.

'As you wish, darling, but first you must break your fast, and that of yesterday and the day before, for you haven't done so these three days past.'

So we went to the scullery and began to make tea and toast and boil eggs until Cecilia, discovering us there, told Nathaniel that it was women's matters to undertake such a task, and dismissed us.

And we found not the night coach, but the coach to Darlington, which was about to leave, and fresh straw already on the floor; and those travelling waiting to board, and the postilion fastening down the box. And we gave him the letter.

Under our Roof

The watchman was still on his rounds, calling out three hours of the morning when Cecilia tapped on my room door.

'The master has been in the garden wi' Mr Walsh this hour past, mun, an' he knows not what to do wi' him,' she said. ''Tis becoming a regularity with him, mun.' Outside, the next day, being the seventh in the month of June, was hovering in the eastern sky and a soft breeze entered in at the window. 'Saving your honour, mun, but Jack Walsh has bin in yon garden this week past in the dark hours an' did I not know it were him I would be frighted, mun, which happen I am, for he has a staring look about his eyes which I like not. Happen Mr Walsh ha' need of Sainte Agathe house, men's ward, for his wits are near gone, pardon my plain speaking, yet I canna say so to the master. If you are to go down, miss, I will call on Bertie-mun also, for I like not the look o' Mr Walsh, not that he is a violent man, but he has not his right wits about him.'

So I put on my wrap and shoes and went down, finding Jack Walsh and Nathaniel in the garden, and Bertie-mun looking over the grown turnips and greens, though there was barely light enough to distinguish one from another.

'Ah, Mrs Chark,' Mr Walsh said, seeing me coming through the rose garden, 'it is going to be a fine day again.'

Then he went on to talk of the roses and the last of the bluebells which were still out in the shaded part at the end of the garden, until I doubted what Cecilia had told me, that his wits were gone.

'Pardon me for being in thy garden at so young an hour, Mrs Chark,' Mr Walsh continued, 'an' you also, Nat my friend, for I had no wish to raise you from your slumbers. As I were telling your husband, Mrs Chark, 'twas in my mind to come an' bid farewell to Felicity's tree, that being the only part o' her left yet in this world. Yet I ask o' myself, an' I told Nat the same just this hour past, 'tis a poor fellow who talks to yon tree as if his wits were gone. An', as I were telling my friend Nat, 'tis in my mind that a fellow can do no more than say out loud his remorse, Mrs Chark, for I were ever irascible wi' Felicity, though she tried my patience sorely wi' her incessant coughing. And at the end twere my doing that she passed out o' this world, on account of the lack of indemnity for Charles Spence, on account o' which he were obliged to flee his dwellinghouse, an' on account o' which he took yon Blennowe path wi' strong liquor upon him an slipped ovver yon edge, whether by accident or by design I know not, but he did so, Mrs Chark. An' here I come to the nub o' my tale, for 'tis in my mind to seek out my sister Felicity, though we never did enjoy a meeting o' minds, an' humbly beg her pardon.'

'She is passed out of this world, Jack, my dear friend,' said Nathaniel. 'You can do no better than place your grief in the hands of the Lord.'

''Tis no use, Nat,' said Jack Walsh. ''Tis a poor substitute. Your good husband has been speaking thus for an hour gone an' I will not be persuaded, Mrs Chark. I mus' needs apologise in person an' that I intend to do, an' would ha' done it by now but that Nat found me here bidding farewell to a tree like an addle-headed fellow.'

'It was the sneck on the gate, darling,' said Nathaniel. 'I heard Jack come into the garden. I have told him that he may come and live here until such time as he feels more at peace.'

'But I willna, Mrs Chark,' said Jack Walsh. 'For I would then be bringing my bad soul to dwell here under your roof.'

'We would welcome you, Mr Walsh,' I said.

'Aye,' he said, 'I keep a poor home now that yon bairn ha' gone, for 'twas not seemly that I should harbour a married woman under my roof.'

The first of the sun was by that time touching the top branches of the sycamore and falling in long golden ribbons into the garden.

'Aye, a fine day,' said Mr Walsh. 'A fine season for turnips. On question o' them indemnities, Nat, happen they mus' be paid in trust to the bairn.'

'That is a matter we may discuss, Jack,' said Nathaniel. 'Are you persuaded to dwell under our roof for the present?'

'Aye, thanking ye,' said Jack Walsh. 'I mus' needs fetch a change o' shirt. I will be back betimes. Thanking ye for your hospitality, Mrs Chark.' With which Mr Walsh was gone.

'We do not know whether he will be back before Sunday service,' said Nathaniel.

'I had forgotten it is Sunday,' I said.

'We must ask Cecilia to prepare a room for him,' Nathaniel continued. 'We cannot let him come back to an empty house, and we cannot let one person have charge of him. Bertie-mun must stay behind with Cecilia.'

'We must all stay behind, Nathaniel,' I said. 'Perhaps Bertie-mun may go and leave our apologies with Mr Tregowan.'

'I fear Barbara will think I have taken offence. Go inside, darling, and I will talk to Bertie-mun.'

'He is not here, Nathaniel. He was in the garden but he is not here now.'

'I will find him. Pray go back to your rest, darling. You are tired.'

'And you also, Nathaniel,' I said, for the daylight had drained away the last vestige of colour from his face. 'We can do nothing. It is to be hoped that Bertie-mun has taken to his bed again, and Cecilia also.'

Then my husband took me into the drawing room and laid me on the sofa, placing a cushion under my head, and fetching from the closet his heavy cloak, the same that he had wrapped round my shoulders on the first morning we had gone to Sunday service, and which had about it part the scent of the coal mine, as do the clothes of all in Durham, and part the scent of sweet lavender, which fills the house on wash day.

For my husband would have counted it an intrusion to take me to my room, and the words of Cecilia came back to me, 'He likes not women's matters', which I know not whether it is true or not, for he sat by me in a chair until the chill of the morning had left me and I drifted into a sleep. And I awoke to find him still seated there, with his head sunk on his chest and his lame arm dropped by his side, and with every hair of his head awry.

'We are not lovely this morning, sir,' I said. 'We had best get ready for the Sunday service if we are going, for Mr Walsh has not yet come back and no doubt he is going also.'

'Pardon my presence, mun,' said Cecilia's voice, which was at once also in the room, 'for I heard you had awoken. I ha' taken up hot water, an' for the master also if you would be so kind as to tell him. An if you would be so kind as to tell the master also that Bertie-mun is gone.'

'Has Mr Walsh returned, Cecilia?' I said.

'Why, no, mun,' she said. 'I knew not that he was expected.'

'He was to have gone home for a change of shirt and come back, Cecilia,' I said. 'Nathaniel has invited him to stay with us until he is more himself. Unless I dreamt it.'

'You dreamt it, mun,' said Cecilia. 'The master will get a crick in his neck an it will be his own doing.' Then I fetched a hairbrush from the closet and brushed my husband's hair until he came to himself.

'Cecilia says to tell you she has taken up hot water, Nathaniel,' I said, 'and she says to tell you also that Bertie-mun has gone. He may have followed Mr Walsh home.'

'May the Lord forgive me,' said Nathaniel. 'I did not think of that.'

And it came to me that the Lord must also be tired, being called upon for forgiveness at all hours of the day and night.

'The Lord is yet abed, Nathaniel,' I said. 'You must let him be and forgive yourself.' My husband's eyes widened in astonishment.

'Forgive myself,' he said. 'I had best go and search for Bertie-mun, darling.'

'Then I will come with you, Nathaniel.' I said.

'You need not, darling,' he said, 'but I know you will do as you wish.'

'We are not tired, Nathaniel.'

'No, indeed we are not, darling.'

'And when we have availed ourselves of the hot water Cecilia has taken up we shall be lovely, though we are not lovely at this moment.'

'You are always lovely, darling,' said Nathaniel. 'I knew that the first time I set eyes on you, though you have always failed to see it yourself. But it is a poor thing to go forth on a morning, even in the company of my lovely wife, knowing that the Lord is not yet woken up. What was the word you used, darling?'

'Abed, sir.'

'It is a fine word,' he said. 'I must remember it.'

Then presently we set off, going down through the lanes of Durham, which were by then, as the watchman went on his last round, paved in sunlight. And coming eventually to the Wear Bridge we could see from far off that a crowd had been gathered there, but was dispersing even as we approached, going off in their ones and twos in all directions, as if there had been an occasion but it had now passed.

As we came nearer to the river we could see them winding up the ropes, yet there was no talk by which we might know what had taken place. And we might have remained in ignorance, for none were willing to enter into conversation with the coal master, but that the watchman, going home from his night's labours, drew my husband aside, saying that his words were not fit hearing for a lady.

319

'A poor fellow went into the Wear,' said Nathaniel when the watchman had gone. 'They have taken him to Sainte Agathe.'

'It is Mr Walsh, Nathaniel' I said.

'That was my thought also, darling,' said Nathaniel.

'Does he live?' I said.

'He was alive when they brought him out,' said Nathaniel.

Then we went by the back streets of Durham, which I did not know, but which my husband knew as if he could have walked there blindfolded, and arrived at the house of Sainte Agathe. And it came to me, not for the first time, that all who go there do not so directly but by the most circuitous means, as if they would go in secret.

We made our way round to the outbuilding known as the men's ward, finding there the doorkeeper, who said in answer to my husband's enquiry that there had been one brought in, who was quiet enough yet in a locked room, for he had been brought up out of the Wear and conveyed to Sainte Agathe by order of the justice, who had lately gone back to his dwellinghouse, having been alerted in the small hours of the morning.

'And I know not if it is the gentleman you seek, sir,' said the doorkeeper, though Nathaniel had not said he was seeking anyone, but had merely asked if anyone had been brought in. 'Happen if I were to let you into the room you would be none the wiser for the gentleman rambles about seeking out a lady, though to my mind tis an odd place for a tryst int middle o' River Wear, if you take my meaning, sir. Yet I may not let you in, sir, for he who holds yon key is gone to his dwellinghouse to break his fast. I may send for him if you so wish, sir.'

To which Nathaniel said no, for we may easily return later in the day, and to let the good man break his fast in peace.

And we went home, not finding Bertie-mun on the way back, nor indeed any other one, for those who had been out at night had gone and those whose habit it was to be out by day were not yet abroad, it being still several hours short of the time for Sunday service. Then entering in by the scullery door we found Bertie-mun, dressed already for chapel, yet occupied with the mangle, putting through it what looked like the same shirt he had been wearing as he tended the garden earlier, while in the sink lay the dregs of the River Wear, with its leaves and twigs and ordure.

'Begging your pardon, sir,' Bertie-mun said as best he may, 'for the Lord bids us not to labour on the Sabbath day.'

'Happen the Lord does not know, for he is still abed,' said Nathaniel.

'Aye, sir,' said Bertie-mun, after which no more words were to be drawn from him.

Because Bertie-mun was dressed for chapel we had no option but to do likewise and set off. So we went all five of us through the same streets we had walked but a matter of hours before, as if a whole day had passed by already, even though it was still two hours before noon, and intending when we reached the chapel to seat ourselves unobtrusively on the back two benches. But Mrs Tregowan was waiting at the door which stood wide open on account of the hot weather, although the service had already begun.

'Claribell, my dear,' she said. 'I feared you were not recovered and were unable to come to holy service. Yet here you are, looking a little peaky, perhaps, but better

321

than you were. Nathaniel, my dear, I will have a word with you after the service, if I may.'

'You may talk in front of my wife, Barbara,' said Nathaniel. Then seeing Mrs Tregowan's poor face flush with hurt and bewilderment he took her hand. 'May the Lord forgive me for my ill manners, Barbara,' he said. 'We have all of us been awake for the better part of the night. Except the Lord, who Clara says has been abed,' he added when Mrs Tregowan had gone to her place. And I dared not catch his eye through all of the service, knowing that if his merriment began it would not stop, in spite of the reason for our all-night wakefulness.

'I have a matter to tell you, dear Nathaniel,' Mrs Tregowan said after the service, 'and I would have wished not to say this in the presence of dear Claribell, yet since you wish that I do, it must be done. Poor Jack has been taken badly and is in the men's ward of Sainte Agathe, which I would not have known but that I was awake early and thought to pay a visit to my girls. And I have no more on the matter, dear Nathaniel. Yet this I do have, which was given to me before I left.' Here Mrs Tregowan took from her reticule a letter addressed to Felicity Walsh. 'It is from poor Hilda,' she continued, 'and the dear souls at Sainte Agathe knew not to whom to entrust it. It may well concern the little bairn, but we do not know for it is not ours.'

'What does Patrick say?' said Nathaniel.

'He advised me to entrust the matter to you, Nathaniel, since you and dear Claribell and Bertie-mun are the kindred in Christ of the little bairn. Otherwise it must needs be given to poor Jack, but that he is at Sainte Agathe.'

'Then it must be given to the justice, Barbara,' said Nathaniel.

'Whom you will likely find coming forth from,' she dropped her voice, 'the established church a quarter of the hour from now, dear. He will not mind being waylaid, I am sure. I will let it be known that you are not well, dear Claribell, so that you will not be importuned by the scholars.'

'You were right, we are not lovely today, darling,' said my husband, as we waited outside the church. And, indeed, for all that we felt ourselves to be decent enough in chapel, and much like everyone else, we were but drab dissenters among those coming out of the established church.

'You are lovely anywhere, Nathaniel,' I said.

'That is not true, darling,' he said. And he said rightly, it was not true, for to those above him in station the coal master is no more than grime and uncouth manners, and to those below him in station he is one who deals unjustly with those who labour in the mine.

'But all is not gloom,' Nathaniel continued, 'as I perceive that the Lord has awoken and sent to us Mr Morfew.' For the justice was even then emerging from the church, on his own, so that we might waylay him. 'I pray the Lord, who is now awake, that I do not appear defective,' he added.

'We meet in a less contentious place,' said Mr Morfew, who, catching sight of us, approached with his hand extended. 'What have we here, Mr Chark, sir?'

For he had seen the letter addressed to Felicity which my husband held in his hand. Nathaniel told Mr Morfew of what had happened to Jack Walsh, that he had been brought up out of the Wear and was now in the house of Sainte Agathe, as if the justice had no knowledge of the matter, Mr Morfew scratched his head, raising a little tuft of red hair.

'I will think about it, Mr Chark, for she to whom this letter is addressed is passed out of this world and he who is her kindred is taken badly and is in the care of Sainte Agathe,' he said. 'Who do you suppose is the writer of this letter?'

Nathaniel looked at me.

'We believe it is Hilda Spence, for Felicity was good to her and she and I saw Hilda in Sainte Agathe when she herself was in her last days,' I said.

'Spence, ah yes,' said Mr Morfew. 'Spence, Spence, Spence, all passed out of this world, and Felicity Walsh also. I will lay it before the better judgement of my fellow justice in Darlington, who is impartial in this matter as he does not know any person involved, and I will let you know of our deliberation. Which latter word I use advisedly because these matters without recent precedent are like to last out a night in Russia when nights are longest there, to borrow from Mr Shakespeare.'

Then Mr Morfew invited us to take refreshment at his house, which my husband declined, saying that we were on our way to visit Mr Walsh.

'Well, another time, Mr Chark,' said Mr Morfew, begging my husband to convey his best regards to each of his lady servants, whom he feared had been used off-handedly at the hearing.

'Maybe we should have accepted Mr Morfew's invitation to take refreshment at his house, Nathaniel,' I said, when he had bid us good-day.

'We could not, darling,' he said.

'How so? We did not say to the doorkeeper when we were going back to see Mr Walsh.'

'I do not know why exactly, darling, but we could not. It would not have sat well with us to receive hospitality of the justice when Jack left the hearing a disappointed man. Yet the justice meant well, darling,' he added.

'And we may have seen again his periwig, which diverted Willow so much,' I said.

'And the Lord, being yet abed, would not have saved us from our merriment,' said Nathaniel.

'And were we not so tired, we would not be talking in this way on the Lord's day,' I said.

'I do not well with a double negative, darling, for I am defective in such respects,' which word "defective" redoubled my husband's merriment and we were obliged to take the long way round to Sainte Agathe; finding there the superintendent returned from his dwelling, who said his doorkeeper had told him of our forthcoming visit, and that we might see the patient.

'Yet I have to beg you to be prepared to see some other person than he you expect to see, sir,' he went on. 'For we find generally that folks come here expecting to see those with whom they are acquainted, and that is not always the case.'

And I was still reflecting on what Nathaniel was making of these curious words when we came to the room of Jack Walsh, which the superintendent entered, leaving us outside. 'He will see you, sir. Do you wish the lady to wait here?'

'I will go in if I may, sir, for Mr Walsh is a friend to us both,' I said. And we went in, finding Jack Walsh standing to greet us.

'Welcome, Nat, welcome, Mrs Chark,' he said. 'A fine season for turnips, Nat.'

Then Nathaniel asked Jack Walsh how he fared. 'Well enough, thanking ye, Nat,' he said. 'And Enid, happen the bairn will be a fine young lad by now.' Nathaniel's hand tightened round mine.

'He is, thank you, Jack,' I said. 'He is a fine young lad.' And we took our leave presently, finding that those few words from an unforgotten past had drained the strength of poor Mr Walsh.

'How did you find him?' said the superintendent, who was waiting a little way down the passage with a key.

'Very much as he was four years ago, sir,' said Nathaniel, thinking no doubt to forestall any further enquiries. Yet the good man was wise to my husband's meaning and said that it was not unknown for those who had been immersed to lose the recent memory, which would most likely return as the water left the brain.

'We will go back by the fields, darling,' said Nathaniel when we were away from the house of Sainte Agathe. 'It is a shorter way, and I fear you are very tired.'

'So tired that I made light of the Lord,' I said.

'And I also,' said Nathaniel. 'The Lord will not mind, darling.'

'If you say so, sir,' I said.

We went into the Wear meadows where the hot, quiet afternoon settled on the silvered grass and shining buttercups. And Nathaniel took off his coat, then my bonnet, and then loosed my hair, knowing well how the clip works, for all that he does not like women's matters. And it was as if we were no longer drab dissenters, but lovers; though we are not.

'We have a letter from York,' he said presently. 'Bertie-mun brought it up from the night coach, and with

326

Jack taking badly it went out of my mind. I have not opened it. Say something, darling,' he added presently.

'I had best put my hair back, sir,' I said.

'Allow me, darling,' he said, 'but first let me gaze at you a little longer, for you are lovely though you do not know it.' Then with the same alacrity as he had loosed my hair Nathaniel restored it to the clip, replacing also my bonnet and tying the strings under my chin.

'We have yet more visitors,' he said as we neared the Rose Pavement. 'Do not ask me how I know. I feared this.'

'Then as you know we have visitors, you will suggest that they are Mr Beech and Mr Pennell or Mr Darbyshire, of other of the scholars,' I said, 'even though Mrs Tregowan let it be known that there was not a Sabbath day school. Or all of the scholars, perhaps.'

And indeed, it was all the scholars, whom Cecilia said she had shown to the schoolroom and given refreshment.

''Tis no good tidings, mun,' she said as we entered. 'Happen they come not to study but to see the master, for Mrs Tregowan had let it abroad that you are not well. But happen you have a bit more colour to you this afternoon, mun.'

Then we went to the schoolroom, finding there the scholars, who stood as we entered and would, I believe, have recited their names, but that my husband gestured to them to be seated.

'We would han you to study this, Mr Chark, sir,' said Colin Beech, rising to his feet and handing Nathaniel a folded paper. 'We would han you to give an ear to our grievances. And we know, sir, that Mrs Chark is not in good health, an ye han had troubles enough, sir, and for tha reason we han writ out our grievances so as not to encumber you ovver long wi' our presences. Our grievances being these, sir:

'yon rent arrears following on from half time pay after fire,

'the matter of indemnity for one Charles Spence, though there are certain hereabouts an I count mysen not one who condisered he led a lewd life an got his wown sister in trouble, saving your presence, Mrs Chark,

'the matter o' wimmin wi' child as canna work, which 'tis right an' proper, sir, but them wages ha' not bin med up,

'the matter o' firedamp in pit for 'tis said yon Speddin mill is broke an none other ha' been brought up fro Blennowe, which could ha' been done.

''Tis all writ down here, sir.'

And all might have been, though contentious, less so, but that Colin Beech had not finished his discourse.

'We will bid you good-day, sir, wi' our best respects, an' to ye, Mrs Chark, for we mean no ill, for ye are kindred in Christ to the bairn an' the pit gives us our daily bread such as it is, but happen we would ask for our rights, sir.'

Then my husband, after the scholars had left, went to the closet in a white fury, and finding Mr Paine's work entitled *The Rights of Man* still in the pocket of his coat, took it to the scullery and hurled it onto the fire, which had been lit to boil water, as if the volume were a poisoned thing.

'I love them as my brothers, darling,' he said. 'But they are misguided. They see not the mine, but only the furlong of it on which they themselves stand.'

"Best to Return It to the Fire"

I awoke to the sneck on the gate before the first bird of the morning had begun his song and, looking out, expected to see again the woeful figure of Jack Walsh. Yet there was no one. And it was broad daylight with the hot sun streaming into the room through a gap I had left in the curtains when Cecilia knocked.

'The master asked for this to be gave to you, mun,' she said, handing me a note. 'He was gone out early, mun. Happen 'tis something to do wi' Mr Beech that he is gone, though I am not asking. 'Tis just what I surmise, saving your honour.'

'What is it you surmise, Cecilia?' I said.

'Why, mun, that Mr Beech was after making certain requests, for the master is disconcerted.'

'And why do you surmise that, Cecilia?'

''Tis all about at the scripture class tha' Mr Beech were to make requests, and I ha' my reasons to think so also, for Bertie-mun brought to my attention an item in the fire that he found while raking them ashes, mun. Which item will no doubt be known to you, mun.' Saying which, Cecilia slipped out of the door and came back with the charred remains of Mr Paine's book displayed on a shovel. 'What do I do with it, mun?' she said. Then, as I made no answer, she went on. 'Happen 'tis best to return it to the fire, mun, if the master intended that for it, for he thinks what he thinks an' none can change tha', for all that Mr Beech is an eloquent gentleman.'

'You were about to say that the master is an obdurate gentleman, Cecilia,' I said.

'I were so, mun,' she said, 'but I know ye canna say naught for the master is your lawful wedded husband. I will return it to the scullery fire, mun. 'Tis strange tha' the last word to be burned be that one.'

'Perhaps it is the hard cover that made it slow to burn, Cecilia,' I said, for indeed one word remained legible, and that was "Rights".

'Happen it is, mun,' said Cecilia, 'though I would ha ventured there were purpose in it.'

'What do you mean, Cecilia?' I said, and a sudden chill ran over me in spite of the heat of the morning.

''Tis just a hunch, mun,' said Cecilia. 'For some would say 'tis the purpose o' the Lord, though I know not for myself, for the master also is a follower of the Lord an' yet he will ha' none of those requests o' Mr Beech.'

'You may sit down and rest the shovel on the floor, Cecilia,' I said, for Cecilia showed no signs of finishing her discourse.

'Thank you, mun,' she said, and remained standing holding the shovel. 'And even the master ha' not always been a follower o' the Lord,' she continued, 'for when Mistress Enid passed out o' this world he were like to ha' gone the same way as Mr Walsh, but for yoursen, mun, for I ha' seen the light come back into his eyes; an' some would say, though I know not for myself, for I know his dark humours, that there is no man in the

county of Durham more blessed in his countenance tha'
the master. Which brings me to the nub o' my tale, mun,
saving your honour, for I see the dark humour come
again upon the master lately, an' yourself peaky, mun,
though less so lately, pardon my plain speaking. An 'tis
known, yet I know not how, tha' Bertie-mun brought up
a letter from York, which happen 'tis yon physician,
mun.'

Saying which, Cecilia went out of the room with the
shovel, leaving me still holding Nathaniel's letter, which
I had forgotten about. "Darling, I am gone to Blennowe
to search out a Spedding," it said.

So I went down, having little to do for it was
Monday wash day, with all the household occupied, and
I took up *Sense and Sensibility*, which had lain idle for
many a long week, for we had not had the heart to read.

And I came to the last part where all the foregoing
confusion looked likely to end in happiness, which
brought on a weeping fit, a foolish and watery state,
which was still upon me when Mrs Tregowan came in;
who, taking one look at me, said, 'Where is dear
Nathaniel?' as if he were inevitably the cause of my low
spirits. 'And how is poor Mr Walsh?' she continued,
when I had told her that Nathaniel had, as I thought,
gone to Blennowe because the Spedding mill brought to
Shackleton from Thayne was not working. 'And the men
are agitating on account of the firedamp,' said Mrs
Tregowan, by which I understood that she had heard of
the grievances.

'We saw Mr Walsh,' I said.

'And how did you find him, my dear Claribell?' she
said.

'He spoke to me as if he were speaking to Enid, and
the superintendent said that the near memory may be

affected in cases of immersion, but will be restored as the water leaves the brain.'

'Such matters are known only to the Lord,' said Mrs Tregowan. 'Dear Cecilia is of the opinion that Nathaniel should take you to the physician in York, darling Claribell, for Felicity's passing has brought you very low, and I know not what else is grieving you, my dear, but the untoward words of Jack Walsh cannot have helped, although he is not in possession of his proper wits. It would be but a three day excursion,' she continued, 'and Patrick and I will watch over dear Jack.'

'And Cecilia will watch over the mine,' I said.

'Well, no doubt she will, dear,' said Mrs Tregowan. Which matters we were engaged with when the doorbell rang and we heard Cecilia's voice in the hallway, then her steps on the landing as she returned.

'It was Mr Beech asking for the master, mun, and he would not come in seeing the master were away an it were Monday wash day. An' I said he may speak to you, mun, but he said he wouldna, for he wished not to put the matter on you. An' though it be forward of me to say this, saving your presence, to my mind when he knew he couldna deliver what message he had brought, whether of his own or that of others, a giant weight were lifted from his shoulders. But I know not whether I be right or no, mun. Happen 'tis the master come in now, mun.'

'I would see dear Nathaniel on the matter of the physician,' said Mrs Tregowan.

Yet whether Nathaniel heard her words through the walls and doors of the house or whether he indeed had a pressing matter to attend to, or whether it was both, he went out again immediately.

'If you please, Mrs Tregowan, I will send Bertie-mun after him,' said Cecilia.

'No, dear,' said Mrs Tregowan. 'I fear he has not forgiven me, and the Lord has delivered me from intruding on matters which are rightly between dear Claribell and Nathaniel.'

'You mean well, mun,' said Cecilia. 'I wonder, mun, and also Mistress Willow, does thy kinsman wear his curls when he is in his dwellinghouse?'

'I do not know, my dear,' said Mrs Tregowan, 'but I will find out and inform you. Now, my dear Claribell, we can do no better than to take ourselves away from under Cecilia's feet on Monday wash day and call upon Julia Beech, for the little bairn will cheer your heart. If I might use your privy, Cecilia, my dear, while Claribell is getting ready.'

So Cecilia conducted Mrs Tregowan out to the privy, coming back presently with a small paper packet concealed in her hand.

''Tis from Bertie-mun for the bairn,' she said, which I knew, from the feel and weight of it, that the parcel contained a florin. And it came to me of a sudden that Bertie-mun, more even than Nathaniel or I, wished for the little bairn not to be put to work in the pit. 'I know not the answer, mun,' said Cecilia, though she can have read nothing of my thoughts. 'The little bairn might ha' been raised in the household o' Mistress Felicity an ha' escaped yon mine, yet they did ever war among themselves, Mistress Felicity an Mr Walsh, which Mistress Beech an Mr Beech do not to the best o' my knowledge. An' moreover the Lord ordained the bairn's life before he ha' been born, mun, for 'tis writ down in them scriptures. An if the scriptures says aught, happen we need na fret. 'Tis in the psalm, mun.'

Then Mrs Tregowan and I went, not straight away to Shackleton, but to the dwelling of Mr Morfew, finding him in his garden seated under an oak tree reading the *Times*, and wearing eyeglasses, which would have diverted Willow no less than his periwig.

'We are not stopping, James, dear,' said Mrs Tregowan before he could so much as greet us. 'I come with a question from dear Cecilia, as to whether you wear your hair in your dwellinghouse.'

Then Mr Morfew, without saying anything, laid down the *Times* and led us into the house and into the hallway. And as our eyes became accustomed to the shade we saw ranged on pegs a whole flock of periwigs, one of which Mr Morfew lifted from its hook and gave to me.

'Mrs Chark, you will see that I am overly blessed with these little fellows,' he said. 'Pray take one to your good lady servants, my dear. As to the question, you may tell Cecilia that I do not wear them in my dwellinghouse. It is enough that they are under my roof, for my housekeeper says they harbour ticks, yet they do not. It is long since this one was worn by a sheep.'

'It is not dear James who has to do with the rentals in Shackleton,' said Mrs Tregowan as we left. 'And I know not how much he may be prevailed upon to approach the kindred, for as you see, dear, he is a little unusual.'

'We are all of us unusual,' I said.

'Indeed, dear Claribell,' said Mrs Tregowan. 'It took us not long to discover that dear Nathaniel, for all his sweet nature, is a most obdurate gentleman. He will not bend, Claribell. He may listen to the grievances of Mr Beech, yet he will not bend.'

'His hands are tied, Mrs Tregowan,' I said.

'Yes, I do believe Nathaniel is of that opinion, dear.'

334

And no more was said on the matter, as we were coming into Shackleton, which slept under a thin mist of coal dust in the hot sun. And there were few bairns, and few women at home, being only the youngest bairns and those women far gone with child.

'They will not cease their toil in the mine until they show,' Mrs Tregowan whispered, laying emphasis on the last word; and indeed, all those women we saw, who were few, were not only far gone with child, but nearing their time.

Julia Beech rose to her feet on seeing us, for she was seated and engaged in turning sides into middle of a sheet, which Mrs Tregowan picked up so that she might admire the stitchwork, while I searched for Bertie-mun's parcel under the periwig in my reticule, being reminded of it on seeing the little bairn Moses in his cradle by the window.

'He must needs catch the sun,' said Julia Beech. 'For he will be down pit in the blinking of an eye, an' there is no sun in the pit, an' on the Sabbath folks are in chapel where there is no sun neither. An' likely he will be stunted in his growth for want o' sun. I ha' lost three bairns o' my own, mun,' she added, turning to me, 'which is nothing out o' the ordinary hereabouts, for even them wi' child ha' needs toil in pit to mek up wages till they show an then they canna, an wi'out wages folks canna pay rental.'

And Julia Beech said this all without rancour as if there was no more to be done about the mine than about the sun itself which would shine on some days and on others be hidden in a pall of black smoke. Then Mrs Tregowan asked how the little bairn Moses fared, sleeping as he was in the sun in his cradle, and if he cried much after the manner of little bairns, for he must surely be cutting his teeth.

'He cries not at all, mun,' said Julia Beech. 'An' there is many a time by day and by night when I go to look at him to pacify myself that he is yet in this world, for he is so still I sometimes ask myself if he lives. An' I know not his age, mun, yet there is others who tell me there should be more movement about him, though I know not for myself for my other bairns were hardly in this world afore they passed out of it.'

Mrs Tregowan took up a little hand, and the tiny fingers closed round hers.

'I believe he smiles, Julia, my dear,' she said.

'He does so,' said Julia Beech. 'An' if the physician gentleman, though I know he were disgraced, were yet with us I would ask of him. For happen he were not allowed to practise the profession, mun, on account o' one evil deed they tell of, which happen drove him to strong liquor out o' remorse, or else that he did the evil deed while in a state of strong liquor, but he were not evil in the eyes of the folks o' Shackleton on account o' his dispensing his knowledge free o' charge. Yet he is gone out o' this world, mun, for reasons known to all, which are too woeful to be spoke of. An' I may speak in front of you also, mun,' Julia Beech continued, turning to me, 'when I say tha the same gentleman attended upon Miss Felicity, which were not the first time he were to tend one whose afflictions he caused, may the Lord rest his soul, for he lived evil an he passed out o' this world, though I do not say it myself, in an evil fashion.'

During all of which time Mrs Tregowan was using every means at her disposal to halt the discourse of Julia Beech, saying when Julia stopped to draw breath that we must be away.

'You did not hear that, Claribell, my darling,' she said as we made our way back from Shackleton. 'Yet I fear you did and I must tell dear Nathaniel at the risk of bringing on his displeasure again, for he has not forgiven me for the last time, which I remember not the occasion of and I doubt if he does, yet he has not forgiven me for being a meddlesome woman.'

'Perhaps the little bairn would have liked Mr Morfew's periwig,' I said.

Then Mrs Tregowan, seeing that I was not to be drawn on Julia's discourse, said that happen he would, for little bairns like comforts, and that dear Bertie-mun might take it once Willow and Cecilia have examined it, only so long as there were no ticks in it.

And arriving back at the Rose Pavement, for Mrs Tregowan would not let me go on my own, and finding Nathaniel was at home, she went to seek him out, coming back a few moments later saying that there had been a letter from the physician in York who speaks the French language.

'Am I a meddlesome woman, my dear Claribell?' she said. Yet before I could reply, though she knew well the answer and also knew well that I would not give it, Mrs Tregowan said herself that she is indeed a meddlesome woman. 'Yet I mean well, Claribell, my dear,' she added.

Then Cecilia brought in tea, and I gave to her Mr Morfew's periwig, and she said she would call Willow, who looked also at it, but I fear it had lost its humour without the wearer of it.

When Mrs Tregowan had gone my husband came into the drawing room.

'You are in the doldrums, Nathaniel,' I said.

''Tis not I but you who should be in the doldrums, darling,' he said, turning me towards the light, for the curtains were pulled almost closed against the afternoon sun. 'We are both of us in the doldrums,' he continued. 'I went to Blennowe and they say the Spedding will be at the disposal of Shackleton in three days. I have told Mr Higgs and Mr Thorley, who have always been of the opinion that we have no need for the Spedding. It is nevertheless the consensus that we might hold out with the mine still working until the week's end. We should go to York, darling, for Julia has spoken of matters we were trying to keep from you, though she meant no ill.'

So it is arranged that we go to York, which might just as well be on the moon, for neither Nathaniel nor I have ever in our lives set foot outside the county of Durham.

"As If You Are Bound for
the Dissenting Chapel"

Yet far from the three day excursion that Mrs Tregowan
had predicted, we are to be away from the county of
Durham only a single day, travelling overnight to York
one night and back from York the following night, for
the reason that Nathaniel does not wish to be out of the
sight of the mine.

And I have to say that the arrangement does not
displease me, for into my soul there has crept a fear and
sickness of leaving the house on the Rose Pavement,
even for so much as one day, although it has been my
home for less than a year. And the disquiet in our minds,
for Nathaniel is no less fearful than I am, has transferred
itself to our household, as much as if we had spoken of it
out loud, which we have not.

For every hour Cecilia comes to me with some tale
of the privations of a journey by coach, which she has
never in her life made, and Willow has brought from the
apothecary cupboard the remedy of bistort, which
Cecilia assures me is, 'For those that be bilious, mun,
though I have doubts the master will partake. An'
happen also you may take sweet lavender, for you know
not if those of your fellow travellers have bathed or no.

An' happen juniper also for the self-same reason, lest they may pass on to you the itch.'

All this, until the excursion has become an insurmountable upheaval in my mind, for all that the town of York is but an inch down the road on the map, and we will travel as most others do, without mishap, leaving the fair city of Durham and the sparkling Wear on the one day and arriving in the town of York the day after, which is to my mind as all the ensuing pages of my book are, with nothing written upon them. And I do not know if what is eventually written will be for harm or healing, or if I will have the heart for the writing of either.

'We will come with you and the master to see you on your journey, mun,' said Cecilia, on whose face the frown has deepened as the day has gone by. 'An' I do wish the master would hurry himself to be back from yon mine, for the coach sets off at five after mid-day. Happen you need not look as if you are bound for the dissenting chapel, mun,' she added, 'for happen they in the town of York are ladies, though I know not, mun.'

Yet that was how I was dressed, and Nathaniel, when he entered the drawing room ready to set off, looked also as if he were bound for the dissenting chapel, which brought back into my mind the time we could not enter the chapel on account of our merriment and had to take a turn around Chivenor Square, thinking that whatever else passed in the chapel it was bound to make us feel worse rather than better. And that day, though recent enough, is as a hundred years in the past.

Having All the Appearance
of a Friar

My husband had gone when I woke, yet his cloak was there, covering me and tucked around my ankles, so that the hem of it had collected stalks of straw. And my bonnet was on the seat beside me, having been replaced by a shawl. A pencil of light came in through a crack in the blind, and accompanying it the din as of a great crowd, with the creak of carts and the stamping of horses, and the whole world, as it seemed, within an arm's length. And the heat battered me as I pulled down the blind, finding there, looking back at me and at close quarters, not the whole world but the amiable face of the coachman.

'You did not tell me that a carriage is like a rolling ship to you, Nathaniel,' I said as we made our way to the Monk-bar. 'We should not have come here, and we still have to make the journey back.'

'I am much recovered, darling,' said Nathaniel, 'and we have a day on dry land before we must go on board ship again.'

'It is as well that we go to see a physician, Nathaniel.'

'We go for you, darling, not for me,' he said. 'I pray the Lord that I will not be so prodigal with my words that I give you no time. It is a failing I was born with, for I never could use one word where ten would suffice. I am all failings.'

Then seeing the gloom descend upon my husband, as if a black curtain had been drawn between him and the sunny streets of York with their crowds and chatter, I told him of the periwig Mr Morfew had sent to Cecilia and Willow, and how there had been a veritable flock of periwigs hanging on pegs in his hallway, and that even now, as we walked through York, Cecilia would be asking Bertie-mun to inspect the periwig in the safety of the garden for ticks before it was brought into the house, which last part of the tale I had invented.

And I might have continued with my fable, seeing the merriment in Nathaniel's eyes, but that too soon we were standing beneath the Monk-bar, looking up at its several storeys, as if a high window would open and a voice summon us to go in. Yet it did not, and we were still standing there when a young man appeared as if from the thin air and asked us to follow him, advising us to mind our heads at the turning of the stairs, and not to be dismayed by the darkness, for the dispensary itself was light and not dark.

It mattered little that we had arrived in the town of York as drab dissenters and in our black chapel garments, for the gentleman who stood before us in the room at the top of the stairs was no different, having all the appearance of a friar, dressed, as he was, in a black robe, and tall and spare out of the ordinary.

And all of a sudden the city of Durham with its mines of Shackleton, Thayne and Blennowe, and the house on the Rose Pavement, and our household of Cecilia, and Willow, and Bertie-mun, seemed as far away as if in a different life. And there was only my dear husband, yet even he, away from home, was someone other whom I did not know; who, before he had said any other word, was already begging the physician to forgive him for his prodigality with words, for he never could use one word where ten would suffice, and, moreover, the visit was on behalf of his darling wife and not himself.

Then the physician, looking from one to another of us in some bewilderment and merriment, asked if he might call us by the names our Lord had given us.

'You see that we are dissenters, sir,' said my husband, 'yet I know not whether the dissenting chapel makes us feel better or worse, for often we have come away with the sins of the world on our shoulders as well as our own. I speak only for myself, sir, for my darling Clara is as blameless as any may aspire to be in this life. I told you that I could never make do with one word where a multitude would suffice. Pray forgive me, sir. I will hold my peace now, for the climb up your staircase after so recently spending a night pitching on the open sea has near on taken away my breath.'

'Nathaniel did not take kindly to the carriage and sat for most of the journey outside on the box, sir,' I said. 'We did not come by sea.'

Then I asked the physician in the French tongue if he could look to my husband's seasickness before attending to me. The physician continued to look from one to another of us, and as he did so the light kindled in his eyes, which were dark, and sat deep in a remarkable face, young and yet old, and both merry and serious together.

'I will, if I may, give you some tincture for your ills, Nathaniel, and while that is working we may look to

Clara,' he said. 'You have suffered a wound to the lung, and I notice a partial paralysis of your left arm also. I have observed from your letters that your script is accomplished with difficulty, for I surmise you write with the left hand.'

'We never fail to admire your script, sir,' said Nathaniel as he unlaced his shirt.

'It is Luke whom you should praise,' said the physician. And I saw for the first time that most of the fingers of his right hand and also his thumb had been sorely hurt.

Then the young man who had brought us into the building, as if summoned by the mention of his name, set down on the table a jug of water and some phials, much like those in Willow's apothecary cupboard, but that they bore the same fine calligraphy as the letters we had received, and were written upon in the Latin tongue.

'It is *Pulmonaria* for the lungs and a tincture for the seasickness,' the physician continued. 'You have been in the care of a fine surgeon. He who mended you knew well that the lung may be saved by allowing the upper part to collapse in the case of a wound there. And he knew also to keep your left arm still to let the sinews mend. Yet I see that my careless words, far from bringing you comfort, have brought pain to your spirit, Nathaniel,' he added. 'I am sorry.'

'I am much recovered, sir,' said Nathaniel presently. 'We give *Pulmonaria* to those who suffer with their lungs in the mines.'

The morning sun had meanwhile climbed over the sill and was lying across the floor as if it were a river, with my husband and I on the one side and the French physician on the other. Drifting in through the open window were the voices of the crowd and the creak of carts in the street below, and, suddenly, also, the clang of a great bell, such that the shutters at the window were set rattling.

Then I asked the physician if my husband might speak, saying that we both of us came to him with the doldrums, yet my husband had also seasickness and his need was the greater; which words my husband understood well enough, though he does not know the French tongue. And he said he would speak, only so that we might not last out a night in Russia when nights are longest there with our deliberations on the matter of who should speak first, knowing that the physician had many calls upon his time. For Nathaniel had realised, as I had, that we were in the presence of a rare and good soul.

So Nathaniel began, turning first to me and saying, 'Forgive me for what I have to say, darling.' And he would likely have begun and finished in few words, but for the physician's silence. 'He who mended my wound was the same who inflicted it, sir, though Clara does not know that. She knows only that some person was coming into the house, whose presence caused her considerable anguish, although she could not have seen him, and did not know the cause of her disquiet. Sir, she did not see this person, neither did I know of her distress at the time, may the Lord forgive me. We were but recently wed, sir.

'The person who inflicted the wound was the same one as he who had been surgeon in Durham, whom I, being the master of Shackleton mine, assisted in appointing, for we have always much need of the services of a surgeon among those who work in the mine, and, indeed, few came forward for the position on account of the rigours of the post. Yet this man did,

345

having come up from the county of Lincoln, where he had held a series of appointments in asylums.

'I was wed before, sir. My first wife passed out of this world at the moment our bairn came into the world. The bairn lived but a half hour before he also passed out of this world. And I will forever hold myself to blame, sir,' saying which Nathaniel buried his head in his hands, and there came to me again and I know not from where, the words of Cecilia, that the master does not like women's matters; which saying went round in my mind until I wondered whether it was so or not, or even if I had heard Cecilia's words rightly.

He recovered himself and continued.

'In a word, sir, though I never could use one word where a volume would suffice, the newly appointed surgeon, unknown to me, though I have no doubt that the whole of the county of Durham knew of it, entertained a,' Nathaniel hesitated as if he were to give voice to an unseemly word, 'passion for my first wife Arabella. And one winter's day, as the streets were sinking into shadow,' Nathaniel hesitated again, 'he manhandled my wife, as he thought, to some kind of dwelling and hurt her.

'Yet who am I to condemn the act, sir,' he added then, 'having done no less, albeit with God's blessing; and indeed worse, for my lawful act led to my wife Arabella passing out of this world, so injurious was the birth to her, though I did not dream it could be so, may the Lord forgive me.'

'No, no, Nathaniel, my good man, do not lay the blame on yourself,' said the physician. 'Forgive me, I break in on your story.'

'The day following,' Nathaniel continued, 'he who had done the deed came to the house in a state of abject contrition. He was by then in a state of insobriety, and was met at the door by our good housekeeper, who, noting that he was the worse for strong liquor, bid him good-day, knowing little from what he said but that he had dishonoured the mistress.

'Yet it was not the mistress, sir. It was another young woman of equal loveliness whom many have said is like my first wife, though I do not see it myself. It was some time before I found her, for she had been cast off by her employer and taken to the refuge of Sainte Agathe.

'My wife and I made it our life's intention and our dearest wish to cherish and watch over this young woman, whom after Arabella passed out of this world I continued to visit, intending eventually to take her into my household as further domestic help. Yet as time went on I knew I could not, for I had come to love her deeply, though I will as long as I live be unworthy of her. She is the young lady you see seated here before you, sir, my darling Clara.'

While Nathaniel was speaking the sun had moved round, and touched the sleeve of the physician's robe as he poured water into glasses.

'You have suffered much, Clara, my dear,' he said, 'and you also, Nathaniel, my good man. I have seen others also who are of a tender and gracious spirit and count themselves at fault when a dear wife passes away in childbirth. Yet it is not so that you are at fault, Nathaniel. The scripture says that we cannot alter so much as a hair on our heads. How much less do we ordain who passes out of this world. There is a tincture of feverfew and thyme for the melancholy in the water,' he went on presently. 'It will not take away your griefs, but it may help you to bear them, for in the telling you have suffered greatly.'

347

'Thank you, sir,' said Nathaniel. 'I would like to be able to say that we are not accustomed to being waited upon, yet to my shame we are, sir, for we have Cecilia.'

'Who is watching over the mine while my husband is away, and who also insisted that we see you, sir,' I added.

The physician again looked from one to another of us, not knowing, as I thought, whether we were being merry or not.

'It is no less arduous being the master than being the man in these times,' he said.

'I did not know at the time that Nathaniel was master of Shackleton, sir,' I said, yet whether I was speaking in the French tongue or my own I did not know. 'I was companion to a lady from Amiens who had fled France at the time of the terror, sir. I was abroad in Durham at dusk one day when that event which Nathaniel has told you of took place, though God has been merciful to me and taken away much of the memory of it. My employer placed me in the refuge of Sainte Agathe, yet she could not take me back when I was recovered on account of the shame she felt. The gentleman who is seated here before you came to see me in the company of his wife, though I did not know why. There were many things then that I did not know. Later on there was a time when they no longer came to Sainte Agathe, and I took the fault to be in myself, sir, for the gentleman's wife was by that time with child, and I told myself that they wished not to be associated with a fallen woman such as I was. Yet the gentleman eventually returned to the refuge, wearing that same mask of sorrow on his face as you see now. He has told you the rest, sir.'

'I tell Clara every day that she is lovely, but she does not believe me,' said Nathaniel.

'And neither does Nathaniel believe me when I tell him the same thing,' I said, not knowing whether I addressed my husband or the physician, who continued to look from one to the other of us with kind, quizzical eyes.

'You have not yet finished your story, Clara, my dear,' he said.

'The person who had done the deed was all the time abroad in the streets of Durham, yet I did not know, only that from time to time I felt a fearful presence in the house, which I now know to be at those times he was under our roof attending Nathaniel for the wound he had inflicted. And there was a time also when I was abroad in the city of Durham that a voice spoke to me that I had heard before, though I could not place it. Yet he had been under our roof even before he came back as a dresser of wounds, for he was always a helper of the poor and would continually beleaguer my husband about the affairs of the mine.

'At that time also, sir, which Nathaniel has not told you, there were many camped at our gate who wished him harm. This state of affairs went on, with occasional letters of ill-intent arriving, until a poor soul from Shackleton who had been evicted from his dwelling was lost on the Wear path near a precipitous place called Blennowe crag. And, because Nathaniel was one of the search party, a trip wire was laid at the edge of the cliff. Yet it was not Nathaniel who tripped, but our dear friend Felicity, who ran forwards to warn them of an impending peril. I do not remember when, but it can have been no more than two days after the accident on Blennowe crag that the same gentleman who had been surgeon in Durham, and who had caused the hurt I have spoken of, arrived when I was alone in the house, to say farewell and speak of his remorse and beg forgiveness. He did not wait for my response, sir, and I had not at the time any to give. Yet after that meeting, sir, and I did not know why until some days later, I felt that a spirit of dread had left me, yet I did not feel joyful. The remains of the surgeon, who, you will know now, sir, was the same who laid the trip wire, and offered the earlier assault to Nathaniel, and he who also who looked to the good of the poor and treated the colliers, were found in a garret at the inn near Blennowe crag. Felicity also passed out of this world, being already seriously ill with consumption when she suffered the accident. My story is finished, sir.'

'The telling of which was your purpose in coming here,' said the physician. 'Do you now know what you might have said to the visitor at your door when he asked for your forgiveness, which you could not think of at the time?'

'Yes, sir,' I said.

'If I say farewell to you now I will have done you great harm,' the physician said presently. 'I will have sent you away with heavier hearts than you had on arriving here.' He walked across the room to where a butterfly struggled against the window pane and let it out. 'See, that simple, beautiful creature speaks to us of the soul,' he said, 'for we are trapped in this world fluttering against a window glass until such time as we are set free. Those who have left this world are as the butterfly is; liberated into the clear air.'

Then I told the physician how, after Felicity had passed away, Mr Tregowan led me to the pond in his garden, and finding the brown duck there swimming with her bairns he had taken one of the little creatures out of the water and shown me its tiny wings and feet, so that I might believe in life again.

'He is a good and wise man,' said the physician. 'He encouraged you to hold on to life after the loss of your dear friend Felicity, who was indeed a friend to you, and you to her, in spite of what you judged, and no doubt rightly so, to be her ardent feelings for your beloved husband, which though she did not speak of such in many words, you knew well, Clara, my dear; and of which feelings on the part of Felicity Nathaniel knew nothing for he does not count himself worthy of esteem, from yourself or from any other.

'Only our dear Saviour knows whether Felicity ran deliberately into the trip wire to save your life, Nathaniel,' the physician continued, although that had not been spoken of, by either of us. 'She might well, and more rationally, have summoned help to discover the wire, yet I have seen often that those in the final journey of consumption act not with what this world perceives as reason, for we know only in part.'

Then I believe, for I do not remember well, I heard my own voice in the dispensary room, yet I do not know if I spoke or not.

'*Monsieur?*'

'Clara, *ma chère?*'

'My tongue has run away with me. Pray forgive me.'

'You have something to say.'

'*Monsieur, mon cher mari et moi-même, nous sommes entre-nous come le frère et la soeur.*'

'*Comprends-tu pourquoi?*'

'*Oui, monsieur, je comprends bien.*'

'*Et* Nathaniel?' I looked across at my husband and saw that the sorrow had fallen away and that the light had returned to his eyes. *'Oui, il comprend bien, monsieur. Merci.'*

'Puis-je parler en anglais, ma chère?'
'Oui, monsieur, je vous prie.'
'I believe that all will be well, Clara, my dear.'

Then he took us down to the dispensary garden, and I do not know whether it was the cold water we had lately been given, or the sweet breath of the plants, or the words of the physician, who was part healer, part friar, but I felt the life return to me. And I do not know whether I had heard or dreamed the words, 'All will be well,' but they would not leave me.

A Dream I Was In

The same words were with me when I woke to the crash of thunder. And I did not know where I was until the sound of wheels told me that we were in a carriage on the north road with a great storm riding over our heads. The coach came to a halt, and we could hear the coachman jump down.

'We are in Durham, darling,' Nathaniel said, for he had stayed inside the carriage, the seasickness having passed, and there having been another passenger on the box as far as Darlington.

'Happen you had best take a look, sir,' the coachman was saying, hammering on the door as he spoke. 'Happen ye had best leave the lady inside an tek a look thyself. 'Tis no sight for a lady. 'Tis enough to mek heaven weep, sir. Happen ye have a muffler against the smoke, an' the lady also, for I am on point of opening the door for ye directly.' And as he did so a cloud of smoke poured into the interior of the carriage.

'I'm coming with you, Nathaniel,' I said, yet not knowing if I was still in my dream.

'You need not, darling,' he said.

'Leave the lady inside, sir, I beg you,' the coachman said again. ''Tis no sight for a lady. 'Tis enough to make all the angels in heaven weep, dear Jesus. Pray mind thy footing, mun, if thou wilt come out, though it were better ye did not, for thou wilt not see aught out here for yon smoke.'

And indeed I could not, for although the sky above our heads was paling into a leaden stormy light all below was smoke and rain, and far off in the valley was a great arc of fire with forks of lightning striking down into it.

''Tis Thayne, sir,' said the coachman.

'No, sir, it is Shackleton,' said Nathaniel. 'They will have been down the pit this last hour. I would that you take us as near to there as is possible, sir, for they are my brothers.'

'Thy kindred, sir?' said the coachman. 'Then if you would, sir, I beg you to hold them hosses the while I blinker them an we will go down by way of Wycliffe hollow, for there the poor beasts may not see yon fire. Thy kindred, you say, sir?'

Nathaniel did not answer.

''Tis the gentleman's kindred, mun?' said the coachman, turning to me.

I told him that the gentleman was master of Shackleton and those who laboured there were like brothers to him, though not his kindred.

'Aye,' said the coachman. 'An' ye had best be inside, mun, for thou be fair drenched an smothered in yon soots.'

So we climbed back inside the coach, where the rain drummed with a gathering vehemence on the roof, and we did not speak. And I could still hear in my mind the same words repeating themselves over and over, "All will be well." "All will be well." Yet I knew that matters could not be well because the approaching day, for all that it was dark with the storm, told the whole of the county of Durham that men would have been down the pit an hour and more.

We travelled for some furlongs, hearing still the crash of the thunder and the thrumming of the rain, until the coach stopped and the face of the coachman was again at the window.

'Sir, I canna go no further for the wheels will sink i' the mire. If ye are willing, I may tek the lady back to Wycliffe an ye go on foot to Shackleton for 'tis but a step if yon footway be not down.'

'I'm coming with you, Nathaniel,' I said.

'Nay,' the coachman said, ''tis no sight for a lady. Ye mus' ought be sat nigh the hearth an dry out, mun.' Then to Nathaniel he said, 'Happen the lady is set on going wi' you, sir, an I mus get yon hosses rubbed down.'

And so we came on foot round by Wycliffe hollow, which was by then well rutted, finding the footway across the shallows of the Wear still intact, and finding suddenly, rising out of the storm the hamlet of Shackleton, and its mine but a furlong in front of us. Then letting go of my hand Nathaniel kissed me and ran, before I could detain him, to where the smoke billowed from the pit head, and was lost to view. And I tried to follow but I could not, nor could I see who or what was impeding me, or make sense of any sound, until I heard, as I thought, a cry go up.

'There is a fellow gone in!'

Then every voice fell silent but those of the crashing timbers and the seething fires and the storm over our heads. Yet still the same words echoed in my mind, "All will be well", as if I were imprisoned in a dream and could not wake.

And I turned to see Frederick Pennell, being one of the scholars at the Sabbath day school, who should rightly have been at that time down the pit, but was all of a sudden standing by my side.

'Ye needna fret, mun,' he said, as I thought, 'for they han got the master out, for he would ha' gone in. Thy man ha' brooght him out.'

Then there were with Frederick Pennell those others of the scholars, half lost in the smoke, and all who had their living in Shackleton, coming out of their dwellings, who should rightly have been down the mine, every one. And Colin Beech also, speaking to me, though I could not hear what he said. And he said the words again, and yet a third time, until his voice was carried to me on a lull in the storm.

'Asking your pardon, mun, for we han all on us withdrawn our labour on this day, being the eleventh in the month of June in the year of our good Lord 1812. They be none down pit, mun. An' likely we would han informed yon master of our intentions, but that he were not at home, mun.'

And I saw, as I thought, my husband Nathaniel passing between those colliers who should rightly have been down the pit but were not, shaking them each one by the hand, for I heard from somewhere the same words, "All will be well". And whether I was still in my dream or not, or where the words came from, I could not tell.